Textbook written according to revised syllabus of S.Y.B.Com. (Semister III & IV, Paper I & II) prescribed by Dr. Babasaheb Ambedkar Marathwada University, Aurangabad from June 2014-2015. Also useful for other universities in Maharashtra.

I0681672

CORPORATE ACCOUNTING

Prin. Dr. Kishor N. Jagtap

Dr. Sunil D. Zagade

Diamond Publications

CORPORATE ACCOUNTING

Prin. Dr. Kishor N. Jagtap
Dr. Sunil D. Zagade

First Edition : July 2014

ISBN : 978-81-8483-594-6

© Diamond Publications

Type Setting :
Diamond Publications

Printed by :
Repro Knowledgecast Limited, Thane

Cover Page :
Sham Bhalekar

Published by :
Diamond Publications
264/3 Shaniwar Peth, 302 Anugrah Apartment
Near Omkareshwar Temple, Pune - 411 030
☎ 020-24452387, 24466642

info@diamondbookspune.com
www.diamondbookspune.com

Sale Distributor :
Diamond Book Depot
661 Narayan Peth
Appa Balwant Chowk
Pune 411 030
Tel. - 24480677, 66020282

PREFACE

It is a matter of great pleasure for us to present this book to our esteemed readers and students. This book has been designed as standard text on 'Corporate Accounting' for Second Year B. Com.

This book comprehensively covers the entire syllabus of S. Y. B. Com. Course of Dr. Babasaheb Ambedkar Marathwada University, Aurangabad w. e. f. June-2014. It has been written to meet the requirement of students. The special features of the book are :

- Full coverage of the revised syllabus.
- Chapter outline at the beginning of each chapter to give a bird's eye view of the topics covered in the chapter.
- Point wise explanation of each topic in the chapter.
- Topics are logically arranged in numbered paragraphs exactly according to the modified syllabus.
- Proposed questions at the end of each chapter.
- Extensive use of diagrams, tables and various forms to give visual view of key concepts and techniques.
- Conversional, lucid and simple language.

Every effort has been made to provide the readers with most up-to-date and authentic material on the subject.

We are very grateful to our publisher Mr. Dattatray Pashte of Diamond Publication, Pune who have rendered all possible assistance in bringing out this book. We wish to acknowledge our deep gratitude to staff who have assisted and helped us in preparing this book.

We will consider our efforts amply rewarded in case the book proves useful to the students and Faculty Members of the subject.

Suggestions of readers are welcome and shall be acknowledged with gratitude.

With best wishes.

Prin. Dr. Kishor N. Jagtap
Dr. Sunil D. Zagade

Contents

CHAPTER 1

Issue and Forfeiture of Shares, Re-issue of Forfeited Shares

1:1.1 Introduction :

A Company is a particular kind of Association. It is a voluntary association of persons. A company is formed for carrying out large-scale business for profit. It is a voluntary and autonomous association of certain persons with capital divided into numerous transferable shares formed to carry out a particular purpose in common. A company is an artifical person created by law having a common seal and perpetual succession.

A company needs capital on a very large scale. Naturally, very few persons can raise such a huge capital needed by a company, enabling to carry out a large-scale business with the object of earning profits on behalf of the members supplying such capital to it. A company, therefore, has to collect its required capital from the public at large by inviting them to subscribe towards capital of the company, by contributing their worth.

A joint stock company, therefore, has to invite the general public to raise its capital by way of issuing shares and debentures of the company.

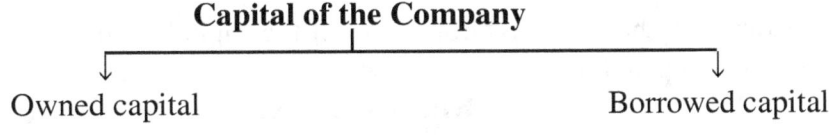

Capital of the Company

Owned capital   Borrowed capital

(Through issue of shares for public subscription) (Through issue of debentures to public)

1) Share Capital :

A capital raised by the company through the issue of shares is called as "Share Capital". Such shares are issued to the public through public subscription in the form of shares. Thus, the required capital is collected. The capital of a company is divided into small parts called as "shares". The shareholders are the owners of the company, and hence, the capital contributed by them is also termed as "owned capital".

A company needs large funds, both for its existence and development. A company, has therefore, to borrow by inviting public by open declaration to lend money, for a fixed period at a declared rate of interest to be paid on such money. Issue of Debentures is a type of borrowing and holders of these debentures are called Debentureholders. They are creditors of the company. Hence, the amount given by them is termed as "borrowed capital".

The main divisions of share capital are :

1. **Authorised capital :** It is also termed as "Nominal Capital" or "Registered Capital". It is the maximum amount of share capital which the company is authorised to raise by way of public subscription. This amount is stated in the "Memorandum of Association".

2. **Issued capital :** It is represented by the number of shares that have been issued to the public for cash and to the vendors as fully or partly paid-up against purchase consideration. This capital may be equal or less than the authorised capital.

3. **Subscribed capital :** It is that part of the issued capital for which the applications are received from the public. It is called "subscribed capital".

4. **Un-issued capital :** It is that portion of authorised capital which has not yet been allotted and which is available for issue, if required.

5. **Called-up capital :** The amount on the shares which is actually demanded by the company to be paid is known as called-up capital.

6. **Uncalled capital :** It is the amount of share capital remaining uncalled on the shares.

7. **Paid-up capital :** The part of the called-up capital which is actually paid by the shareholders is known as paid-up capital.

8. **Unpaid capital :** It is the amount though called-up but not paid by the shareholders. It is nothing but "calls in arrears" which is to be shown on the liability side of balance sheet by way of deduction.

9. **Reserve capital :** It is the amount of authorised capital which the company as determined by special resolution shall not be capable of being called-up, except in the event of and for the purpose of winding-up.

SHARES

Definition : "A share is a fractional part of the capital of the company which forms the basis of ownership and interest of a subscriber in the company."

Kinds of Shares

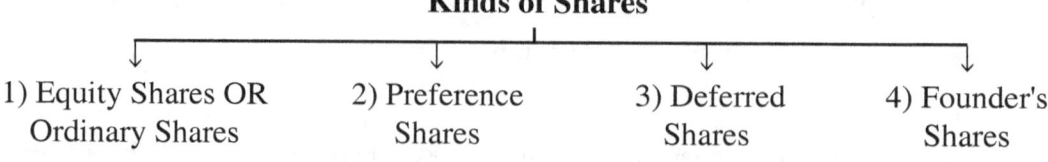

| 1) Equity Shares OR Ordinary Shares | 2) Preference Shares | 3) Deferred Shares | 4) Founder's Shares |

Shares are divided into different classes according to their respective rights. A company issues the above mentioned distinct classes of shares to satisfy the requirements of the investor so as to induce the investors and collect capital.

1) Equity shares : Those shares, the holders of which are entitled to profits after all prior charges have been paid, namely, preference dividend etc. are known as equity shares. There will be no fixed rate of dividend to be paid to the equity shareholders and this rate may vary from year to year, even more than the rate attached to preference shares. Such shareholders may go without any dividend if no profit is made.

2) Preference shares : Shares which enjoy the preferential rights as to dividend and repayment of capital in the event of winding up of the company over the equity shares or any other shares are called preference shares. The preference shares will get a fixed rate of dividend.

Types of Preference Shares

a) **Cumulative preference shares :** If the company does not earn adequate profit in any year, dividend on preference shares may not be paid for that year. In the case of cumulative preference shares, such unpaid dividends are treated as arrears and become payable out of profits of the company in subsequent years. They are sure to receive dividend.

b) **Non-cumulative preference shares :** These type of shares do not have the privilege of the accumulation of the unpaid dividends; if the profit during that particular year is not adequate for paying the guaranteed dividends, the balance left over lapses. Even though these preference shares will be treated on the same footing as other preference shareholder as regards repayment of capital is concerned.

c) **Redeemable preference shares :** The capital raised through the issue of redeemable preference shares is to be paid back by the company to such shareholders after the expiry of stipulated period, whether the company is wound up or not.

d) **Participating preference shares :** These shares carry the right of sharing profits left after paying preference and equity dividends at a fixed rate,

e) **Non-Participating preference shares :** These are shares which do not carry the right of sharing in the surplus left after paying equity dividend.

f) **Convertible preference shares :** These are shares which can be converted into equity shares.

g) **Non-convertible preference shares :** These are shares which can not be converted into equity shares.

h) **Guaranteed preference shares :** It is those which carry the right to a fixed dividend even if the company makes no or insufficient profits. If the company itself cannot pay the dividend, the vendor or some outsider undertakes to pay the dividend.

3) Deferred shares : Are those which receive dividend only after preference and equity dividends have been paid. Under Section 90 (b) of the Companies Act, 1956, these shares can now by issued by independent private companies only. In other words, no Public

Ltd. Company or a subsidiary thereof, or a private company deemed to be a public company u/s 43(A), can issue deferred shares.

4) Founder's shares : Are those shares which are entitled to one-quarter or one-half of the net profits after a fixed percentage has been paid on preference, equity and deferred shares and a certain amount is credited to a Reserve Fund.

1:1.2 Issue of Shares :

Shares can be issued for cash to public, friends, relatives and other important organisations like Life Insurance Corporation, Unit Trust of India, etc. Also, shares can be issued for consideration other than cash to the vendors.

Procedure : To obtain capital, it is usually necessary for a public company to issue a prospectus. A private company is prohibited to invite public for the purchase of its shares / debentuers. The prospectus is an invitation to offer. Besides other information, the prospectus discloses the number, type and amount of shares. It also mentions the manner in which the amount of shares is payable by the public.

i) Application : The prospectus contains a printed letter of application. A person who intends to buy shares in the company has to fill in the application form and forward it to the company's banks with a cheque for the amount payable on the application, The money payable with the application form is known as the "application money" and must not be less than 5% of the nominal value of the shares.

ii) Allotment : The directors fix the last date for the receipt of application. After the last date expires, the company's bankers forward all the applications and the pass book to the company's office. The directors then proceed to allot the shares.

The applicants to whom shares are allotted, will be sent this information. After allotment, they become the shareholders of the company. Those to whom shares could not be allotted will be sent a letter of regret along with the refund of their application money.

The shareholders will be required to pay the "allotment money" on allotment of shares which will be recorded in the application and allotment book. (Form is given below)

iii) Calls : (First call, Second call, Final call)

Definition : Call is a demand made by the company on its shareholders to pay the whole or part or the balance remaining unpaid on each share after the allotment of shares, at any time during its lifetime.

Instalments payable after the allotment of shares are technically known as calls.

Rules :

The Regulation No. 13 of the Table 'A' of the Companies Act, has provided for the following rules :-

   a) The maximum amount of call should not be for more than 25% of the nominal value of the shares.

b) There should be at least one month's interval between two successive calls.

Generally, the prospectus gives the dates of different calls.

The directors have the discretion to call it in one call or more than one call. The notice is sent to the shareholders with a request to pay the amount of the call. Then particulars are entered in a share call book (Form is given below)

FORMS
Share Application And Allotment Book

Application No.	Date of Application	Name of Applicant	Address	Occupation	No. of shares applied for	Amount paid on Application	C. B. Folio	Distinctive No. From	Distinctive No. To	Allotment Letter No.	Amount due on Allotment	Date of Receipt of cash	Allotment Money C. B. Folio	Cash in Advance	Amount of cash Return	C. B. Folio	Member's Register Folio	Share Certificate No.	Remarks

Share Call Book

Serial No.	Name of Shareholder	Address	Member's Register Folio	No. of shares held	Amount due	Date of Receipt	Amount Received	C. B. Folio	Amount	Date of Receipt	C.B. Folio	Date of Adjustment	Amount	Day	Interest	Remarks

Kinds Of Subscription of Shares by Public

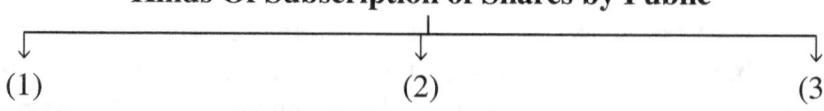

(1)	(2)	(3)
Exact Subscription	**Under Subscription**	**Over Subscription**
e. g. X Ltd. issued 10,000 equity shares and applications received from public for subscription of 10,000 equity shares.	e. g. Y. Ltd. issued 50,000 preference shares and applications received for subscription of 40,000 preference shares only.	e. g. Z Ltd. issued 15,000 equity shares and applications received for subscription of 20,000 equity shares.
↓	↓	↓
In this case, entries are to be passed for 10,000 shares.	In this case, entries are to be passed for 40,000 shares only.	In this case, entries are to be passed for 15,000 shares only from allotment.

Shares Issued at Par; Premium and Discount

Sr. No.	Face value of one share Rs.	Issued at Rs.	Meaning
1.	100	100	Issued at par / face value.
2.	100	120	Issued at premium
3.	100	95	Issued at discount

Kinds of Allotment

(1)	(2)	(3)
Allotment in full with no excess application money i.e. 100% allotment	Allotment in part and balance Applications rejected	Allotment on pro-rata basis e.g. Issued 50,000 shares, applications received for 60,000 shares. The Board of Directors allotted all the shares on pro-rata basis amongst all applicants (Excess application money is transferred to Allotoment A/c and Calls in Advance A/c respectively)
↓	↓	
e.g. issued and subscribed 10,000 shares. Board of Directors allotted all the shares amongst all the applicants	e.g. Issued 20,000 shares, applications received for 25,000 shares. Board of Directors rejected applications for 5,000 shares and allotted 20,000 shares amongst remaining applicants.	

Treatment of Excess Application Money

| Excess application money may be refunded to those applicants whose shares are rejected | Excess application money may be transferred to Share Allotment A/c when pro-rata allotment is made | Excess application money may be transferred to Calls in Advance A/c after transferring the amount to share allotment |

Calls-in-Advance : When an applicant sends more money than required, the excess money is called Calls-in-Advance. According to Sec 92, the company can accept money on Calls-in-Advance only if it's Articles authorise it to do so. The amount received on calls in advance should be credited to Calls-in-Advance A/c and not to Share Capital A/c.

The company is required to pay interest on Calls-in-Advance amount if the company has adopted Table 'A', then it is required to pay 6% p. a. interest on such calls in advance amount from the date of receipt of such money to the due date of call for which this money is used.

Interest paid on Call-in-Advance is an expense and is transferred to P & L A/c debit. If Interest on Calls-in-Advance is outstanding, it will appear on the liability of B/S under "Current Liabilities" heading.

Calls-in-Arrears : If a Shareholder makes a default in sending call money according to terms and conditions, then the money not so sent is called Calls-in-arrears. The amount not received on any call is transferred to a "Calls-in-Arrears A/c." This account is shown on the liability side by way of deduction from Called-up Capital.

The company is authorised to charge interest on all Calls-in-Arrears. If the company has adopted Table 'A', it can charge interest on such Calls-in-Arrears from the day appointed for payment to the date of actual payment @ 5% p.a.

Accounting Treatment
Model Journal Entries
I Upon Application

Date	Particulars	L.F.	Dr. Rs.	Cr. Rs.
1.	Bank A/c Dr To Equity Share Application A/c (Being application money received on... shares at Rs... each)			

2.	Equity Share Application A/c Dr.
	    To Equity Share Capital A/c
	    To Bank A/c (Refunded)
	    To Equity Share Allotment A/c
	    To Calls in Allotment A/c (if any)
	    (Being application money on... shares transferred to capital, on... shares refunded, as applications rejected, on... shares transferred to allotment money which is excess application money and remaining transferred to calls in advance A/c.)			

	II. Upon Allotment			
3.	Equity Share Allotment A/c Dr. To Equity Share Capital A/c (Being allotment made on... shares)			

	OR
	Equity Share Allotment A/c Dr.
	    To Equity Share Capital A/c
	    To Equity Share Premium A/c
	(Being allotment made on... shares including Premium)			

	OR Equity Share Allotment A/c Dr. Discount on Issue of Shares A/c Dr. To Equity Share Capital A/c (Being allotment made on... shares and discount adjusted)			

Date	Particulars		L.F.	Dr. Rs.	Cr. Rs.
4.	Bank A/c Dr. To Equity Share Allotment A/c (Being allotment money received on... shares after adjusting excess application money, if any)				
	III. Upon First Call				
5.	Equity Share first call A/c Dr. To Equity Share Capital A/c (Being first call made on... shares)				
6.	Bank A/c Dr. Calls in Advance A/c Dr. To Equity Share first call A/c (Being first call money received, call in advance adjusted)				
	OR Bank A/c Dr. Calls in Arrears A/c Dr. To Equity Share first call A/c (Being first call money received except on... shares)				

* Note :

  (1) If the shares are not forfeited then it is convenient to transfer arrears to Calls in Arrears A/c as in the above entry. If the shares are being forfeited, then the first call A/c can be closed in Forfeiture Entry and Calls in Arrears A/c need not be opened.

  (2) Similar entries are to be passed for second, third or final call as the case may be.

  (3) When a company issues both Equity Shares and Preference Shares, entries should be separately passed for each type of share. Words "Equity" and "Preference" be used.

Problem : Calls-in-Arrears and Calls-in-Advance

A Limited Company with a nominal capital of Rs. 5,00,000 in shares of Rs. 10 each, issued 20,000 shares payable at Rs. 2.50 per share on application, Rs. 2.50 per share on allotment, and Rs. 5 per share on first and final call three months later. All monies payable on allotment were duly received but one shareholder failed to pay the amount due on allotment on his 250 shares; while another shareholder who held 200 shares, paid for the shares right up in full.

Make the necessary journal entries.

Solution :

Journal Entries in the books of ....

	Particulars		L.F.	Dr. Rs.	Cr. Rs.
1.	Bank A/c	Dr.		50,000	
	To Share Application A/c				50,000
	(Being Share application money of 20,000 shares @ Rs. 2.50 received.)				
2.	Share Application A/c	Dr.		50,000	
	To Share Capital A/c				50,000
	(Being Share application money of 20,000 shares @ Rs. 2.50 transferred to Share Capital A/c as per Board's resolution dated...)				
3.	Share Allotment A/c	Dr		50,000	
	To Share Capital A/c				50,000
	(Being share allotment money of 20,000 shares @ Rs. 2.50 transferred to Share Capital A/c as per Board's resolution dated.....)				
4.	Bank A/c	Dr.		50,375	
	Calls-in-Arrear A/c	Dr.		625	
	To Share Allotment A/c				50,000
	To Calls-in-Advance A/c				1,000
	(Being share allotment money of 19,750 shares @ Rs. 2.50 together with the advance money of 200 shares @ Rs. 5 received.)				
5.	Share First and Final Call A/c	Dr.		2,50,000	
	To Share Capital A/c				2,50,000
	(Being first and final call money of 1,00,000 shares @ Rs. 2.50 transferred to Share Capital Account as per Board's resolution dated...)				
6.	Bank A/c	Dr.		2,00,000	
	Calls-in-Arrear A/c	Dr.		50,000	
	To Share First and Final Call A/c				2,50,000
	(Being first and final call money of 80,000 shares @ Rs. 2.50 received.)				
7.	Sundry Assets A/c	Dr.		1,50,000	
	To Vendors A/c				1,50,000
	(Being assets purchased from vendors.)				

8.	Vendors A/c Dr.	1,00,000	
	To Share Capital A/c		1,00,000
	(Being 10,000 shares of Rs. 10 each issued to vendor company as fully paid.)		
9.	Vendors A/c Dr.	50,000	
	To Bank A/c		50,000
	(Being balance of purchase price paid in cash.)		

Terms of Issue

The shares may be issued in any one of the following manner :

1) **Issue of Shares at Par :** When the applicant of shares has to pay the amount which is equal to the face value of shares, the same is known as shares issued at par.

2) **Issue of Shares at Premium :** Sometimes shares are issued at a premium i.e. applicant has to pay more than the face value of shares. Hence, the premium is the difference between the issue price and the face value of shares. Generally, a premium is payable on allotment and/or application.

Accounting Entry :

a) When the premium is payable with application money

Share Application A/c	Dr.	(with the total amount received)
To Share Capital A/c		(with the face value)
To Share Premium A/c		(with the amount of premium)

b) When the premium is payable with Allotment

Share Allotment A/c	Dr.	(with the total allotment money)
To Share Capital A/c		(with the amount of allotment)
To Share Premium A/c		(with amount of premium)

There is, however, no restrictions in the Companies Act, 1956, on the issue of shares at a premium but the disposal of the same is restricted as per Section 78 of the said Act. The share premium account may be utilised for the following purposes (Section 78.)

i) in issuing fully paid bonus shares.

ii) in writing off preliminary expenses.

iii) in writing off expenses of, or the commission paid or discount allowed on any issue of shares or debentures of the company; or

iv) in providing for preminum payable on the redemption of redeemable preference shares or any debentures of the company.

Note : The Share Premium Account is shown in the liability side of the Balance Sheet under the head "Reserve and Surplus."

c) Issue of Shares at a discount

Sometimes, shares are issued at a discount, i.e. an applicant has to pay less than the face value of share. So, the discount is the difference between the face value and the issue price of the shares. According to Sec. 79 of the Companies Act, 1956, the shares may be issued at a discount when the following conditions are satisfied :

i) The share must belong to a class already issued.

ii) The issue is authorised by a resolution passed by the general meeting and sanctioned by the Company Law Board.

iii) The issue is made at a discount specified in the above resolution but in no case the rate of discount should exceed 10% or such higher rate as permitted by the Company Law Board.

iv) At least one year has elapsed since the date on which the company was entitled to commence business.

v) Issues are made within two months from the date of receiving sanctions of the Company Law Board or within such extended time as the Board may allow.

Note : The discount on issue of shares is shown (till it is written off) in the asset side of the Balance Sheet under the head "Miscellaneous Expenditures."

Accounting Entries

The entry for discount is generally passed at the time of allotment of shares. The entry is :

Share Allotment A/c	Dr.	- With the amount of allotment.
Discount on Issue of Shares A/c	Dr.	- With the amount of discount.
To Share Capital A/c		- With the amount of total.

1.1.3 Forfeiture of Shares

Forfeiture of shares means compulsory termination of membership as a penalty for non-payment of any call money. In short, if any shareholder fails to pay any call within the stipulated period on his shareholdings, the board of directors may forfeit his shares, if so, empowered by the Articles of the Company.

Rules

a) A notice must be issued to the holder, demanding to pay call (with interest, if any) within a fixed period, failing which the shares will be forfeited.

b) This notice must specify a future date (not earlier than 14 days from the date of issuing (such notice) on or before the payment should be made.

c) The board of directors will pass a resolution to forfeit the shares if the requirements of the said notice are not complied with.

Accounting Entries

For Forfeiture of Shares :

Share Capital A/c	Dr.	(No. of forfeited shares × called up values)	**
To Share Allotment A/c		(amount unpaid)	**
To Share First Call A/c		(amount unpaid)	**
To Share Final Call A/c		(amount unpaid)	**
To Share Forfeiture Call A/c		(amount received)	**

Alternatively :

If the Share Allotment Account, Share First Call and Share Final Call Account are closed by debiting Calls-in-Arrear Account, in that case, instead of crediting respective calls account, Calls-in-Arrear account will be credited.

We know that a company can issue shares either at par, or at a discount or at a premium. Similarly, at the time of forfeiture of shares all the above three categories may also be applied. Consider the following problems one by one.

Case 1. Forfeiture of Shares issued at Par

Problem :

Mr. A held 25 shares of Rs. 10 each, out of which he paid Rs. 3 on application but could not pay Rs. 3 on allotment and Rs. 2 on first call. Directors forfeited his shares. Show forfeiture entries.

Solution

In the books of ....

Journal Entries

Date	Particulars		L.F.	Dr. Rs.	Cr. Rs.
	Share Capital A/c Dr.	(25 × Rs. 8)		200	
	To Share Allotment A/c	(25 × Rs. 3)			75
	To Share First Call A/c	(25 × Rs. 2)			50
	To Share Forfeiture A/c	(25 × Rs. 3)			75
	(Being ....)				

Case 2. Forfeiture of shares issued at a discount

If the forfeited shares were originally issued at a discount, a proportionate amount of discount allowed on such shares should be cancelled if the discount on Issue of Shares Account has already been debited at the time of forfeiture of shares. Therefore, discount account is to be credited for this purpose. The entry will be:

On forfeiture :

Share Capital A/c	Dr.	(No. of forfeited shares × called up values)	**
To Share Allotment A/c		(amount unpaid)	**
To Share First Call A/c		(amount unpaid)	**
To Share Final Call A/c		(amount unpaid)	**
To Discount on issue of Shares A/c		(the amount discount)	**
To Share Forfeiture A/c		(the amount received on forfeiture)	**

Note : The balance of discount on issue of Share Account is to be shown in the asset side of the Balance Sheet under the head "Misc. Expenditures."

Problem : 'X' Ltd. issued 20,000 Equity Shares of Rs. 10 each at a discount of 10%. The amount payable as : Rs 2 on application, Rs. 3 on allotment, Rs. 5 on first and final call. Mr. Y, the holder of 1,000 shares did not pay the amount due on call and his shares were forfeited by the company.

Show the entries.

Solution : **In the books of 'X' Ltd.**

Journal Entries

Date	Particulars	L.F.	Dr. Rs.	Cr. Rs.
	Bank A/c (20,000 × Rs. 2) Dr. To Share Application A/c (Being Application money received on 20,000 shares @ Rs. 2)		40,000	40,000
	Share Application A/c Dr. To Share Capital A/c (Being transfer of application money to share capital account as per Board's resolution dated...)		40,000	40,000
	Share Allotment A/c Dr. Discount on Share A/c To Share Capital A/c (Being transfer of allotment money to Share Capital A/c and discount allowed as per Board's resolution dated....)		40,000 20,000	60,000
	Bank A/c Dr. To Share Allotment A/c (Being allotment money received on 20,000 shares @ Rs. 2)		40,000	40,000
	Share First and Final call A/c Dr. To Share Capital A/c (Being transfer of share of first and final call money to Share Capital Account as per Board's resolution dated...)		1,00,000	1,00,000
	Bank A/c (19,000 × 5) Dr. To Share Capital A/c (Being amount received on first and final call on 19,000 shares @ Rs. 5)		95,000	95,000

Date	Particulars	L.F.	Dr. Rs.	Cr. Rs.
	Share Capital A/c, (1,000 × 10) Dr.		10,000	
	To Share First and Final Call A/c			5,000
	To Discount on Shares A/c (1,000 × 1)			1,000
	To Share Forfeiture A/c			4,000
	(Being shares forfetied for non-payment of share of first and final call as per Board's resolution dated...)			

Case 3. Forfeiture of Shares issued at a Premium

Section 78 of the Companies Act, 1956, states that once the premium money is collected, it cannot be cancelled later on. Therefore, if the forfeited shares were issued at a premium and the premium money had already been received on those forfeited shares, Share Premium Account will not be cancelled or debited but the same will remain in the Share Premium Account, i.e., the entry will be same as in the case of shares issued at par.

On the contrary, if the premium remains in arrears, but the Share Premium Account has already been credited, in that case, the amount of such premium should be cancelled by debiting Share Premium Account. The entry will be -

(For Forfeiture of Shares)

Share Capital A/c	Dr.	(No. of forfeited shares × called up value)	**
Share Premium A/c	Dr.	(No. of forfeited shares × premium)	**
To Share Allotment A/c		(amount unpaid)	**
To Share First Call A/c		(amount unpaid)	**
To Share Final A/c		(amount unpaid)	**
To Share Forfeiture A/c		(amount received)	**

Problem : A Ltd. Co. had its issued capital comprising of 20,000 equity shares of Rs. 10 each payable as Rs. 2 on application, Rs. 3 on allotment (including premium) Rs. 3 on 1st call and Rs. 3 on final call.

The shares were called upto the 1st call stage. All the share money was received except from 'A', holding 300 shares, who paid only upto application, and except 'B', holding 100 shares, who paid upto allotment. All these shares are forfeited.

Journalise the entries for forfeiture only.

Solution :

In the books of 'A' Ltd.
Journal Entries

Date	Particulars	L.F.	Dr. Rs.	Cr. Rs.
	Share Capital A/c (400 × Rs. 7) Dr.		2,800	
	Share Premium A/c (300 × Rs. 1) Dr.		300	
	To Share Allotment A/c (300 × Rs. 3)			900
	To Share First Call A/c (400 × Rs. 3)			1,200
	To Share Forfeiture A/c			1,000
	(Being forfeiture of 300 shares for non-payment of allotment and first call money and 100 shares for non-payment of first call money, as per Board's resolution dated ....)			

1.1.4 Re-Issue of Forfeited Shares

The Board of Directors may re-issue the forfeited shares if they think fit, if so empowered by Table 'A'. It has already been pointed out earlier that forfeited shares may either be re-issued at par or at a discount or at a premium subject to the following conditions:

a) The Board must have to pass a resolution sanctioning the re-issue of forfeited shares.

b) If the forfeited shares are re-issued at a discount, the amount of such discount can in no case exceed the amount credited to Share Forfeiture Account during forfeiture. The entry, in that case, will be :

For re-issue of Shares :

Bank A/c	Dr.	(Amount received)	**
Share Forfeiture A/c	Dr.	(Loss on re-issue)	**
To Share Capital A/c		(Nominal value of forefeited shares)	**

c) The balance left in Share Forfeiture Account (i.e. if the discount allowed is less than the amount which has earlier been received) after the re-issue of shares will be transferred to Capital Reserve Account which will be shown in the liabilities side of the Balance Sheet under the head "Reserves and Surplus'. The entry will be :

For transferring to Capital Reserve :

Share Forfeiture A/c	Dr.	(With the amount of credit)
To Capital Reserve A/c		(balance of share forfeiture account)

Note : If the forfeited shares are re-issued at a premium, Share Forfeiture Account will not be debited but Share Premium Account will be credited.

Accounting Entries : Now, to sum up :

Case 1. Re-issue of forfeited shares which were originally issued at par

A) If the forfeited shares are re-issued at par :

i) On re-issue of shares -

Bank Account	Dr.	With the amount received
To Share Capital Account		With the amount credited as paid-up

ii) On transfer of Forfeited Shares Account to Capital Reserve Account -

Forfeited Shares Account	Dr.	With the entire amount standing
To Capital Reserve Account		to the credit of Forfeited Shares Account.

B) If the forfeited shares are re-issued at premium:

i) On re-issue of shares -

Bank Account	Dr.	With the total amount received
To Share Capital Account		With the amount credited as paid-up
To Share Premium Account		With the premium money

ii) On transfer of Forfeited Shares Account to Capital Reserve Account -

Forfeited Shares Account	Dr.	With the entire amount standing
To Capital Reserve Account		to the credit of Forfeited Shares Account.

C) If the Forfeited Shares are re-issued at discount:

i) On re-issue of Shares -

Bank Account	Dr.	With the amount received on
Forfeited Shares Account	Dr.	re-issue
To Share Capital Account		With the amount credited as paid-up

ii) On transfer of Forfeited Shares Account to Capital Reserve Account -

Forfeited Shares Account	Dr.	With the net gain, if any, on re-issue
To Capital Reserve Account		

Problem :

Show the forfeiture and pre-issue entries (without narration) in each of the following cases :

i) 'X' Ltd forfeited 300 shares of Rs. 10 each, Rs. 8 called up held by Mr. 'A' for non-payment of second call money of Rs. 3 per share. These shares were re-issued to Mr. 'Z' for Rs. 10 per share as fully paid up.

ii) 'Y' Ltd forfeited 400 shares of Rs. 10 each, fully called up, held by Mr. 'B' for non-payment of final call money of Rs. 4 per share. These shares were re-issued to Mr. 'T' at Rs. 12 per share as fully paid-up.

iii) 'Z' Ltd. forfeited 250 shares of Rs. 10 each, fully called up, held by Mr. 'C' for non-payment of allotment money of Rs. 3 per share and first and final call money of Rs. 4 per share. These shares were re-issued at Rs. 8 per share to Mr. 'P'.

Solution : **In the books of.....**
Journal Entries

	Particulars		L.F.	Dr. Rs.	Cr. Rs.
a)	Share Capital A/c Dr. (300 × Rs. 8)	Dr.		2,400	
	To Share Second call A/c (300 × 3)				900
	To Share Forfeiture A/c (300 × 5)				1,500
	Bank A/c	Dr.		3,000	
	To share Capital A/c				3,000
	Share Forfeiture A/c	Dr.		1,500	
	To Capital Reserve A/c				1,500
b)	Share Capital A/c (400 × Rs. 10)	Dr.		4,000	
	To Share Final Call A/c (400 × 4)				1,600
	To Share Forfeiture A/c				2,400
	Bank A/c (400 × Rs. 12)	Dr.		4,800	
	To Share Capital A/c				4,000
	To Share Premium A/c				800
	Share Forfeiture A/c	Dr.		2,400	
	To Capital Reserve A/c				2,400
c)	Share Capital A/c (250 × Rs. 10)	Dr.		2,500	
	To Share Allotment A/c (250 × 3)				750
	To Call A/c (250 × 4)				1,000
	To Share Forfeiture A/c (250 × 3)				750
	Bank A/c (250 × Rs. 8)	Dr.		2,000	
	Share Forfeiture A/c (250 × Rs. 2)	Dr.		500	
	To Share Capital A/c				2,500
	Share Forfeiture A/c	Dr.		250	
	To Capital Reserve A/c				250

Problem :

'X' held 100 shares of Rs. 10 each on which he has paid Re. 1 per share as application money, 'Y' holds 200 shares of Rs. 10 each on which he has paid Re. 1 and Rs. 2 per share as application and allotment money, respectively. 'Z' holds 300 shares of Rs. 10 each and has paid Re. 1 on application, Rs. 2 on allotment and Rs. 3 on first call.

They all failed to pay their arrears and the final call of Rs. 4 per share and the directors, therefore, fofeited their shares. Share were re-issued subsequently for Rs. 8 per share as fully paid.

Show the forfeiture and re-issue entries in the books of the company.

Solution :

In the books of .....

Journal Entries

Date	Particulars	L.F.	Dr. Rs.	Cr. Rs.
	Share Capital A/c (600 × 10) Dr.		6,000	
	To Share Allotment A/c (100 × 2)			200
	To Share First Call A/c (300 × 3)			900
	To Share Final Call A/c (600 × 4)			2,400
	To Share Forfeiture A/c (bal-figure)			2,500
	(Being 600 shares were forfeited for non-payment of allotment money on 100 shares, first call money of on 300 shares and final call money on 600 shares, as per Board's resolution dated....)			
	Bank A/c (600 × 8) Dr.		4,800	
	Share Forfeiture A/c Dr.		1,200	
	To Share Capital A/c			6,000
	(Being forfeited shares re-issued as fully paid at Rs. 8 per share as per Board's resolution dated...)			
	Share Forfeiture A/c Dr.		1,300	
	To Capital Reserve (Rs. 2,500 - Rs. 1,200)			1,300
	(Being balance of Share Forfeiture A/c transferred to Capital Reserve A/c.)			

* Share Forfeiture Account may be calculated as under:

'X' has paid only application money i.e.   = 100 × Re. 1 =   100

'Y' has paid only application + allotment i.e.   = 200 × Rs. 3 =   600

'Z' has paid only application + allotment + 1st call i.e. = 300 × Rs. 6 = $\underline{1,800}$

                                                               2,500

Case 2. Re-issue of Forfeited Shares which were originally issued at a discount.

Sometimes shares, which were originally issued at a discount may be re-issued after forfeiture. In that case, the discount account is re-recorded. Needless to mention that any loss in excess of the old rate is debited to Share Forfeiture Account. The entry will be.

Bank A/c   Dr.   (Amount received)

Discount A/c   Dr.   (at old rate)

Share Forfeiture A/c   Dr.   (excess over old rate)

   To Share Capital A/c

Problem :

'X' Ltd. issued 20,000 equity shares of Rs. 10 each at a discount of 10% payable at Rs. 2 on application, Rs. 3 on allotment, Rs. 4 on first and final call. Mr. 'Y' holding 1,000 shares did not pay the call money. His shares were forfeited and re-issued at Rs. 7 per share to Mr. 'Z' show the re-issue entry (without narration)

Solution -

In the books of X Ltd.
Journal Entries

Date	Particulars	L.F.	Dr. Rs.	Cr. Rs.
	Bank A/c (1,000 × Rs. 7)		7,000	
	Discount Issue of Shares A/c (1,000 × Re.1)		1,000	
	Share Forfeiture A/c (1,000 × Rs. 2)		2,000	
	To Share Capital A/c			10,000
	Share Forfeiture A/c Dr		4,000	
	To Capital Reserve A/c (6,000 - 2,000)			4,000

Case 3. Re-issue of Forfeited Shares originally issued at Premium :

Under the circumstances, the amount of premium which has already been realised should remain in Share Premium Account and must not be transferred to Share Forfeiture Account since the amount of share premium can only be utilised as per Sec. 78 (2) of the Companies Act. But if the amount of premium remains in arrear, in that case, Share Premium Account should be debited in order to cancel the same. As such, it is suggested that Share Premium Account should not be credited at the cost of Forfeited Shares Account even when the premium on shares was not received during forfeiture of shares. Hence, entries for re-issue of share and transfer to Capital Reserve Account will be similar to the method discussed earlier for re-issue of shares which were originally issued at par.

Problem :

Beta Ltd made an issue of 10,000 equity shares of Rs. 15 each payable as follows :
  i) Rs. 4 per share on "Application."
 ii) Rs. 7 per share (including Rs.2 per share as premium).
iii) Rs. 6 per share on first call.

Mr. Sen holding 50 shares failed to pay the "Allotment and Call" money. Mr. Gupta holding 80 shares failed to pay the "Call" money.

All these shares were forfeited and subsequently re-issued to Mr. Bose as fully paid-up at a discount of Rs. 3 per share.

Pass journal entries (without narration) to record the above "Issue", "Forfeiture" and "Re-issue" of shares in the books of the company.

Solution :

In the books of Beta Ltd.
Journal Entries

Date	Particulars		L.F.	Dr. Rs.	Cr. Rs.
	Bank A/c	Dr.		40,000	
	To Share Application A/c				40,000
	Share Application A/c	Dr.		40,000	
	To Share Capital A/c				40,000
	Share Allotment	Dr.		70,000	
	To Share Capital A/c				50,000
	To Share Premium A/c				20,000
	Bank A/c (70,000 - 50 × 7)	Dr.		69,650	
	To Share Allotment A/c				69,650
	Share First Call A/c	Dr.		60,000	
	To Share Capital A/c				60,000
	Bank A/c (60,000 - 130 × 6)	Dr.		59,220	
	To Share First Call A/c				59,220
	Share Capital A/c (130 × Rs.15)	Dr.		1,950	
	Share Premium A/c (50 × Rs. 2)	Dr.		100	
	To Share Allotment A/c (50 × Rs.7)				350
	To Share First Call A/c (130 × Rs. 6)				780
	To Share Forfeiture A/c (50 × Rs. 4 + 80 × Rs. 9)				920
	Bank A/c (130 × Rs.12)	Dr.		1,560	
	Share Forfeiture A/c (130 × Rs. 3)	Dr.		390	
	To Share Capital A/c				1,950
	Share Forfeiture A/c	Dr.		530	
	To Capital Reserve A/c (Rs. 920 - Rs. 390)				530

Note : Needless to mention that out of the total of 130 forfeited shares, only 50 shares premium money remained in arrears and the balance were realised. Hence, Share Premium A/c must be debited with such arrears premium i.e. Rs.100 (50 × Rs. 2)

When all forfeited shares are not re-issued :

Special attention must be given when only a portion of the forfeited shares are re-issued. In that case, only profit made on re-issue of such shares will be transferred to Capital Reserve. That is, the amount of forfeited Shares which are not re-issued will remain intact in the Forfeited Shares Account. The following illustration will make the above principle clear :

Problem :

X Ltd. issued 10,000 equity shares of Rs.10 each payable at Rs.3 - on application, Rs.3 on allotment and the balance by two calls. All the calls were duly made and the amount so realised with the exception of the following :

   i) Mr. 'A' holding 100 shares did not pay the amount due on first call ; and

  ii) Mr. 'B' holding 100 shares did not pay the amount due on final call.

All the shares were forfeited and only 150 shares were re-issued (full shares of 'A' and balance of 'B') to Mr. 'D' at Rs. 8 per share. Show the forfeiture and re-issue entries.

Solution :

In the books of 'X' Ltd.
Journal Entries

Date	Particulars	L.F.	Dr. Rs.	Cr. Rs.
	Share Capital A/c (200 × Rs.10) Dr.		2,000	
	To Share First Call A/c (100 × Rs. 2)			200
	To Share Final Call A/c (200 × Rs. 2)			400
	To Share Forfeiture A/c			1,400
	(Being 200 shares forfeited for non-payment of first call money of 100 shares and non-payment of final call money of 100 shares as per Board's resolution dated ....)			
	Bank A/c (150 × Rs. 8) Dr.		1,200	
	Share Forfeiture A/c Dr.		300	
	To Share Capital A/c			1,500
	(Being 150 forfeited shares re-issued at Rs. 8 as per Board's resolution dated ....)			
	Share Forfeiture A/c Dr.		700	
	To Capital Reserve A/c			700*
	(Being required balance of share forfeiture account transferred to Capital Reserve Account.)			

    *   Calculation of the amount to be transferred to Capital Reserve :

Credit balance of Share Forfeiture A/c	1,400
Less : Loss on re-issue	300
	1,100

Less : Profit on remaining 50 shares (out of 100)

$$\frac{Rs.\,8\times100}{100} = \frac{800\times50}{100} \text{ shares } = \frac{40,000}{100} = 400$$

$$\therefore 1,100 - 400 = 700$$

1.2 PROBLEMS :

Problem 1 : (Forfeiture and re- issue) Wonders Ltd. has issued 10,000 shares of Rs. 20 each on which the amount payable is as follows :-

On Application	Rs. 5	per Share
On Allotment	Rs. 4	per Share
On 1st call	Rs. 3	per Share
On 2nd call	Rs. 5	per Share
On 3rd call	Rs. 3	per Share

From the particulars given, journalise the transactions in respect of calls, forfeiture and re-issue of shares only.

Name of the Shareholder	Shares held	Amount Paid on
Mr. 'A'	200	Application and Allotment
Mr. 'B'	400	Application, Allotment and First Call.
Mr. 'C'	600	Application, Allotment, 1st Call and 2nd Call.

The Company made all the calls. The call money was received in full except from the above persons. The directors forfeited the shares of the above shareholders on their failure to pay the last call. These shares were re-issued to Mr. 'X' as fully paid-up for Rs. 22 per share. Mr. 'X' paid the amount in full.

Solution

Wonders Ltd's Journal Book
On Application

Date	Particulars	L.F.	Debit Rs.	Credit Rs.
	Bank A/c Dr.		50,000	
	To Equity Share Application A/c			50,000
	(Being application money received on 10,000 shares at Rs. 5 each)			
	Equity Share Application A/c Dr.		50,000	
	To Equity Share capital A/c			50,000
	(Being application money transferred to capital)			

On Allotment

Date	Particulars	L.F.	Debit Rs.	Credit Rs.
	Equity Share Allotment A/c Dr.		40,000	
	To Equity Share Capital A/c			40,000
	(Being allotment money called on 10,000 shares at Rs. 4 each.)			
	Bank A/c Dr.		40,000	
	To Equity Share Allotment A/c			40,000
	(Being allotment money received in full.)			

On 1st Call

Date	Particulars	L.F.	Debit Rs.	Credit Rs.
	Equity share 1st call A/c Dr.		30,000	
	To Equity Share Capital A/c			30,000
	(Being 1st call made on 10,000 shares at Rs. 3 each)			
	Bank A/c Dr.		29,400	
	To Equity Share 1st Call A/c			29,400
	(Being 1st call money reccived on 9,800 shares as Mr. A failed to pay on his 200 shares)			

On 2nd Call

Date	Particulars	L.F.	Debit Rs.	Credit Rs.
	Equity Shares 2nd Call A/c Dr.		50,000	
	To Equity Share Capital A/c			50,000
	(Being 2nd call made on 10,000 shares at Rs.5 each)			
	Bank A/c Dr.		47,000	
	To Equity Share 2nd call A/c			47,000
	(Being 2nd call money received on 9,400 shares as Mr 'A' failed to pay on 200 Shares and Mr. 'B' on 400 shares)			

ON 3rd Call

Date	Particulars		L.F.	Debit Rs.	Credit Rs.
	Equity Share 3rd call A/c	Dr.		30,000	
	To Equity Share Capital A/c				30,000
	(Being 3rd call made on 10,000 shares at Rs. 3 each)				
	Bank A/c	Dr.		26,400	
	To Equity Share 3rd Call A/c				26,400
	(Being 3rd Call money received on 8,800 shares as Mr. 'A', 'B' & 'C' failed to pay on 200, 400 & 600 shares respectively.)				

Note : In the above entries "Calls in Arrears A/c" is not debited.

Forfeiture Table

Name	Shares held	Application Rs. 5	Allotment Rs. 4	1st Call Rs. 3	2nd Call Rs. 5	3rd Call Rs. 3	Total Received Rs.
'A'	200	5	4	×	×	×	1,800* (200 × 9)
'B'	400	5	4	3	×	×	4,800** (400×12)
'C'	600	5	4	3	5	×	10,200*** (600×17)
	1,200 × 20	–	–	200 × 3	600 × 5	1,200 × 3	16,800 Forfeited A/c
	=24,000 (Dr.)			= 600 (Cr.)	= 3,000 (Cr.)	=3,600 (Cr.)	(Cr.)

*200 × (5 + 4) = 200 × 9 = Rs. 1,800 received from 'A'.

**400 × (5 + 4 + 3) = 400 × 12 = Rs. 4,800 received from 'B'.

***600 × (5 + 4 + 3 + 5) = 600 × 17 = Rs.10,200 received from 'C'.

Forfeiture Entry

Date	Particulars	L.F.	Debit Rs.	Credit Rs.
	Equity Share Capital A/c Dr.		24,000	
	To Equity Share forfeiture A/c			16,800
	To Equity Share 1st Call A/c			600
	To Equity Share 2nd Call A/c			3,000
	To Equity Share 3rd Call A/c			3,600
	(Being forfeiture of 1,200 equity shares held by 'A', 'B' & 'C' upon non-payment of various calls)			

Re-issue Entry

Date	Particulars	L.F.	Debit Rs.	Credit Rs.
	Bank A/c Dr.		26,400	
	To Equity Share Capital A/c			24,000
	To Equity Share Premium A/c			2,400
	(Being re-issue of 1,200 shares to Mr. 'X' at Rs. 22 each i e. at a premium of Rs. 2 each)			

Transfer Entry

Date	Particulars	L.F.	Debit Rs.	Credit Rs.
	Equity Share Forfeiture A/c Dr.		16,800	
	To Capital Reserve A/c			16,800
	(Being balance on Forfeiture A/c transferred to Capital Reserve Account)			

Problem 2 : (Premium, Forfeiture, Re-issue)

Madras Minerals Limited was registered on 1st Jan. 2009 with an authorised capital of Rs.15,00,000 divided into 15,000 equity shares of Rs.100 each. The company went for allotment on 1st April, 2009, when 5,000 shares of Rs.100 each were allotted at a premium of Rs. 5 per share, payable Rs. 25 on application, Rs. 30 (including premium) on allotment and the balance in two equal instalments of Rs. 25 each on 1st July and 1st October, 2009 respectively. All the allotment and call money was paid when due, except in the case of one shareholder who failed to pay the final call on 100 shares held by him. His shares were forfeited on 1st November, 2009 after giving him due notice.

Show the necessary entries in the books of the company to record the transactions.

Solution 2:

Madras Minerals Ltd.
Journal Entries (on Application)

Date	Particulars	L.F.	Debit Rs.	Credit Rs.
1-4-09	Bank A/c Dr. To Equity Share Application A/c (Being application money received on 5,000 shares at Rs. 25 each)		1,25,000	1,25,000
1-4-09	Equity Share Application A/c Dr. To Equity Share Capital A/c (Being application money transferred to Capital A/c)		1,25,000	1,25,000

Issue of Shares, Forfeiture and Re-issue of Shares
On Allotment

Date	Particulars	L.F.	Debit Rs.	Credit Rs.

1-4-09	Equity Share Allotment A/c Dr.
	    To Equity Share Capital A/c
	    To Equity Share Premium A/c
	(Being allotment made on 5,000 Shares with a
	premium Rs. 5)
			1,50,000	1,25,000
				25,000

1-4-09	Bank A/c Dr. To Equity Share Allotment A/c (Being allotment money received in full)		1,50,000	1,50,000

On 1st CALL

Date	Particulars	L.F.	Debit Rs.	Credit Rs.
1-7-09	Equity Share 1st call A/c Dr. To Equity Share Capital A/c (Being 1st call made on 5,000 shares at Rs. 25 each)		1,25,000	1,25,000
1-7-09	Bank A/c Dr. To Equity Share 1st Call A/c (Being 1st call money received in full)		1,25,000	1,25,000

On 2nd and Final Call

Date	Particulars	L.F.	Debit Rs.	Credit Rs.
1-10-09	Equity Share Final Call A/c Dr. To Equity Share Capital A/c (Being final call made on 5,000 shares at Rs. 25 each)		1,25,000	1,25,000
1-10-09	Bank A/Cc Dr. To Equity Share Final Call A/c (Being final call money received in full except on 100 Shares)		1,25,000	1,25,000

Forfeiture Entry

Date	Particulars	L.F.	Debit Rs.	Credit Rs.
1-10-09	Equity Share Capital A/c Dr. To Equity Share Forfeiture A/c To Equity Share Final Call A/c (Being forfeiture of 100 equity shares upon non-payment of final call)		10,000	7,500 2,500

Note: The balance on Share Forfeiture A/c is not transferred to Capital Reserve Account as shares are not re-issued.

Problem 3 : (Equity and Preference, Issue, Forfeiture Re-issue)

Kolhapur Steel Ltd., was registered with a capital of Rs.10,00,000 divided into 6,000 equity shares of Rs.100 each, 2,000, 6% preference shares of Rs.200 each. The amounts on these shares were payable as follows :

	Equity Shares Rs.	Preference Shares Rs.
On Application	10	30
On Allotment	25	60
On First Call	15	30
On Second Call	30	40
On Third & Final Call	20	40

All the shares were duly subscribed. The final call money on 50 equity shares and 40 preference shares was not received, and therefore, the directors decided to forfeit them. After due notice, these shares were forfeited. Equity shares, however, were re-issued at Rs. 85 per share.

Give the necessary journal entries and prepare the Cash Book. Create a Reserve Account by transferring the balance of Forfeited Shares A/c after the re-issue of shares.

Solution 3 :

Kolhapur Steel Ltd.
Journal Book On Application

Sr.No.	Particulars	L.F.	Debit Rs.	Credit Rs.
1.	Bank A/c Dr.		1,20,000	
	To Equity Share Application A/c			60,000
	To 6% Preference Share Application A/c			60,000
	(Being application money received on 6,000 equity shares at Rs.10 each and on 2,000 preference shares at Rs. 30 each.)			
2.	Equity Share Application A/c Dr.		60,000	
	6% Preference Share Application A/c Dr.		60,000	
	To Equity Share Capital A/c			60,000
	To 6% Preference Share Capital A/c			60,000
	(Being application money transferred to Capital A/c)			

On Allotment

Sr.No.	Particulars	L.F.	Debit Rs.	Credit Rs.
1.	Equity Share Allotment A/c Dr.		1,50,000	
	6% Preference Share Allotment A/c Dr.		1,20,000	
	To Equity Share Capital A/c			1,50,000
	To 6% Preference Share Capital A/C			1,20,000
	(Being allotment made on 6,000 equity Shares at Rs. 25 each and on 2,000 pref. shares at Rs.60)			
2.	Bank A/c Dr.		2,70,000	
	To Equity Share Allotment A/c			1,50,000
	To 6% Preference Share Allotment A/c			1,20,000
	(Being allotment money received in full.)			

On First Call

Sr.No.	Particulars		L.F.	Debit Rs.	Credit Rs.
1.	Equity Share First Call A/c	Dr.		90,000	
	6% Preference Share First Call A/c Dr.			60,000	
	To Equity Share Capital A/c				90,000
	To 6% Preference Share Capital A/c				60,000
	(Being first call made on 6,000 Eq. sh. at Rs.15 each & on 2,000 pref. sh. at Rs.30 each)				
2.	Bank A/c	Dr.		1,50,000	
	To Equity Share First Call A/c				90,000
	To 6% Preference Share First Call A/c				60,000
	(Being first call money received in full.)				

On Second Call

Sr.No.	Particulars		L.F.	Debit Rs.	Credit Rs.
1.	Equity Share Second Call A/c	Dr.		1,80,000	
	6% Preference Share Second Call A/c	Dr.		80,000	
	To Equity Share Capital A/c				1,80,000
	To 6% Preference Share Capital A/c				80,000
	(Being second call made on 6,000 Equity shares at Rs. 30 each & on 2,000 Preference shares at Rs.40 each)				
2.	Bank A/c	Dr.		2,60,000	
	To Equity Share Second Call A/c				1,80,000
	To 6% Preference Share Second Call A/c				80,000
	(Being second call money received in full.)				

On Third & Final Call

Sr.No.	Particulars		L.F.	Debit Rs.	Credit Rs.
1.	Equity Share Final Call A/c	Dr.		1,20,000	
	6% Preference Share Final Call A/c	Dr.		80,000	
	To Equity Share Capital A/c				1,20,000
	To 6% Preference Share Capital A/c				80,000
	(Being final call made on 6,000 Equity shares at Rs. 20 each and on 2,000 preference shares at Rs. 40 each)				

Sr.No.	Particulars	L.F.	Debit Rs.	Credit Rs.
2.	Bank A/c Dr. (1,20,000 - 1,000) + (80,000 - 1,600) To Equity Share Final Call A/c To 6% Preference Share Final Call A/c (Being final call money received in full except on 50 equity shares and on 40 preference shares)		1,97,400	 1,19,000 78,400

Equity Forfeiture Entry

Sr.No.	Particulars	L.F.	Debit Rs.	Credit Rs.
	Equity Shares Capital A/c Dr. (50 × 100) To Equity Share Forfeiture A/c (50 × 80) To Equity Share Final Call A/c (50 × 20) (Being forfeiture of 50 Equity shares upon non-payment of final call)		5,000	 4,000 1,000

Equity Re-issue Entry

Sr.No.	Particulars	L.F.	Debit Rs.	Credit Rs.
	Bank A/c (50 × 85) Dr. Equity Share forfeiture A/c (50 × 15) Dr. To Equity Share Capital A/c (Being re-issue of 50 equity Shares at a discount of Rs. 15 each)		4,250 750	 5,000

Transfer

Sr.No.	Particulars	L.F.	Debit Rs.	Credit Rs.
	Equity Share Forfeiture A/c (4,000 - 750) Dr. To Capital Reserve A/c (Being balance on Forfeiture Account transferred to Capital Reserve Account)		3,250	 3,250

Preference Forfeiture Entry

Sr.No.	Particulars	L.F.	Debit Rs.	Credit Rs.
	6% Preference Share Capital A/c (40×200) Dr.		8,000	....
	To 6% Preference Share Forfeiture A/c (40×160)		....	6,400
	To 6% Pref. Share Final Call A/c (40 × 40)		....	1,600
	(Being forfeiture of 40 6% preference Share			
	up on nonpayment of final call.)			

Note : Balance on Preference Share Forfeiture A/C can be transferred to Capital Reserve after re-issue of the same.

Cash Book (Bank Column)
(for issue of shares only.)

Dr.   Cr.

Date	Receipts	L.F.	Rs.	Date	Payments	L.F.	Rs.
	To Balance B/d	-	?	...	By Balance C/d	-	10,01,650
	To eq. share Application	-	60,000				
	To 6% pref sh. Application	-	60,000				
	To eq. share Allotment	-	1,50,000				
	To 6% pref share Allotment	-	1,20,000				
	To eq. share first call	-	90,000				
	To 6% pref share first call	-	60,000				
	To eq. share second call	-	1,80,000				
	To 6% pref. share second call	-	80,000				
	To eq. share final call	-	1,19,000				
	To 6% pref. share final call	-	78,400				
	To eq. share capital						
	(Re-issue)	-	4,250				
			10,01,650				10,01,650
	To Balance Bld		10,01,650				

Problem : 4 (Forfeiture and Re-issue)

Anand holds 100; Babubhai holds 200; & Chandrakant holds 3,000 equity shares of Rs.10 each of ALPHA CHEMICALS LTD.

Anand has paid Re. 1 per share as application money.

Babubhai has paid Re. 1 & Rs. 2 per share as application and allotment money, respectively.

Chandrakant has paid Re. 1 on application, Rs. 2 on allotment & Rs. 3 per share on first call.

They failed to pay their arrears and final call of Rs. 4 per share and the Directors, therefore, forfeited their shares.

Give entries in the books of company regarding forfeiture assuming that the above forfeited shares are re-issued to Dinakar at Rs.7 per share as fully paid.

Solution : 4

Forfeiture Table :

Name	Shares held	Application Re. 1	Allotment Rs. 2	First Call Rs. 3	Final Call Rs. 4	Total Received Rs.
Anand	100	1	×	×	×	100
Babubhai	200	1	2	×	×	600 *
Chandrakant	300	1	2	3	×	1,800 **
	600 × 10		100 × 2	300 × 3	600 × 4	2,500
	6,000 (Dr.)		200 (Cr.)	900 (Cr.)	2,400 (Cr.)	Forfeiture A/c (Cr.)

* (200 × 1) + (200 × 2) = Rs. 600 received from Babubhai

** (300 × 1) + (300 × 2) + (300 × 3) = Rs.1,800 received from Chandrakant.

Forfeiture Entry

Date	Particulars	L.F.	Debit Rs.	Credit Rs.
	Equity Share Capital A/c Dr.		6,000	
	To Equity Share Forfeiture A/c			2,500
	To Equity Share Allotment A/c			200
	To Equity Share First Call A/c			900
	To Equity Share Final Call A/c			2,400
	(Being forfeiture of 100 shares of Anand, 200 Shares of Babubhai, 300 Shares of Chandrakant upon non-payment of call money)			

Re-issue Entry

Date	Particulars	L.F.	Debit Rs.	Credit Rs.
	Bank A/c (600 × 7) Dr.		4,200	
	Equity Share Forfeiture A/c Dr.		1,800	
	(Discount : 600 × 3)			
	To Equity Share Capital A/c			6,000
	(Being re-issue of shares at a discount of Rs. 3 each)			
	Equity Share Forfeiture A/c Dr.		700	
	(Rs.2,500-1,800)			
	To Capital Reserve A/c			700
	(Being balance on Forfeited A/c transferred to Capital Reserve)			

Problem 5

Dynamics Ltd. makes an issue of 5,000 equity shares of Rs. 100 each at a premium of Rs. 12.50 per share payable as follows :

1. Rs. 12.50 on Application
2. Rs. 25.00 on Allotment (including Premium)
3. Rs. 50.00 on First Call
4. Rs. 15.00 on Second Call
5. Rs. 10.00 on Final Call

The application and allotment monies are duly received and in addition holders of 2,500 shares pay in full on allotment. Holders of 100 shares fail to pay the first call and after due notice their shares are forfeited. The amounts payable on second call (made after the forfeiture) are paid in full except that a holder of 50 shares fail to pay. 75 of 100 shares forfeited are re-issued, credited with Rs. 90 paid for Rs. 65 per share. The new holder pays for these shares in full. The balance of Rs. 10 per share being treated as calls-in-advance. The final call is met in full including the arrears of the second call.

Show the necessary journal entries including cash in the books of Dynamics Ltd.

Solution :

In the books of Dynamics Ltd
Journal Entries

Date	Particulars	L.F.	Debit Rs.	Credit Rs.
	Bank A/c Dr.		62,500	
	To Share Application A/c			62,500
	(Being application money of 5,000 shares @ Rs. 12.50 received)			

Date	Particulars	L.F.	Debit Rs.	Credit Rs.
	Share Application A/c Dr.		62,500	
	To Share Capital A/c			62,500
	(Being application money of 5,000 shares @ Rs. 12.50 transferred to Share Capital A/c as per Board's resolution dated...)			
	Share Allotment A/c Dr.		1,25,000	
	To Share Capital A/c			62,500
	To Share Premium A/c			62,500
	(Being allotment money of 5,000 shares @ Rs. 12.50 transferred to Share Capital A/c and the premium money as per Board's resolution dated....)			
	Bank A/c Dr.		3,12,500	
	To Share Allotment A/c			1,25,000
	To Calls-in-Advance A/c			1,87,500
	(Being allotment money together with premium of 5,000 shares @ Rs. 25.00 and advance payment of call monies on 2,500 shares @ Rs. 75 received.			
	Share First Call A/c Dr.		2,50,000	
	To Share Capital A/c			2,50,000
	(Being share first Call money of 5,000 shares @ Rs. 50, transferred to Share Capital A/c as per Board's resolution dated....)			
	Bank A/c Dr.		1,20,000	
	Calls-in-Advance A/c (2,500 × Rs.50) Dr.		1,25,000	
	Calls-in Arrear A/c Dr.		5,000	
	To Share First Call A/c			2,50,000
	(Being share first call money received except on 100 shares.)			
	Equity Share Capital A/c (100 × Rs. 75) Dr.		7,500	
	To Calls-in-Arrear A/c			5,000
	To Share Forfeited A/c			2,500
	(Being 100 were forfeited for non-payment of share, first call money of Rs. 50 per share as per Board's resolution dated...)			

Date	Particulars	L.F.	Debit Rs.	Credit Rs.
	Share Second Call A/c (4,900 × Rs. 15) Dr.		73,500	
	To Share Capital A/c			73,500
	(Being share second call money of 4,900 shares @ Rs. 15 transferred to Share Capital A/c as per Board's resolution dated...)			
	Bank A/c Dr.		35,250	
	Calls-in-Advance A/c (2,500 × Rs. 15 Dr.		37,500	
	Calls-in-Arrear A/c (50 × Rs. 15) Dr.		750	
	To Share Second call A/c			73,500
	(Being share second call money received except on 50 shares.)			
	Bank A/c (75 × Rs. 65) Dr.		4,875	
	Share Forfeiture A/c Dr.		1,875	
	To Share Capital A/c (75 × Rs. 90)			6,750
	(Being 75 out of 100 forfeited shares shares re-issued at Rs. 65 each, credited to Rs. 90 per share as per Board's resolution dated....)			
	Bank A/c (75 × Rs. 10) Dr.		750	
	To Calls-in-Advance A/c Dr.			750
	(Being new holders paid in full, i.e. Rs. 10 per share in advance.)			
	Share Final Call A/c (4,975 × Rs. 10) Dr.		49,750	
	To Share Capital A/c			49,750
	(Being share final call money of 4,975 shares @ Rs. 10 transferred to Share Capital A/c as per Board's resolution dated...)			
	Bank A/c Dr.		49,750	
	Calls-in-Advance A/c Dr.		750	
	To Share Final Call A/c			49,750
	To Calls in Arrear A/c			750
	(Being share final call money received on 4,900 shares @ Rs. 10 together with the arrears of share second call money)			

Pro-rata Allotment

It has already been discussed earlier that at the time of oversubscription of shares, the directors have got the right either to reject or to refund the excess application money or to adjust the excess application money against the sum due on allotment. In other words, when smaller number of shares are allotted to a holder who had applied for more shares, the excess application money will not be refunded to him but will be adjusted against the sum due on allotment or even calls, i.e. it is applicable particularly when the partial allotment is made. So, in order to adjust the excess application money, the company may make pro-rata allotment (i.e., in proportion). Sometimes, the Company may also make a full allotment to some applicants. The entry for this purpose has also been discussed earlier. The only entry given here is when the excess application money is adjusted against the share call money. The entry is :

Share Application A/c   Dr.
To Share Call A/c

Problem 6 :

A Ltd. Co. invited application for 10,000 shares of Rs. 10 each at a premium of Rs. 5 per share payable as follows :

On application Rs. 3 per share, on allotment Rs. 6 per share (including premium) and the balance by two calls of equal amount.

Applications were received for 18,000 shares and allotment was made on applications of 15,000 shares at the rate of two shares for every three applied for. Mr. Sen failed to pay the allotment money for the forty (40) shares allotted to him and these shares were forfeited when he failed to pay the first call. Mr. Basu failed to pay the calls in respect of 120 shares allotted to him and these shares were forfeited after the second call.

40 shares were allotted to Mr. Sen originally and another 40 shares allotted to Mr. Basu were later issued to Mr. Ghosh as fully paid on payment of Rs. 9 per share.

Show the relevant entries in the Cash Book and Journal of the Company.

Solution.

Workings :

Share Allotted	Shares Applied for
2	3
10,000	$\dfrac{3 \times 10,000}{2} = 15,000$ shares

∴ (15,000 - 10,000) = 5,000 shares' excess application to be adjusted against allotment.

	No. of shares
Application received	18,000
Less : Issued	10,000
Over Subscription	8,000
Less :Adjusted against allotment	5,000
Refunded	3,000

Solution :

In the books of A Ltd.
Journal Entries

Date	Particulars	L.F.	Dr. Rs.	Cr. Rs.
	Bank A/c (18,000 × Rs. 3) Dr. To Share Application A/c (Being application money received on 18,000 shares @ Rs. 3)		54,000	54,000
	Share Application A/c (10,000 × Rs. 3) Dr. To Share Capital A/c (Being share application money of 10,000 shares @ Rs. 3 transferred to Share Capital A/c as per Board's resolution dated.....)		30,000	30,000
	Share Application A/c (5,000 × Rs.3) Dr. To Share Allotment A/c (Being surplus application money of 5,000 shares adjusted to Share Allotment A/c.)		15,000	15,000
	Share Application A/c (3,000 × Rs. 3) Dr. To Bank A/c (Being application money of 3,000 shares refunded)		9,000	9,000

	Share Allotment A/c Dr.
	     To Share Capital A/c
	     To Share Premium A/c
	 (Being share allotment money of 10,000 Shares @ Rs. 1 transferred to Share Capital A/c, Premium transferred to Share Premium A/c as per Board's resolution dated...)
			60,000	10,000
				 50,000

	Bank A/c Dr. To Share Allotment A/c (Being share allotment money received.)		44,820	44,820
	Share First Call A/c Dr. To Share Capital A/c (Being share first call money of 10,000 shares @ Rs. 3 transferred to share capital A/c, as per Board's resolution dated....)		30,000	30,000

Date	Particulars	L.F.	Dr. Rs.	Cr. Rs.
	Bank A/c (9,840 × Rs. 3) Dr.		29,520	
	To Share First Call A/c			29,520
	(Being first call money of 9,840 shares @ Rs. 3 received)			
	Share Capital A/c (40 × Rs. 7) Dr.		280	
	Share Premium A/c (40 × Rs. 5) Dr.		200	
	To Share Allotment A/c			180
	To Share First Call A/c (40 × Rs. 3)			120
	To Share Forfeiture A/c			180
	(Being 40 shares forfeited for non-payment of share allotment money and share first call money as per Board's resolution dated....)			
	Share Final Call A/c (9,960 × Rs. 3) Dr.		29,880	
	To Share Capital A/c			29,880
	(Being share final call money of 9,960 shares @ Rs.3 transferred to Share Capital A/c as per Board's resolution dated....)			
	Bank A/c (9,840 × Rs. 3) Dr.		29,520	
	To Share Final Call A/c			29,520
	(Being share final call money received on 9,840 shares @ Rs.3)			
	Share Capital A/c (120 × Rs. 10) Dr.		1,200	
	To Share First Call A/c			360
	To Share Final Call A/c			360
	To Share Forfeiture A/c			480
	(Being 120 shares forfeited for non-payment of first and final call as per Board's resolution dated....)			
	Bank A/c (80 × Rs. 9) Dr.		720	
	Share Forfeiture A/c Dr.		80	
	To Share Capital A/c			800
	(Being 80 shares re-issued at Rs. 9 per share)			
	Share Forfeiture A/c Dr.		260	
	To Capital Reserve A/c			260
	(Being profit on forfeited shares transferred to Capital Reserve A/c)			

Notes -

1. Amount received on allotment	Rs.	2. Amount tranferred to Capital Reserve	Rs.
Total amount due 10,000 × Rs. 6	60,000	Credit balance of Share Forfeiture A/c	
Less : Already received with		(Rs. 180 + Rs. 480)	660
application (5,000 × Rs. 3)	15,000	Less : Loss on Re-issue	80
Balance due on allotment	45,000		580
Less : Amount due from Sen	180*	Less : Profit on remaining 80 Shares	
Actual amount received		(Out of 120) $\left(\dfrac{80\times480}{120}\right)$	320
on allotment.	44,820		260
* Shares allotted Shares Applied			
10,000 15,000			
i.e. 2 3			
For 40 $=\dfrac{3\times40}{2}$	= 60		
i.e 60 Shares were applied by Sen.			
	Rs.		
Now, the application money received			
from Sen (60 × Rs. 3)	180		
But, he should pay on application			
(40 × Rs. 3)	120		
Excess application money was			
adjusted against allotment	60		
Again, he should pay on allotment			
(40 × Rs. 6)	240		
Less : Already paid with application	60		
∴ Failed to pay on allotment	180		

Problem 7

'X' Co. Ltd. invited application for 20,000 of its equity shares of Rs. 10 each at a premium of Rs. 2 per share, payable Rs. 3 on application, Rs. 7 on allotment including premium and the balance on first and final call.

Applications for 25,000 shares were received. It was decided –
a) to refuse allotment to the applicants for 1,000 shares,
b) to allot in full to applicants for 4,000 shares,
c) to allot the balance of the available shares in pro-rata among the other applicants, and
d) To utilise excess application money in part payment of allotment money.

Mr. 'X' holding 200 shares to whom shares had been allotted on pro-rata basis failed to pay the amount due on allotment and call and Mr. 'Y' holding 100 shares to whom full allotment was made - failed pay the amount due on call only. These shares were forfeited.

160 forfeited shares of Mr. 'X' and 40 forfeited shares of Mr. 'Y' were re-issued at a discount of Re. 1 per share to Mr. 'Z'.

Show the necessary journal entries including cash in the books of 'X' Co. Ltd.

Solution :

Workings :

Shares applied	Shares allotted
1,000	Nil
4,000	4,000
20,000 (bal. fig.)	16,000 (bal. fig.)
25,000	20,000

So, pro-rata allotment is 20,000 : 16,000 or 5 : 4.

In the books of 'X' Co. Ltd.
Journal Entries

Date	Particulars	L.F.	Dr. Rs.	Cr. Rs.
	Bank A/c (25,000 × Rs. 3) Dr. To Share Application A/c (Being application money received for 25,000 share @ Rs. 3)		75,000	75,000
	Share Application A/c Dr. To Share Capital A/c (Being share application money of 20,000 shares @ Rs. 3 transferred to Share Capital A/c as per Board's resolution dated...)		60,000	60,000
	Share Application A/c (4,000 × Rs. 3) Dr. To Share Allotment A/c (Being surplus application money of 4,000 shares adjusted against allotment.)		12,000	12,000
	Share Application A/c (1,000 × Rs. 3) Dr. To Bank A/c (Being application money refunded.)		3,000	3,000

	Share Allotment A/c Dr.
	    To Share Capital A/c (20,000 × Rs. 5) A/c
	    To Share Premium A/c (20,000 × Rs. 2) A/c
	 (Being share allotment money of 20,000 shares @ Rs. 5 transferred to Share Capital Account, premium transferred to Share Premium A/c as per Board's resolution dated....)
			1,40,000	1,00,000
				 40,000

Date	Particulars		L.F.	Dr. Rs.	Cr. Rs.
	Bank A/c	Dr.		1,26,750*	
	To Share Allotment A/c				1,26,750
	(Being balance of allotment money received except from the shareholder Mr. X. for 200 shares.)				
	Share First & Final Call A/c	Dr.		40,000	
	To Share Capital A/c				40,000
	(Being first and final call money of 20,000 shares @ Rs. 2 transferred to Share Capital Account as per Board's resolution dated...)				
	Bank A/c (19,700 × Rs. 2)	Dr.		39,400	
	To Share First and Final call A/c				39,400
	(Being amount received on first and final call of 19,700 shares @ Rs. 2)				
	Share Capital A/c (200 × Rs. 10)	Dr.		2,000	
	Share Premium A/c (200 × Rs. 2)	Dr.		400	
	To Share Allotment A/c				1,250
	To Share First and Final Call A/c				400
	To Share Forfeiture A/c				750
	(Being 200 shares forfeited for the non-payment of share allotment and first and final call money of Rs. 7 and 2 respectively.)				
	Share Capital A/c (100 × Rs. 10)	Dr.		1,000	
	To Share First and Final Call A/c				200
	To Share Forfeiture A/c				800
	(Being 100 shares forfeited for the non-payment of first and final call money of Rs. 2 per share.)				
	Bank A/c (200 × Rs. 9)	Dr.		1,800	
	Share Forfeiture A/c			200	
	To Share Capital A/c				2,000
	(160 forfeited shares of 'X' and 40 shares of 'Y' were re-issued at Rs. 2)				
	Share Forfeiture A/c	Dr.		720	
	To Capital Reserve A/c				720
	(Being profit on forfeited shares transferred to Capital Reserve A/c.)				

Note: **Amount transferred to Capital Reserve**

	Rs.
Credit balance of Share Forfeiture A/c - (Rs. 750 + Rs. 800)	1,550
Less : Loss on re-issue	200
	1,350

Less : Profit made on the remaining shares.

$$'X' - \left(\frac{40 \times 750}{200}\right) = 150$$

$$'Y' - \left(\frac{60 \times 800}{100}\right) = 480$$

630

720

* Method of calculation will be similar to Problem No. 21, showed earlier.

Problem 8

A Ltd. issued 1,00,000 shares of Rs. 10 each payable as follows : Rs. 3 on application, Rs. 2 on allotment, Rs. 3 on first call and Rs. 2 on final call. Applications were received for 1,60,000 shares out of which letters of regret were issued for 30,000 shares. Full allotment was made to applicants for 40,000 shares. Pro-rata allotment was made on the balance.

A shareholder holding 100 shares to whom full allotment was made failed to pay allotment money. Another shareholder holding 2,000 shares to whom pro-rata allotment was made also failed to pay allotment money. On first call, there was further default on 300 shares. All these shares were forfeited. The first lot of 300 was re-issued at the rate of Rs. 8 per share as fully paid-up shares.

Pass necessary journal entries.

Solution : **In the books of A Ltd.**
Journal Entries

Date	Particulars	L.F.	Dr. Rs.	Cr. Rs.
	Bank A/c. Dr.		4,80,000	
	To Share Application A/c			4,80,000
	(Being application money received @ Rs. 3 on 1,60,000 shares.)			
	Share Application A/c Dr.		3,00,000	
	To Share Capital A/c			3,00,000
	(Being application money of 20,000 shares transferred to Share Capital A/c as per Board's resolution dated...)			
	Share Application A/c Dr.		90,000	
	To Bank A/c			90,000
	(Being application money of 30,000 shares refunded)			

Date	Particulars	L.F.	Dr. Rs.	Cr. Rs.
	Share Application A/c Dr.		90,000	
	To Share Allotment A/c			90,000
	(Being surplus application money of 30,000 shares adjusted against Share Allotment Account.)			
	Share Allotment A/c Dr.		2,00,000	
	To Share Capital A/c			2,00,000
	(Being share allotment money of 1,00,000 shares @ Rs. 2 transferred to Share Capital Account as per Board's resolution dated....)			
	Bank A/c Dr.		1,09,700	
	To Share Allotment A/c			1,09,700
	(Being allotment money received after adjusting excess application money)			
	Share First Call A/c Dr.		3,00,000	
	To Share Capital A/c			3,00,000
	(Being first call money of 1,00,000 shares @ Rs. 3 transferred to Share Capital Account as per Board's resolution dated....)			
	Bank A/c Dr.		2,98,200	
	To Share first call A/c			2,98,200
	(Being first call money received on 99,400 shares @ Rs. 3)			
	Share Capital A/c (600 × Rs. 8) Dr.		4,800	
	To Share Allotment A/c			300
	To Share First Call A/c (600 × Rs. 3)			1,800
	To Share Forfeiture A/c			2,700
	(Being 600 shares forfeited as per Board's resolution dated....)			
	Bank A/c (300 × Rs. 8) Dr.		2,400	
	Share Forfeiture A/c Dr.		600	
	To Share Capital A/c			3,000
	(Being 300 forfeited shares re-issued at Rs. 8 as per Board's resolution dated....)			
	Share Forfeiture A/c Dr.		600	
	To Capital Reserve A/c			600
	(Being profit on forfeited shares transferred to Capital Reserve.)			

Workings -

1) **Amount received on allotment :**

			Rs.
Total amount due			2,00,000
Less : Already received with application			90,000
			1,10,000
Less : Amount due from a shareholder	200	}	
Amount due from another shareholder	100*		300
			1,09,700

*Share Allotted	Share Applied
60,000	90,000
2	3
200	$\dfrac{3 \times 200}{2}$ = 300

		Rs.
Therefore, application money received from the shareholder	300 × 3	900
He should pay	200 × 3	600
Excess to be adjusted against allotment		300
Now, He should pay on allotment 200 × 2		400
Less : Excess payment on application		300
failed to pay		100

2) **Amount transferred to Capital Reserve**

	Rs.
Credit balance of Share forfeiture A/c	2,700
Less : Loss on re-issue	600
	2,100
Less : profit on remaining 300 Shares (300 × 5)	1,500
	600

Problem 9

2,000 shares of Rs. 10 each were issued at a premium of Rs. 2 per share payable on application, Rs. 2 per shares on allotment, Rs. 5 (including premium), a first call Rs. 3 and on final call Rs. 2. Applications for 3,000 shares were received and allotment was made pro-rata to applicants of 2,400 shares. Money overpaid on application was employed on account of sums due on allotment.

Kailash, to whom 40 shares were allotted, failed to pay allotment money and on his subsequent failure to pay 1st call, his shares were forfeited. Romen, the holder of 60 shares, failed to pay the two calls and his shares were forfeited after the 2nd and final call. Of these shares forfeited, 80 shares were sold to Karim credited as fully paid for Rs. 9 per share, the whole of Kailash's shares being included.

Show journal entries to record the above.

Solution -

In the books of Company
Journal Entries

Sr.No.	Particulars	L.F.	Dr. Rs.	Cr. Rs.
	Share Application A/c Dr. To Share Capital A/c (Being allotment of 2,000 shares @ Rs. 2 to the application of 2,400 shares on pro-rata basis as per Board's resolution dated....)		4,000	4,000

	Share Allotment A/c Dr.
	    To Share Capital A/c
	    To Share Premium A/c
	 (Being amount due on allotment of 2,000 shares @ Rs. 3 at a premium of Rs. 2 per share as per Board's resolution dated....)
			10,000	6,000
				 4,000

	Share Application A/c Dr. To Share Allotment A/c (Being excess application money on 400 shares adjusted against allotment.)		800	800
	Share First Call A/c Dr. To Share Capital A/c (Being first call money on 2,000 shares @ Rs. 3 transferred to share capital A/c as per Board's resolution dated....)		6,000	6,000

	Share Capital A/c (40×8) Dr.
	 Share Premium A/c (40×2) Dr.
	    To Share Allotment A/c
	    To Share First Call A/c
	    To Share Forfeiture A/c
	 (Being 40 shares held by Kailash forfeited for non-payment of allotment and first call money as per Board's resolution dated....)
			320
			 80
				184
				 120
				 96

	Share Final Call A/c $(1,960 \times 2)$ Dr. To Share Capital A/c (Being Amount due on final call of 1,960 Shares @ Rs. 2 as per Board's resolution dated....)		3,920	3,920

Sr.No.	Particulars	L.F.	Dr. Rs.	Cr. Rs.
	Share Capital A/c (60 × 10) Dr.		600	
	To Share First Call A/c			180
	To Share Final Call A/c			120
	To Share Forfeiture A/c			300
	(Being 60 shares held by Romen forfeited for non-payment of first call and final call money as per Board's resolution dated...)			
	Share Forfeiture A/c Dr.		80	
	To Share Capital A/c			80
	(Being 80 Shares re-issued at a discount as per Board's resolution dated...)			
	Share Forfeiture A/c Dr.		216	
	To Capital Reserve A/c			216
	(Being profit on re-issue of 80 shares transferred to Capital Reserve.)			

Workings -

                                                   Rs.

1) Total amount due on allotment of 40 shares held by Kailash = 40 × Rs. 5   = 200

   Less : Excess amount paid by Kailash on application $\left(\dfrac{40 \times 800}{2,000}\right)$ = 16

                                                      184

2) Amount transferred to Capital Reserve -   **Rs.**
   Credit balance of Share Forfeiture Account (96 + 300)   396
   Less : Loss on re-issue   80

                                                   316

   Less : Profit on remaining 20 shares of Romen $\left(\dfrac{20 \times 300}{60}\right)$ 100

                                                   216

Problem 10

North Electronics Ltd. issued for public subscription 20,000 equity shares of Rs. 10 each at a premium of Rs. 3 per share payable as under :

On application Rs. 3 per share;

On allotment Rs. 8 per share; (including premium); and

On final call Rs. 2 per share.

Applications were received for 18,000 shares and allotment was made in full.

Shri Sharma to whom 120 shares were allotted, failed to pay the allotment money and as a consequence his shares were forfeited. Shri Sohan holder of 180 shares, failed to pay both the allotment and final call monies and his shares were also subsquently forfeited. Besides the above, all monies due were received in full.

Of the shares forfeited, 80 shares of Shri Sharma and 100 shares of Shri Sohan were sold to shri Naresh as fully paid-up at Rs. 8 per share.

Show necessary joumal entries (without narration) including those relating to cash in the books of the company.

Solution -

In the books of North Electronics Ltd.

Journal Entries

Date	Particulars		L.F.	Dr. Rs.	Cr. Rs.
	Bank A/c (18,000 × Rs. 3)	Dr.		54,000	
	To Share Application A/c				54,000
	Share Application A/c	Dr.		54,000	
	To Share Capital A/c				54,000
	Share Allotment A/c	Dr.		1,44,000	
	To Share Capital A/c				90,000
	To Share Premium A/c				54,000
	Bank A/c	Dr.		1,41,600	
	Calls-in-Arrear A/c (300 × 8)			2,400	
	To Share Allotment A/c				1,44,000
	Share Capital A/c (120 × 8)	Dr.		960	
	Share Premium A/c (120 × 3)	Dr.		360	
	To Calls-in-Arrear A/c				960
	To Share Forfeiture A/c				360
	Share Final Call A/c (17,880 × Rs. 2)	Dr.		35,760	
	To Share Capital A/c				35,760
	Bank A/c (17,700 × Rs. 2)	Dr.		35,400	
	Calls-in-Arrear (180 × Rs. 2)			360	
	To Share Final call A/c				35,760

Date	Particulars		L.F.	Dr. Rs.	Cr. Rs.
	Share Capital A/c (180 × Rs. 10)	Dr.		1,800	
	Share Premium A/c (180 × Rs. 3)	Dr.		540	
	To Calls-in-Arrear A/c				1,800
	To Share Forfeiture A/c				540
	Bank A/c (180 × Rs. 8)	Dr.		1,440	
	Share Forfeiture A/c	Dr.		360	
	To Share Capital A/c				1,800
	Share Forfeiture A/c	Dr.		180	
	To Capital Reserve A/c				180

Note :

1. Amount transferred to Capital Reserve.

	Rs.
Credit balance of Share Forfeiture A/c (360 + 540)	900
Less : Loss on re-issue	360
	540

Less : Profit on remaining shares -

$$\text{Sharma } 360 \times \frac{40}{120} = 120$$

$$\text{Sohan } 540 \times \frac{80}{180} = 240 \quad \bigg\} \qquad 360$$

	180

Problem 11 :

A Ltd. Co. issued 10,000 equity shares of Rs. 10 each at a premium of Rs. 2 per share payable Rs. 2 per share on application, Rs. 4 (including premium) on allotment, Rs. 3 on first call and Rs. 3 on final call. Subscription was received for 11,000 shares and directors while making allotment adjusted the excess received on applications to the allotment money due in respect of 500 shares. Three months after the date of allotment, the first call was made. The company received all monies due except in the case of a holder of 200 shares from whom nothing other than application money was received and in respect of another holder of 100 shares in whose case the call money became overdue. The directors, after giving proper notice, forfeited the defaulting shares and re-issued them to a shareholder for a consideration of Rs. 2,000 duly received.

Show journal entries (including cash transactions) in respect of forfeiture and re-issue of forfeited shares in the books of the company.

Solution -

In the books of Co ....
Journal Entries.

Date	Particulars		L.F.	Dr. Rs.	Cr. Rs.
	Share Capital A/c (300 × Rs. 7)	Dr.		2,100	
	Share Premium A/c (200 × Rs. 2)	Dr.		400	
	To Share Allotment A/c				780
	To Share First Call A/c (300 × Rs. 3)				900
	To Share Forfeiture A/c				820
	(Being 300 shares forfeited for the non-payment of shares allotment and first call money Rs. 4 and Rs. 3 respectively as per Board's resolution dated...)				
	Bank A/c	Dr.		2,000	
	Share Forfeiture A/c	Dr.		100	
	To Share Capital A/c				2,100
	(Being 300 forfeited shares re-issued for Rs. 2,000 as per Board's resolution dated....)				
	Share Forfeiture A/c	Dr.		720	
	To Capital Reserve A/c				720
	(Being profit on re-issue of 3,000 shares transferred to Capital Reserve.)				

Note :

1) Share Allotted   Share Applied
   10,000   10,500

   200     $\frac{10,500}{10,000} \times 200 = 210$

2) Amount of arrears on allotment.   Rs.

 Application money received 210 × Rs. 2   420

 Less : Payable on application 200 × Rs. 2   400

 Excess application money adjusted against allotment money 20

                       Rs.

 Amount payable on allotment 200 × Rs. 4   800

 Less : Already paid with application   20

 Arrears on allotment   780

1.3 EXERCISES

Issue and Forfeiture of Shares

1. Apex Co. Ltd. was registered with a capital of Rs. 5,00,000 divided into 5,000 equity shares of Rs. 100 each. On 1.1.09, the Company offered to the public 2,500 shares payable as follows :-

On Application	Rs. 20
On Allotment (1.3.09)	Rs. 40
On first call (1.5.09)	Rs. 20
On Second & final call (1.7.09)	Rs. 20

    Applications totalled 4,000 shares. Applications for 500 shares were rejected and the money received on applications was returned to the applicants. Remaining applications were accepted and 2,500 shares were issued on a pro-rata basis.

    The company received all the monies due on allotment, first call and final call except two calls on 200 shares held by Amit. These shares were forfeited on 31-12-2009. Give the necessary journal entries.

2) Bharat company Ltd. offered for public subscripion 3,000 equity shares of Rs. 100 each at a premium of Rs. 30 per share on the following terms :
    a) Application money to be paid before 30/4/08 at Rs. 60 per share (including the premium).
    b) Allotment money to be paid before 31/7/08 for Rs. 30 per share.
    c) 1st & final call money to be paid before 30th Sept. 2008 balance amount.

    Applications for 6,000 shares were received. The Company decided to -
    1) Allot in full 800 shares to 4 applicants who had applied for the same.
    2) Reject the applications for 800 shares applied by persons who in the opinion of Board of Directors are undesirable.
    3) Allot the balance number of shares proportionately to the applicants and refund the excess paid after deducting the allotment dues.

    Morarjee who was allotted 100 shares on proportion basis could not pay the first & final call. After due notices, all such shares were forfeited and re-issued at a discount of 20% of the face value of the shares, to Mr. Diskshit.

    Pass the necessary journal entries.

    (Ans. Capital Reserve Rs. 4,000)

3) The Bombay Shipping Company Ltd. with an authorised capital of Rs. 20,00,000 in 20,000 equity shares of Rs. 100 each, issued 15,000 equity shares to public for subscription. The terms of issue were -

On Application	15-1-2008	Rs. 20	per	share
On Allotment	15-3-2008	Rs. 20	per	share
On 1st call	15-6-2008	Rs. 30	per	share
On final call	15-12-2008	Rs. 30	per	share

All the amounts were duly received except the following -

a) From Shri Nandlal holding 30 shares on which allotment, 1st call and final call money was in arrears.

b) From Shri Madanlal holding 20 shares on which first and final call money was in arrears.

c) For Shri Chandanmal holding 100 shares out of which final call amount on 10 shares only was in arrears.

The Directors forfeited the shares on which amounts were in arrears and re-issued the same to Shri Gupta on the following terms :-

i) Nandanlal's shares issued at Rs. 90 per share.

ii) Madanlal's shares issued at Rs. 70 per share.

iii) Chandanlal's shares issued at Rs. 50 per share.

Shri Gupta paid the whole amount.

Give journal entries and Balance Sheet for the above.   (P.U.)

4) Mahila Graha Udyog Ltd. issued 1,000 equity shares of Rs. 100 each at a premium of Rs. 20 per share. The share amount was collected as follows :-

On application Rs. 15; on allotment Rs. 55 including premium, on first call Rs. 25 and final call Rs. 15.

Shri Careless to whom 200 shares were allotted, failed to pay both the calls. Shri Misfortune failed to pay final call on his 100 shares. Shares were forfeited on which both the calls were not paid.

The Directors re-issued these forfeited shares to Mr. Lucky at Rs. 80 per share, fully paid.

Give journal entries.   (S.U.)

           (**Ans.** 200 Shares of Careless only are forfeited. Capital Reserve Rs. 6,000.)

5) ABC Co. Ltd. had called up Rs. 100 per share on the whole of subscribed capital of 50,000 equity shares of Rs. 100 payable as follows :

Rs. 10 on application,

Rs. 20 on allotment,

Rs. 30 on first call,

Rs. 40 on final call,

'X', 'Y' & 'Z' were the holders of 100 shares. 200 shares and 300 shares respectively in the above company.

'X' failed to pay the final call, 'Y' failed to pay the first as well as the final call while 'Z' failed to pay the amounts on allotment, first & final calls.

The Directors after giving due notice, forfeited all the shares held by 'X', 'Y' & 'Z' and re-issued all the shares to 'D' for cash at a discount of 10%.

Pass the journal entries regarding forfeiture & re-issue only.   (S.U.)

           (**Ans.** Capital Reserve Rs. 9,000)

6) On 1-1-2009, a company with an authorised capital of Rs. 20,00,000 divided into 1,00,000 equity shares of Rs. 10 each and 50,000 6% preference shares of Rs. 20 each offered its shares to the public on the following terms :

Equity Shares - Rs. 2-50 on application,

Rs. 2-50 on allotment,

Rs. 2-50 on 31st March &

Rs. 2-50 on 31st May

Preference Shares - Rs. 7-50 on application,

Rs. 7-50 on allotment,

Rs. 5-00 on 31st March.

75,000 equity shares and 27,500 preference shares were applied for and allotted on 31-1-2009. By 1st of June, the following sums were received :

Equity Shares - On 69,000 shares - full amount,

On 5,000 shares - Rs. 7-50 each,

On 1,000 shares - Rs. 5-00 each.

Preference shares - On 25,000 shares - full amount,

On 2,500 shares - Rs. 15 each.

The Directors forfeited the equity shares on which only Rs. 5 had been paid and the preference shares upon which full amount due was not paid.

The forfeited equity shares were re-issued on 25th June at a premium of Rs. 2 per share together with the amount due on such shares.

Give Journal entries and Balance Sheet

(**Ans.** 1,000 equity shares and 2500 preference shares are forfeited. Total Capital Reserve Rs. 27,500.) (Eq. 5,000 + Pref. 22,500)

Objective Type

A. State whether the following statements are True or False :

1) The discount on re-issue of forfeited shares should not exceed 10% as specified in Section 75 of the companies Act.

2) Dividend is payable on the calls paid in advance by a shareholder.

3) When shares originally issued at a discount are forfeited, the discount account in respect of them is to be cancelled.

4) A shareholder unable to pay the calls forgoes his right to such shares is called forfeiture of shares.

5) Discount on issue of shares is a revenue loss, hence debited to P & L A/c.

6) Share Premium Account appears on the liability side of the Balance Sheet.

7) On forfeiture of shares, amount called by the company and paid for is forfeited.

8) Any balance left on "Forfeited Shares Account" after re-issue is transferred to Capital Reserve.

9) Forfeited shares are not re-issued by the company.

10) The difference between subscribed capital and called up capital is called paid-up capital.

11) When shares are forfeited, the share capital account is debited by called-up amount.

12) Premium on issue of shares can be used for writing-off preliminary expenses.

Answer : (1) False (2) False (3) True (4) False (5) False (6) True (7) True (8) True (9) False (10) False (11) True (12) True

B) Fill in the blanks :

1) Shares enjoying disproportionate voting rights are called....

2) Profit on re-issue of forfeited shares is to be transfered to .....

3) Calls in advance do not form part of....

4) When shares are forfeited, the share capital account is debited by .....

5) The profit on re-issue of forfeited shares is transferred to.....

6) Discount on issue of shares is a ..... loss.

Answer : (1) Deferred / Founder shares (2) Capital reserve (3) Paid-up capital (4) Called-up amount (5) Capital reserve (6) Capital

C) Theory Questions

1) State the legal provisions as to the utilisation of share premium.

2) Define "share". State its different kinds.

3) When can a company issue shares at a discount? What conditions must a company satisfy for issuing shares at a discount?

4) What is forfeiture of shares? When can shares be forfeited?

5) What is issue of shares? Explain the different steps involved in connection with the issuing and allotment of shares.

6) On what conditions can forfeited shares be received?

D) Write Short Notes on :

a) Allotment of shares

b) Call-on-shares

c) Forfeiture of shares

d) Re-issue of forfeited shares

CHAPTER
2

Redemption of Debentures

2.1 Redemption of Debentures

In the case of Redeemable Debentures, redemption must be effected on the expiry of the fixed period or on the happening of contingency.

Redemption means repayment . Redemption of debentures means to discharge the liability on acount of debentures.

Generally, the terms on which debentures are to be redeemed are given in the prospectus.

A company can redeem debentures : i) at par; ii) at premium; or iii) at discount.

The following three problems require attention when a company wants to redeem or repay the debentures.

1) Time of redemption of debentures

2) Amout to be paid on redemption.

3) Source of finance for redemption.

1) Time of redemption : Generally, debentures are redeemed at the expiry period by making a payment of the amount promised for. If authorised by Articles of Association, a company may have right to redeem debentures even before the date of redemption either by instalments or by purchasing them in the open market. The following are the main methods of redemption of debentures :-

i) **Redemption after a fixed period :** Under this method, the debentures will be redeemed on a specified date mentioned under the terms of issue.

ii) **Redemption by periodical drawings :** Under this method, a certain portion of debentures are redeemed either at the end of each year or any other fixed period. This is generally done by having a draw of lottery. Slips will be put in a drum and out of it, required slips will be taken as the number of debentures to be redeemed.

iii) **Redemption by purchase in open market :** Purchase by a company of its own debentures in the open market is one way of redeeming debentures. In order to avail the opportunity of less prices prevailing in the market of such debentures, the company may decide to purchase its own debentures in the open market. Own Debentures may be purchased for (a) cancellation, (b) for re-issue, or (c) for investment.

iv) **Redemption by conversion :** Sometimes, the shareholders of a company are given the option to convert their debentures into shares within a stipulated period.

v) **Redemption at the option of the company :** The company can also redeem the debentures at its option, provided the terms of issue allows it to do so.

vi) **Sinking fund for redemption :** It is desirable to make some arrangement for their redemption, otherwise it will be very difficult for the company to pay the lumpsum at the time when the redemption is due. For this purpose, a sinking fund is created, so that with accumulated interest and regular yearly provision it may amount to a sum necessary to pay off the debentures on the due date.

vii) **Insurance policy method :** Sinking fund insurance policy can also be taken to make provision for redemption of debentures. Under this method, a fixed amount of premium is paid every year to the insurance company, which in turn, agrees to pay the necessary amount for redemption of debentures at the end of a specific period.

Premium paid is debited to Sinking Fund Policy A/c and credited to Bank A/c. When on maturity, the policy amount is received from insurance company, the reverse entry is passed.

2) Amount to be paid on redemption : The amount to be paid on redemption of debentures depends upon the terms and conditions of issue and redemption and also on circumstances of the case. The journal entries of issue of debentures under different cases are already given in earlier part i.e. 1:3

It should be remembered and noted that -

Premium on issue of debentures is a profit.

Premium on redemption of debentures is a loss.

Discount on issue of debentures is a loss.

Discount on redemption of debentures is a profit.

3) Source of finance of redemption : The funds for redemption come from the following sources :-

a) Out of profits.

b) Out of provision made for redemption.

c) Out of capital

d) By converting debentures into shares or new debentures.

Provision for Redemption of Debentures

In order not to cripple the financial resources of the company on the repayment of debentures, it is advisable to set aside a particular portion from the profits of each year, so that with accumulated interest and regular yearly provision, it may amount to a sum necessary to pay off the debentures on due date.

Necessary journal enries are as under :

1) When provision is made at the end of the year out of profits.
   P & L Appropriation A/c   Dr.
       To Debenture Redemption Fund A/c

2) When this provision is invested in gilt-edged securities outside the business.
   Debenture Redemption Investment A/c   Dr.
       To Bank A/c

3) When interest from such investment is received.
   Bank A/c   Dr.
       To Debenture Redemption Fund A/c

4) When the interest amount together with appropriated amount from profit is further invested.
   Debenture Redemption Fund Investment A/c   Dr.
       To Bank A/c

   This procedure is continued for all the years till the debentures mature and are paid off.

   On repayment of debentures, the Debenture Redemption Fund Investment should be realised and debentures paid off. The entries will be as under.

5) When the investments are sold off :
   Bank A/c   Dr.
       To Debenture Redemption Fund Investment A/c

6) When Debentures are paid off :
   Debentures A/c   Dr.
       To Bank A/c

7) The balance Debenture Redemption Fund Investment A/c will either show a profit or loss, whatever it is, the balance must be transferred to Debenture Redemption Fund A/c, thus closing the Debenture Redemption Fund Investment Account.
   If there is profit, an entry will be
   Debenture Redemption Fund Investment A/c   Dr.
       To Debenture Redemption Fund A/c
   If there is loss, a reverse entry is passed.

8) When debentures are paid off in full or in part, Debenture Redemption Fund or proportionate amount thereof should be transferred to General Reserve A/c. The entry is :
   Debenture Redemption Fund A/c   Dr.
       To General Reserve A/c

Notes :

1) **In the first year,** two entries .... one for keeping aside a certain amount out of profits, and second, for investing the same amount in gilt-edged securities to be passed.

2) **From second and subsequent years,** three entries are to be made.
   a) For interest received on investment (last year balance i.e. opening balance)
   b) For setting aside annual contribution (annual provision), and
   c) Investing the annual provision together with interest to be passed.
3) **In the last year :** First three entries as above; fourth entry for the investment sold, fifth entry for transferring profit or loss on sale of investment; sixth entry for repayment of debentures; and seventh entry (final) for Transferring Fund A/c to General Reserve.
4) Debentures may be redeemed at par, premium or discount. If at premium - it is a loss to be debited to "loss on Issues of Debentures" written off against Debenture Redemption Fund (Sinking Fund) Account.

Problems

Problem 1 : Agra Chemicals Limited issued 1,000 debentures of Rs. 100 each @ 5% on 1st Jan 2006 redeemable at a premium of 10%. Terms of issue provided that the company should set aside every year a sum of Rs. 34,893 to be invested at 5% outside the business. The investments were sold at Rs. 71,580 at the end of the third year and debentures were paid off.

Give journal entries and prepare Sinking Fund A/C. (S.U.)

Solution 1 :

Agra Chemicals Ltd
Journal Book (First Year)

Date	Particulars	L.F.	Dr. Rs.	Cr. Rs.
1-1-06	Bank A/c Dr. Loss on Redemption of Debentures A/c Dr. 　　To 5% Debentures A/c 　　To Premium on Redemption of Debentures A/c (Being issue of 5% debentures at par and repayable after 3years at 10% premium)		1,00,000 10,000	 1,00,000 10,000
31-12-06	Profit & Loss Appropriation A/c Dr. 　　To Sinking Fund A/c (Being set aside for sinking fund)		34,893	 34,893
31-12-06	5% Sinking fund Investment A/c Dr. 　　To Bank A/c (Being amount set aside and invested in 5% securities)		34,893	 34,893
31-12-06	Profit & Loss A/c Dr. 　　To Loss on Redemption of Deb. A/c (Being 1/3rd of loss written off)		3,333	 3,333

Second Year

Date	Particulars	L.F.	Dr. Rs.	Cr. Rs.
31-12-07	Bank A/c Dr. To Sinking Fund A/c (Being interest @ 5% p.a. received on investments of Rs. 34,893)		1,744.65	1,744.65
31-12-07	Profit & Loss Appropriation A/c Dr. To Sinking Fund A/c (Being amount set aside - for Sinking Fund)		34,893	34,893
31-12-07	Profit & Loss A/c Dr. To Loss on Redemption of Deb. A/c (Being 1/2 of Loss written off)		3,333	3,333
31-12-07	Sinking Fund Investment A/c Dr (34,893 + 1,744.65) To Bank A/c (Being amount set aside and interest received is invested in 5% securities)		36,637.65	36,637.65

Third year : (Last year)

Date	Particulars	L.F.	Dr. Rs.	Cr. Rs.
31-12-08	Bank A/c Dr. To Sinking Fund A/c (Being interest @ 5% received on investments of Rs. 34,893 + 36,637.65) i.e. 71,530.65		3,576.53	3,576.53
31-12-08	Profit & Loss Approrriation A/c Dr. To Sinking Fund A/c (Being amount set aside for sinking fund)		34,893	34,893
31-12-08	Bank A/c Dr. To Sinking fund Investments A/c (Being 5% securities sold)		71,580	71,580
31-12-08	Sinking Fund Invesment A/c Dr. To Sinking Fund A/c (Being profit on sale of investment transferred to sinking fund i.e. 71,580-71530.65		49.35	49.35

Date	Particulars		L.F.	Dr. Rs.	Cr. Rs.
31-12-08	5% Debentures A/c Dr.			1,00,000	
	Premium on Redemption of Debentures A/c Dr.			10,000	
	To Bank A/c				1,10,000
	(Being redemption of 5% Debentures at 5% premium)				
31-12-08	Profit & Loss A/c Dr.			3,334	
	To Loss on Redemption of Debentures A/c				3,334
	(Being balance of loss written off)				
31-12-08	Sinking Fund A/c Dr.			1,10,049.53	
	To General Reserve A/c				1,10,049.53
	(Being balance transferred to General Reserve)				

Ledger :

Sinking Fund Account

Dr. Cr.

		Rs.			Rs.
31-12-06	To Balance C/d	34,893	31-12-06	By P & L Appropriation A/c	34,893
			1-1-07	By Bal. B/d	34,893
31-12-07	To Balance C/d	71,530.65	31-12-07	By P & L Appropriation A/c	34,893
				By Bank (int.@5% on 34,893)	1,744.65
		71,530.65			71,530.65
			1-1-08	By Balance B/d	71,530.65
31-12-08	To General Reserve (Transferred)	1,10,049.53	31-12-08	By P & L Appropriaition A/c	34,893
				By Bank (int. @ 5% on 71,530.65)	3,576.53
				By Sinking Fund Investment A/c (Profit on Sale)	49.35
		1,10,049.53			1,10,049.53

Note : This much answer / solution of the problem is required in the examination as stated,

But for the purpose of better understanding, prepare "Additional Accounts"

Problem 2 :

Choundeshwari Weavers Ltd issued 5% Debentures of Rs. 2,00,000 on 1st Jan. 2005 For the redemption of these debentures, it created a Debenture Redemption Fund by transferring Rs. 20,000 out of profits to it at the end of each year. This amount is invested immediately at par in 5% Government securities. The interest of these investments was re-invested in the same securities at par every year. The accounts were closed on 31st December every year.

You are required to write Debenture Redemption Fund Account and Debenture Redemption Fund Investment Account for the four years ending 31-12-2008

(Note : Fractional interest is to be rounded to next digit) (S.U.)

Solution 2 : **Debenture Redemption Fund A/C**
(i.e. Sinking Fund A/C)

Dr. Cr.

		Rs.				Rs.
31-12-05	To Balance c/d	20,000	31-12-05	By P & L Appropriation		20,000
			1-1-05	By Balance b/d		20,000
			31-12-05	By P & L		20,000
31-12-06	To Balance c/d	41,000		Appropriation		
			31-12-06	By Bank (int @ 5% p.a on 20,000)		1,000
		41,000				41,000
31-12-07	To Balance c/d	63,050	1-1-06	By Balance b/d		41,000
			31-12-07	By P & L Appropriation		20,000
				By Bank (int @ 5% p.a.on 41,000)		2,050
		63,050				63,050
31.12.08	To Balance c/d	86,203	1.1.08	By Balance b/d		63,050
			31.12.08	B P&L Appropriation		20,000
			31.12.08	By Bank (int.@ 5% p.a. on 63,050)		3,153
		86,203				86,203
			1.1.09	By Bal. b/d		86,203

5% Debenture Redemption Fund Investment A/c
(i.e.Sinking Fund Investment A/c or Govt securities A/c)

Dr. Cr.

		Rs.			Rs.
31.12.05	To Bank	20,000	31.12.05	By Bal. c/d	20,000
1.1.06	To Bal. b/d	20,000	31.12.06	By Bal. c/d	41,000
31.12.06	To Bank	21,000			
	(20,000 + 1,000)				
		41,000			41,000
1.1.07	To Bal. b/d	41,000	31.12.07	By Bal c/d	63,050
31.12.07	To Bank	22,050			
	(20,000 + 2,050)				
		63,050			63,050
1.1.08	To Bal b/d	63,050	31.12.08	By Bal c/d	86,203
31.12.08	To Bank	23,153			
	(20,000 + 3,153)				
		86,203			86,203
1.1.09	To Balance b/d	86,203			

Problem 3 :

The Swastik Engineering Co. Ltd. had issued 6% debentures of Rs.2,00,000. They were redeemable at 5% premium on 31-12-09. On that date, other concerned ledger accounts showed the following balances:

		Rs.
i)	Debentures Redemption Fund	2,10,000
ii)	Debenures Redemption Fund Investments	
	(5% Maharashtra Govt. Loan 2022 of the face value of Rs. 1,85,000)	1,85,000
iii)	Bank Account	2,21,500
iv)	Premium on Redemption of Debentures A/c	10,000

On 31st Dec - 2009, the investments were sold at 101% and all the debentures were duly redeemed.

Write up all the concerned ledger accounts and show the redemption of debentures Account.

(S.U.)

Solution 3:

The Swastik Engineering Co. Ltd.

Dr.   6% Debentures A/c   Cr.

		Rs.			Rs.
31-12-09	To Bank (Redeemed)	2,10,000	31-12-09	By Bal. b/d	2,00,000
				By Premium on Redemption of Deb.	10,000
		2,10,000			2,10,000

Premium on Redemption of DebentureA/C

Dr.   Cr.

		Rs.			Rs.
31-12-09	To 6% Debentures	10,000	31-12-09	By Balance b/d	10,000

Debenture Redemption Fund A/c

Dr.   (Sinking Fund A/c)   Cr.

		Rs.			Rs.
31.12.09	To General Reserve (Transferred)	2,15,850	31.12.09	By Balance b/d By Debenture Redemption Fund Investment A/c (profit)	2,10,000 5,850
		2,15,850			2,15,850

Debenture Redemption Fund Investment A/c

Dr.   (Sinking Fund Investment A/c)   Cr.

		Rs.			Rs.
31.12.09	To Bal b/d To Debenture Redemption Fund A/c (profit)	1,81,000 5,850	31.12.09	By Bank (sold : Rs. 1,85,000 @ 101%	1,86,850
		1,86,850			1,86,850

Problem 4 : (Sinking Fund Method)

On 1st January, 2005, Supreme Ltd. issued 30,000, 10% redeemable debentures of Rs. 100 each at 5% discount, redeemable at 10% premium on 31st December 20. The amount is to be invested in 10% N.G. Bonds (2006) in multiples of Rs. 100. Amount of annual appropriation is fixed at Rs.4,00,000.

Pass necessary journal entries and show sinking fund account and sinking fund investments account for first 5 years.

Solution :

Journal

Date	Particulars		L.F.	Dr. Rs.	Cr. Rs.
2005 Jan.1	Bank A/c	Dr.		28,50,000	
	Expenses on issue of Debentures A/c	Dr.		3,00,000	
	Discount on issue of Debentures A/c	Dr.		1,50,000	
	To 10% Redeemable Debenture A/c				30,00,000
	To Premium on Redemption of Debentures A/c				3,00,000
	(Being 10% redeemable debentures issued at 5% discount and redeemable at 10% premium)				
2005 Dec.31	At the end of the year				
	Profit & Loss Appropriation	Dr.		4,00,000	
	To Sinking Fund A/C				4,00,000
	(Being annual amount transferred to sinking fund account)				
Dec.31	Sinking Fund Investment A/c	Dr.		4,00,000	
	To Bank A/c				4,00,000
	(Being sinking fund investments purchased)				
2006 Dec.31	At the end of the 2nd year				
	Bank A/C	Dr.		40,000	
	To Sinking Fund A/c				40,000
	(Being interest collected)				
Dec.31	Profit & Loss Appropriation A/c	Dr.		4,00,000	
	To Sinking Fund A/c				4,00,000
	(Being annual amount transferred to sinking fund account)				
Dec.31	Sinking Fund Investment A/c	Dr.		4,40,000	
	To Bank A/c				4,40,000
	(Being investments purchased)				

Date	Particulars	L.F.	Dr. Rs.	Cr. Rs.
2007 Dec.31	At the end of the 3rd year Bank A/c Dr. To Sinking Fund A/c (Being interest collected)		84,000	84,000
Dec.31	Profit & Loss Appropriation A/c Dr. To Sinking Fund A/c (Being annual appropriation amount transferred to Sinking Fund Account)		4,00,000	4,00,000
Dec.31	Sinking Fund Invesments A/c Dr. To Bank A/c (Being investments purchased)		4,84,000	4,84,000
2008 Dec.31	At the end of the 4th year Bank A/c Dr. To Sinking Fund A/c (Being interest collected)		1,32,400	1,32,400
Dec.31	Profit & Loss Appropriation A/c Dr. To Sinking Fund A/c (Being annual set aside)		4,00,000	4,00,000
Dec.31	Sinking Fund Investment Dr. To Bank A/c (Being investment made)		5,32,400	5,32,400
2009 Dec.31	Bank A/c Dr. To Sinking Fund A/c (Being interest collected)		1,85,640	1,85,640
Dec.31	Profit & Loss Appropriation A/c Dr. To Sinking Fund A/c (Being annual appropriation amount transfened to sinking fund account)		4,00,000	4,00,000
	Sinking Fund Investments A/c Dr. To Bank A/c (Being investments purchased)		4,85,600	4,85,600

Ledger Accounts
Sinking Fund A/c

Dr.   Cr.

		Rs.			Rs.
2005			2005		
Dec. 31	To Balance c/d	4,00,000	Dec. 31	By Profit andLoss Appropriation A/c	4,00,000
2006 Dec. 31	To Balance c/d	8,40,000	2006 Jan 1	By Balance b/d	4,00,000
			Dec. 21	By Bank (Interest)	40,000
			Dec. 31	By Profit and Loss Appropriation A/c	4,00,000
		8,40,000			8,40,000
2007 Jan. 1	To Balance c/d	13,24,000	2007 Jan.1	By Balance b/d	8,40,000
			Dec. 31	By Bank (Interest)	84,000
			Dec. 31	By Profit and Loss Appropriation A/c	4,00,000
		13,24,000			13,24,000
2008 Dec. 31	To Balance c/d	18,56,400	2008 Jan. 01	By Balance b/d	13,24,000
			Dec. 31	By Bank (Interest)	1,32,400
			Dec. 31	By Profit and Loss Appropriation A/c	4,00,000
		18,56,400			18,56,400
2009 Dec. 31	To Balance c/d	24,42,040	2009 Jan. 1	By Balance b/d	18,56,400
			Dec 31	By Bank (Interest)	1,85,640
			Dec. 31	By Profit and Loss Appropriation A/c	4,00,000
		24,42,040			24,42,040

Sinking Fund Investments A/c
In 10% N.G. Bonds (2006)

Dr.   Cr.

		Rs.			Rs.
2005			2005		
Dec. 31	To Bank A/c	4,00,000	Dec. 31	By Balance c/d	4,00,000
2006			2006		
Jan. 1	To Balance b/d	4,00,000	Dec. 31	By Balance c/d	8,40,000
Dec. 31	To Bank A/c	4,40,000			
		8,40,000			8,40,000
2007			2007		
Jan 1	To Balance	8,40,000	Dec. 31	By Balance c/d	13,24,000
Dec. 31	To Bank A/c	4,84,000			
		13,24,000			13,24,000
2008			2008		
Jan. 1	To Balance b/d	13,24,000	Dec. 31	By Balance c/d	18,56,400
Dec. 31	To Bank A/c	5,32,400			
		18,56,400			18,56,400
2009			2009		
Jan. 1	To Balance b/d	18,56,400	Dec. 31	By Balance c/d	24,42,000
Dec. 31	To Bank	5,85,600			
		24,42,000			24,42,000

Problem 5 :

On 1st January 2009, the following Ledger Accounts appear in the books of Supreme Ltd. 10% Redeemable Debentures Account Rs. 30,00,000 (redeemable on 31st December 2009 @ 10% premium) :

Sinking Fund Account   24,42,040

Sinking Fund Investment Account   24,42,000

(in 10% N.G. Bonds 1999)

Annual appropriation amount was fixed at Rs. 4,00,000. On 31st December, 2009 all investment were sold at Rs. 24,60,000 and all debentures are redeemed.

You are required to show the following Ledger Accounts :

1. 10% Redeemable Debentures Account;
2. Sinking Fund Account;
3. Sinking Fund Investments Account;
4. 10% Debentureholders Account; and

5. Premiun on Redemption of Debentures Account.

Also pass necessary journal entries.

Solution

Dr.   **10% Debentures A/c**   Cr.

		Rs.			Rs.
2009 Dec. 31	To Debentureholders	30,00,000	2009 Jan 1	By Balance b/d	30,00,000

Dr.   **Sinking Fund A/c**   Cr.

		Rs.			Rs.
2009 Dec. 31	To General Reserve A/c	31,04,240	2009 Jan 1 Dec. 31 Dec. 31 Dec. 31	By Balance b/d By Bank (Interest) By Profit and Loss Appropriation A/c By Sinking Fund Investment A/c	24,42,040 2,44,200 4,00,000 18,000
		31,04,240			31,04,240

Sinking Fund Investment A/c

Dr.   **In 10% N.G. Bonds 2005**   Cr.

		Rs.			Rs.
2009 Jan. 1 Dec. 31	To Balance b/d To Sinking Fund A/c	24,42,000 18,000	2009 Dec. 31	By Bank A/c	24,60,000
		24,60,000			24,60,000

Dr.   **Debentureholders A/c**   Cr.

		Rs.			Rs.
2009 Dec. 31	To Bank A/c	33,00,000	2009 Dec. 31 Dec. 31	By 10% Debenture A/c By Premium on Redemption of Debentures	30,00,000 3,00,000
		33,00,000			33,00,000

Dr. **Premium on Redemption of Debentures A/c** Cr.

		Rs.			Rs.
2009 Dec. 31	To 10% Debenture holders A/c	3,00,000 3,00,000	2009 Jan. 1	By Balance b/d	3,00,000 3,00,000

Solution : **Journal Entries**

Date	Particulars	L.F.	Dr. Rs.	Cr. Rs.
2009 Dec. 31	Bank A/c Dr. To Sinking Fund A/c (Being interest collected)		2,44,200	2,44,200
	Profit & Loss Appropriation A/c Dr. To Sinking Fund A/c (Being annual appropriation amount transferred to sinking fund account)		4,00,000	4,00,000
	Bank A/c Dr. To Sink Fund Investment A/c (Being all investments sold out)		24,60,000	24,60,000
	Sinking Fund Investment A/c Dr. To Sinking Fund A/c (Being profit on sale of investments transferred to sinking fund account)		18,000	18,000
	10% Debentures A/c Dr. Premium on Redemption A/c Dr. To Debentureholders A/c (Being 10% debentures account and premium on redemption of debentures account transferred to debentureholders account)		30,00,000 3,00,000	33,00,000
	Dsebentureholders A/c Dr. To Bank A/c (Being debentures redeemed)		33,00,000	33,00,000
	Sinking Fund A/c Dr. To General Reserve A/c (Being balance on sinking fund account transferred to general reserve account		31,04,240	31,04,240

Problem 6 : (Redemption of all the Debentures)

The following balances stood in the books of the company on 31st December 2009

	Dr.	Cr.
12 per cent First Mortgage Debentures		5,00,000
Debenture Redemption Find		5,00,000
Debentures Redemption Fund Investments :		
Rs. 2,40,000 Government loan	2,45,000	
Rs. 1,80,000 Port Trust Debentures	1,75,000	

The above investments were sold on the above date to redeem the debentures:

Govt. loan at par.

Port Trust Debentures at 95 percent.

The company had sufficient bank balance. The debentures were redeemed on 1st Januray 2010.

You are required to prepare the necessary ledger accounts.

Solution :

Ledger of a Company

Dr.   **12% Mortgage Debentures A/c**   Cr.

Date	Particulars	Rs.	Date	Particulars	Rs.
2009 Jan.1	To Bank	5,00,000 –	2009 Dec. 31	By Balance b/d	5,00,000 –
		5,00,000			5,00,000

Dr.   **Debentures Redemption Fund A/c**   Cr.

Date	Particulars	Rs.	Date	Particulars	Rs.
2009 Dec. 31	To Debentures Redemption Fund Investments A/c	9,000	2009 Dec. 31	By Balance b/d	5,00,000
2010 Jan.1	To General Reserve	4,91,000			
		5,00,000			5,00,000

Dr.		Debentures Redemption Fund Investment A/c				Cr.
Date	**Particulars**	**Rs.**	**Date**	**Particulars**		**Rs.**
2009 Dec. 31	To Balance b/d To Govt. loan To Port Trust Debentures	2,45,000 1,75,000	2009 Dec. 31	By Bank (Govt. loan Sold) By Bank (Port Trust Debentures Sold) By Debentures Redemption Fund A/c (Loss)		2,40,000 1,71,000 9,000
		4,20,000				4,20,000

Explanatory Note :

On redemption of all the debentures, the balance on debenture redemption fund should be transferred to General Reserve.

Problem 7 : (Redemption partly by conversion and by cash)

A Limited Company has an authorised capital of Rs. 10,00,000 in shares of Rs. 10 each of which 60,000 shares have been issued and are fully paid :

A summary of its balance sheet on 31st March 2009 is as follows :

Liabilities	**Rs.**	**Assets**	**Rs.**
Share Capital	6,00,000	Fixed Assets (Net)	11,00,000
Debenture Redemption Fund	4,80,000	Debenture Redemption	
Profit and Loss A/c	1,90,000	Fund Investment (Cost)	
9% Debentures		(Market Value Rs. 4,08,000)	4,80,000
Redeemable at 102%	5,00,000	Current Assets	3,00,000
Current Liabilities	1,10,000		
	18,80,000		18,80,000

Interest on the debentures had been paid upto 31st March 2009. On 1st April, 2009, the directors gave notice to redeem the 9% debentures. On 1st July, 2009; giving the holders the option to be repaid either wholly in cash or by issue of four shares of Rs. 10 each fully paid for every Rs. 100 debentures.

Sixty per cent of holders exercised the option to take the shares, and the cash for the remainder was obtained by realising a suffcient amount of the investments at their market value on 31st March 2009.

Draft journal entries to record these transactions and any consequential transfers which you consider necessary. (P.U.)

Solution : **Journal of a Limited Company**

Date	Particulars	L.F.	Dr. Rs.	Cr. Rs.
2009 July 1	Debentures A/c Dr. Premium on Redemption of Debentures A/c Dr. To Debentures Redemption A/c (Being the amount due on redemption of debentures at 102%)		5,00,000 10,000	5,10,000
July 1	Bank A/c Dr. Debenture Redemption Fund A/c Dr. To Debenture Redemption Fund Investment A/c (Being the sale of investments of Rs. 2,40,000 at a loss of Rs. 36,000)		2,04,000 36,000	2,40,000
July 1	Debentures Redemption A/c Dr. To Share Capital A/c (12,000 × 10) To Securities Premium A/c (3,06,000 - 1,20,000) To Bank A/c (Being the redemption of Rs. 3,00,000 debentures by conversion and of Rs. 2,00,000 in cash)		5,10,000	1,20,000 1,86,000 2,04,000
July 1	Debentures Redemption Fund A/c Dr. To General Reserve A/c (Being transfer of balance to general reserve account)		4,44,000	4,44,000
July 1	Securities Premium A/c Dr. To Premium on Redemption of Debentures A/c (Being premium on redemption written off)		10,000	10,000

Explanatory Note :

No. of Shares to be issued for redemption of debentures = 3,000 × 4 = 12,000 Shares

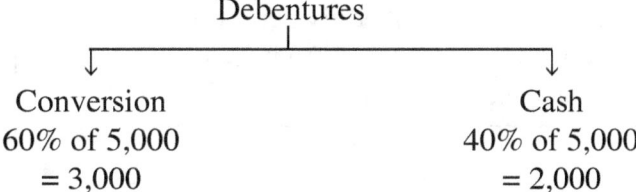

Debentures

Conversion	Cash
60% of 5,000	40% of 5,000
= 3,000	= 2,000

Problem 8 :

(Redemption by purchasing debentures in the open market)

On 1st April, 2008, debentures account showed a balance of Rs. 1,50,000 in the books of R Ltd. A Sinking Fund exists to redeem the debentures which the trustees empowered to utilise in cancelling the debentures by open market purchase at below par. The sinking fund stood at Rs. 48,750 on 1st April, 2008 and the entire amount has been invested. During the year 2008-09, trustees sold to investments and redeemed the debentures as noted below:

Date	Investments Cost Rs.	Realised Rs.	Debentures Face Value Rs.	Cost Rs.
31-05-2008	18,000	17,562	18,800	17,210
31-12-2008	10,000	11,050	11,200	10,980

Interest received on 31st March, 2009 was Rs. 1,070 and the annual contribution was Rs. 17,200.

Pass the necessary entries to record the above transactions.

Solution :   **Journal of R Ltd.**

Date	Particulars	L.F.	Dr. Rs.	Cr. Rs.
2008 May 31	Bank A/c Dr.		17,562	
	Sinking Fund A/c Dr.		438	
	To Sinking Fund Investment A/c			18,000
	(Being the Sale of investnents and loss there on transferred to Sinking fund accounts)			
May 31	Debentures A/c Dr.		18,800	
	To Bank A/c			17,210
	To Sinking Fund A/c			1,590
	(Being the redemption of debentures by purchase from open market)			

May 31	Sinking Fund A/c	Dr.		18,800	
	To General Reserve				18,800
	(Being transfer of amount equivalent to face value of debentures redeemed from sinking fund account to general reserve)				
Dec. 31	Bank A/c	Dr.		11,050	
	To Sinking Fund Investment A/c				11,050
	(Being sale of investments)				
Dec. 31	Sinking Fund Investments A/c	Dr.		1,050	
	To Sinking Fund A/c				1,050
	(Being transfer of profit on sale of investments)				
Dec. 31	Debentures A/c	Dr.		11,200	
	To Bank A/c				10,980
	To Sinking Fund A/c				220
	(Being the redemption of debentures by purchase from open market)				
Dec. 31	Sinking Fund A/c	Dr.		11,200	
	To General Reserve				11,200
	(Being transfer of amount equivalent to face value of debentures redeemed from sinking fund to general reserve)				
2009 Mar 31	Bank A/c	Dr.		1,070	
	To Sinking Fund A/c				1,070
	(Being receipt of interest on sinking fund investment account)				
Mar. 31	Profit and Loss Appropriation A/c	Dr.		17,200	
	To Sinking Fund A/c				17,200
	(Being the annual fund instalment appropriated)				

Ledger Accounts

Dr. **Debentures A/c** **Cr.**

Date	Particulars	Rs.	Date	Particulars	Rs.
2008			2008		
May 31	To Bank	17,210	April 1	By Balance b/d	1,50,000
May 31	To Sinking Fund	1,590			
Dec. 31	To Bank	10,980			
Dec. 31	To Sinking Fund	220			
2009					
Mar. 31	To Balance c/d	1,20,000			
		1,50,000			1,50,000

Dr. **Sinking Fund A/c** **Cr.**

Date	Particulars	Rs.	Date	Particulars	Rs.
2008			2008		
May 31	To Sinking Fund		April 1	By Balance b/d	48,750
	Investments A/c	438	May 31	By Debentures A/c	1,590
May 31	To General Reserve	18,800	Dec. 31	By Sinking Fund	
Dec/ 31	To General Reserve	11,200		Investments A/c	1,050
			Dec. 31	By Debentures A/c	220
2009			2009		
Mar. 31	To Balance c/d	39,442	Mar 31	By Bank	1,070
			Mar 31	By Profit and Loss	
				Appropriation A/c	17,200
		69,880			69,880

Dr. **Sinking Fund Investment A/c** **Cr.**

Date	Particulars	Rs.	Date	Particulars	Rs.
2008			2008		
April 1	To Balance b/d	48,750	May 31	By Bank A/c	17,562
Dec. 31	To Sinking Fund A/c		May 31	By Sinking Fund A/c	
	(Profit on Sale)	1,050		(Loss on sale)	438
			Dec. 31	By Bank A/c	11,050
			2009		
			Mar. 31	By Balance c/d	20,750
		49,800			49,800

2.2 Issue of Debentures

Meaning : Like shares, debentures too are issued by the company. It does so, by inviting the public to apply for its debentures by way of issuing prospectus.

The word "Debenture" is used to signify the acknowledgement of a debt, given under the seal of the company and containing a contract for the repayment of the principal sum at specified date and for the payment of interest either on yearly or half yearly basis.

The interest must be paid on the face value of the debenture whether there is profit or loss to the company and is debited to P & L A/c.

Debentures can be issued by the company for various purposes :

e.g :-

i) Debentures can be issued for "cash".

ii) Debentures can be issued for "purchase of assets".

iii) Debentures can be issued as "collateral security".

Difference between Debentures and Shares

	Debentures		Shares
1)	Debenture is a debt of the company.	1)	Share is a part of the capital of the company.
2)	Debenture-holder is not a member of the company.	2)	Shareholder is a member of the company.
3)	Debentureholder receives interest.	3)	Shareholder receives a dividend.
4)	Interest on Debenture is payable even if there may or may not be a profit to the company.	4)	Dividend is payable to the shareholders only when there is a profit to the company.
5)	Debentureholders have no right of voting.	5)	Shareholders have a right of voting.

Kinds Of Debentures

1) Redeemable debentures are those which are paid out at the expiry of a fixed period.

2) Irredeemable debentures are those which are not repaid during the life of the company.

3) Simple or Naked debentures are those where no security is given.

4) Mortgage debentures are those which are secured by fixed charge on the assets of the company.

5) Floating debentures are those which are secured not against any specific fixed or floating asset but by a floating charge on company's property belonging to the company at the time of settling the claim.

6) Bearer debenture i.e. Debentures payable to a bearer.

7) Registered debentures are debentures registered in the names of the holders in the books of the company.

Debenture and Debenture Stock

Debenture Stock is a debt owed by a company and is usually secured by a Trust Deed on the property of the company.

Difference :

i) Debentures are payable after a expiry of certain period, but debenture stock becomes payable only in the event of winding up.

ii) Debenture stock must always be fully paid but debentures of other classes may be partly paid.

Procedure :

The public will apply for debentures just as they apply for shares.

After receipt of applications, the directors will consider them and will make the allotment according to their discretion.

The face value of one debenture may be divided into various instalments : e.g. Debenture of Rs. 100 each may be divided us under :

on application	Rs. 20
on allotment	Rs. 30
on first call	Rs. 25
on final call	Rs. 25

The debentures can be issued at par, premium and discount like shares.

Accounting Entries

On application :	i)	Bank A/c	Dr.
		To Debenture Application A/c	
		(Being application money received on Debentures)	
	ii)	Debenture Application A/c	Dr.
		To Debentures A/c	
		(Being application money transferred to Debentures A/c)	
On allotment :	i)	Debenture Allotment A/c	Dr.
		To Debentures A/c	
		(Being allotment made on ..... Debentures.)	
	ii)	Bank A/c	Dr.
		To Debenture Allotment A/c	
		(Being Allotment money received)	
On call :	i)	Debenture first / second / finall call A/c	Dr.
		To Debentures A/c	
		(Being call made on ...... Debentures)	

ii) Bank A/c   Dr.
     To Debenture first / second / final call A/c
     (Being call money received)

It is usual to put the rate of interest before debentures, if the debentures carry interest at the rate of 8% for e.g., the account will be headed as '8% debentures account.'

Debentures account appear on the liability side of Balance Sheet under the head "secured loans".

Example : Suppose, 1,000 8% Debentures of Rs. 100 are issued at par payable as to Rs. 20 on application. Rs. 30 on allotment and Rs. 50 on call.

The above mentioned journal entries are passed with the respective amounts.

The students are requested to fill up the above journal entries with Rs. 20,000, Rs. 30,000 and Rs. 50,000.

Then, balance sheet will appear as under :

Balance Sheet

Liabilities	Rs.	Assets	Rs.
Secured Loans : 8% Debentures of Rs. 100 each fully paid	1,00,000	Bank	1,00,000

Various cases of Issue and Redemption of Debentures
Cases Table

No.	Face Rs.	Issued at Rs.	Redemption at Rs.	Meaning
1.	100	100	100	It means issued at par and redemption at par,
2.	100	95	100	It means issued at Discount and Redemption at par,
3.	100	102	100	It means issued at premium and Redemption at par,
4.	100	100	102	It means issued at par and Redemption at premium,
5.	100	95	102	It means issued at discount and redemption at premium,
6.	100	100	95	It means issued at par and redemption at discount.

Problems

Case No. 1 : Issued at par, redemption at par.

Problem 1 : AB Ltd. issued 1,000 8% debentures of Rs. 100 each at par and redeemable after 5 years at par. Give journal entries on issue and redemption.

Solution 1 :   **Journal Book**
                                    On Issue

			Rs.	Rs.
Entry :	Bank A/c Dr.		1,00,000	....
	To 8% Debentures A/c		......	1,00,000
	(Being issue of 8% debentures at par and redeemable after 5 years at par.)			

On Redemption

			Rs.	Rs.
Entry :	8% Debentures A/c Dr.		1,00,000	.....
	To Bank A/c			1,00,000
	(Being redemption of 8% debentures at par.)			

Case No. 2 : Issued at Discount and Redemption at par

Problem 2 : BC Ltd. issued 2,000 10% debentures of Rs. 10 each at 5% discount and redeemable after 10 years at par.

Give journal entries on issue and redemption.

Solution 2 :   **Journal Book**
                                    On Issue

			Rs.	Rs.
Entry :	Bank A/c Dr.		1,90,000	....
	Discount on Issue of Debentures A/c Dr.		10,000	.....
	To 10% Debentures A/c		......	2,00,000
	(Being issue of 10% debentures at 5% discount and redeemable after 10 years.)			

On Redemption

			Rs.	Rs.
Entry :	10% Debentures A/c Dr.		2,00,000	.....
	To Bank A/c			2,00,000
	(Being redemption of 10% debentures at par.)			

Note : "Discount on Issue of Debentures A/c" is a loss to the company. This loss is written off gradually every year during the life of debentures. The unwritten off portion appears in the balance sheet on the asset side under the heading "miscellaneous expenditure."

Here, every year Rs. 1,000 (10,000 ÷ 10 years) will be written off against P & L A/c and balance appears on assets side, till it is fully written off.

Problem 3 : Case No. 3 : Issued at Premium and Redemption at Par.

CD Ltd. issued 3,000, 9% debentures of Rs. 100 each at 15% premium and redeemble after 10 years at par.

Give journal entries on issue and redemption.

Solution 3 : **Journal Book**
On Issue

			Rs.	Rs.
Entry :	Bank A/c	Dr.	3,45,000	.....
	To 9% Debentures A/c		.....	3,00,000
	To Premium on Issue of 9%			
	Debentures A/c		......	45,000
	(Being issue of 9% debentures at 15% premium and redeemable at par).			

On Redemption

			Rs.	Rs.
Entry :	9% Debenture A/c	Dr.	3,00,000	.....
	To Bank A/c		.....	3,00,000
	(Being redemption of 9% debentures at par)			

Note : Premium on Issue of Debentures is a capital profit but it shall not be added in the share capital of the company : "Debenture premium on Issue" appears in the B/s under the heading "Reserves and Surplus."

Case No. 4 : Issued at Par and Redemption at Premium.

Problem 4 : DE Ltd. issued 4,000, 7% Debentures of Rs. 100 each at par and redeemable after 10 years at 10% premium.

Give journal entries on issue and redemption.

Solution 4 : **Journal Book**
On Issue

			Rs.	Rs.
Entry :	Bank A/c	Dr.	4,00,000	.....
	Loss on Redemption of Debentures A/c	Dr.	40,000	...
	To 7% Debentures A/c			4,00,000
	To Premium on Redemption of Debentures A/c			40,000
	(Being issue of 7% debentures at par and redeemable after 10 years at 10% premium.)			

On Redemption

			Rs.	Rs.
Entry :	7% Debentures A/c	Dr.	4,00,000	.....
	Premium on Redemption of Debentures A/c Dr.		40,000	.....
	To Bank A/c		......	4,40,000
	(Being redemption of 7% debentures at 10% premium.)			

Notes :

i) If debentures are issued on the condition that they will be redeemed at premium, then company stands to lose the amount of premium when the repayment of loan takes place. It must be very carefully noted that the loss will accrue only when the actual redemption of debenture takes place. But in keeping with the convention of conservatism, the company records the loss in anticipation by debiting "Loss on Redemption of Debentures A/c."

ii) "Loss on Redemption" Rs. 40,000 will be written off against P & L proportionately every year Rs. 4,000 (40,000 ÷ 10 years) till it is fully written off and balance will appear in Balance sheet's asset side.

iii) Premium on redemption of debentures is a personal A/c because there is a liability on the part of the company to pay the debenture holders at a premium. This account appears in the Balance sheet's liability side under the head "Current Liabilities." until repayment is made.

Case No. 5 : Issued at Discount and Redemption at Premium

Problem 5 :

FG Ltd. issued 5,000, 6% debentures of Rs. 100 each at 5% discount redeemable after 20 years at a premium of 2%. Give journal entries on issue and redemption.

Solution 5 :   Journal Book
On Issue

			Rs.	Rs.
Entry :	Bank A/c	Dr.	4,75,000	.....
	Discount on issue of Debentures	Dr.	25,000	.....
	Loss on Redemption of Debentures A/c	Dr.	10,000	
	To 6% Debentures A/c		....	5,00,000
	To premium on Redemption of Debentures A/c		......	10,000
	(Being issue of 6% debentures at 5% discount and redeemable after 20 years at 2% premium)			

On Redemption

			Rs.	Rs.
Entry :	6% Debentures A/c	Dr.	5,00,000	.....
	Premium on Redemption of Debentures A/c	Dr.	10,000	.....
	To Bank A/c		......	5,10,000
	(Being redemption of 6% debentures at 2% premium)			

Note : Please see for notes, cases No. 2 and 4 above.

2.3 EXERCISE

Objective Type

A) State whether the following statements are True or False :

1) Debentureholders are the owners of a company.
2) Interest on debentures is to paid at a pre-determined fixed rate.
3) Premium on issue of debentures is a profit while premium on redemption of debentures is a loss.
4) Discount on redemption of debentures is a loss.
5) Debentureholders can influence the management the affairs of the company.
6) Discount on issue of debentures appears on the asset side of balance sheet under the words "miscellaneous expenditure."
7) A Company cannot buy its on debentures.

Answer : (1) False (2) True (3) True (4) False (5) False (6) True (7) True

B) Fill in the blanks :

1) Debentureholders are ..... of a company.
2) Interest on debentures is to be paid at pre - determined.....
3) Premium on issue of debentures is a....
4) Discount on issue of debentures is a....
5) After redemption of debentures, the balance on sinking fund account is to be transferred to....
6) If debentures are redeemed at a premium, it is a loss and to be debited to.....

Answer : (1) Creditors (2) Fixed rate (3) Profit (4) Loss (5) General reserve (6) Debentures account.

C) Theory Questions

1) Define "debenture." Distinguish it from debenture stock.
2) What are the types of debenture?

3) Enumerate and describe the various ways of issuing debentures.

4) Write Short Notes on :

a)   Redemption of debentures

a) Issue of Debentures

1) Rajkumar Ltd. makes a public issue of 20,000 shares of Rs. 10 each payable as follows.

On application	Rs.1
On allotment	Rs. 2
On first Call	Rs. 3
On 2nd & final call	Rs. 4

All the shares were duly subscribed and all shareholders paid the money due on shares except Shri Jayraman holding 400 shares did not pay the 2nd call. His shares were then forfeited. These were re-issued as fully paid @ Rs. 5 per share.

The Company also issued 1,000 debentures of Rs. 100 each at a discount of 5% redeemable at a premium of 10% after 10 years.

Set out the journal entries.

2) The Iceland company issued 10,000 6% debentures of Rs. 100 each at par repayable after a period of 10 years at a premium of 5%. Give journal entries on issue and redemption. (P.U.)

(Hint - Refer Case No. 4)

3) Dawson Ltd. issued 1,000, 6% debentures of Rs. 100 each, payable as to Rs. 20 on application and the balance on allotment. Applications were received for 1,500 debentures out of which applications for 900 shares were allotted fully, applicants for 400 were allotted 100 debentures and the remaining rejected.

All sums due were received journalise the above. (S.U.)

4) ABC Ltd has an authorised capital of Rs. 4,50,000 in shares of Rs. 20 each, of which shares of the face value of Rs. 3,00,000 have been issued and paid up. The company has also issued Rs. 1,00,000 of debentures bearing interest at 8% and redeemable at the option of the company at any time at a premium of 5%. The company decides to redeem the debentures and to issue the remaining shares at Rs. 25 each. The premium on shares is to be used in paying the premium on redemption of debentures and the balance transferred to capital reserve account.

The shares are all taken up and paid for as follows. Rs. 5 on application, Rs. 15 on allotment (including premium) and Rs. 5 on first and final call. The debentures are paid off.

Give journal entries and show the debentures and share capital accounts after the transactions are completed. (S.U.)

(Hints & Answers)

 i) Take balance on Share Capital A/c & Debentures A/c at Rs. 3,00,000 and Rs. 1,00,000 respectively on credit side,

 ii) Balance on Share Capital A/c Rs. 4,50,000 & balance on Debentures A/c. Nil.)

 5) Honest Efforts Ltd. had issued 6% Debentures of Rs. 25,50,000 in the past on condition to redeem the same at a premuim of 2% on 31st Dec. 2008, the company offered the debentureholders the following options :

 a) To accept 8% cumulative preference shares of Rs. 100 each at a premium of Rs. 10 per share.

OR

 b) To accept 5% new debentures at a discount of 4% repayable at par.

OR

 c) To accept cash.

Holders of Rs. 11,00,000 debentures opted for the first option. Holders of Rs. 10,00,000 debentures opted for the second option, and the rest opted for the third option.

Show journal entries to record the redemption of 6% debentures under first, second and third options as exercised by the debentureholders. (S.U)

Hints -

 i) In every case debit "Premium on Redemption of Debentures A/c" at 2% on Rs. 11,00,000; Rs. 10,00,000 & Rs. 4,50,000 (25,50,000 - 11,00,000 - 10,00,000)

 ii) In every case, 1st entry will be for crediting debentureholders A/c with their amount due + 2% premium.

 iii) In every case, the second entry will be for redemption of debentures and crediting with the respective option they have opted.

 iv) In first case, entries can be passed as -

 a) 6% debentures A/c Dr. 11,00,000
    Premium on Redemption of Deb. A/c Dr. 22,000
    To 6% debentureholders A/c 11,22,000.

 b) 6% debentureholders A/c Dr. 11,22,000.
    To 8% cumulative preference share capital A/c 10,20,000.
    To preference share premium A/c 1,02,000.

b) Redemption of Debentures

 1) On 1-1-2007, a Company issued 1,000 debentures of Rs. 100 each at par, the whole of that amount being received. For the redemption of these debentures, it provided a sinking fund of Rs. 10,000 at the end of every year. This amount is invested immediately at par - 4% Govt. securities. The interest of these investments was reinvested in the same securities at par every year.

On 31-12-2008, the company redeemed Rs. 7,000 debentures at 3% premium and the required amount was realised by selling Rs. 8,000 Govt. securities at 98%.

On 31-12-2009, the company sold Rs. 6,000 securities at 4% premium and used the proceeds to redeem Rs. 5,000 debentures at 983.

Write the necessary accounts in the books of the company for 2007, 2008 and 2009.

(P.U.)

(**Ans.** i) Balance on debentures A/c Rs. 88,000,

ii) Loss on sale of security Rs. 160,

iii) Profit on sale of security Rs. 240.)

2) On June 30, 2009 the following balances stood in the books of PQR Co. Ltd.

6% Mortgage Debentures.	Rs. 4,00,000
Debenture Redemption Reserve Fund	Rs. 4,26,160

The above fund was invested in the following securities :

Rs. 2,40,000 4¾ % Govt. Loan 2007	Rs. 2,42,520
Rs. 1,90,000 4½% Govt. Loan 2012	Rs. 1,83,640

To redeem the debentures on June, 30, 2004, the above investments were sold on the same as detailed below

4¾% Govt. Loan 2007 at par.

4½% Govt. Loan 2007 at Rs. 96

Draw up the necessary ledger accounts, bring down their balances, if any, after the redemption of debentures and state how they will be disclosed in the Balance Sheet

(P.U.)

(**Ans.** i) Loss on sale of investments Rs. 7600.

ii) Transfer or sinking fund to general reserve Rs. 4,18,560)

3) A Limited Co. had issued 7% mortgage debentures of the sum of Rs. 10,00,000 on 1st Feb. 1999 at a discount of 5% redeemable in 20 years at par. but with the right to redeem at any time after ten years at a premium of 5% upon three months notice to exercise its option on 1st Feb. 2009. The sinking fund investments by then amounted half the amount of the liability and were realised at a premium of 10%. The whole of the debentures were paid off on 1st May 2009, half the amount required being satisfied by a loan on mortagage from Union Bank Ltd.

Give the journal entries relating to the redemption. (S.U.)

4) X Ltd. issued 5,000, 7% redeemable debentures of Rs. 100 each at a discount of 2% repayable after 10 years at a premium of 5%. The entire issue was subscribed and paid for. On 1st Jan. 2003. It was decided by the company to set up a sinking fund for the purpose of the redemption of debentures and set aside Rs. 40,000 at the end of every year out of profits. The sinking fund is invested in 5% Government securities. You are required to show the necessary ledger accounts in the books of X Ltd. for the year ending on 31st December 2003 and 2004 to record the above transactions. (P.U.)

CHAPTER
3

Redemption of Preference Shares

3.1 Redemption of Preference Shares
3.2 Problems
3.3 Exercises

3.1 Redemption of Preference Shares :

When the capital is raised by issuing redeemable preference shares, it is to be paid back by the company to such shareholders after the expiry of stipulated period whether the company is to wound up or not.

A company limited by shares may (if authorised by its articles) issue redeemable preference shares in accordance with Sec. 80.

Provisions of Sec. 80 :

  (i) Redeemable preference shares can be redeemed out of the profits of the company which would otherwise be available for; dividend or;

 (ii) Redeemable preference shares can be redeemed out of the proceeds of fresh issue of shares made for the purpose of redemption,

(iii) Redeemable preference shares can be redeemed if they are fully paid;

 (iv) Premium if any, payable on redemption must have been provided for out of the profits of the company or out of the company's Share Premium Account before the shares are redeemed;

  (v) Where redeemable preference shares are to be redeemed out of profits, then an amount equal to nominal amount of shares so redeemed must, out of profits (available for dividends) be transferred to a reserve called the "Capital Redemption Reserve Account.";

 (vi) The redemption of preference shares by a company will not be taken as reducing the amount of its authorised share capital ;

(vii) The Capital Redemption Reserve Account may be applied by the company in paying up un-issued shares of the company to be issued to the members of the company as "fully paid bonus shares" otherwise the provisions relating to the reduction of the share capital will apply as if the Capital Redemption Reserve A/c were paid-up share capital.

Accounting Entries

1) Transfer of redeemable preference share capital and premiums, if any, payable on redemption to shareholder's account.

Redeemable Preference Share Capital A/c   Dr.
Premium on Redemption of Pref. Shares A/c (if any)   Dr.
    To Sundry members (shareholders) A/c

2) Issue and allotment of shares for the purpose of redemption.

Bank A/c   Dr.
    To Share Application A/c

3) Transfer the account to share capital A/c :

Share Application A/c   Dr.
    To Share Capital A/c
    To Share Premium A/c (if any)

4) For providing the amount of premium payable on redemption from the profits of the company or Share Premium A/c if any, existing.

Profit & Loss A/c   Dr.
OR
Share Premium A/c   Dr.
    To premium on redemption of Pref. Shares A/c

5) Transfer an amount equal to the nominal value of shares redeemed out of profits of the company to Capital Redemption Reserve A/c :

Profit and Loss A/c   Dr.
OR
General Reserve A/c   Dr.
    To Capital Redemption Reserve A/c

Important Note : If they are to be redeemed out of proceeds of fresh issue of shares, then there is no necessity of creating Capital Redemption Reserve A/c

6) For amount paid to shareholders :

Sundry members (or Shareholders) A/c   Dr.
    To Bank A/c

Important Points :

1) If in the example, the shares are to be redeemed without issue of fresh shares, existence of profit should be assumed, and a sum equal to the nominal value of shares redeemed be transferred to the "Capital Redemption Reserve A/c."

2) If the shares to be redeemed are partly paid, they are to be made fully paid by making a find call and presuming that the call is received on all shares before redemption is effected.

3) The term "proceeds" will not include, for the purpose of redemption of preference shares, the amount of share premium from the fresh issue. Thus, the term "proceeds" will correspond with the nominal value. But when fresh issue is at a discount, actual

proceeds after deducting will be considered.

4) The term "profits", for the purpose of redemption of preference shares, has been qualified by the wording "Otherwise available for dividend." Hence, profits which are not free for distribution cannot be utilised for the purpose of redemption.

5) It should be noted that an issue of debentures is not to be considered for this redemption purpose.

6) Transfer to Capital Redemption Reserve A/c is not to be made from share premium, Forfeited Shares A/c profits prior to incorporation and Capital Reserve.

Effects of Redemption of Preference Shares on the Balance Sheet

1) Profits otherwise available for dividend will be reduced by the amount transferred.

2) Capital Redemption Reserve A/c created.

3) Share Premium A/c or Profit and Loss A/c will be reduced by the amount transferred to premium on redemption.

4) Equity share capital or Preference share capital will be increased by fresh issue.

5) Preference share capital given in the Balance Sheet will not be shown in the new Balance Sheet.

6) Cash/Bank balance will be increased by the amount of fresh issue and reduced by the amount paid to preference shareholders.

7) Sale of investment and issue of debentures, if any, will increase the bank balance. Investments sold will not be shown in the new Balance Sheet while debentures will be shown on the liability side of the Balance Sheet.

8) New share premium (if any) will be added to old share premium.

9) Discount on issue of shares / debentures, if any, will be shown on the asset side of the new Balance Sheet.

10) Debenture premium, if any, will be shown on the liability side of the new Balance Sheet.

11) Profit on sale of investment will be added to P. & L A/c balance while loss on sale of invesment will be deducted from P. & L A/c balance.

12) If instruction is given in the problem to keep any balance to the credit of Profit and Loss A/c, the amount used for redemption will be calculated as follows :

	Rs.
Profit and Loss A/c Balance as per B/S	....
	....
Add profit on sale of Investments (if any)	....
Less : loss on sale of Investments (if any)	....
Less : Amount transferred to premium on redemption	....
Less : Balance to be kept (required)	....
Amount to be used for redemption of Pref. shares	....

3.2 PROBLEMS

Problem 1 : Bombay Burma Ltd. issued on 1st July, 1997, 10,000 redeemable preference shares of Rs.10 each. Such shares were redeemable at a premium of 10%

Two-fifths of this issue was redeemed out of profits on 20th Jan. 2002.

On 20th Dec. 2009, the company issued 20,000 equity shares of Rs.10 each at a premium of Rs. 4 per share. Out of the proceeds of such issue, the balance of redeemable preference shares were redeemed.

Give necessary journal entries.

Solution 1 : **Bombay Burma Ltd.**
Journal Book

Date	Particulars	L.F.	Dr. Rs.	Cr. Rs.
20-1-09	Profit & Loss A/c Dr.		4,000	
	To Premium on Redemption A/c			4,000
	(Being provision made for premium on redemption.)			
20-1-09	Profit & Loss A/C (1,00,000 × 2/5) Dr.		40,000	
	To Capital Redemption Reserve A/c			40,000
	(Being provision made out of profits for redemption of capital)			
20-1-09	Redeemable Pref. Share Capital A/c Dr.		4,0000	
	Premium on Redemption A/c Dr.		4,000	
	To Redeemable Pref. share holders A/c			44,000
	(Being amount payable is credited)			
20-1-09	Redeemable Pref. Shareholders A/c Dr.		44,000	
	To Bank A/c			44,000
	(Being redemption of Pref. shares at 10% premium)			
20-12-09	Bank A/c Dr.		2,80,000	
	To Equity Share Capital A/c			2,00,000
	To Equity Share Premium A/c			80,000
	(Being 20,000 equity shares issued at premium of Rs. 4 per share)			
20-12-09	Equity Share Premium A/c Dr.		6,000	
	To premium on Redemption A/c			6,000
	(Being premium payable is provided out of equity share premium)			
20-12-09	Redeemable Preference Share Capital A/c Dr.		60,000	
	Premium on Redemption A/c Dr.		6,000	
	To Redeemable pref. Shareholders A/c			66,000
	(Being amount payable credited to its holders)			
20-12-09	Redeemable Pref. Shareholders A/c Dr.		66,000	
	To Bank A/c			66,000
	(Being redemption of pref. shares at 10% premium)			

Note :	2/5th on 20-1-02 = 1,00,000 × 2/5 =	40,000
	Add : 10% premium	4,000
	Paid out of profits on 20.1.02	44,000
	3/5th on 20.12.09 = 1,00,000 × 3/5 =	60,000
	Add : 10% premium	6,000
	Paid out by fresh issue on 20.12.09	66,000

Problem 2 :

A company has 4,000 6% Redeemable preference shares of Rs. 100 each fully paid. The company decides to redeem the shares on December 31st 2008 at a premium of 5%

The company makes the following issues :

a) 1,000 equity shares of Rs. 100 each at a premium of 10%

b) 1,000 6% debentures of Rs. 100 each.

The issue was fully subscribed and all amounts were received. The redemption was duly carried out. The company has sufficient profits.

Give journal entries.

Solution 2 :   **Journal Book**

Date	Particulars	L.F.	Dr. Rs.	Cr. Rs.

a)
31-12-08
	Bank A/c Dr.
	   To Equity Share Capital A/c
	   To Equity Share Premium A/c
	(Being issue of 1,000 eq. shares at 10% premium)
			1,10,000	
				1,00000
				10,000

b) 31-12-08	Bank A/c Dr. To 6% Debentures A/c (Being issue of debentures at par)		1,00,000	 1,00,000
31-12-08	Profit & Loss A/c Dr. To premium on Redemption of Pref. Shares A/c (Being provision made out of profits for redemption of pref shares of Rs. 4,00,000 at 5% premium)		20,000	 20,000
31-12-08	Profit & Loss A/c Dr. To Capital Redemption Reserve A/c (Being the amount uncovered by issue of equity shares only (not debentures) i.e. Rs. 3,00,000 (4,00,000 - 1,00,000) is transferred from profit to Redempition Reserve.)		3,00,000	 3,00,000
31-12-08	6% Redeemable Pref. Share Capital A/c Dr. Premium on Redemption A/c Dr. To Redeemable Pref. Share Holders A/c (Being amount payable credited to redeemable Pref. Share Holders A/c)		4,00,000 20,000	 4,20,000

Date	Particulars	L.F.	Dr. Rs.	Cr. Rs.
31-12-08	Redeemable Pref. Shareholders A/c Dr. To Bank A/c (Being redemption of 6% pref. sh. at 5% premium)		4,20,000	4,20,000

Note : Issue of debentures is not to be considered for redemtpion of preference shares, only, issue of equity shares is to be considered for ascertaining amount required from Profit & Loss A/c.

Problem 3 :

Dhanapal Ltd. has as a part of share capital, 500 Redeemable preference shares of Rs. 100 each fully paid-up and these have become due for redemption.

The company having Rs. 45,000 to its reserve fund, issued equity shares of the face value of Rs. 30,000 at a premium of 5% especially for the purpose of such redemption and received cash for the full amount of the issue.

The redeemable preference shares are then paid out of the proceeds of the new issue, the balance having been met out of the balance to the credit of Reserve fund.

Pass journal entries.

Solution 3 :   **Dhanapal Ltd.**
                    Journal Book

Sr.No.	Particulars	L.F.	Dr. Rs.	Cr. Rs.
1.	Bank A/c Dr. To Equity Share Capital A/c To Equity Share Premium A/c (Being issue of eq. shares at 5% premium)		31,500	30,000 1,500
2.	Reserve Fund A/c Dr. To Capital Redemption Reserve A/c (Being provision made from Reserve fund equal to amount uncovered by issue of eq. shares i.e. 50,000 - 30,000 (not Rs. 31,500)		20,000	20,000
3.	Redeemable Pref. Share Capital A/c Dr. To Redeemable pref. Shareholders A/c (Being amount payable to holders)		50,000	50,000
4.	Redemable Pref. Shareholder A/c Dr. To Bank A/c (Being redemption of pref. shares at par.)		50,000	50,000

Problem 4 : (Partly Paid Preference Shares)

X Co. decides to redeem its 40,000 6% redeemable pref. shares of Rs. 10 each on which Rs. 7 per share have been called up and paid up. The redemption was carried out of profits.

Journalise.

Solution 4 :

X Co. Journal Book

Sr.No.	Particulars	L.F.	Dr. Rs.	Cr. Rs.
1.	6% Redeemable Pref. Share Final Call A/c Dr.		1,20,000	
	To 6% Redeemable Pref. Share Capital A/c			1,20,000
	(Being final call made on 4,0000 Pref. shares at Rs. 3 each (10-7))			
2.	Bank A/c Dr.		1,20,000	
	To 6% Redeemable Pref. Sh. Final Call A/c			1,20,000
	(Being final call received in full)			
3.	Profit & Loss Appropriation A/c Dr.		4,00,000	
	To Capital Redemption Reserve A/c			4,00,000
	(Being provision made from profit)			
4.	6% Redeemable Pref. Sh. Capital A/c Dr.		4,00,000	
	To Redeemable Pref. Sh. Holder's A/c			4,00,000
	(Being capital payable credited)			
5.	6% Redeemable Pref. Sh. Holder's A/c Dr.		4,00,000	
	To Bank A/c			4,00,000
	(Being redemption of pref. sh. at par.)			

Problem 5 : (Redemption partly out of fresh issue and out of profits)

The Balance sheet of M Ltd. contained the following items as on 31st March, 2009

$7\frac{1}{2}$ preference share Capital (shares of Rs. 100 each)   4,00,000

Securities Premium Account   18,000

General Reserve Account   3,20,000

The company redeemed the preference shares at a premium of 5% on 1st April, 2009. For the purpose of redemption, it issued 20,000 equity shares of Rs. 10 each at a premium of 4%

Show journal entries in the books of the company to give effect to the above transactions.

Solution 5 :

M Ltd.
Journal (1.4.2009)

Sr.No.	Particulars		L.F.	Dr. Rs.	Cr. Rs.
1.	Bank A/c	Dr.		2,08,000	
	To Equity Share Capital A/c				2,00,000
	To Securities Premium A/c				8,000
	(Being issued 20,000 equity shares of Rs. 10 each at a premium of 4% for the purpose of redemption of preference shares)				
2.	$7\frac{1}{2}$ Preference Share Capital A/c	Dr.		4,00,000	
	Premium on Redemption of Preference Shares A/c	Dr.		20,000	
	To Preference Shareholders' A/c				4,20,000
	(Being the claim of preference shareholders transferred to their account)				
3.	Securities Premium A/c	Dr.		20,000	
	To Premium on Redemption of Preference shares A/c				20,000
	(Being provided premium on redemption of preference shares @ 5% from out of share premium account)				
4.	General Reserve A/c	Dr.		2,00,000	
	To Capital Redemption Reserve A/c				2,00,000
	(Being created capital redemption reserve out of general reserve)				
5.	Preference shareholder's A/c	Dr.		4,20,000	
	To Bank A/c				4,20,000
	(Being settled the claim of preference shareholders)				

Working Note -

$$CRR = \frac{\text{N.V. Preference Shares}}{\text{to be redeemed}} - \text{Proceeds of fresh issue of shares}$$

$$= 4,00,000 - 2,00,000$$

$$= 2,00,000$$

Problem 6 -

Bajaj Electronics Ltd. has an authorised capital of Rs. 50,00,000/-. Its Balance sheet as at 31st March, 2009 is as follows.

Balance Sheet
as at 31-3-2009

Liabilities	Rs.	Assets	Rs.
Share Capital :		Fixed Assets	9,80,000
Issued & Paid-up Capital		Investment	2,00,000
60,000 equity shares of		Current Asset	5,40,000
Rs. 10/- each	6,00,000	Cash at Bank	1,80,000
30,000, 5% Redeemable			
Preference Shares of			
Rs. 10/- each	3,00,000		
Securities Premium A/c	2,70,000		
General Reserve	4,00,000		
Profit and Loss A/c	2,30,000		
Creditors	1,00,000		
	19,00,000		19,00,000

The Company decided to redeem on 1st April, 2009 the whole of the preference share capital at a premium of 10% In order to pay off the preference shareholders, it sold the investments realising Rs. 1,95,000/-

Pass necessary journal entries and prepare Balance sheet after redemption.   (P.U.)

Solution 6 : **Bajaj Electronics Ltd.**
Journal

Date	Particulars	L.F.	Dr. Rs.	Cr. Rs.
2009 April 1	Bank A/c Dr.		1,95,000	
	Profit and Loss A/c Dr.		5,000	
	To Investments A/c			2,00,000
	(Being sale of investments at a loss of Rs. 5,000)			
April 1	5% Redeemable Preference Share Capital A/c Dr.		3,00,000	
	Premium on Redemption of			
	Preference Shares A/c Dr.		30,000	
	To 5% Redeemable Preference Shareholders A/c			3,30,000
	(Being claim of preference shareholders			
	transferred to their account)			

Date	Particulars	L.F.	Dr. Rs.	Cr. Rs.
April 1	Securities Premium A/c Dr. To Premium on Redemption of Preference Share A/c (Being premium on redemption of preference shares provided out of share premium account)		30,000	 30,000
April 1	Profit and Loss A/c Dr. General Reserve A/c Dr. To Capital Redemption Reserve A/c (Being amount transferred to capital redemption reserve account equivalent to the nominal value of shares redeemed out of profits)		2,25,000 75,000	 3,00,000
April 1	5% Redeemable Preference Shareholder's A/c Dr. To Bank A/c (Being settled the claim of preference shareholders)		3,30,000	 3,30,000

Balance sheet of Bajaj Electronics Ltd.
(After Redemption)
as on 1-4-2009

Liabilities	Rs.	Assets	Rs.
Share Capital		Fixed Assets	9,80,000
60,000 Equity shares of		Current Assets	5,40,000
Rs. 10 each fully paid	6,00,000	Cash at Bank	45,000
Securities Premium A/c	2,40,000		
Capital Redemption Reserve A/c	3,00,000		
General Reserve	3,25,000		
Profit and Loss A/c	1,00,000		
S. Creditors	–		
	15,65,000		15,65,000

Problem 7 - Minimum reduction in Revenue Reserve

The Balance sheet of Malhotra Ltd. as at 31st December, 2008 is as follows.

Balance sheet

Liabilities	Rs.	Assets	Rs.
Share Capital		Land and Building	10,00,000
500 Redeemable		Plant	3,00,000
Preference Shares of		Furniture	20,000
Rs. 100 each	5,00,000	Stock	3,00,000
90,000 Equity Shares of		Debtors	1,50,000
Rs. 10 each	9,00,000	Investment	2,80,000
Securities Premium A/c	1,00,000	Bank A/c	2,00,000
General Reserve	2,00,000		
Profit and Loss A/c	2,50,000		
Sundry Creditors	3,00,000		
	22,50,000		22,50,000

The Company decided to redeem its preference shares at a premium of 10% on 1st January, 2009.

A fresh issue of 10,000 equity shares of Rs. 10 each was made at Rs. 12 per share payable in full on 1st January, 2009. These shares were fully subscribed and all monies were duly collected. All the investments were sold realising Rs. 2,70,000. The Directors wish that only a minimum reduction should be made in the revenue reserves.

You are required to give journal entries to record the above transactions and draw up the balance sheet as it would appear after redemption of preference shares.

Solution 7 :   **Malhotra Ltd.**

Journal

Date	Particulars	L.F.	Dr. Rs.	Cr. Rs.
2009 Jan. 1	Bank A/c Dr.		1,20,000	
	To Equity share Capital A/c			1,00,000
	To Securities Premium A/c			20,000
	(Being 10,000 equity shares issued at a premium of Rs. 2 per share)			
Jan. 1	Bank A/c Dr.		2,70,000	
	Profit and Loss A/c Dr.		10,000	
	To Investments A/c			2,80,000
	(Being sale of investment at a loss of Rs. 10,000)			

Date	Particulars	L.F.	Dr. Rs.	Cr. Rs.
Jan. 1	Redeemable Preference Share Capital A/c Dr. Premium on Redemption of Preference Shares A/c Dr. To Preference Shareholders A/c (Being the amount due to preference sharehloders for capital and premium transferred.)		5,00,000 50,000	 5,50,000
Jan. 1	Profit and Loss A/c Dr. General Reserve A/c Dr. To Capital Redemption Reserve A/c (Being the amount transferred to capital redemption reserve account equivalent to the nominal value of shares redeemed out of profits)		2,40,000 1,60,000	 4,00,000
Jan. 1	Securities Premium A/c Dr. To Premium on Redemption of Preference Shares A/c (Being the amount of securities premium account transferred to Redemption of preference shares account.)		50,000	 50,000
Jan. 1	Preference Shareholders A/c Dr. To Bank A/c (Being payment made to shareholders on redemption)		5,50,000	 5,50,000

Balance Sheet of Malhotra Ltd. (After Redemption)
as on 1-1-2009

Liabilities	Rs.	Assets	Rs.
Share Capital		Land and Building	10,00,000
1,00,000 equity shares of		Plant	3,00,000
each fully paid	10,00,000	Furniture	20,000
Securities Premium A/c	70,000	Stock	3,00,000
General Reserve A/c	40,000	Debtors	1,50,000
Capital Redemption Reserve A/c	4,00,000	Bank A/c	40,000
Sundry Creditors	3,00,000		
	18,10,000		**18,10,000**

Problem 8 -

The Balance Sheet of Ashok Limited as on 31st December, 2008 stood as follows.

Liabilities	Rs.	Assets	Rs.
Share Capital 3,000 9% Redeemable Preference Shares of Rs. 100 each	3,00,000	Land and Building	3,00,000
		Plant and Machinery	2,00,000
40,000 Equity Shares		Stock	1,50,000
Rs. 10 each	4,00,000	Debtors	75,000
General Reserve	1,05,000	Cash at Bank	2,50,000
Profit and Loss A/c	25,000		
Securities Premium	20,000		
Sundry Creditors	1,25,000		
	9,75,000		9,75,000

The redeemable preference shares were redeemed on 1st January, 2009 at a premium of 5%. Not having sufficient profits available to redeem the whole issue, the company issued 2,000 8% preference shares of Rs. 100 each. Payable as to Rs. 20 on application and the balance on allotment. These shares were duly taken up.

Pass the necessary journal entries and balance sheet of the company thereafter.

Solution 8 : **In the Books of Ashok Limited**
Journal Entries

Date	Particulars	L.F.	Dr. Rs.	Cr. Rs.
2009 Jan. 1	Bank A/c Dr. To Preference Share Application A/c (Being received share application money at Rs. 20 per share on 8% 2,000 preference shares.)		40,000	40,000
	Preference Share Application A/c Dr. To Preference Share Capital A/c (Being share application money transferred)		40,000	40,000
	Preference Share Allotment A/c Dr. To Preference Share Capital A/c (Being preference share allotment money transferred)		1,60,000	1,60,000

Date	Particulars	L.F.	Dr. Rs.	Cr. Rs.
	Bank A/c Dr.		1,60,000	
	To Preference Share Allotment A/c			1,60,000
	(Being preference share allotment money received)			
	Profit and Loss A/c Dr.		25,000	
	General Reserve A/c Dr.		75,000	
	To Capital Redemption Reserve A/c			1,00,000
	(Being amount due for redemption of preference shares transferred to capital reserve)			
	9% Redeemable Preference Share Capital A/c Dr.		3,00,000	
	Premium on Redemption of Preference Shares Dr.		15,000	
	To 9% Redeemable Preference Shareholders A/c			3,15,000
	(Being amount due on redemption transferred)			
	Securities Premium A/c Dr.		15,000	
	To Premium on Redemption of Preference Shares			15,000
	(Being Premium payable on redemption provided out of share premium account)			
	9% Redeemable Preference Shareholders A/c Dr.		3,15,000	
	To Bank A/c			3,15,000
	(Being amount payable to preference shareholders paid)			

Balance Sheet of Ashok Ltd. as on 1-1-2009
(After Redemption)

Liabilities	Rs.	Assets	Rs.
Share capital		**Fixed Assets**	
2,000. 8% Pref Shares of		Land & Building	3,00,000
Rs. 100 each	2,00,000	Plant and Machinery	2,00,000
4,000 Equity Shares of		**Current Assets**	
Rs. 10 each	4,00,000	Stock	1,50,000
Reserve & Surplus		Debtors	75,000
General Reserve	30,000	Cash Bank	1,35,000
Capital Redemption Reserve A/c	1,00,000		
Securities Premium A/c	5,000		
Sundry Creditors	1,25,000		
	8,60,000		8,60,000

Problem 9 -

The Balance Sheet of Saurabh Ltd. as on 31st December, 2008 was as follows.

Balance Sheet

Liabilities	Rs.	Assets	Rs.
6,000 5% Redeemable Preference Shares of Rs. 100 each	6,00,000	Land and Building	8,00,000
		Plant and Machinery	4,00,000
30,000 Equity Shares of		Cash at Bank	6,00,000
Rs. 10 each	3,00,000		
Securities Premium A/c	1,50,000		
Profit and Loss A/c	4,50,000		
Sundry Liabilities	3,00,000		
	18,00,000		18,00,000

The company decided to redeem on 1st January, 2009 the whole of the preference share capital at a premium of 5%. It was decided to arrange that as for as possible out of company's resources subject to leaving a balance of Rs. 80,000 to remain in the credit of profit and loss account. It was also decided to raise the balance of funds required by the issue of sufficient number of equity shares of Rs. 10 each at a premium of Rs. 2 per share.

Pass necessary journal entries giving effect to the above arrangement. Also draw up the balance sheet of the company as it would appear after redemption of preference shares.

(P.U.)

Solution 9 :   In the Books of Saurabh Ltd.
Journal Entries

Date	Particulars	L.F.	Dr. Rs.	Cr. Rs.
2009 Jan. 1	5% Redeemable Preference Share Capital A/c Dr.		6,00,000	
	Premium on Redemption of Preference Shares A/c Dr		30,000	
	To Preference Shareholoders A/c			6,30,000
	(Being the total amount due to redeemable preference shareholders on redemption of shares)			
	Bank A/c Dr.		2,76,000	
	To Equity Share Capital A/c			2,30,000
	To Securities Premium A/c			46,000
	(Being received cash on issue of 23,000 equity shares of Rs. 10 each at a premium of Rs. 2 per share)			

Date	Particulars	L.F.	Dr. Rs.	Cr. Rs.
	Profit and Loss A/c Dr. To Capital Redemption Reserve (Being made provision out of profits for redemption of preference shares)		3,70,000	3,70,000
	Securities Premium A/c Dr. To Premium on Redemption of Preference Shares A/c (Being premium payable on redemption of preference shares is charged to share premium account)		30,000	30,000
	Preference Shareholders A/c Dr. To Bank A/c (Being repayment of preference shareholders)		6,30,000	6,30,000

Balance Sheet
as on 1-1-2009

Liabilities	Rs.	Assets	Rs.
Share Capital		**Fixed Assets**	
53,000 Equity Shares		Land and Building	8,00,000
of Rs. 10 each	5,30,000	Plant and Machinery	4,00,000
Reserves and Surplus		**Current Assets**	
Securities Premium	1,66,000	Cash at Bank	2,46,000
Capital Redemption Fund	3,70,000		
Profit and Loss A/c	80,000		
Current Liabilities			
Sundry Liabilities	3,00,000		
	14,46,000		14,46,000

Problem 10 -

The following is the summarised Balance Sheet of Patil Cement Ltd. as on 31st March, 2009.

Liabilities	Rs.	Assets	Rs.
Share Capital		Plant and Machinery	3,00,000
50,000 Equity Shares of		Land and Building	2,00,000
Rs. 10 each fully paid	5,00,000	Debtors	60,000
2,000, 2% Redeemable		Stock	40,000
Preference Shares of		Cash at Bank	3,00,000
Rs. 100 each fully paid	2,00,000		
Securities Premium	5,000		
Profit and Loss A/c	85,000		
General Reserve	20,000		
6% Debentures	50,000		
Creditors	40,000		
	9,00,000		9,00,000

On 1st April, 2009, the company decided to redeem its preference shares at a premium of 5%. The company issued for cash so many but no more equity shares of Rs. 10 each at par as were necessary to provide for redemption of 5% redeemable preference shares which could not otherwise be redeemed. The issue was fully subscribed and all the amounts were fully received.

Pass necessary journal entries for recording the above transactions in the books of the company. (P.U.)

Solution 10 : **In the Books of Patil Cement Ltd.**
Journal Entries

Date	Particulars	L.F.	Dr. Rs.	Cr. Rs.
2009 April 1	Bank A/c Dr. To Equity Share Application and Allotment A/c (Being Received application and allotment money for 10,000 equity shares at Rs. 10 per share)		1,00,000	1,00,000
	Equity Share Application and Allotment A/c Dr. To Equity Share Capital A/c (Being application and Allotment money is transferred to share capital account)		1,00,000	1,00,000

Date	Particulars	L.F.	Dr. Rs.	Cr. Rs.
	2% Redeemable Preference Share Capital A/c Dr. Premium on Redemption of Preference Shares A/c Dr. To Redeemable Preference Shareholders A/c (Being amount payable to preference shareholders on account of their capital and premium)		2,00,000 10,000	2,10,000
	Profit and Loss A/c Dr. Securities Premium A/c Dr. To Premium on Redemption of Preference Shares (Being premium on redemption of preference shares is written off against share premium and profit & loss account)		5,000 5,000	10,000
	Profit & Loss A/c Dr. General Reserve A/c Dr. To Capital Redemption Reserve A/c (Being made necessary provision for redemption of redeemable preference shares)		80,000 20,000	1,00,000
	Redeemable Preference Shareholders A/c Dr. To Bank A/c (Being repayment of amount due to redeemable preference shareholders)		2,10,000	2,10,000

Problem 11 -

Uday Ltd. has an authorised capital of Rs. 60,00,000. Its balance sheet as on 31-12-2008 is as follows :-

Liabilities	Rs.	Assets	Rs.

Issued and
Paid-up Capital
1,50,000 Equity Shares of
   Rs. 10 each
60,000 8% Redeemable
Preference Shares of
   Rs. 10 each
Securities Premium A/c
General Reserve
Profit and Loss A/c
Creditors
	
	15,00,000
	
	6,00,000
	3,00,000
	2,00,000
	3,10,000
	2,00,000
		Fixed Assets
		Investments
		Current Assets
		Bank Balance
			20,00,000
			4,00,000
			3,40,000
			3,70,000

	31,10,000		31,10,000

The company decided to redeem on 1st January, 2009 the whole of the preference share capital at a premium of 10%. The company issued for cash so many but no more equity shares of Rs. 10 each at par as were necessary to provide for redemption of 8% redeemable preference shares which could not otherwise be redeemed. The issue was fully subscribed and all the amounts were fully received. In order to pay-off preference shareholders, it sold the investments realising Rs. 3,90,000.

Journalise the above transactions in the books of Uday Ltd. and Balance sheet after redemption of redeemable preference shares.

Solution 11 : **In the books of Uday Ltd.**

Journal Entries

Date	Particulars	L.F.	Dr. Rs.	Cr. Rs.
2009 Jan. 1	8% Redeemable Preference Share Capital A/c Dr. Premium on Redemption of Preference Share A/c Dr. To 8% Redeemable Preference Shareholders A/c (Being amount due to preference shareholder for capital and premium transferred)		6,00,000 60,000	6,60,000
	Bank A/c Dr. To Equity Share Capital A/c (Being 10,000 equity Shares issued at par)		1,00,000	1,00,000
	Profit and Loss A/c Dr. General Reserve A/c Dr. To Capital Redemption Reserve A/c (Being the amount transferred to C.R.R. A/c equivalent to the nominal value of shares redeemed out of profits)		3,00,000 2,00,000	5,00,000
	Bank A/c Dr. Profit and Loss A/c Dr. To Investment (Being investment sold)		3,90,000 10,000	4,00,000
	Securities Premium A/c Dr. To Premium on Redemption of Preference Share A/c (Being premium on redemption provided out of the share premium account)		60,000	60,000
	8% of Redeemable Preference Shareholder A/c Dr. To Bank A/c (Being payment made to shareholders on redemption)		6,60,000	6,60,000

Balance Sheet of Uday Ltd. as on 1-1-2009

Liabilities	Rs.	Assets	Rs.
Share Capital		**Fixed Assets**	20,00,000
1,60,000 Equity Shares		**Current Assets**	3,40,000
of Rs. 10 each	16,00,000	Bank Balance	2,00,000
Reserves and Surplus			
Capital Redemption Reserve A/c	5,00,000		
Securities Premium A/c	2,40,000		
Current Liabilities			
Creditors	2,00,000		
	25,40,000		25,40,000

3.3 EXERCISES

Redemption of Preference Shares

1) **The following is the Balance Sheet of H Ltd. as on 30th June, 2009.**

Liabilities	Rs.	Assets		Rs.
Share capital		**Fixed assets**		100,000
3,000, 6% Redeemable		Investments		21,000
Preference Shares of Rs. 10		**Current Assets**		
each fully paid.	30,000	Stock	44,000	
6,000 Equity Shares of		S. Debtors	16,000	
Rs. 10 each fully paid	60,000	Cash at Bank	22,000	
Securities Premium A/c	29,000			82,000
General Reserve	40,000			
Profit & Loss A/c	24,500			
Sundry Creditors	19,500			
	2,03,000			2,03,000

The company exercised its option to redeem on 1st July 2009, the whole of the preference share capital at a premium of 5%.

To assist in financing the redemption, all the investments were sold, realising Rs. 19,500. On 1st September, 2005, the company made a bonus issue of five equity shares fully paid for every six equity shares held on that date.

The appropriate resolutions having been passed, the above transactions were duly completed.

You are required to show the journal entries to record the transactions in the books of the company and the balance sheet as it would appear after the completion of the transactions.

(**Ans.** Balance Sheet Total Rs.1,70,000)

Redemption at a premium and sale of investment.

2) **The Balance Sheet of P Ltd. as on 31st December, 2008 was as follows -**

Liabilities		Rs.	Assets	Rs.
6% Redeemable			Fixed Assets	1,32,000
Preference shares of Rs. 100			Stock	22,000
each fully paid	50,000		Debtors	15,000
Equity shares of Rs. 10			Investments	36,000
each	90,000	1,40,000	Bank	20,000
Capital Reserve		5,000		
Securities Premium		10,000		
General Reserve		20,000		
Profit & Loss A/c		30,000		
Creditors		20,000		
		2,25,000		2,25,000

The preference shares were due for repayment on 31st January 2009 and the company decided to redeem them at a premium of 5%. For the purpose of redemption, the Company made a fresh issue of 1,000 new equity shares of Rs. 10 each, at Rs. 12 per share, payable in full on 15th January, 2009. These shares were fully subscribed and all cash was collected. Then, the company sold 75% of the investments for Rs. 26,000. The directors wish that only a minimum reduction should be made in the revenue reserves. The redemption was duly made on 31st January. 2009.

Write journal entries for above transactions and draw up the balance sheet after the redemption of preference shares was over.

(**Ans.** CRR Rs. 40,000 Balance sheet Total Rs. 1,83,500)

Redemption out of fresh issue and profit with minimum reduction in reserve

3) **The following are the balances of P Co. Ltd. as on 31st December, 2008.**

Redeemable Preference Share Capital	
2,50,000 shares of Rs. 100 each, fully called up.	2,50,000
Less : Calls-in-Arrear (final call of Rs. 20 on 60 shares)	1,200
	2,48,800
Equity Share Capital.	
30,000 shares of Rs. 10 each fully called-up	3,00,000
General Reserve	1,12,000
Securities Premium	15,000

Preference shares were redeemable on 1st July, 2009 at a premium of 10% On getting a reminder about payment of calls-in-arrear, shareholders holding 50 shares paid their dues by 31st May, 2009. The shareholder, holding the remaining 10 shares on which calls were due, became insolvent and was unable to pay the balance. Consequently, the directors forfeited those shares and re-issued them as fully paid on 10th June, 2009 on receiving Rs. 500.

Repayments were completed by 30th September, 2009 except in the case of one shareholder holding 100 shares, who was out of India.

Further 15,000 equity shares of Rs. 10 each were issued at par for the purpose of the above transaction.

Show the entries and prepare the balance sheet assuming that minimum reduction is to made in revenue reserve.

(Ans. CRR Rs. 1,00,000)

Calculation of sufficient amount of equity shares for redemption.

4) Spotlight Ltd. has issued share capital of 60,000 8% Redeemable Cumulative Preference Shares of Rs. 20 each and 4,00,000 Equity Shares of Rs. 10 each. The Preference Shares are redeemable at a premium of 5% on 1st January, 2009. As at 31st December, 2008 the company's Balance Sheet showed the following Position.

Liabilities	Rs.	Assets	Rs.
Issued share Capital		Plant & Machinery	25,00,000
60,000 8% redeemable		Furniture & Fixtures	9,00,000
cumulative preference		Stock	15,00,000
shares of Rs. 20 each,		Debtors	14,00,000
fully paid up	12,00,000	Investments	3,50,000
4,00,000 equity shares of		Balance at Bank	3,50,000
Rs. 10 each, fully paid	40,00,000		
Profit & Loss A/c	7,00,000		
Sundry Creditors	11,00,000		
	70,00,000		70,00,000

In order to facilitate the redemption of preference shares it was decided –

a) to sell the investments for Rs. 3,00,000.

b) to finance part of the redemption from company funds subject to leaving of balance of profit and loss account of Rs. 2,00,000.

c) to issue sufficient equity shares of Rs. 10 each at a premium of Rs. 2 per share to raise the balance of funds required.

The preference shares were redeemed on due date. New equity shares were fully subscribed.

You are required to prepare –

i) Journal entries to record the above transactions, and

ii) A memorandum balance sheet as on completion of redemption.

(**Ans.** CRR Rs. 4,50,000; Fresh Issue Rs. 75,000 shares)

Hint.

1) Calculation of fresh issue of equity shares.

   Total fund required for redemption   Rs. (12,00,000) + 60,0000   12,60,000

2) Less :   Available balance from Profit and Loss Account

            by creating Capital Redemption Reserve.

   Profit and Loss (Balance) Account   7,00,000

   Less :   Loss on sale of Investment   50,000

                                                                   6,50,000

   Less :   Minimum balance to be retained in

   Profit and Loss Account   2,00,000   4,50,000

   ∴ Total amount required   8,10,000

   Less :   Premium payable on redemption   60,000

            Total fund to be raised by the issue of equity shares   7,50,000

   ∴ No. Shares to be issued $\dfrac{Rs.7,50,000}{Rs.10}$ = 75,000

3) Balance Sheet Total.   Rs. 65,90,000.

Redemption of preference shares with dividend due.

5) The Balance Sheet of P Q Ltd. on 31st December 2008 was as follows.

Liabilities	Rs.	Assets	Rs.
8% Redeemable		Fixed Assets	20,00,000
Preference Shares of		Current Assets	3,80,000
Rs. 100 each fully paid	9,00,000	Investments	2,70,000
Equity shares of		Bank Balance	2,00,000
Rs. 10 each fully paid	9,00,000		
General Reserve	3,60,000		
Securities Premium	27,000		
Profit & Loss A/c	5,40,000		
Creditors	1,23,000		
	28,50,000		28,50,000

The preference shares are to be redeemed at 10% premium along with the dividend due for 2008. The company issued 45,000 equity shares of Rs. 10 at a premium of Rs. 5 per share. All shares were subscribed and cash duly received. The investments were sold for Rs. 3,50,000. Payment was made to the preference shareholders and thereafter, the directors decided to issue bonus shares in the ratio of one share for every four shares held. For this purpose, the revenue reserves were utilised to the minimum extent possible.

Give the necessary journal entries and the balance sheet after redemption.

(**Ans.** CRR = Rs. 4,50,000, balance sheet total Rs. 2,54,300 bonus shares 33,750)

Conversion of partly paid-up equity shares into fully paid-up.

6) The Following is the Balance Sheet of Redeemer Ltd. as on 31st March, 2009.

Liabilities	Rs.	Assets	Rs.
Authorised Capital		Fixed Assets	10,00,000
1,00,000 Equity Shares of		Current Assets	4,10,000
Rs. 10 each	10,00,000	Cash at Bank	75,000
5,000 7% Preference			
Shares of Rs. 100 each	5,00,000		
	15,00,000		
Paid up Capital			
80,000 Equity Shares of			
Rs. 10 each			
Rs. 7.50 paid up	6,00,000		
2,500 7% Preference			
Shares of Rs. 100 each	2,50,000		
Securities Premium	10,000		
Capital Reserve	1,00,000		
General Reserve	3,50,000		
Profit & Loss A/c	1,25,000		
Sundry Creditors	50,000		
	14,85,000		14,85,000

It was decided to –

a) redeem the 7% preference shares at a premium of 5%.

b) issue 1,000 6% debentures of Rs. 100 each.

c) convert the partly paid-up equity shares into fully paid up without requiring the shareholders to pay for the same.

d) issue fully paid right shares of Rs. 10 each at a premium of Rs. 2 per share in the proportion of one share for every four shares held for the purpose of redemption of preference shares.

You are required to pass necessary entries keeping in view the prudent utilisation of profits, to effect the aforesaid decision.

       (Ans. CRR = Rs. 50,000)

Objective Type

A) State whether the following statements are True or False :

1) A preferential share is one which enjoys a preferential right regarding payment of dividend.

2) Share premium account can be uitilised to write off premium payable on redemption of preference shares.

3) Share Premium Account is to be debited on issue of shares at premium

Answer : (1) True (2) True (3) False

B) State whether the following statements are True or False :

1) A company cannot redeem its preference shares.

2) Redemption of preference shares can be made from out of the proceds of fresh issue of debentures.

3) A company can redeem only fully paid preference shares.

4) Premium payable on redemption of preference-shares must be debited against profits only.

5) Capital Redemption Reserve Account can be utilised for writing off Miscellaneous expenditure and losses.

6) Transfer to Capital Redemption Reserve can be made from General Reserve.

7) If fresh issue is made for the purposse of redemption of preference shares it will be treated as increase of share capital.

8) Capital Redemption Reserve A/c can be utilised for issue fully paid bonus shares.

Answer : (1) False (2) False (3) True (4) False (5) False (6) True (7) False (8) True

C) Fill in the blanks :

1) Unless otherwise stated, a preference share is always deemed to be cumulative, non - convertible and...

2) Premium on issue of shares can be used for....

3) Share premium account is to be .... on issue of shares at premium.

4) Preference shares cannot be redeemed unless they are....

5) Capital Redemption Reserve A/c can be utilised for issuing fully paid .....

6) Any premium payable on redemption of preference share must be met either from out of .... of the company or out of the company's ..... account.

7) Redemption means .....

Answer : (1) Non - participating (2) Writing off preliminary expenses (3) Credited (4) Fully paid (5) Bonus shares (6) Share premium (7) Repayment

Theory Questions

1) What are preference shares? Explain the different types of preference shares.

2) Write Short Notes on :
     a)   Issue of shares at premium
     b)   Redeemable Preference Shares

CHAPTER 4

Final Accounts of Joint Stock Company

4.1 Introduction

One of the norms of modern business dictates al business entities to prepare a set of Financial statements with a two-fold purpose - for assessing periodically profits earned and for getting conversant with the financial position of the business concern in question on a specified date. Joint stock companies, simply referred to as companies in India, are no exception to this prescription.

A Profit and loss Account and a Balance Sheet are essential for all business concerns except the single-ownership ones. In the case of joint stock companies, the Companies Act, 1956 further prescribes books of Account to be maintained and lays down the format and content of financial statments to be made. In addition, the accounts should be statutorily audited by external/s who are called Autitor/s - person or persons legally qualified to do the work. It is the auditor's duty to submit a report in the prescribed format for the shareholder's to see.

Since the introduction of the limited liability system, it has become procedural to appoiont a board of directors, through election by the sharholders, which board is supposed to protect and promote their interest to the best of its ability. However, a complete reliance on the board of directors may not be an adequate safeguard of shareholders' interest.

The Companies Act, therefore, Prescribes a few provisions under which financial Statements are to be prepared and presented. The purpose is to lay before the shareholders adequate information for enabling them to judge the performance of the company and, thus, the role of the directors during a specified period, Called the "accounting period'

As the preparation of the financial statements of a company requires the observation of the legal prescriptions, it acquires much importance for the shareholders in their efforts to assess the business unit's health.

Books of Accounts to be kept by Company

Section 209 of the Companies Act, 1956 requires that every company shall keep at its registered office proper books of account regarding -

a) All sums of money received and expended by the company and the matters in respect of which the receipt and expenditure take place.

b) All sales and purchases of goods by the company.

c) the assets and liabilities of the company; and

d) in the case of a company pertaining to any class of companies engaged in production, processing, manufacturing or mining activities, such particulars relating to utilisation of material or labour or to other items of cost as may be prescribed, if such class of companies is required by the Central Government to include such particulars in the books of account.

Proper books of account shall not be deemed to be kept with respect to the matters specified above -

a) if there are not kept such books as are necessary to give a true and fair view of the state of affairs of the company or branch office, as the case may be, and to explain its transactions; and

b) if such books are not kept on accrual basis and according to the double entry system of accounting.

The books of account of every company relating to a period of not less than eight years immediately preceding the current year together with the vouchers relevant to any entry in such books of account shall be preserved in a good order.

The books of account and other books and papers of every company shall be open to inspection by any director during business hours.

To satisfy the different requirements of the Companies Act, generally the following books of account are maintained by companies.

1. Cash book to record cash and bank transactions, discounts allowed and received.
2. Purchases Day Book to record credit Purchases.
3. Sales Day Book to record credit sales.
4. Returns Inwards Book or Sales Returns Book to record goods returned by customers.
5. Returns Outwards Book or Purchases Returns Book to record goods returned by the Company to suppliers.
6. Bills Receivable Book to record the details of Bills receivable
7. Bills Payable Book to record the details of Bills Payable.
8. Journal Proper to record opening entries, closing entries, adjustment entries and such residual transactions for which there is no separate book of primary entry.

9. General Ledger showing all accounts other than the accounts of customers and suppliers.
10. Debtors' Ledger or Customers' Ledger showing accounts of customers.
11. Creditors' Ledger or Suppliers' Ledger showing accounts of suppliers.

4.2 Statutory Books

As per the provisions of different sections of the Companies Act, the following records are also to be maintained in addition to the above books of account.
1. Register of Investments no held inthe compnay's name (Section 49)
2. Register of Charges (Section 143)
3. Register of Members (Section 150)
4. Index of Members (Section 151)
5. Register of Debenture-holders with Index (Section 152)
6. Copies of Annual Returns (Section 163)
7. Minute Books - of the G.M and of the meetings of the board and its Committees (Section 193)
8. Register of Contracts, Companies and Firms in Which Directors are Interested (Section 301)
9. Register of Directors, Managing Director, Manager and Secretary (Section 303)
10. Register of Directors' Shareholdings etc. (Section 307)
11. Register of Loans made to other companies under the same management (Section 370)
12. Register of Investments in Shares and Debentures of bodies corporate (Section 372)
13. Directors' Attendance Book (Regulation 71 of Table A)

4.3 Statistical Books

In addition to books of account and statutory books. companies usually maintain the following books which give details information regarding holding and transfer of shares and debentures, calls made on shareholders and debentureholders, interest paid to debenturholders, Share warrants issued and surrendered and such other matters not covered by the books of account and statutory books.
1. Share Application and Allotment Book
2. Share Call Book
3. Debenture Application and Allotment Book
4. Debenture Call Book
5. Register of Share Transfers;
6. Shareholders' Dividend Book
7. Debenture Interest Book;
8. Register of Cerfitication and Balance Tickets;
9. Debenture Transfer Register;
10. Register of Share Certificates;

11. Register of Probates;
12. Register of Share Warrants;
13. Register of Dividend Mandates;
14. Agenda Book;
15. Register of Sealed Documents;
16. Register of Powers of Attorney.

4.4 Annual Accounts and Balance Sheet

As per the provision of Section 210 of the Companies Act 1956, at every annual general meeting of a company held in pursuance of Section 166, the Board of Directors of the company shall lay before the company
  a) a Balance Sheet as at the end of the period specified in sub - section (3); and
  b) a Profit and Loss Account for that period.

In the case of a company not carrying on business for Profit, an Income and Expenditure Account shall be laid before the company at its annual general meeting instead of a Profit and Loss Account, and all references to 'Profit and Loss Account', 'Profit' and 'Loss' in this section and elsewhere in this Act, Shall be construed, in relation to such a company, as a references respectively to the 'Income and Expenditure Acount', 'The excess of income over expenditure', and 'the excess of expenditure over income'.

The Profit and Loss Account Shall relate -

  a) in the case of first annual general meeting of the company. to the period beginning with the incorporation of the company and ending with a day which shall not precede the day of the meeting by more than nine months; and
  b) in the case of any subsequent annual general meeting of the company. to the period beginning with the day immediatly after the period for which the account was last submitted and ending with a day. which shall not precede the day of the meeting by more than six months, or in cases where an extension of time has been granted for holding the meeting under the second provision to sub-section (I) of section 166 by more than six months and the extension so granted.

The period to which the account aforesaid relates in referred to in this Act as a 'Financial year' and it may be less or more than a calendar year but it shall not exceed fifteen months.

Form and Contents of Balance Sheet and Profit and Loss Account

Section 211 of the Companies Act. 1956 states that :
  1) Every Balance Sheet of a company shall give a true and fair view of the state of affairs of the company as at the end of the financial year and shall, subject to the provisions of this section, be in the form set out in Part I of Schedule VI, or as near therto as circumstances admit or in such other form as may be approved by the Central Government either generally or in any particular case; and in preparing the Blanace

Sheet due regard shall be had, as far as may be, to the general instructions for preparation of Balance Sheet under the heading "Notes' at the end of that Part.

Provided that nothing contained in this sub- section shall apply to any insurance or banking company or any company engaged in the generation or supply of electricity or to any other class of company for which a form of Balance Sheet has been specified in or under the Act governing such class of company.

2) Every Profit and Loss Account of a company shall give a true and fair view of the profit and loss of the company for the financial year and shall, subject as aforesaid, comply with the requirements of Part II of Schedule VI,so far as they are applicable thereto

Provided that nothing contained in this sub-section shall apply to any insurance or banking company or any company engaged in the generation or supply of electricity or to any other class of company for which a form of Profit and Loss Account has been specified in or under the Act governing such class of company.

3) The Central Government may, be notification in the Official, Gazette, exempt any class of companies from compliance with any of the requirements in Schedule VI, if, in its opinion, it is necessary to grant the exemption in public interest.

Any such exemption may be granted either unconditionally or subject to which conditions as may be specified in the notification.

3A) Every profit and loss account and balance sheet of the company shall comply with the accounting standards.

3B) Where the profit and loss account and the balance sheet of the company do not comply with the accounting standards, such companies the disclose in its profit and loss account and balance sheet, the following namely.

a) the deviation from the accounting standards;

b) the reasons for such deviation; and

c) the financial effect, if any, arising due to such deviation.

3C) For the purposed of this section, the expression "accounting standards" means the standards of accounting recommended by the Institute of Chartered Accountants of India constituted under the Chartered Accountants. Act 1949 (38 of 1949) as may be prescribed by the Central Government in consultation with the National advisory Committee on Accounting Standards. established under sub-section (1) of section 210A Provided that the standard of accounting specified by the Institute of Chartered Accountants of India Shall be deemed to be the Accounting Standards unitl the accounting standards are prescribed by the Central Government under this sub-section.

4) The Central Government may, on the application or with the consent of the Board of Directors of the company, by order, modify in relation to that company any of the requirements of this Act as to the matters to be stated in the company's Balance Sheet

or Profit and Loss Account for the purpose of adapting them to the circumstances of the company.

Contents of Revised Schedule VI

1. General Instructions for Preparation of Balance Sheet and Statement of Profit and Loss of a company.
2. Form of Balance Sheet (only vertical format) with General Instructions for preparation of Balance Shet (PART - I) The privilege of having a balance Sheet under horizontal or vertical format has been done away with. Option of only one format i.e Vertical format is now available for preparation of the Balance Sheet.
3. Form of Statement of Profit and Loss with General Instructions for preparation of Statement of Profit and Loss (PART - II)
4. The general format does not apply to Insurance Companies, Banking Companies, Electricity Companies or any other company governed by a separate Act, Where a form has been specified under that Act.

4.5 Disclosures

1. The Revised Schedule VI has eliminated the concept of "Schedule' and such information is now to be furnished in the notes to accounts.
2. **Proposed Dividend :** Part I of Revised Schedule VI does not require the provision for Proposed dividend to be made and only desires disclosure of same in notes to accounts. Although Revised Schedule VI does not require provision for proposed dividend, however, the accounting Standards have an overriding effect over Revised Schedule VI and Accordingly companies will have to account for the same until revision to this effect is made in AS 4.
3. **Share Capital :** Shareholder holding more than 5% Shares specifying the number of Shares held, etc.
4. **Long Term Borrowing :** Shall be stated in descending order of maturity or conversion. Further Period and amount of continuing default as on balance sheet date in repayment of loans and interest also needs to be disclosed.
5. **Trade Receivables :** The term Sundry debtor has been replaced with trade receivables.
6. **Cash and cash equivalents :** Bank deposits with more than 12 months maturity to be disclosed separately. The difurcation of bank deposits among scheduled and non scheduled banks has been dispensed with.
7. **Contingent liabilities and commitments :** These were required to be disclosed as footnote to balance Sheet under old Schedule VI and are now required to be disclosed in notes to accounts.
8. Income or expenditure exceeding 1% of the revenue from operations or ₹ 1,00,000 whichever is higher, need to be disclosed by way of notes.
9. The limits of rounding off (on the basis of turnover) are as follows

Turnover	Rounding off
Less than 100 Crores	To the nearest hundereds, thousands, lakhs or millon, or decimals thereof
More than 100 Crores	To the nearest Lakhs, millions or Crores, or decimals therof.

10. An asset shall be classified as current when it satisfies any of the following criteria.
    a) It is expected to be realized within twelve months after the reporting date; or
    b) Used to settle a liablility for at least twelve month after the reporting date.
11. A liablility Shall be classified as current when it is due to be settled within twelve months after the reporting date;
12. Reserves & Surplus : The balance of 'Reserves and Surplus' after adjusting negative balance of surplus (Profit & Loss Account), if any, shall be shown under the head 'Reserves and Surplus' even if the resulting figure is in the negative. Earlier, any debit balance in profit and Loss Account was required to be shown as the last item on the asset side of the Balance Sheet.
13. The Old Schedule VI required Separate presentation of debtors outstanding for a period exceeding 6 months based on date on which the bill / invoice was raised whereas, the Revised Schedule VI requires separate disclosure of "trade receivables outstanding for a period exceeding six months from the date the bill / invoice is due for payment."
14. The name has been changed to "Statement of Profit and Loss" as against "Profit and Loss Account' as contained in the Old Schedule VI

4.6 Part I :   Form of Balance Sheet

Name of the Company			
Balance Sheet as at 31 March 2014			
Particulars	Note No.	As at 31 March, 2014 ₹	As at 31 March, 2013 ₹
A. **Equity and Liabilities**			
1. **Shareholder's funds**			
a. Share Capital	1		
b. Reserves and Surplus	2		
c. Money received against share Warrants			

2	Share application money pending allotment			
3	**Non-current liablities**			
	(a) Long-term borrowings	3		
	(b) Deferred tax liabilities (net)			
	(c) Other long-term liabilities	4		
	(d) Long-term Provisions	5		
4	**Current liabilities**			
	(a) Short-term borrowings	6		
	(b) Trade Payables			
	(c) Other current liabilities	7		
	(d) Short-term provisions	8		
	Total			
B	**Assets**			
1	**Non-current assets**			
	(a) Fixed assets			
	(i) Tangibls assets	9		
	(ii) Intangible assets	10		
	(iii) Capital work-in-progress			
	(iv) Intangible assets under developments			
	(v) Fixed assets held for sale			
	(b) Non-current investments	11		
	(c) Deferred tax assets (net)			
	(d) Long-term loans and advances	12		
	(e) Other non-current assets	13		
2	**Current Assets**			
	(a) Current Investments	14		
	(b) Inventories	15		
	(c) Trade receivables	16		
	(d) Cash and cash equivalents	17		
	(e) Short-term loans and advances	18		
	(f) Other current assets			
	Total			

Part II : **Form of Statment of Profit and Loss**

	Particulars	Note No.	For the year ended 31 March, 2014 ₹	For the year ended 31 March, 2013 ₹
	Name of the Company			
	Statement of Profit and Loss for the year ended 31 March, 2014			
	A Continuing Operations			
1	**Revenue from operations (gross)**			
	Less : Excise duty			
	Revenue from operations (net)	20		
2	**Other income**	21		
3	**Total revenue (1+2)**			
4	**Expenses**			
	(a) Cost of materials consumed			
	(b) Purchase of stock-in-trade			
	(c) Changes in inventories of finished goods, work-in-progress and stock-in-trade			
	(d) Employee benefits expense	22		
	(e) Finance costs	23		
	(f) Depreciation and amortisation expense			
	(g) Other expenses	24		
	Total expenses			
5	**Profit / (Loss) before exceptional and extraordinary items and tax (3-4)**			
6	**Exceptional items**			
7	**Profit / (Loss) before extraordinary items and tax (5 ± 6)**			

8	**Extraordinary items**			
9	**Profit / (Loss) before tax (7 ± 8)**			
10	**Tax expense :**			
	(a) Current tax expense for current year			
	(b) (Less) : MAT credit (where applicable)			
	(c) Current tax expense relating to prior years			
	(d) Net current tax expense			
	(e) Deferred tax			
11	**Profit / (Loss) from continuing operations (9 ± 10)**			
B	**Discontinuing Operations**			
12.i	Profit / (Loss) from discontinuing operations (before tax)			
12.ii	Gain / (Loss) on disposal of assets / settlement of liabilities attributable to the discontinuing operations			
12.iii	Add / (Loss) : Tax expense of discontinuing operations			
	(a) on ordinary activities attributable to the discontinuing operations			
	(b) on gain / (Loss) on disposal of assets / settlement of liabilities			
13	**Profit / (Loss) from discontinuing operations (12.i ± 12.ii ± 12.iii)**			
C	**Total Operations**			
14	**Profit / (Loss) for the year (11 ± 13)**			
15	**Earnings per equity share :**			
	(1) Basic			
	(2) Diluted			

Note 1 : Share Capital		
Particulars	**As at 31 March, 2014**	**As at 31 March, 2013**
	₹	₹
Authorized Share Capital ..... Equity Share of ₹ ... each (Pr. Yr. ... Equity Shares) .... Preference Shares of ₹ .... each (Pr. Yr. .... preference Share)		
Issued Share Capital .... Equity Share of ₹ .... each (Pr. Yr. .... Equity Shares) .... Preference Shares of ₹ ... each (Pr. Yr. .... Preference Share)		
Subscribed & Fully Paid up ..... Equity Share of ₹ ... each (Pr. Yr. .... Equity Shares) .... Preference Shares of ₹ ... each (Pr. Yr. .... preference Share)		
Subscribed & not fuliy Paid up ..... Equity Share of ₹ ... each (Pr. Yr. .... Equity Shares) .... Preference Shares of ₹ ... each (Pr. Yr. .... preference Share)		
Less : Calls Unpaid • By Directors • By Officers		
Less : Forfeited Shares (Amount ordinarily paid-up) (....... Shares (Equity / Preference) issued for a Considerations other than Cash) (.... Shares (Equity / preference) issued as Bonus Shares & for this purpose .... (Reserves) is used		
Total		

Note 2 : Reserves and Surplus		
Particulars	**As at 31 March, 2014**	**As at 31 March, 2013**
	₹	₹
Capital Reserves		
Capital Redemption Reserve		
Securities Premium Reserve		
Debenture Redemption Reserve		
Revaluation Reserve		
Share Options Outstanding Account		
Other Reserves (specify the nature and purpose of reserve and the amount in respect there of)		
Total		

Note 3 : Long - term borrowings		
Particulars	**As at 31 March, 2014**	**As at 31 March, 2013**
	₹	₹
Bonds / debentures		
Term loans • From banks • Form other parties		
Deferred payment liabilities		
Deposits		
Loans and advances from related parties		
Long term maturities of finance lease obligations		
Other loans and advances (specify nature)		
Total		

Note 4 : Other Long-term liabilities

Particulars	As at 31 March, 2014	As at 31 March, 2013
	₹	₹
Trade Payables		
Others		
Total		

Note 5 : Long-Term Provisions

Particulars	As at 31 March, 2014	As at 31 March, 2013
	₹	₹
Provision for employee benefits		
Others		
Total		

Note 6 : Short-term borrowings

Particulars	As at 31 March, 2014	As at 31 March, 2013
	₹	₹
Loans repayable on demand		
• From banks		
• From others parties		
Loans and advances from related parties		
Deposits		
Others loans and advances (specify nature)		
Total		

Note 7 : Other Current Liabilities

Particulars	As at 31 March, 2014	As at 31 March, 2013
	₹	₹
Current maturities of long-term debt		
Current maturities of finance lease obligations		
Interest accrued but not due on borrowings		
Interest accrued and due on borrowings		
Income received in advance		
Unpaid dividends		
Application money received for allotment of securities and due for refund and interest accrued thereon		
Unpaid matured deposits and interest accrued thereon		
Unpaid matured debentures and interest accrued thereon		
Other payables (specify nature)		
Total		

Note 8 : Short - Term Provisions

Particulars	As at 31 March, 2014	As at 31 March, 2013
	₹	₹
Provision for employee benefits		
Other (specify nature)		
Total		

Note 9 : Tangible Assets

Particulars	As at 31 March, 2014	As at 31 March, 2013
	₹	₹
Land		
Buildings		
Plant and Equipment		
Furniture and Fixtures		
Vehicles		
Office equipment		
Others (specify nature)		
Total		

Note 10 : Intangible Assets

Particulars	As at 31 March, 2014	As at 31 March, 2013
	₹	₹
Goodwill		
Brands / trademarks		
Computer software		
Mastheads and publishing titles		
Mining rights		
Copyrights and patents and other intellectual property rights, services and operating rights		
Recipes, formulae, models, designs and prototypes		
Licenses and franchise		
Others (specify nature)		
Total		

Note 11 : Non-current Investments		
Particulars	**As at 31 March, 2014**	**As at 31 March, 2013**
	₹	₹
Investment property		
Investment in Equity Instruments		
Investment in preference shares		
Investment in Governmnet or trust securities		
Investment in debentures or bonds		
Investment in Mutual Funds		
Investment in Partnership firms		
Other Non-Current Investments (specify nature)		
Aggregate amount of quoted investments and market value thereof		
Aggregate amount of unquoted investments		
Aggregate provision for diminution in value of investments		

Note 12 : Long-term Loans and Advances		
Particulars	**As at 31 March, 2014**	**As at 31 March, 2013**
	₹	₹
Capital Advances		
Security Deposits		
Loans and advances to related parties (giving details thereof)		
Other loans and advances (a) Secured, considered good (b) Unsecured, considered good (c) Doubtful		
Total		

Note 13 : Other Non-Current Assets		
Particulars	**As at 31 March, 2014**	**As at 31 March, 2013**
	₹	₹
Long Term Trade Receivable (including trade receivables on defferred credit terms)		
Others (specify nature)		
Total		

Note 14 : Current Investments		
Particulars	**As at 31 March, 2014**	**As at 31 March, 2013**
	₹	₹
Investments in equity Instruments		
Investments in Perference Shares		
Investments in Government or Trust Securities		
Investments in Debentures or Bonds		
Investments in Mutual Funds		
Investments in Partnership Firms		
Other Investments (specify nature)		
Total		

Note 15 : Inventories		
Particulars	**As at 31 March, 2014**	**As at 31 March, 2013**
	₹	₹
Raw materials		
Work-in-progress		
Finished goods		
Stock-in-trade (in respect of goods acquired for trading)		
Stores and spares		
Loose tools		
Others (specify nature)		
Total		

Note 16 : Trade Receivables			
Particulars		**As at 31 March, 2014**	**As at 31 March, 2013**
		₹	₹
Trade Receivable > 6 month from the due date of Payment			
Secured, considered good	××		
Unsecured considered good	××		
Doubtful	××		
	××		
Less : Provision for Bad debt	××	××	
Trade Receivable ≤ 6 month from the due date of Payment			
Secured considered good	××		
Unsecured considered good	××		
Doubtful	××		
	××		
Less : Provision for Bad debts	××	××	
Total			

Note 17 : Cash and Cash Equivalents		
Particulars	**As at 31 March, 2014**	**As at 31 March, 2013**
	₹	₹
Balances with bank • Unpaid Dividend • Margin Money • Bank deposits with more than 12 months maturity		
Cheques, darfts on hand		
Cash on hand		
Others (specify nature)		
Total		

Note 18 : Short-term Loans and Advances			
Particulars		**As at 31 March, 2014**	**As at 31 March, 2013**
		₹	₹
Loans and advances to related parties (giving detalis thereof)			
Secured, considered good	××		
Unsecured, considered good	××		
Doubtful	××		
	××		
Less : Provision for Bad debt	××	××	
Others (specify nature) Loans and advances to related parties (giving details thereof)			
Secured, considered good	××		
Unsecured, considered good	××		
Doubtful	××		
Less : Provision for Bad debt	××	××	
Total			

Note 19 : Contingent Liabilities and Commitments		
Particulars	**As at 31 March, 2014**	**As at 31 March, 2013**
	₹	₹
Contigent liabilities shall be classified as : (a) Claims against the company not acknowledged as debt (b) Guarantees (c) Other money for which the company is contingently liable		
Commitments shall be classified as : (a) Estimated amount of contracts remaining to be executed on capital account and not provided for (b) Uncalled liability on shares and other investments partly paid (c) Other commitments (specify nature)		
Total		

Note 20 : Revenue from Operations		
Particulars	**As at 31 March, 2014**	**As at 31 March, 2013**
	₹	₹
In Respect to Non-finance Company Sale of Products Sale of Services Other Operating Revenues Less : Excise Duties		
In Respect to Non-finance Company Interest Other Financial Services		
Total		

Note 21 : Other Income		
Particulars	**As at 31 March, 2014**	**As at 31 March, 2013**
	₹	₹
Interest Income (other than a Finance company)		
Dividend Income		
Net Gain/Loss on Sale of Investments		
Other Non-Operating Income (net of expenses directly attributable to such income)		
Adjustment to the carrying value of Investments (Write-back)		
Net Gain/Loss on foreign currency translation and transaction (other than considered as finance cost)		
Total		

Note 22 : Employee Benefits Expense		
Particulars	**As at 31 March, 2014**	**As at 31 March, 2013**
	₹	₹
Salaries & Wages		
Contribution to Provident & Other Funds		
Expenses on Employee Stock Option Scheme (ESOP)		
And Employee Stock Purchase Plan (ESPP)		
Staff Welfare Expenses		
Total		

Note 23 : Finance Cost

Particulars	As at 31 March, 2014	As at 31 March, 2013
	₹	₹
Interest Expense		
Other Borrowing Costs		
Applicable Net Gain/Loss of Foreign Currency translations & transactions.		
Total		

Note 24 : Other Expenses

Particulars	As at 31 March, 2014	As at 31 March, 2013
	₹	₹
Consumption of Stores and spare parts		
Power and fuel		
Rent		
Repairs to Buildings		
Repairs to Machinary		
Insurance		
Rates & Taxes (excluding Income tax)		
Miscellaneous Expenditure		
Payment to Auditors • As Auditors • For Taxation Matters • For Company Law Matters • For Management Services • For Other Services • For Reimbursement of Expenses		
Total		

Provisions of law in relation to Transfer to Reserves [Sec. 205(2A)]

1. No dividend shall be declared or paid by a company for any financial year out of the profits of the company for that year arrived at after providing for depreciation u/s 205(2), except after the transfer to reserves of the company of the prescribed percentage of its profit for that year, not exceeding 10%.

2. Under the companies (Transfer of Profits to Reserves) Rules, 1975, the percentage of profits required to be transferred to reserves have been related to the rate of dividend proposed for the year. These are as under -

Rate of dividend	Percentage of profit required to be transfereed to reserves
Upto 10%	Nil
Exceeding 10% but not exceeding 12.5%	Not less than 2.5% of the current profits.
Exceeding 12.5% but not exceeding 15%	Not less than 5% of the current profits.
Exceeding 15% but not exceeding 20%	Not less than 7.5 of the current profits.
Exceeding 20%	Not less than 10% of the current profits.

Note :

1. Transfer to Reserve u/s 205(2A) does not include any transfer to Development Rebate Reserve, Capital or any special Reserve. The reserves contemplated are only "Free Reserve"

2. Arrears of depreciation mentioned in section 205(1) should also be provided in determining the profit for the purpose of transfer to reserves.

3. Profit for the above purpose should be (a) after tax and (b) after debit for statutory Reserve, wherever applicable.

4. The rates of dividend mentioned in the table above relate to the rates of Equity Dividend and the portion of dividend in excess of the fixed rate of dividend in respect of participating Perference shares.

5. Companies are free to carry the residual profit, irrespective of the amount, after dividend and transfer to reserves, in the Profit and Loss Account.

Managerial Remuneration

1. Total Managerial Remuneration – 11% of Net Profit computed u/s 349. Sitting Free excluded.

2. Individual Limits

   - MD, WTD or Manager - 5% to any one and 10% to all.

- Director
  - If company has MD, WTD or Manager - 1%
  - If company does not have MD, WTD or Manager - 3%

Profit u/s 349

Profit before Tax as per P/L A/c	××
+ Depreciation in books	××
+ Managerial Remuneration charged in books	××
+ Provision for Bad debt	××
	××
– Depreciation u/s 350	××
Profit u/s 349	××

Requirements contained in schedule XIII for remuneration to managerial personnel if the company has inadequate profits or losses.

1. Quantum of Remuneration

Range of Effective capital of the company	Maximum Monthly Remuneration per MD/WTD/ Director Payable in ₹		
	Situation I	Situation II	Situation III
Less than ₹ 1 Crore	75,000	1,50,000	Above the
₹ 1 Crore or more, but less than ₹ 5 Crores	1,00,000	2,00,000	limits under
₹ 5 Crores or more, but less than ₹ 25 Crores	1,25,000	2,50,000	situation II
₹ 25 Crores or more, but less than ₹ 50 Crores	1,50,000	3,00,000	
₹ 50 Crores or more, but less than ₹ 100 Crores	1,75,000	3,50,000	
₹ 100 Crore of more	2,00,000	4,00,000	
2. Conditions to be fulfiled :			
• Approval Remuneration Commitee by a resolution.	Yes	Yes	Yes
Company should not default in repayment of its Debts (including public Deposits & Debentures) or Interest thereon for continuous period of 30 days or more in the preceding financial year before the appointment of such Managerial person	Yes	Yes	Yes

• Special Resolution at Company's General Meeting authorizing payment of Remuneration for a period not exceeding a period of three years.	Not Applicable	Yes	Yes
• Statement containing prescribed particulars to be sent to shareholders, along with notice to general meeting.	Not Applicable	Yes	Yes
• Central Government's Approval	Not Applicable	Not Applicable	Yes

Effective Capital is computed as under -

Paid Up Share Capital (excluding share Application Money or Advances against Shares)	××
Add : Securities Premium Account	××
Reserves and Surplus (excluding Revaluation Reserve)	××
Long Term loans repayable after one year (See Note 1)	××
Deposits repayable after one year	××
Less : Investments, (for Non-Investment Companies only) (See Note 2)	××
Accumulated losses	××
Preliminary Expenses not written off	××
Effective Capital	

Note :

1. Working capital Loans, Overdrafts, Interest due on loans unless funded, Bank Guarantee etc., and other short-term arrangements shall not be included in "Long Term Loans"

2. Investments shall not be "deducted" in the case of an Investment Company whose principal business in acquisition of Shares, Stock, Debentures or Other Securities.

4.7 PROBLEMS

Problem No. 1 : Shruti Ltd., Mumbai is in the midst of finalizing its accounts for the year-ended 30th September 2012. A Profit and Loss Account has been prepared in draft, the account balances as rounded off to the nearest thousands, are listed below :

Particulars	(₹)	Particulars	(₹)
Shares Capital	25,00,000	Finished Goods	1,41,400
General Reserve	6,03,100	Stores and Spares	2,77,100
Development Rebate Reserve	6,27,100	Tools Jigs and Dies	9,18,700
Land	2,22,500	Cash Credit from Banks	30,67,200
Buildings	9,31,600	Acceptances	2,64,500
Plant and Machinary	64,28,200	Sundry Creditors	6,16,200
Furniture, Fixtures & Office Equipment	1,59,400	Other Current Liabilities	10,31,700
Vehicles	45,400	Interest Accured but not due on loans	58,900
Depreciation Reserve		Provisions for Gratuity and Pension	24,100
Building	2,19,300	Interest Accured on Deposits	200
Plant and Machinary	30,32,800	Sundry Debtors	24,23,100
Furniture	56,800	Cash in Hand	3,700
Vehicles	24,500	Bank Balance	
Loan from State government	57,500	On Current Accounts	3,900
Other Secured Loans	32,46,000	On Deposit Accounts	2,700
Fixed Deposits from Public	2,40,000	Loans and Advance	4,51,800
Unsecured Loans	1,11,400	Preliminary Expenses	800
Raw Materials and Components	42,01,400	Advance Income - Tax paid	3,48,900
Work in Progress	6,11,600	Capital Work-in-Progress	59,600
		Profit & Loss A/c (Profit for the year)	14,50,900

In arriving at the profit for the year, the following have been charged :

Particulars	₹
Depreciation	12,42,400
Salary and perquisite to Managing Director	7,200
Director's fee	400

The Authorized capital is 3,50,000 Equity shares of ₹ 100 each. The from the State Government is secured by a charge on the land, cash credits by hypothecation of stocks and book Debts and the other Secured Loans on the Buildings and Plant and Machinary.

The following adjustments are yet to be made -

(i) Investment Allownce Reserve to be created ₹ 5,40,000

(ii) Provision to be made for Income-Tax in ₹ 4,40,000

(iii) Provision to be made for Managing Director's Commission at 1% of the profits.

(iv) Proposed Dividend at 10%.

Depreciation as per section 350 of the Companies Act is ₹ 10,42,400

Required :

(i) Show the computation of commission payable to the Managing Director; and

(ii) Prepare the Balance sheet of the company, based on all the above.

Solution :

Profit and Loss Adjustment Account

Particulars	₹	Particulars	₹
To Commission to MD	16,600	By Profit for the year	14,50,900
To Investment Allownce Reserve	5,40,000	(as per Draft P & L A/c)	
To Provision for Tax	4,40,000		
To Proposed Dividends (10% × 25,00,000)	2,50,000		
To Balance carried to Balance Sheet	2,04,300		
	14,50,900		14,50,900

Computation of Commission to the Managing Director

Particular	₹ Amount	₹ Amount
Profit as per draft Profit and Loss Account		14,50,900
Add : Depreciation charged in the Profit and Loss Account	12,42,400	
Salary and Remuneration to Managing Director	7,200	
Director Fees	400	12,50,000
		27,00,900
Less : Depreciation u/s 350 of the Companies Act		(10,42400)
Profit u/s 349 for the purpose of Managerial Remuneration		**16,58,500**
Maximum Remuneration (5%)		82,900
Less : Salaries and Remuneration Paid (Director's Fees is excluded for this purpose)		(7200)
Maximum Commission Payable to Managing Director		**75,700**
Commission to be provided for at 1% on Net Profits (1% of ₹ 16,585)		16,600

Dollar Ltd		
Balance Sheet as at 30th September, 2012		
Particulars	**Note No.**	**As at 30 September, 2012**
		₹
A EQUITY AND LIABILITIES		
1 Shareholder's funds		
(a) Share Capital	1	25,00,000
(b) Reserves and Surplus	2	19,74,500
(c) Money received against share warrants		
2 Share application money pending allotment		

3	**Non-current liabilities**		
	(a) Long-term borrowings	3	36,54,900
	(b) Deferred tax liabilities (net)		
	(c) Other long-term liabilities		
	(d) Long-term Provisions		
4	**Current liabilities**		
	(a) Short-term borrowings	4	30,67,200
	(b) Trade Payables	5	8,80,700
	(c) Other current liabilities	6	11,07,200
	(d) Short-term provisions	7	3,65,200
	Total		1,35,49,700
B	**ASSETS**		
1	**Non-current Assets**		
	(a) Fixed assets		
	(i) Tangible assets	8	44,53,700
	(ii) Intangible assets		
	(iii) Capital work-in-progress		59,600
	(iv) Intangible assets under developments		
	(v) Fixed assets held for sale		
	(b) Non-current investments		
	(c) Deferred tax assets (net)		
	(d) Long-term loans and advances		
	(e) Other non-current assets		800
2	**Current Assets**		
	(a) Current Investments		
	(b) Inventories	9	61,50,200
	(c) Trade receivables		24,23,100
	(d) Cash and cash equivalents	10	10,300
	(e) Short-term loans and advances		4,51,800
	(f) Other Current Assets		200
	Total		1,35,49,700

Note 1 : Share Capital

Particulars	As at 30 Sept, 2012
	₹
Authorized Share Capital	
3,50,000 Equity Share of ₹ 100 each	35,00,000
Issued, Subscribed & Fully Paid up Shares Capital	
2,50,000 Equity Share of ₹ 100 each	25,00,000
Total	25,00,000

Note 2 : Reserves and Surplus

Particulars	As at 30 Sept, 2012
	₹
General Reserves	6,03,100
Development Rebate Reserve	6,27,100
Investment allowance Reserve	5,40,000
Profit & Loss	2,04,300
Total	19,74,500

Note 3 : Long - term Borrowings

Particulars	As at 30 Sept, 2012
	₹
Loan from state Govt. (Secured by Charge on assets)	57,500
Other Secured Loan (Secured by Charge on building & Plant & Machinery)	32,46,000
Fixed Deposit From Public	2,40,000
Unsecured Loans	1,11,400
Total	36,54,900

Note 4 : Short - term Borrowings	
Particulars	**As at 30 Sept, 2012**
	₹
Cash Credit From Bank (Secured by hypothecation of Stock & book debts)	30,67,200
Total	30,67,200

Note 5 : Trade Payables	
Particulars	**As at 30 Sept, 2012**
	₹
Acceptances	2,64,500
Trade Creditors	6,16,200
Total	8,80,700

Note 6 : Other Current Liabilities	
Particulars	**As at 30 Sept, 2012**
	₹
Other Current Liabilities	10,31,700
Interest Accrued	58,900
MD Commission Payable	16,600
Total	11,07,200

Note 7 : Short-term Provisions	
Particulars	**As at 30 Sept, 2012**
	₹
Provision for Taxation (4,400 - 3489)	91,100
Proposed Dividends	2,50,000
Provision for Gratuity & Pension	24,100
Total	3,65,200

Note 8 : Tangible Assets	
Particulars	**As at 30 Sept, 2012**
	₹
Land	2,22,500
Buildings	7,12,300
Plant and Equipment	33,95,400
Furniture and Fixtures	1,02,600
Vehicle	20,900
Total	44,53,700

Note 9 : Inventories	
Particulars	**As at 30 Sept, 2012**
	₹
Raw Material & Consumables	42,01,400
Work in progress	6,11,600
Finished goods	1,41,400
Stores & Spares	2,77,100
Tools jigs and Dies	9,18,700
Total	61,50,200

Note 10 : Cash and Cash Equivalents	
Particulars	**As at 30 Sept, 2012**
	₹
Balances with bank on current account	3,900
Balances with bank on deposit account	2,700
Cash on hand	37,00
Total	10,300

Problem No. 2 : From the following particulars furnished by Uday Limited, Pune prepare the Balance sheet as at 31st March, 2012 as required by Part I, Schedule VI of the Companies Act.

(in ₹)

Particulars	Debit	Credit
Equity Capital (Face Value of ₹ 100)		20,00,000
Calls in Arrears	2,000	
Land	4,00,000	
Building	7,00,000	
Plant and Machinary	10,50,000	
Furniture	1,00,000	
General Reserve		4,20,000
Loan from State Financial Corporation		3,00,000
Stock : Finished goods	4,00,000	
Raw Material	1,00,000	5,00,000
Provision for Taxation		1,36,000
Sundry Debtors	4,00,000	
Advances	85,400	
Proposed Dividend		1,20,000
Profit and Loss Account		2,00,000
Cash Balance	60,000	
Cash at Bank	4,94,000	
Preliminary Expenses	26,600	
Loans (Unsecured)		2,42,000
Sundry Creditors (for goods and expenses)		4,00,000
Total	**38,18,000**	**38,18,000**

The following additional information is also provided :
   (i) 4,000 Equity shares were issued for consideration other than cash.
   (ii) Debtors of ₹ 1,04,000 are due for more than six months from the due date of payment.
   (iii) The Balance of ₹ 3,00,000 in the loan account with state finance corporation includes 15,000 interest accured but not due.
   (iv) Balance at Bank includes ₹ 4,000 with Elite Bank Limited, which is not a scheduled Bank.
   (v) Bills Receivalbe for ₹ 5,50,000 maturing on 30th June have been discounted.
   (vi) The company had Contract for the erection of Machinary at ₹ 3,00,000 which is still incomplete.

Solution :

			Note No.	As at 31 March, 2012
	XYZ Limited			
	Balance Sheet as at 31 March, 2012			
	Particulars		**Note No.**	**As at 31 March, 2012**
				₹
A	**EQUITY AND LIABILITIES**			
1	**Shareholder's funds**			
	(a) Share capital		1	19,98,000
	(b) Reserves and Surplus		2	6,20,000
	(c) Money received against share Warrants			
2	**Share application money pending allotment**			
3	**Non-current liabilities**			
	(a) Long-term borrowings		3	5,27,000
	(b) Deferred tax liabilities (net)			
	(c) Other long-term liabilities			
	(d) Long-term Provisions			
4	**Current liabilities**			
	(a) Short-term borrowings			
	(b) Trade Payables			4,00,000
	(c) Other current liabilities		4	15,000
	(d) Short-term provisions		5	2,56,000
	Total			**38,16,000**
B	**ASSET**			
1	**Non-current assets**			
	(a) Fixed assets			
	(i) Tangible assets		6	22,50,000
	(ii) Intangible assets			

		(iii) Capital work-in-progress		
		(iv) Intangible assets under developments		
		(v) Fixed assets held for sale		
	(b)	Non-current investments		
	(c)	Deferred tax assets (net)		
	(d)	Long-term loans and advances		
	(e)	Other non-current assets	7	26,600
2	**Current Assets**			
	(a)	Current Investments		
	(b)	Inventories	8	5,00,000
	(c)	Trade receivables	9	4,00,000
	(d)	Cash and cash equivalents	10	5,54,000
	(e)	Short-term loans and advances		85,400
	(f)	Other current assets		
		Total		**38,16,000**

Note 1 : Share Captial	
Particulars	**As at 31 March, 2012**
	₹
Issued Subscribed & Fully Paid up Shares Capital	
10,000 Equity Share of ₹ 100 each	20,00,000
Less : Calls Unpaid	2,000
{2,000 Equity Shares issued for a Consideration other than Cash}	
Total	19,98,000

Note 2 : Reserves and Surplus

Particulars	As at 31 March, 2012
	₹
General Reserves	4,20,000
Profit & Loss	2,00,000
Total	6,20,000

Note 3 : Long-term borrowings

Particulars	As at 31 March, 2012
	₹
Unsecured Loan	2,42,000
Loan from State Financial Corporation	2,85,000
Total	5,27,000

Note 4 : Other Current Liabilities

Particulars	As at 31 March, 2012
	₹
Interest accrued but not due on borrowings	15,000
Total	15,000

Note 5 : Short-term Provisions

Particulars	As at 31 March, 2012
	₹
Provision for Taxation	1,36,000
Proposed Dividends	1,20,000
Total	2,56,000

Note 6 : Tangible Assets	
Particulars	**As at 31 March, 2012**
	₹
Land	4,00,000
Buildings	7,00,000
Plant and Equipment	10,50,000
Furniture and Fixtures	1,00,000
Total	22,50,000

Note 7 : Other Non-Current Assets	
Particulars	**As at 31 March, 2012**
	₹
Preliminary Expenses	26,600
Total	26,600

Note 8 : Inventories	
Particulars	**As at 31 March, 2012**
	₹
Raw Materials	1,00,000
Finished goods	4,00,000
Total	5,00,000

Note 9 : Trade Receivable

Particulars		As at 31 March, 2012
		₹
Trade Receivable > 6 month from the due date of Payment		
Unsecured considered good	1,04,000	
Less : Provision for Bad debt...		1,04,000
Trade Receivable ≤ 6 month from the due date of Payment		
Unsecured considered good	2,96,000	
Less : Provision for Bad debt....		2,96,000
Total		4,00,000

Note 10 : Cash and Cash Equivalents

Particulars	As at 31 March, 2012
	₹
Balances with bank	4,94,000
Cash on hand	60,000
Total	5,54,000

Note 11 : Contigent Liabilities and Commitments

Particulars	As at 31 March, 2012
	₹
Contigent liabilities shall be classified as :	
Other money for which the company is contingently liable	5,50,000
Commitments shall be classified as :	
Estimated amount of contracts remaining to be executed on capital account and not provide for	3,00,000
Total	8,50,000

Problem No. 3 : Following are the balance from the books Amrut Ltd Nagar as at 31st March 2013

Particulars	₹	Particulars	₹
Sales	1,33,94,000	Other Expenses	22,52,800
Depreciation	71,000	General Reserve	5,16,000
Other Income (Operation)	57,600	Sundry Debtors	11,80,000
Development Rebate Reserve	46,800	Share Capital	4,00,000
Investment Allowance Resreve	85,000	Secured Loans	2,69,600
Fixed Assets at Cost	12,77,400	Cash at Bank	6,400
Investments (Long Term)	3,800	Loan & Advances (Short term)	11,600
Interest Accrued	500	Fixed Deposits	3,20,000
Purchases (Raw Material)	89,68,000	Depreciation Reserve	5,60,000
Salaries and Wages	6,94,200	Provision for Doubtful Debts	1,200
		Sundry Creditors	22,15,500

Calculate Managing Director's Remuneration and Prepare in the proper from the profit and loss Account and Balance Sheet as at 31st March 2013 with the help of the following information.

Particulars	₹	₹
Stocks	Opening	Closing
- Raw Material and stores	10,00,400	5,00,200
- Work in progress	19,01,600	4,00,800
- Finished goods	4,98,000	16,19,000
Depreciation as per schedule XIV to the companies Act, 1956		80,000
Market value of Investments		2,900
Sundry debtors due for more than 6 months		7,200
Out of above, provision made this year for Doubtful debts		800
Included in other expenses are		
- Audior's fee for audit		1,200
- Payment to Auditors for other services		400

- Income Tax to the provided at 36.6%
- Managing Directors Remuneration is at 5% of Net Profit as per law subject to maximum of ₹ 2,40,000 p.a.
- Provide Dividends at 25% on capital and transfer the Balance of profits to general Reserve.
- Authorised capital of the company is 60,00,000 equity Shares of ₹ 100 each. Out of this 4 lakhs shares have been issued and fully paid.
- Provision for Doubtful debts is made in respect of Debotors due for more than 6 months.
- Debtors due for less than 6 months is secured to the extent of ₹ 60,000

Solution :

Fundoo Ltd			
Balance Sheet as at 31st March 2013			
	Particulars	**Note No.**	**As at 31 March, 2013**
			₹
A	**Equity and Liabilities**		
1	**Shareholder's Funds**		
	(a) Share capital	1	4,00,000
	(b) Reserves and Surplus	2	9,20,550
	(c) Money received against share Warrants		

2	Share application money pending allotment		
3	**Non current liabilities**		
	(a) Long - term borrowings	3	5,89,600
	(b) Deferred tax liabilities (net)		
	(c) Other Long-term liabilities		
	(d) Long - term Provisions		
4	**Current Liabilities**		
	(a) Short term borrowings		
	(b) Trade Payables		22,15,500
	(c) Other Current liabilities		2,400
	(d) Short term provisions	4	3,10,450
	Total		44,38,500
B	**Assets**		
1	**Non Current Assets**		
	(a) Fixed Assets		
	(i) Tangible assets	5	7,17,400
	(ii) Intangible assets		
	(iii) Capital work in progress		
	(iv) Intangible assets under developments		
	(v) Fixed assets held for sale		
	(b) None - Current investments		3,800
	(c) Deferred tax assets (net)		
	(d) Long term loans and advances		
	(e) Other non current assets		
2	**Current Assets**		
	(a) Current Investments		
	(b) Inventories	6	25,20,000
	(c) Trade receivables	7	11,78,800
	(d) Cash and cash equivalents		6,400
	(e) Short term loans and advances		11,600
	(f) Other current assets		500
	Total		44,38,500

Statements of Profit and Loss for the year ended 31 March 2013		
Particulars	**Note No.**	**For the year ended 31 March, 2013**
		₹
A	**Continuing Operations**		
1	**Revenue from operations (gross)**	8	1,34,51,600
	Less : Excise duty		
	Revenue from Operations (net)		1,34,51,600
2	**Other income**		
3	**Total revenue (1 + 2)**		1,34,51,600
4	**Expenses**		
	(a) Cost of materials consumed	9	94,68,200
	(b) Purchase of stock in trade		
	(c) Changes in inventories of finished goods, work in progress and stock in trade		3,79,800
	(d) Empolyee benefits expense	10	6,96,600
	(e) Finance costs		
	(f) Depreciation and amortisation expense		71,000
	(g) Other expenses	11	22,52,800
	Total expenses		1,28,68,400
5	**Profit / (Loss) before exceptional and extraordinary items and tax (3 -4)**		5,83,200
6	**Exceptional items**		
7	**Profit / (Loss) before extraordinary items and tax (5 ± 6)**		5,83,200
8	**Extraordinary items**		
9	**Profit / (Loss) before tax (7 ± 8)**		5,83,200
10	**Tax expenses :**		
	(a) Current tax expense for current year		2,10,450

	(b) (Less) : MAT credit (where applicable)		
	(c) Current tax expense relating to prior years		
	(d) Net current tax expense		
	(e) Deferred tax		
11	**Profit / (Loss) From continuing operations (9 ± 10)**		3,72,750
B	**Discountinuing Operations**		
12.i	Profit / (Loss) from discontinuing operations (before tax)		
12.ii	Gain / (Loss) on disposal of assets / settlement of liabilities attributable to the discontinuing operations		
12.iii	Add / (Loss) : Tax expense of discontinuing operations		
(a)	On ordinary activities attributable to the discontinuing operations		
(b)	On gain / (Loss) on disponsal of assets / settlement of liabilities		
13	**Profit / (Loss) from discontinuing Operations (12i ± 12.ii ± 12.iii)**		
C	**Total Operations**		
14	**Profit / (Loss) for the year (11 ± 13)**		3,72,750
15	**Earnings per equity share :** (1) Basic (2) Diluted		

Working Notes :

1. Other expenses   22,52,800

    (-) Provision for doubtful debts   800

    (-) Auditors Remuneration

       Audit fees   1200

       Other Service   400

                            (1600)

                           22,50,400

2. Profit u/s 349

Net Profit before MD remuneration	5,85,600
+ Depreciation	71,000
+ Prov. for BD	800
(-) Dep. Sch. XIV	80,000
	5,77,400
5% of 5,77,400	28,870

Subject of Max of 2400

3. Prov for doubtful debt is not allowad under income tax.

Let us assume depreciation under income tax is ₹ 80,000 i.e. similar to depreciation under companies Act.

Taxable Profit

Profit before to as per books	5,83,200
+ Dep. Charged in books	71,000
+ Prov.for BD (not allowed in IT)	300
(-) Dep. under IT Act	80,000
	5,75,000
36.6% of 5,75,000	2,10,450

Note 1 : Share Capital	
Particulars	**As at 31 March, 2013**
	₹
Authorized Share Capital 6,00,000 Equity Share of ₹ 100 each	6,00,000
Issued Subscribed & Fully Paid up Shares Capital 4,00,000 Equity Share of ₹ 100 each	4,00,000
Total	4,00,000

Note 2 : Reserves and Surplus

Particulars	As at 31 March, 2013
	₹
Development Rebate Reserve	46,800
Investment Allowance Reserve	85,000
General Reserve	5,16,000
Profit & Loss	2,72,750
Total	9,20,550

Note 3 : Long - term Borrowings

Particulars	As at 31 March, 2013
	₹
Secured Loan	2,69,600
Unsecured Loan	3,20,000
Total	5,89,600

Note 4 : Short - term Provisions

Particulars	As at 31 March, 2013
	₹
Provision for Tax	2,10,450
Proposed Dividend	1,00,000
Total	3,10,450

Note 5 : Tangible Assets

Particulars	As at 31 March, 2013
	₹
Fixed Assets at Cost	12,77,400
Less : Depreciation Reserve	5,60,000
Total	7,17,400

Note 6 : Inventories	
Particulars	**As at 31 March, 2013**
	₹
Raw Material & Stores	5,00,200
Work in progress	4,00,800
Finished goods	16,19,000
Total	25,20,000

Note 7 : Trade Receivables		
Particulars		**As at 31 March, 2013**
		₹
Trade Receivables > 6 month from the due date of Payment Unsecured Considered good Less : Provisiong for Bad debt	7200 1200	6000
Trade Receivables < 6 month from the due date of Payment secured considered good Unsecured considered good	6,00,000 5,72,800	11,72,800
Total		11,78,800

Note 8 : Revenue from Operations	
Particulars	**As at 31 March, 2013**
	₹
Sales of Products	1,33,94,000
Other Operating Revenues	57,600
Total	1,34,51,600

Note 9 : Cost of Material Consumed	
Particulars	**As at 31 March, 2013**
	₹
Raw Material Purchases	89,68,000
Opening Stock of Raw Material	10,00,400
Less : Closing Stock	5,00,200
Total	94,68,200

Note 10 : Employees Benefit Expenses	
Particulars	**As at 31 March, 2013**
	₹
Salaries and Wages	6,94,200
MD Remuneration	2,400
Total	6,96,600

Note 11 : Other Expenses		
Particulars		**As at 31 March, 2013**
		₹
Auditors Remuneration		
For Audit	1200	
For Other Services	400	1,600
Provision for Baddebts		800
Other Expenses (WN1)		22,50,400
Total		22,52,800

Problem No. 4 : Prepare a Balance Sheet of Kartiki Ltd, Nasik as at 31st March, 2012 required under schedule VI of the companies Act, 1956, from the following information of Honeymoon Ltd.

Particulars	Amount (₹)	Particulars	Amount (₹)
Terms Loans (Secured)	20,00,000	Investments (Long term)	4,50,400
Sundry Creditors	22,90,000	Loss for the year	6,00,000
Advances	7,44,000	Sundry Debtors	24,50,000
Cash and Bank Balances	5,50,000	Miscellaneous expenses	1,16,000
Staff Advances	1,10,000	Loan from debtors	4,00,000
Provision for Taxation	3,40,000	Provision for doubtful debtors	40,400
Securities Premium	9,50,000	Stores	8,00,000
Loose Tools	1,00,000	Fixed assets (WDV)	1,03,00,000
General Reserve	41,00,000	Finished goods	15,00,000
Capital work in progress	4,00,000		

Additional Information :

i) Share Capital Consists of :
   - 60,000 Equity shares of ₹ 100 each fully paid up.
   - 20,000 10% Redeemable preferences shares of ₹ 100 each fully paid up.

ii) Depreciation on assets ₹ 10,00,000

Solution :

	Balance Sheet as at 31 March, 2012		
	Particulars	**Note No.**	**As at 31 March, 2012**
			₹
A	**EQUITY AND LIABILITIES**		
1	**Shareholder's funds**		
	(a) Share capital	1	80,00,000
	(b) Reserves and Surplus	2	44,50,000
	(c) Money received against share warrants		
2	**Share application money pending allotment**		

3	**Non-current liabilities**		
	(a) Long-term borrowings	3	20,00,000
	(b) Deferred tax liabilities (net)		
	(c) Other long-term liabilities		
	(d) Long-term Provisions		
4.	**Current liabilities**		
	(a) Short-term borrowings	4	4,00,000
	(b) Trade Payables		22,90,000
	(c) Other current liabilities		
	(d) Short-term provisions	5	3,40,000
	Total		1,74,80,000
B	**ASSETS**		
1	**Non-current assets**		
	(a) Fixed assets		
	(i) Tangible assets		1,03,00,000
	(ii) Intangible assets		
	(iii) Capital work-in-progress		4,00,000
	(iv) Intangible assets under developments		
	(v) Fixed assets held for sale		
	(b) Non-current investments		4,50,400
	(c) Deferred tax assets (net)		
	(d) Long-term loans and advances		
	(e) Other non-current assets	6	1,16,000
2	**Current Assets**		
	(a) Current Investments		
	(b) Inventories	7	24,00,000
	(c) Trade receivables	8	24,09,600
	(d) Cash and cash equivalents		5,50,000
	(e) Short-term loans and advances	9	8,54,000
	(f) Other current assets		
	Total		1,74,80,000

Note 1 : Share Capital	
Particulars	**As at 31 March, 2012**
	₹
Issued, Subscribed & Fully Paid up Shares Capital	
60,000 Equity Share of ₹ 100 each	60,00,000
20,000 Redeemable Preference Share of ₹100 each	20,00,000
Total	80,00,000

Note 2 : Reserves and Surplus	
Particulars	**As at 31 March, 2012**
	₹
General Reserves	41,00,000
Securities Premium	9,50,000
Profit & Loss A/c	6,00,000
Total	44,50,000

Note 3 : Long-term borrowings	
Particulars	**As at 31 March, 2012**
	₹
Term Loan (Secured)	20,00,000
Total	20,00,000

Note 4 : Short-term Borrowings	
Particulars	**As at 31 March, 2012**
	₹
Loan from Debtors	4,00,000
Total	4,00,000

Note 5 : Short-term Provisions

Particulars	As at 31 March, 2012
	₹
Provision for Taxation	3,40,000
Total	3,40,000

Note 6 : Other Non Current Assets

Particulars	As at 31 March, 2012
	₹
Misscellaneous expenses	1,16,000
Total	1,16,000

Note 7 : Inventories

Particulars	As at 31 March, 2012
	₹
Loose Tools	1,00,000
Stores	8,00,000
Finished Goods	15,00,000
Total	24,00,000

Note 8 : Trade Receivables

Particulars		As at 31 March, 2012
		₹
Trade Receivables		
Unsecured considered good	24,50,000	
Less : Provision for Bad debt	40,400	24,09,600
Total		24,09,600

Note 9 : Short term Loans & Advances	
Particulars	**As at 31 March, 2012**
	₹
Staff Advances	1,10,000
Other Advances	7,44,000
Total	8,54,000

Problem No. 5 : Following balance are extracted from the books of the Omkar Industries Ltd, Satara as at 31 st Dec. 2013.

Particulars	Debit	Credit
Sales		27,60,000
Purchases of Materials	12,18,000	
Share capital fully paid		1,00,000
Land purchased in the year as stock	73,000	
Leasehold premises	42,000	
Creditors		4,63,000
Debtors	7,35,000	
Directors Salaries	39,000	
Wages	1,11,000	
Work in progress on 1st january	2,10,000	
Sub contractors cost	8,94,000	
Equipment, Fixtures and fittings at cost on 1st January	2,64,000	
Stock on 1st January	59,000	
Profit and Loss Account, Credit Balaance on 1st January		1,28,000
Secured Loan		1,12,000
Bank Overdraft		1,05,000
Interest on loan and overdraft	22,000	
Depreciation on Equipment on 1st January		1,64,000
Administration Expenses	1,47,000	
Office Salaries	18,000	
Total	**38,32,000**	**38,32,000**

The following further information is furnished to you.

i) On 31st December, Stock in Hand including the land acquired during the year, is valued at 1,42,000 Work progress at that date is valued at 1,40,000

ii) On 1st July, the company moved to a new premise. The premise was taken on a 12 years lease and the lease premium paid amounted to 42,000 The company used sub contract Labour of 40,000 and Materials at cost of 38,000 in the refurbishment of the said premises. These are to be considered as part of the cost leasehold premises.

iii) A review of the Debtors reveals specific doubtful debts of ₹ 35,000 among dues outstanding for more than 6 months and the Directors wish to provide for these together with a provision of 2% of the balance Debtors.

iv) Depreciation on equipment, fixtures and fittings is provided at 15% on the written down value.

v) Uner the income tax Rules, the Depreciation on the companys assets amounts to ₹ 25,000

vi) Elite Ltd. sued Hexa Industries Ltd. for supplying defective materials, which has been written off as valueless. The Directors are confident that Hexa Industries Ltd. will agree for a settlement of ₹ 50,000

vii) The Directors propose a dividend of 25%

viii) ₹ 20,0000 is to be provided as Audit Fee.

ix) The company will provide 10% of Pre-tax Profit as Bonus to Employees in the books before charging Bonus.

x) Income Tax to be provided at 50% of the profits.

xi) Debtor of ₹ 300 had remained outstanding for more than 6 months.

You are required.

1. To prepare the company's Financial Statements for the year ended 31st December as near as possible to proper form of Company Final Accounts; and

2. To prepare a set of Notes to Accounts including significant accounting policies.

Solution :

	Elite Ltd		
	Balance Sheet as at 31st December 2013		
	Particulars	**Note No.**	**As at 31 Dec, 2013**
			₹
A	**Equity and Liabilities**		
1	**Shareholder's funds**		
	(a) Share Capital		1,00,000
	(b) Reserves and Surplus	1	1,89,000
	(c) Money received against share Warrants	-	
2	**Share application money pending allotment**		
3	**Non - current liabilities**		
	(a) Long term borrowings	2	2,17,000
	(b) Deferred tax liabilities (net)		
	(c) Other long-term liabilities		
	(d) Long-term Provisions		
4	**Current liabilities**		
	(a) Short term borrowings		
	(b) Trade Payables		4,63,000
	(c) Other Current liabilities	3	44,000
	(d) Short - term provisions	4	1,55,000
	Total		11,68,000
B	**Assets**		
1	**Non - Current Assets**		
	(a) Fixed assets		
	(i) Tangible assets	5	2,00,000
	(ii) Intangible assets		

	(iii) Capital work in progress			
	(iv) Intangible assets under developments			
	(v) Fixed assets held for sale			
	(b) Non current investments			
	(c) Deferred tax assets (net)			
	(d) Long - term loans and advances			
	(e) Other non - current assets			
2	**Current Assets**			
	(a) Current Investments			
	(b) Inventories		6	2,82,000
	(c) Trade receivables		7	6,86,000
	(d) Cash and cash equivalents			
	(e) Short - term loans and advances			
	(f) Other Current assets			
	Total			11,68,000

Elite Ltd		
Statement of Profit and Loss for the year ended 31 December 2013		
Particulars	**Note No.**	**For the year ended 31 Dec, 2012**
		₹
A Continuing Operations		
1 Revenue from operations (gross)		27,60,000
Less : Excise duty		
Revenue from operations (net)		27,60,000
2 Other income		
3 Total revenue (1 + 2)		27,60,000

4	**Expenses**		
	(h) Cost of materials consumed	8	11,80,000
	(i) Purchase of stock in trade		73,000
	(j) Changes in inventories of finished goods, work in progress and stock in trade	9	13,000
	(k) Employee benefits expense	10	1,92,000
	(l) Finance costs		22,000
	(m) Depreciation and amortisation expense		20,000
	(n) Other expenses	11	10,70,000
	Total expenses		25,70,000
5	**Profit / (Loss) before exceptional and extraordinary items and tax (3 - 4)**		2,16,000
6	**Exceptional items**		
7	**Profit / (Loss) before extraordinary items and tax (5 ± 6)**		2,16,000
8	**Extraordinary items**		
9	**Profit / (Loss) before tax (7 ± 8)**		2,16,000
10	**Tax expense**		
	(a) Current tax expense for current year		1,30,000
	(b) (Less) : MAT Credit (Where applicable)		
	(c) Current tax expense relating to prior years		
	(d) Net Current tax expense		
	(e) Deferred tax		
11	**Profit / (Loss) From continuing operations (9 ± 10)**		86,000
B	**Discontinuing Operations**		
12.i	Profit / (Loss) From discontinuing operations (before tax)		
12.ii	Gain / (Loss) on disposal of assets / Settlement of liabilities attributable to the discontinuing operatiosn		
12.iii	Add / (Loss) : Tax expense of discontinuing operations		

	(a) On ordinary activities attributable to the discontinuing operations			
	(b) on gain / (Loss) on disposal of assets / settlement of liabilities.			
13	**Profit / (Loss) From discontinuing Operations (12.i ± 12.ii ± 12.iii)**			
C	**Total Operations**			
14	**Profit / (Loss) For the year (11 ± 13)**			86,000
15	**Earnings per equity share** (1) Basic (2) Biluted			

Working Notes :

1. Calculation of Depreciation

Furniture (Equipment, fixture & Fittings) Cost	2,64,000
(-) Depreciation	1,64,000
	1,00,000
Depreciation 100 × 15%	= 15,000
Lease hold premises	
Lease Rent	42,000
+ Refurbishment	
Material	38,000
Subcontract	40,000
	1,20,000

Annual depreciation $\dfrac{\cos t}{life} = \dfrac{1,20,000}{12,000} = $ = 10,000

Depreciation for Current year $= 10 \times \dfrac{6,000}{12} = $ = 5000

2. Provision for doubtful debts

Specific Provision	35,000
+ Other Prov. (7,35,000 - 35,000) × 2%	14,000
	49,000

3. **Profit before bonus to employees** = 5,55,000 - (39,000 + 22,000 + 1,47,000 + 18,000 + 20,000 + 49,000 + 20,000) =   2,40,000

Bonus = 10% of 2,40,000 =   24,000

4. **Taxable Profit**

Profit before tax (as per books)	2,16,000
+ Dep. As per books	20,000
(-) Dep. As per IT Rules	25,000
+ provision of doubtful	49,000
Taxable profit	2,60,000
Tax = 2,60,000 × 50%	1,30,000

5. **Transfer to reserve :**

Profit before tax	2,16,000
Tax	1,30,000
PAT	86,000
Transfer to reserve @ 10%	9000
	77,000
Proposed Dividend	25,000
Transfered to B/S	52,000

Note 1 : Reserves and Surplus

Particulars	As at 31 Dec, 2013
	₹
Profit & Loss (128 + 52)	1,80,000
General Reserve	9000
Total	1,89,000

Note 2 : Long - term Borrowings

Particulars	As at 31 Dec, 2013
	₹
Bank Overdraft	1,05,000
Secured Loan	1,12,000
Total	2,17,000

Note 3 : Other Current Liabilities

Particulars	As at 31 Dec, 2013
	₹
Audit Fees Payable	20,000
Bonus Payable	24,000
Total	44,000

Note 4 : Short term Provisions

Particulars	As at 31 Dec, 2013
	₹
Provision for Taxation	1,30,000
Proposed Dividends	25,000
Total	1,55,000

Note 5 : Tangible Assets

Particulars		As at 31 Dec, 2013
		₹
Leasehold Premises	42,000	
Add : Sub - Contract Labour	40,000	
Add : Material Consumed	38,000	
	1,20,00	
Less : Depreciation	5000	1,15,000
Equipment (Gross Block)	2,64,000	
Less : Depreciation	1,79,000	85,000
	Total	2,00,000

Note 6 : Inventories

Particulars	As at 31 Dec, 2013
	₹
Work in progress	1,40,000
Finished goods	1,42,000
Total	2,82,000

Note 7 : Trade Receivables

Particulars		As at 31 Dec, 2013
		₹
Trade Receivables > 6 month from the due date of Payment		
Unsecured considered good	2,65,000	
Doubtful	35,000	
Less:Provision for Bad debt (35,000 + 5,300)	40,300	2,59,700
Trade Receivables < 6 month from the due date of Payment		
Unsecured Considered good	4,35,000	
Less: Provision for Bad debt	8,700	4,26,300
Total		6,86,000

Note 8 : Cost Of Material Consumed

Particulars	As at 31 Dec, 2013
	₹
Raw Material	12,18,000
Less : Material used in refurnishment of new premises	38,000
Total	11,80,000

Note 9 : Changes in Inventories of Finished Goods, WIP & Stock in Trade

Particulars	As at 31 Dec, 2013
	₹
Opening Finished Goods	59,000
WIP	2,10,000
Closing Finished Goods	1,42,000
WIP	1,40,000
Total	13,000

Note 10 : Employees Benefit Expenses

Particulars	As at 31 Dec, 2013
	₹
Wages	1,11,000
Bonus to employees	24,000
Directors salary	39,000
Officer Salaries	18,000
Total	1,92,000

Note 11 : Other Expenses

Particulars	As at 31 Dec, 2013
	₹
Subscontractors Cost (894 - 40)	8,54,000
Administration Expenses	1,47,000
Provision for Bad Debt	49,000
Payment to Auditors	20,000
Total	10,70,000

Problem No. 6 : From the following particulars of Sunrise Limited Pune you are required to calculate the managerial Remuneration in the following situations.

(i) There is only one Whole Time Director.

(ii) There is two Whole Time Directors.

(iii) There are two Whole Time Directors, a part time Director and a Manager.

Liabilities	₹
Net Profit before Income Tax and Managerial Remuneration, but after depreciation and Provision for repairs	87,04,100
Depreciation provided in the books	31,00,000
Provision for Repairs for Machinery during the year	2,50,000
Depreciation Allowable under Schedule XIV	26,00,000
Actual expenditure incurred on Repairs during the year	1,50,000

Solution : Computation of Net Profits u/s 349 of the Companies Act.

Net Profit before Provision for Income tax and Managerial Remuneration, but after Depreciation and Provision for Repairs		87,04,100
Add : Depreciation Provided in the Books	31,00,000	
Provision for Repairs of Machinery	2,50,000	33,50,000
		1,20,54,100
Less : Depreciation allowable under Schedule XIV	26,00,000	
Actual Expenditure income on Repairs	1,50,000	27,50,000
Net Profit under Section 349		**93,04,100**

Note : Excess Provision over and above actually incurred shall be added back in determining the Net Profits.

Computation of Managerial Remuneration u/s 309

Situation	% of Remuneration	Managerial remuneration
One Whole Time Director	5%	4,65,205
Two Whole Time Directors	10%	9,30,410
Two Whole Time Directors and Part Time Director and a Manager	11%	10,23,451

Problem No. 7 : The following extract of Balance Sheet Abhishek Ltd sangli as at 31 st March was obtained.

Liabilities	₹
Authorised Capital :	
10,000 14% Preference shares of ₹ 100 each	10,00,000
1,00,000 Equity Shares of ₹ 100 each	1,00,00,000
	1,10,00,000
Issued and Subsecribed Capital.	
7,500 14% Prefernce Sheres of ₹ 100 each fully paid	7,50,000
60,000 Equity Shares of ₹ 100 each ₹ 80 paid up	48,00,0000
Share Suspense Accoung	10,00,000
Reserves and Surplus	
Capital Reserves(60% is Revaluation Reserve)	1,25,000
Securities Premium	25,000
Secured Loans : 15% Debentures	32,50,000
Unsecured Loans :	
Public Deposits	1,85,000
Cash credit from SBI	2,30,000
Current Liabilities : Surdry Credtitors	1,72,500

Assets	₹
Investment Shares, Debentures etc	37,50,000
Profit and Loss Account	7,62,500
Preliminary Expenses not written off	27,500

Share Suspense Account represents application money received on shares the allotment of which is not yet made. Abhishek Ltd has been sustaining losses for the last few years. The company has only one Whole - Time Director. Find out how much remuneration can the company pay to its managerial person as per the provision of Part II of Schedule XIII to the Companies Act, 1956 Would your answer differ if Abhishek Ltd. is an Investment Compay?

Solution :

Computation of Effective Capital

If Abhishek Ltd is treated as an	Non-Invt. Company	Investment Company
Paid up Share Capital		
15,000 14 % Preference Shares	7,50,000	7,50,000
1,20,000 Equity Shares	4,80,000	4,80,000
Add : Capital Reserve (Excluding Revaluation Reserve 60%)	50,000	50,000
Securities Premium	25,000	25,000
15% Debentures	32,50,000	32,50,000
Public Deposits (Repayable after one year)	1,85,000	1,85,000
(A)	**90,60,000**	**90,60,000**
Less : Items for deduction		
Investment (deducted for a Non Investment as company)	37,50,000	-
Per Expln 1 to Part II of Schedule XIII		
Profit and Loss Account (Dr. Balance)	7,62,500	7,62,500
Preliminary Expenses no written off	27,500	27,500
(B)	**45,40,000**	**7,90,000**
Effective Capital (A - B)	**45,20,000**	**82,70,000**
Slab under which the efective capital falls	Less : than ₹ 1 Crore	₹ 1 Crore or more, but less than ₹ 5 Crores

Maximum Remuneration and conditions to be fulfilled

If Abhishek Ltd is treated as an	Non-Invt. Company	Investment Company
Slab under Which the Effective Capital Falls - Determined above	Less than ₹ 1 Crore	₹ 1 Cror or less More, but than ₹ 5 Crores
Part II (1) (A) of Schedule XII : 2 Conditions to be fulfilled Monthly Remuneration Shall not exceed	37,500	50,000
Annual Managerial Remuneration not to exceed	4,50,000	6,00,000
Part II (1) (B) of Schedule XIII : 4 Conditions to be fulfilled Monthly Remuneration Shall not exceed	75,000	1,00,000
Annual Managerial Remuneration not to exceed	9,00,000	12,00,000

The conditions to be fulfilled are as under Part II (1) (A) First 2 Conditions Part II (1) (B) - all 4 Conditions

- Approval of Remuneration Committee by a resolution

- Company Should not default in repayment of its Debts (including Public Deposits & Debentures) or Interest thereon for Continuous period of 30 days or more in the preceding financial year before the appointment of such Managerial Person.

- Special Resoultion at Company's General Meeting, Authorizing Payament of Remuneration for a period not exceeding a period of three years.

- Statement Containing the particulars Prescribed under Schedule XIII Part II (10) (B) to be sent to Shareholders, along with Notice to General Meeting.

Problem No. 8 : Bright Pune Ltd was incorporated on 1st April to take over the running business of Shri Rockey. The purchase consideration was satisfied by allotment of.

(i) 20,000 Equity Shares of ₹ 10 each at par.

(ii) 10,000 10% Redeemable Preference Shares ₹ 10 each at par, redeemable on 31.03.2010

(iii) ₹ 50,000 paid in cash.

The company issued a prospectus for raising by issue of 30,000 equity shares of ₹ 10 each at par and 15,000 10% Redeemable preference Shares of ₹ 10 each, at par The entrie amount in respect of the issue was received by 30th june, except Final call of ₹ 2.50 per share on 1000 shares issued to Shri Rockey, a Director. Underwriting commission at 2% on Equity Shares and at 3% preference Shares were paid to a merchant banker.

The Preliminary Expenses were estimated at ₹ 50,000 in the prospectus but the actual expenses incurred were as under.

Solicitor's Fee	₹ 10,000
Printingof Memorandum	₹ 15,000 (of which ₹ 5000 remained unpaid)
Stamping and Registration	₹ 20,000
Advertisement Expenses	₹ 30,000

The Company Purchased a plot of land for ₹ 75,000 Further, it advanced ₹ 1,00,000 for construction of office Building and ₹ 1,50,000 to a supplier, being 40% of contract price for supply of Machinery. A part of the investments taken over from Shri. Rockey was sold for ₹ 50,000 (₹ 5,000 in excess of their book value)

Prepare a Receipts and Payments Account and other relevant information to be included in the Statutory Report pursuant to Sec. 165 of the Companies Act. 1956 in respect of Roadshow Ltd made upto 30th June

Solution :

Extracts from the Statutory Report of Bright Ltd.
(Pursuant to Section 165 of Companies Act, 1956)

1. Receipts and Payment A/c upto 30th June

Receipts	₹	Payments	₹	₹
Shares :	2,97,500	Vendor (Shri Rocky)		50,000
- Equity Shares		Preliminary Expenses :		
(3,00,000 - 2,500)	1,50,000	(a) Underwriting Commission :		
- 10% Redeemable	50,000	Equity Shares (2% on 3,00,000)	6000	
Pref. Shares		- Pref. Shares (3% on 1,50,000)	4,500	
		(b) Solicitor's Fees	10,000	
		(c) Printing of Memorandum	10,000	
		(d) Stamping and Registration	20,000	
		(e) Advertisement	30,000	80,500
		Capital Expenditure :		
		Land		75,000
		Building (Advance)		1,00,000
		Machinery (Advance)		1,50,000
		Closing Balance		42,000
Total	**4,97,500**	**Total**		**4,97,500**

2. Financial Information for inclusion in the statutory Report

(a) Shares Allotted subject to payment there of in Cash

Particulars	No of Shares	Nominal value of each Share	Amount received upto 30th june
Equity Shares	30,000	10	2,97,500
10% Redeemable Preference Shares	15,000	10	1,50,000

(b) Shares allotted as fully paid up otherwise than in cash (to Vendor for purchase of running business)

Particulars	No of Shares	Nominal value of each Share	Amount received upto 30th june
Equity Shares	20,000	10	2,00,000
10% Redeemable Preference Shares	10,000	10,	1,00,000

(c) Preliminary Expenses

Particulars	Preliminary Expenses actually incurred up to 30th june
Solicitor's Fee	10,000
Printing of Memorandum	15,000
Stamping	20,000
Advertisement Expensese	30,000
Total	**75,000**

Preliminary Expenses as estimated in the prospectus: **50,000**

(d) Particulars of Contracts entered into by the Company

(a) The Company has advanced ₹ 1,00,000 for construction of Office Building.

(b) The Company has entered into a contract for supply of Machinery costing ₹ 3,75,000 against which a sum of ₹ 1,50,000 has been advanced, being 40% of contract Price.

(e) Arrears due on calls from Directors Shri Rocky, Director ₹ 2,500 is due.

4.8 EXCERCISE

1. From the following particulars furnished by XYZ Limited, Pune prepare the Balance sheet as at 31st March, 2014 as required by Part I, Schedule VI of the Companies Act.

(in ₹)

Particulars	Debit	Credit
Equity Capital (Face Value of ₹ 100)		10,00,000
Calls in Arrears	1,000	
Land	2,00,000	
Building	3,50,000	
Plant and Machinary	5,25,000	
Furniture	50,000	
General Reserve		2,10,000
Loan from State Financial Corporation		1,50,000
Stock : Finished goods	2,00,000	
Raw Material	50,000 2,50,000	
Provision for Taxation		68,000
Sudry Debtors	2,00,000	
Advances	42,700	
Proposed Dividend		60,000
Profit and Loss Account		1,00,000
Cash Balance	30,000	
Cash at Bank	2,47,000	
Preliminary Expenses	13,300	
Loans (Unsecured)		1,21,000
Sundry Creditors (for goods and expenses)		2,00,000
Total	**19,09,000**	**19,09,000**

The following additional information is also provided :
  (i) 2,000 Equity shares were issued for consideration other than cash.
 (ii) Debtors of ₹ 52,000 are due for more than six months from the due date of payment.
(iii) The Balance of ₹ 1,50,000 in the loan account with state finance corporation includes 7,500 interest accured but not due.
 (iv) Balance at Bank includes ₹ 2,000 with Elite Bank Limited, which is not a scheduled Bank.
  (v) Bills Receivalbe for ₹ 2,75,000 maturing on 30th June have been discounted.
 (vi) The company had Contract for the erection of Machinary at ₹ 1,50,000 which is still incomplete.

2. Prepare a Balance Sheet of Sneha Ltd, Nasik as at 31st March, 2014 required under schedule VI of the companies Act, 1956, from the following information of Honeymoon Ltd.

Particulars	Amount (₹)	Particulars	Amount (₹)
Terms Loans (Secured)	10,00,000	Investments (Long term)	2,25,200
Sundry Creditors	11,45,000	Loss for the year	3,00,000
Advances	3,72,000	Sundry Debtors	12,25,000
Cash and Bank Balances	2,75,000	Miscellaneous expenses	58,000
Staff Advances	55,000	Loan from debtors	2,00,000
Provision for Taxation	1,70,000	Provision for doubtful debtors	20,200
Securities Premium	4,75,000	Stores	4,00,000
Loose Tools	50,000	Fixed assets (WDV)	51,50,000
General Reserve	20,50,000	Finished goods	7,50,000
Capital work in progress	2,00,000		

Additional Information :

i) Share Capital Consists of :
- 30,000 Equity shares of ₹ 100 each fully paid up.
- 10,000 10% Redeemable preferences shares of ₹ 100 each fully paid up.

ii) Depreciation on assets ₹ 5,00,000

3. Medha Mumbai Ltd., is in the midst of finalizing its accounts for the year-ended 30th September. A Profit and Loss Account has been prepared in draft, the account balances as rounded off to the nearest thousands, are listed below :

Particulars	(₹ 000's)	Particulars	(₹ 000's)
Shares Capital	25,000	Finished Goods	1,414
General Reserve	6,031	Stores and Spares	2,771
Development Rebate Reserve	6,271	Tools Jigs and Dies	9,187
Land	2,225	Cash Credit from Banks	30,672
Buildings	9,316	Acceptances	2,645
Plant and Machinary	64,282	Sundry Creditors	6,162
Furniture, Fixtures & Office Equipment	1,594	Other Current Liabilities	10,317
Vehicles	454	Interest Accured but not due on loans	589

Particulars	(₹ 000's)	Particulars	(₹ 000's)
Depreciation Reserve		Provisions for Gratuity and Pension	241
Building	2,193	Interest Accured on Deposits	2
Plant and Machinary	30,328	Sundry Debtors	24,231
Furniture	568	Cash in Hand	37
Vehicles	245	Bank Balance	
Loan from State government	575	On Current Accounts	39
Other Secured Loans	32,460	On Deposit Accounts	27
Fixed Deposits from Public	2,400	Loans and Advance	4,518
Unsecured Loans	1,114	Preliminary Expenses	8
Raw Materials and Components	42,014	Advance Income - Tax paid	3,489
Work in Progress	6,116	Capital Work-in-Progress	596
		Profit & Loss A/c (Profit for the year)	14,509

In arriving at the profit for the year, the following have been charged :

Particulars	₹
Depreciation	12,424
Salary and perquisite to Managing Director	72
Director's fee	4

The Authorized capital is 3,50,000 Equity shares of ₹ 100 each. The from the State Government is secured by a charge on the land, cash credits by hypothecation of stocks and book Debts and the other Secured Loans on the Buildings and Plant and Machinary.
The following adjustments are yet to be made -
   (i) Investment Allownce Reserve to be created ₹ 5,400
  (ii) Provision to be made for Income-Tax in ₹ 4,400
 (iii) Provision to be made for Managing Director's Commission at 1% of the profits.
 (iv) Proposed Dividend at 10%.
       Depreciation as per section 350 of the Companies Act is ₹ 10,424

Required :
   (i) Show the computation of commission payable to the Managing Director; and
  (ii) Prepare the Balance sheet of the company, based on all the above.

4. Following are the balance from the books Vaishali Ltd Nagar as at 31st March 2014.

(₹ in 000's)

Particulars	(₹ 000's)	Particulars	(₹ 000's)
Sales	13,39,400	Other Expenses	2,25,280
Depreciation	7,100	General Reserve	51,600
Other Income (Operation)	5,760	Sundry Debtors	1,18,000
Development Rebate Reserve	4,680	Share Capital	40,000
Investment Allowance Resreve	8,500	Secured Loans	26,960
Fixed Assets at Cost	1,27,740	Cash at Bank	640
Investments (Long Term)	380	Loan & Advances (Short term)	1,160
Interest Accrued	50	Fixed Deposits	32,000
Purchases (Raw Material)	8,96,800	Depreciation Reserve	56,000
Salaries and Wages	69,420	Provision for Doubtful Debts	120
		Sundry Creditors	2,21,550

Calculate Managing Director's Remuneration and Prepare in the proper from the profit and loss Account and Balance Sheet as at 31st March 2014 with the help of the following information.

Particulars	₹	₹
Stocks	Opening	Closing
- Raw Material and stores	1,00,040	50,020
- Work in progress	1,90,160	40,080
- Finished goods	49,800	1,61,900
Depreciation as per schedule XIV to the companies Act, 1956		8,000
Market value of Investments		290
Sundry debtors due for more than 6 months		720
Out of above, provision made this year for Doubtful debts		80
Included in other expenses are		
- Audior's fee for audit		120
- Payment to Auditors for other services		40

- Income Tax to be provided at 36.6%
- Managing Directors Remuneration is at 5% of Net Profit as per law subject to maximum of ₹ 2,40,000 p.a.
- Provide Dividends at 25% on capital and transfer the Balance of profits to general Reserve.
- Authorised capital of the company is 6 lakhs equity Shares of ₹ 100 each. Out of this 4 lakhs shares have been issued and fully paid.
- Provision for Doubtful debts is made in respect of Debtors due for more than 6 months.
- Debtors due for less than 6 months is secured to the extent of ₹ 60,000

5. Following balance are extracted from the books of the Rajesh Industries Ltd, Satara as at 31 st Dec. 2013 (₹ in 000's)

Particulars	Debit	Credit
Sales		2,760
Purchases of Materials	1,218	
Share capital fully paid		100
Land purchased in the year as stock	73	
Leasehold premises	42	
Creditors		463
Debtors	735	
Directors Salaries	39	
Wages	111	
Work in progress on 1st january	210	
Sub-contractors cost	894	
Equipment, Fixtures and fittings at cost on 1st January	264	
Stock on 1st January	59	
Profit and Loss Account, Credit Balance on 1st January		128
Secured Loan		112
Bank Overdraft		105
Interest on loan and overdraft	22	
Depreciation on Equipment on 1st January		164
Administration Expenses	147	
Office Salaries	18	
Total	**3,832**	**3,832**

The following further information is furnished to you.

i) On 31st December, Stock in Hand including the land acquired during the year, is valued at ₹ 1,42,000 Work progress at that date is valued at ₹ 1,40,000.

ii) On 1st July, the company moved to a new premise. The premise was taken on a 12 years lease and the lease premium paid amounted to ₹ 42,000 The company used sub contract Labour of ₹ 40,000 and Materials at cost of ₹ 38,000 in the refurbishment of the said premises. These are to be considered as part of the cost leasehold premises.

iii) A review of the Debtors reveals specific doubtful debts of ₹ 35,000 among dues outstanding for more than 6 months and the Directors wish to provide for these together with a provision of 2% of the balance Debtors.

iv) Depreciation on equipment, fixtures and fittings is provided at 15% on the written down value.

v) Uner the income tax Rules, the Depreciation on the companys assets amounts to ₹ 25,000

vi) Elite Ltd. sued Hexa Industries Ltd. for supplying defective materials, which has been written off as valueless. The Directors are confident that Hexa Industries Ltd. will agree for a settlement of ₹ 50,000

vii) The Directors propose a dividend of 25%

viii) ₹ 20,000 is to be provided as Audit Fee.

ix) The company will provide 10% of Pre-tax Profit as Bonus to Employees in the books before charging Bonus.

x) Income Tax to be provided at 50% of the profits.

xi) Debtor of ₹ 300 had remained outstanding for more than 6 months.

You are required.

1. To prepare the company's Financial Statements for the year ended 31st December as near as possible to proper form of Company Final Accounts; and

2. To prepare a set of Notes to Accounts including significant accounting policies.

Theory Questions

1) What is Joint Stock Company? State its features.

CHAPTER 5

Amalgamation of Joint Stock Companies

5.1 Meaning of Amalgamation.
5.2 Vendor and Purchasing Companies.
5.3 Methods of Calculation of P.C.
5.4 Accounting Entries.
5.5 Problems on Amalgamation.
5.6 Exercises.

Very often companies carrying on similar businesses combine with each other to obtain the economics of large scale production or to avoid the effects of cut-throat competition or to earn the benefits of monopoly. Amalgamation, absorption or reconstruction is the form of business combination. Thus, combination of two or more businesses may be done by amalgamation or absorption.

5.1 Meaning

Amalgamation :

The term amalgamation means taking over of the business of two or more companies by newly formed company for this purpose. The existing company or companies are liquidated and their separate legal existence comes to end. The new company is formed to take over the assets and liabilities of amalgamating companies.

For example : Jay Ltd and Vijay Ltd are dissolved and merged into a new company Jayvijay Ltd. In other words Jayvijay company is newly formed to take over the business of Jay Ltd and Vijay Ltd. In short, the companies whose business are taken over, are wound up and a new company is formed.

5.2 Vendor and Purchasing Companies :

The companies involved in case of amalgamation, absorption or external reconstruction can be classified, for accounting purposes, as follows.

(a) Vendor company or companies : In case of amalgamation, the companies to be amalgamated are the vendor companies. Similarly, in case of absorption the company is to be absorbed is the vendor company. In case of external reconstruction, the company to be reconstructed is the vendor company. The vendor companies are to be wound up after sale of their business.

(b) Purchasing Company / Vendee Company : The company purchasing or taking over the business is called as purchasing company or vendee company. It may be already an existing company as is the case with or absorption or a newly formed company as is the case with external reconstruction or amalgamation. The purchasing company acquires the business of vendor company is a purchasing company. It is transferee or vendee company.

Purchase Consideration :

Purchase consideration is the amount which is paid by the purchasing company for the purchase of business of the vendor company. It may, however be noted that, it is not necessary for the purchasing company to take over all assets and liabilities of the vendor company. It may take over all or some of the assets at such values as may be mutually agreed. Similarly it may take over all or some or none of the liabilities of the vendor company.

In order to have a clear understanding about the concept of purchase consideration, students are advised to note the following points.

(1) Purchase or Taking over of the business : The term 'taking over of business' indicates taking over of all assets and all third party liabilities of the vendor company. Sometimes it may be mentioned as "agreed to take over all liabilities". It means that along with liabilities the purchasing company is ready to accept all assets of the company.

(2) Trade Liabilities and Liabilities : The term "Trade Liabilities" means liabilities which are incurred on account of purchasing and selling of goods. For example : Trade creditors and Bills payable. On the other hand the term 'Liabilities' is wider than the term trade creditors. In includes all outsiders or third party liabilities. Such as Sundry Creditors, Bills Payable, Bank Overdraft, Debentures, Outstanding Salaries, Outstanding Expenses, Loan taken etc.

Here, it should be noted that shareholder's claims against the company such as share capital, general reserve, dividend equilisation reserve and all funds are included in the term liabilities.

(3) Taking Over Liabilities and Paying off Liabilities : There is a difference between 'taking over' of the liability and 'paying off' a liability. If it is stated that it is agreed to take over liabilities, it means liabilities are not to be paid immediately, but they are recorded in the books of purchasing company along with the assets taken over.

In case the purchasing company has agreed 'to pay a liability' it means (i) The liability is immediately payable and (ii) it is payable through the vendor company. In other words, the purchasing company will pay sufficient money to vendor company for paying of such liability which the purchasing company has agreed to pay. The amount so paid will become a part of purchase consideration. Such liability will not appear in the balance sheet of the purchasing company, prepared after acquiring the business of the vendor company.

5.3 Methods of Calculation of Purchase Consideration :

Purchase consideration can be calculated by different method. The method to be adopted by the student in the examination problem will depend upon the information given in the problem. Following are the different methods of calculating purchase consideration.

1) Lump Sum Amount or Direct Ascertain Method : When the purchasing company agrees to pay lump sum or fixed amount to vendor company, it is called a lump sum payment of purchase consideration. As the amount of purchase consideration is given in the problem, calculations for purchase consideration are not required. If purchase consideration is ageed at Rs. 200,000; then purchase consideration will be taken as Rs. 200,000.

2) Net Asset Method : In case of this method, purchase consideration is calculated by finding out the net assets or worth of the company. The term net assets refers to vendor company's assets less liabilities taken over by the purchasing company. For this purpose assets and liabilities are to be taken at the value mutually agreed. The purchase consideration is calculated as follows.

Purchase consideration = Assets Taken over - Liabilities taken over

Balance Sheet of 'X' Ltd.

Liabilities	Rs.	Assets	Rs.
Share capital	60,000	Goodwill	28,000
5% Debentures	10,000	Land and building	16,000
Sundry creditors	6,000	Plant and machinery	28,000
Bank overdraft	4,000	Stock	16,000
Bills payable	10,000	Debtors	8,000
General Reserve	10,000	Cash	2,000
		Preliminary Expenses	2,000
	1,00,000		1,00,000

Suppose

(i) B Ltd takes over the business of A Ltd.

(ii) The value agreed for various assets : Goodwill Rs. 22000, Land and Building Rs. 25000, Plant and Machinery Rs. 24000, Stock Rs. 13000 and Debtors Rs. 8000.

(iii) B Ltd does take over cash but agrees to pay sundry creditors Rs. 5000, Bills payable Rs. 8000 and Bank overdraft Rs. 5000.

Purchase consideration is to be paid as under by B Ltd. 5000 equity shares of Rs. 10 fully paid, 200, 6% debentures of Rs. 100 each and the balance in cash.

Solution :

Calculation of purchase consideration

value of assets taken over by B Ltd.	Rs.
Goodwill	22,000
Land and Building	25,000
Plant and Machinery	24,000
Stock	13,000
Debtors	8,000
	92,000

Less liabilities taken over by B Ltd.	Rs.	
Creditors	5,000	
Bills-payable	8,000	
Bank overdraft	5,000	18,000
Purchase consideration		74,000

Discharge of purchase consideration
Rs. 74,000

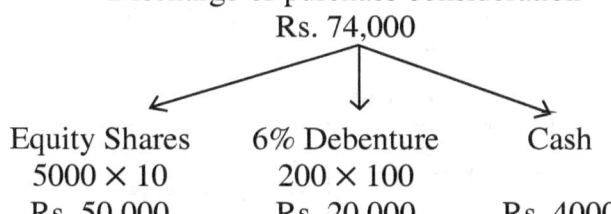

Equity Shares	6% Debenture	Cash
5000 × 10	200 × 100	
Rs. 50,000	Rs. 20,000	Rs. 4000

Important Notes :

While calculating purchase consideration the following points should be taken into consideration.

(1) Only agreed value of those assets are added, which have been taken over by purchasing company.

(2) Fictitious assets and expenses not written off as debit balance of profit and loss account, preliminary expenses, discount on issue of shares or debentures, underwritting commission will not be taken over by the purchasing company and therefore are not added. As these are losses, they should be borne by equity shareholders of old companies.

(3) Goodwill is an intangible asset and its agreed value is added, if taken over by purchasing company.

(4) Only agreed value of those liabilities is deducted which are taken over by purchasing company. These are third party or outsiders liabilities. They include Sundry creditors, Bills payable, Bank overdraft, Outstanding expenses etc. If these liabilities are not taken over by purchasing company, these will be paid off by vendor company.

(5) Undistributed profits like credit balance of profit and loss account, reserve fund, general reserve, sinking fund, share premium, capital Reserve are not deducted. These are transferred to equity shareholders account.

(6) When the expressions 'business' is taken over by the purchasing company is given, then all assets including cash in hand and cash at bank but excluding expenses or losses not written off are taken over and liabilities to outsiders are deducted. Staff provident fund, employee's profit sharing fund and other liabilities to employees of the company are treated as liabilities to outsiders.

(7) Debentures will be paid by the purchasing company separately under payment method or will be taken over by the purchasing company. Of course, it is ultimate liability of vendor company to pay off, if not taken over by purchasing company.

(8) Share capital, both equity and preference, will not be taken over by the purchase

company. The amount of purchase consideration is paid to equity and preference shareholders.

3) Net Payment Method :

Under this method, purchasing company agrees to make payment in the form of shares / debentures / cash to the shareholders / debentureholder / creditors of the vendor company. Thus, the total of all those different forms of payment is the purchase consideration.

The above concept will be clarified with the help of following example.

The following is the balance sheet of 'X' Ltd.

Balance Sheet

Liabilities	Rs.	Assets	Rs.
Share Capital		Sundry Assets	3,58,000
15000 equity shares		Profit & Loss A/C	50,000
of Rs. 10 each.	150,000	Commission on Shares	20,000
10000, 6% preference			
shares of Rs. 10 each	1,00,000		
500, 5% debentures	50,000		
of Rs. 100 each			
Bank Overdraft	28,000		
Sundry Creditors	1,00,000		
	4,28,000		4,28,000

The business of 'X' Ltd is amalgamated with the business of 'Y' Ltd and formed a new company 'A' Ltd on the following terms.

(i) Pay debentureholders at a premium of 10% by issue of 6% preference shares of the face value of Rs. 10 each in A Ltd.

(ii) Issue one equity share of Rs. 10 each and make payment of Rs. 5 in cash in exchange of every two equity shares in Y Ltd.

(iii) Preference share holders to be issued 7% debentures in Y Ltd.

(iv) Sundry creditors to receive 90% of the sum due to them in fully paid equity shares of Rs. 10 each in 'Y' Ltd. in full settlement of their claims.

Calculate the purchase consideration

Solution : **Calculation of purchase consideration**

Whom payable	What payable	How payable	Amt. Rs.
(i) 5% Debenture holders	6% preference Shares	50000 + 10% premium = 50000 + 5000	55000
(ii) Equity Share holders	Equity Share	One share for two old shares i.e.: 2:1, old shares 15000 New shares 7500	
Equity share holders	cash	7500 × 10 = 75000 7500 × 5 = 37500	1,12,500

(3) 6% preference Shareholders	7% debentures	Equal Amount i.e. 1,00,000	1,00,000
(4) Sundry creditors	Equity Shares	90% of 1,00,000 i.e. Rs. 90,000	90,000
		Purchase consideration	3,57,500

Creation of Goodwill or Capital Reserve :

Under lumpsum method and payment method of purchase consideration goodwill or capital reserve may be created. The goodwill is the difference between assets and liabilities taken over and purchase price. It is determined as follows.

Purchase Price (P.C.)   ×××
Add Liabilities taken over   ×××
Less. total of assets taken over ×××

Goodwill   — — —

Capital Reserve :-

If the total of assets taken over are more than the liabilities taken over and purchase price, there is a capital reserve. It is determined as follows.

Total of assets taken over   ×××
Less
(1) Purchase price   ×××
(2) Liabilities taken over   ×××   ×××
Capital Reserve   — — —

4) Share Exchange Method :

In case of this method, the purchase consideration is ascertained on the basis of the ratio in which the shares of purchasing company are to be exchanged for the shares of the vendor company. This exchange ratio is generally determined on the basis of the value of each company's share.

Example :- A Ltd has a share capital of Rs. 1.00 lakh, divided into shares of Rs. 10 each. Its business has been taken over by B Ltd. The purchase consideration is to be satisfied by exchanging shares on the basis that each share of A Ltd. has a market value of Rs. 15 while that of B Ltd has a market value of Rs. 30.

In this case the comparison of the market values of the shares of two companies show that two shares of A Ltd. are equal to one share of B Ltd. This means B Ltd will issue 5000 shares at Rs. 30 each to A Ltd. as purchase consideration. Purchase consideration, therefore, amounts to Rs. 1.50 lakhs (i.e. 5000 × 30).

In case it is desired that the entries are to be made at par, the purchase consideration amounts to Rs. 50000 (i.e. 5000 × 10) only.

Note : While issuing shares to individual shareholders of the selling company, these may be in fraction. A company cannot issue shares in fractions but it can issue fractional certificates or coupons or pay cash for the fraction.

Settlement of Purchase Consideration : The purchasing company may satisfy the purchase consideration in different forms viz. by issue of equity or preference shares of purchasing company or by issue of debentures of purchasing company or by paying cash payment.

Treatment to Funds : In business, variety of funds are created. These funds may be undistributed or accumulated profits or third party liabilities.

(i) Undistributed or Accumulated Profits : Undistributed or accumulated profits belong to shareholders and therefore, they are credited to equity shareholders account. Examples of such funds are as follows :

Reserve fund, General Reserve, Workmen's Compensation fund, Capital Reserve, Sinking Fund, Dividend Equalisation Fund, Share Premium Account, Forfeited Shares Account, Workers Welfare Fund, Fire Insurance Fund, Debenture Redemption Fund, Contingency Reserve etc.

(ii) Third Party or Outsiders Liabilities : The amounts payable to third party or outsiders are treated as third party liabilities. Examples of such funds are as follows :

Employees Profit Sharing Fund, Workmen's Saving Account, Premium On Redemption Of Debentures, Provident Fund, Pension Fund, Superannuation Fund etc.

5.4 Accounting Entries :

There is no difference regarding recording of transaction is the books of account whether, it is a case of Amalgamation, Absorption or External Reconstruction. In each case there are two parties involved i.e. the vendor company or companies and the purchasing company. In the following pages, we are giving the accounting entries to be passed in the books of both the vendor company and the purchasing company.

Entries in the books of Vendor company : Since the vendor company has to wind up its business; it will dispose off all its assets, make payment of all of its liabilities and distribute the surplus if any among its shareholders. The accounting entries to be passed in its books are as follows :

1) For a transfer of assets :

Realisation Account ...Dr.

To Sundry Assets

(Each asset should be credited individually at its book value. All assets have to be transferred. Of course, cash will not be transferred, if it has not been taken over by the purchasing company. Similarly, fictitious assets such as debit balance in the profit and loss account, preliminary expenses, etc. will not be transferred. such assets will be directly transferred to the equity shareholders account. The objective of passing this entry is to close accounts of all assets.)

2) For transfer of liabilities :

Sundry liabilities A/c   ...Dr.

    To Realisation Account

(Each liability should be debited individually at its book value. Only such liabilities are to be transferred which have been taken over by the purchasing company. Items representing shareholders' funds do not constitute liabilities for this purpose).

3) For purchase consideration due :

Purchasing company A/c   ...Dr.

    To Realisation Account

(With the amount of purchase consideration)

4) For receipt of purchase consideration :

Shares in the purchasing company A/c   ...Dr.

Debentures in the purchasing company A/c   ...Dr.

Bank A/c   ...Dr.

    To purchasing company

(The shares and debentures are to be recorded at the price at which they have been received from the purchasing company).

5) For Payment of liabilities not taken over by the purchasing Co.

Sundry liabilities (not taken over) A/c   ...Dr.

    To Bank / Shares in purchasing company A/c

(Liabilities not taken over by the purchasing company will be paid by the vendor company. Any profit or loss on payment of such liability will be transferred to realisation account.)

6) For money due to preference shareholders :

Preference share capital account   ...Dr.

    To preference shareholders A/c

7) For payment to preference shareholders :

Preference shareholders Account   ...Dr.

    To Bank / Shares in the purchasing company A/c

(In case preference shareholders are paid less or more than what is due to them as per the books of the vendor company, any profit or loss on payment to them will be transferred to the realisation account. Alternatively, the amount may be transferred to equity shareholders account.)

8) For liquidation expenses. There can be three situations :

(a) The vendor company may have to meet the liquidation expenses. In such a case, the entry will be as follows :

Realisation Account ...Dr.
 To Bank A/c

(b) The purchasing company may agree to pay to the vendor company a fixed amount by way of liquidation expenses. In such a case, the amount payable as liquidation expenses will be included in the amount of purchase consideration. On payment of such expenses by the vendor company, entry as given in (a) above will be passed in the books of the vendor company.

Alternatively, these liabilities may also be transferred to realisation account and paid through that account. This method is not popular.

(c) The purchasing company may agree to reimburse the vendor company to the extent of liquidation expenses incurred by it. In such a case, the following entries will be passed:

(i) On payment of liquidation expenses :
Purchasing Company A/c ...Dr.
 To Bank A/c

(ii) On reimbursement from the purchasing company :
Bank Account ...Dr.
 To purchasing company A/c

Alternatively, in cases (b) and (c); no entry may be passed in the books of the vendor company. However, this is not adviseable.

9) For transfer of profit on realisation :
Realisation Account ...Dr.
 To Equity Shareholders' A/c.
In case of loss the entry will be reversed.

10) For transfer of Equity Share Capital etc.
Equity Share Capital A/c ...Dr.
General Reserve A/c ...Dr.
Accumulated profits A/c ...Dr.
 To Equity Shareholders A/c.

11) For transfer of fictitious assets :
Equity Shareholders' A/c ...Dr.
 To Profit and Loss A/c. (Debit balance)
 To Preliminary Expenses A/c.
 To Expenses on Issue of Shares A/c.

12) For payment to Equity Shareholders :
Equity Shareholders A/c ...Dr.
 To Shares in purchasing company A/c
 To Bank A/c

Entries in Books of the Purchasing Company

1) For purchase consideration due :

Business Purchase A/c   ...Dr.
  To liquidator of vendor company A/c
(With the amount of purchase consideration).

2) For taking over assets and liabilities :

Assets (Taken over) A/c   ...Dr.
  To Liabilities (Taken over) A/c
  To Business Purchase A/c.

(Each asset and liability is to be debited or credited individually at the values taken over and not at the values at which they are appearing in the books of the vendor company. Goodwill if any, appearing in the vendor company's books, should not be recorded here. In case, the value of net assets is more than the amount of purchase consideration, the balance should be credited to capital reserve. In case the purchase consideration is more than the value of the net assets, the balance should be debited to goodwill.)

3) For payment of purchase consideration.

Liquidator of Vendor Company A/c   ...Dr.
  To Share Capital A/c
  To Share Premium A/c
  To Debentures A/c
  To Bank A/c

(In case the shares or debentures have been issued at premium or discount, the relevant premium or discount account should be credited or debited, as the case may be)

4) For Liquidation Expenses : The entry for liquidation expenses, when payable by the purchasing company, is as follows :

(i) If the purchasing company agrees to pay a fixed amount by way of liquidation expenses to the vendor company. In such a case the amount of liquidation expenses will be included in the purchase consideration and no separate entry will be required.

(ii) If the purchasing company agrees to reimburse the vendor company to the extent of liquidation expenses. In such a case the amount of liquidation expenses will not be included in the amount of purchase consideration. The following entry will be passed separately on payment of such expenses :

Goodwill / capital Reserve A/c   ....Dr.
  To Bank A/c

(The amount of liquidation expenses will be debited to goodwill or capital reserve account, as calculated under entry (2) discussed above.)

5.5 Problems on Amalgamation

Problem No. 1 : X Ltd. and Y Ltd. are two companies carrying on business in the same line of activity. Their balance sheets as on 31-3-2014 are given.

Balance Sheet
As on 31st March, 2014

Liabilities	X Ltd.	YLtd.	Assets	X Ltd.	Y Ltd.
Fully paid up			Land & Building	1,00,000	
Equity shares of			Plant & Machinery	7,00,000	3,00,000
Rs. 10 each	6,00,000	2,00,000	Investments	1,00,000	--
General Reserve	4,00,000	2,00,000	Stock	9,00,000	4,00,000
Secured Loan	6,00,000	1,00,000	Debtors	3,00,000	1,00,000
Current Liabilities	6,00,000	4,00,000	Cash at bank	1,00,000	1,00,000
	22,00,000	9,00,000		22,00,000	9,00,000

The two companies decide to amalgamate into XY Ltd. The following further information is given :

1) X Ltd. holds 8,000 shares in Y Ltd. Rs. 12.50 each.
2) All assets and liabilities of the two companies, except investments are taken over by XY Ltd.
3) Each share in Y Ltd. is valued @ Rs. 25 for the purpose of the amalgamation.
4) Shareholders in X Ltd. and Y Ltd. are paid-off by issuing to them sufficient number of equity shares of Rs. 10 each in XY Ltd. as fully paid up at par.
5) Each share in X Ltd. is valued @ Rs. 15 for the purpose of the amalgamation.
   Show journal entries to close the books of both the companies and Balance Sheet after amalgamation.

Solution :

Statement of purchase consideration

Discharge of P.C.	X Ltd. Rs.	Y Ltd. Rs.	Particulars	X Ltd. Rs.	Y Ltd. Rs.
60000 shares of Rs. 15 each	9,00,000		Assets taken over Land & Building	1,00,000	-
20000 shares of Rs. 25 each		5,00,000	Plant & Machinery	7,00,000	3,00,000
			Debtors	3,00,000	1,00,000
			Stock	9,00,000	4,00,000
			Cash in hand	1,00,000	1,00,000
			Less : Liabilities taken	21,00,000	9,00,000
			Current Liabilities	6,00,000	4,00,000
			Secured Loan	6,00,000	1,00,000
			Goodwill	9,00,000	4,00,000
			(Balancing figure)	-	1,00,000
	9,00,000	5,00,000		9,00,000	5,00,000

Journal Entries in the books of 'X' Ltd.

Particulars		Debite Rs.	Credit Rs.
Realisation A/c	Dr.	21,00,000	
To land & building A/c			1,00,000
To plant & machinery A/c			7,00,000
To stock A/c			9,00,000
To debtors A/c			3,00,000
To cash at bank A/c			1,00,000
(Being assets taken over by XY Ltd. transferred to Realisation A/c).			
Secured Loans A/c	Dr.	6,00,000	
Current Liabilities A/c	Dr.	6,00,000	
To Realisation A/c			12,00,000
(Being the liabilities taken over by XY Ltd. transferred to realisation account.)			
XY Ltd. A/c	Dr.	9,00,000	
To Realisation A/c			9,00,000
(Being purchase consideration agreed to be paid by XY Ltd.)			
Shares in XY Ltd. A/c	Dr.	2,00,000	
To investment A/c			1,00,000
To sundry shareholders A/c			1,00,000
(Being the receipt of shares in XY Ltd., on liquidation of Y Ltd. profit transferred to sundry shareholders A/c.)			
Shares in XY Ltd. A/c	Dr.	9,00,000	
To XY Ltd. A/c			9,00,000
(By the receipt of shares from XY Ltd. on account of purchase consideration.)			
Share capital A/c	Dr.	6,00,000	
General Reserve A/c	Dr.	4,00,000	
To sundry shareholders A/c			10,00,000
(Being the transfer of share capital general reserve to sundry shareholders A/c.)			
Sundry shareholders A/c	Dr.	11,00,000	
To shares in XY Ltd.			11,00,000
(Being the distribution of shares in XY Ltd. among the shareholders.)			

Journal Entries in the books of Y Ltd.

Particulars	Debite Rs.	Credit Rs.
Realisation A/c Dr.	9,00,000	
To plant & machinery A/c		3,00,000
To stock A/c		4,00,000
To debtors A/c		1,00,000
To cash A/c		1,00,000
(Being the assets taken over by XY Ltd. transferred to Realisation Account.)		
Secured Loans A/c Dr.	1,00,000	
Current Liabilities A/c Dr.	4,00,000	
To Realisation A/c		5,00,000
(Being the liabilities taken over by XY Ltd. transferred to realisation A/c.)		
XY Ltd. A/c Dr.	5,00,000	
To Realisation A/c		5,00,000
(Being purchase consideration agreed to be paid by XY Ltd.)		
Share capital A/c Dr.	2,00,000	
General Reserve A/c Dr.	2,00,000	
Realisation A/c Dr.	1,00,000	
To sundry shareholders A/c		5,00,000
(Being the share capital, general reserve & profit on realisation transferred to sundry shareholders A/c.)		
Shares in XY Ltd. A/c Dr.	5,00,000	
To XY Ltd. A/c		5,00,000
(Being the receipt of shares from XY Ltd. on account of purchase consideration.)		
Sundry shareholders A/c Dr.	5,00,000	
To shares in XY Ltd. A/c		5,00,000
(Being the distribution of shares in XY Ltd. among the shareholders.)		

Balance Sheet of XY Ltd. as on 1-4-2014

Liabilities	Rs.	Assets	Rs.
Share capital		Cash at Bank	2,00,000
6000 shares		Land & building	1,00,000
of Rs. 15 each	9,00,000	Plant & machinery	10,00,000
20000 shares		Stock	13,00,000
of Rs. 25 each	5,00,000	Goodwill	1,00,000
Current liabilities	10,00,000	Debtors	4,00,000
Secured Loan	7,00,000		
	31,00,000		31,00,000

Problem No. 2 : The following are Balance Sheets of A Ltd. and B Ltd as on 31st December 2013 which are amalgamated to form a new company AB Ltd.

Liabilities	A Ltd.	B Ltd.	Assets	A Ltd.	B Ltd.
Authorised & Issued			Sundry assets	4,80,000	3,22,000
capital Equity shares			Freehold property	2,00,000	1,00,000
of Rs. 10 each	5,00,000	3,00,000	Investments	50,000	20,000
5% Debentures	2,00,000	1,00,000	Debtors	2,50,000	1,50,000
Reserve Fund-	–	50,000	Preliminary		
Profit & Loss A/c	30,000	20,000	Expenses	20,000	8,000
Mortgage Loan Secured					
on Freehold property	50,000				
Sundry creditors	2,20,000	1,30,000			
	10,00,000	6,00,000		10,00,000	6,00,000

The purchase consideration consisted of :
1) The discharge of the debentures of A Ltd. and B Ltd. by the issue of equivalent amount of 6% debentures in AB Ltd.
2) The assumption of the liabilities of both companies, and
3) The issue of equity shares of Rs. 10 each at a premium of Rs. 2 per share in AB Ltd. For the purpose of the amalgamation the assets are to be revalued as under :

	A Ltd.	B Ltd.
	Rs.	Rs.
Goodwill	1,00,000	75,000
Sundry assets	4,10,000	2,80,000
Freehold property	2,60,000	1,40,000
Investments	51,000	20,000
Debtors	2,25,000	1,35,000

Close the books of A Ltd. and B Ltd. and Balance Sheet of AB Ltd.

Solution :

Calculation of Purchase Consideration

Particulars	A Ltd.		B Ltd.	
	Rs.	Rs.	Rs.	Rs.
Assets taken over -				
Goodwill		1,00,000		75,000
Sundry Assets		4,10,000		2,80,000
Freehold property		2,60,000		1,40,000
Investments		51,000		20,000
Debtors		2,25,000		1,35,000
		10,46,000		6,50,000
Less liabilities taken over				
Mortgage loan	50,000			
Sundry creditors	2,20,000	2,70,000	1,30,000	1,30,000
		7,76,000		5,20,000

Payment of purchase consideration

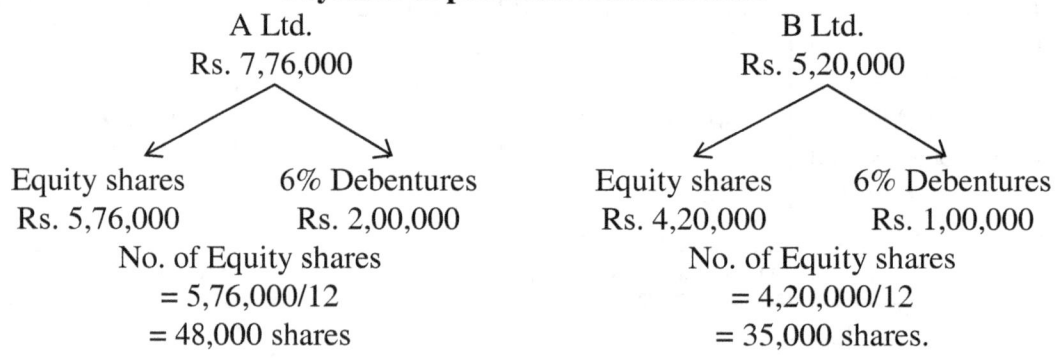

A Ltd.
Rs. 7,76,000

Equity shares Rs. 5,76,000 | 6% Debentures Rs. 2,00,000
No. of Equity shares
= 5,76,000/12
= 48,000 shares

B Ltd.
Rs. 5,20,000

Equity shares Rs. 4,20,000 | 6% Debentures Rs. 1,00,000
No. of Equity shares
= 4,20,000/12
= 35,000 shares.

In the books of A Ltd.

Dr. Realisation A/c **Cr.**

	Rs.		Rs.
To Sundry Assets (Book Value)	9,80,000	By Sundry Liabilities (Book Value)	
To Equity Shareholders A/c	66,000	Mortgage loan	50,000
(Profit)		Sundry Creditors	2,20,000
(Bal. fig.)	–	By AB Ltd A/c (P.C.)	7,76,000
	10,46,000		10,46,000

Dr. **AB Co. Ltd. A/c** **Cr.**

	Rs.		Rs.
To Realisation A/c	7,76,000	By 6% Debentures in AB Ltd.	2,00,000
	–	By Equity Shares in AB Ltd.	5,76,000
	7,76,000		7,76,000

Dr. **6% Debentures in AB Ltd. A/c** **Cr.**

	Rs.		Rs.
To AB Ltd. A/c	2,00,000	By 5% Debentureholder A/c	2,00,000
	–		–
	2,00,000		2,00,000

Dr. **Equity shares in AB Ltd. A/c** **Cr.**

	Rs.		Rs.
To AB Ltd. A/c	5,76,000	By Equity Shareholder A/c	5,76,000
	–		–
	5,76,000		5,76,000

Dr. **5% Debentureholders A/c** **Cr.**

	Rs.		Rs.
To 6% Debentures in AB Ltd.	2,00,000	By 5% Debentures A/c	2,00,000
	–		–
	2,00,000		2,00,000

Dr. **Equity Shareholders A/c** **Cr.**

	Rs.		Rs.
To Equity Shares in AB Ltd.	5,76,000	By Equity Share Capital A/c	5,00,000
To Preliminary Expenses A/c	20,000	By Profit & Loss A/c	30,000
	–	By Realisation A/c	66,000
	5,96,000		5,96,000

In the books of B Ltd.

Dr.   **Realisation A/c**   **Cr.**

	Rs.		Rs.
To Sundry Assets (Book Value)		By Sundry Liab.(Book Value)	
Sundry Assets 3,22,000		Sundry Creditors	1,30,000
Freehold Property 1,00,000		By AB Ltd A/c (P.C.)	5,20,000
Investments 20,000			
Debtors 1,50,000	5,92,000		
To Equity Shareholders A/c	58,000		
(Profit)	–		–
	6,50,000		6,50,000

Dr.   **AB Ltd. A/c**   **Cr.**

	Rs.		Rs.
To Realisation A/c	5,20,000	By 6% Debentures in AB Ltd.	1,00,000
	–	By Equity Shares in AB Ltd.	4,20,000
	5,20,000		5,20,000

Dr.   **6% Debentures in AB Ltd. A/c**   **Cr.**

	Rs.		Rs.
To AB Ltd. A/c	1,00,000	By 5% Debentureholder A/c	1,00,000
	–		–
	1,00,000		1,00,000

Dr.   **5% Debentureholders A/c**   **Cr.**

	Rs.		Rs.
To 6% Debentures in AB Ltd.	1,00,000	By 5% Debentures A/c	1,00,000
	–		–
	1,00,000		1,00,000

Dr.   **Equity Shares in AB Ltd. A/c**   **Cr.**

	Rs.		Rs.
To AB Ltd. A/c	4,20,000	By Equity Shareholder A/c	4,20,000
	–		–
	4,20,000		4,20,000

Dr.		Equity Shareholders A/c		Cr.
	Rs.			Rs.
To Equity Shares in AB Ltd.	4,20,000	By Equity Share Capital A/c		3,00,000
To Preliminary Expenses A/c	8,000	By Reserve Fund		50,000
		By Profit & Loss A/c		20,000
	–	By Realisation A/c (Profit)		58,000
	4,28,000			4,28,000

Balance Sheet of AB Ltd. as on 1st January 2014

Liabilities	Rs.	Assets	Rs.
Share capital		Goodwill	1,75,000
83000 Equity shares		Sundry Assets	6,90,000
of Rs. 10 each.	8,30,000	Freehold property	4,00,000
Share premium	1,66,000	Investments	71,000
6% Debentures	3,00,000	Debtors	3,60,000
Mortgage Loan			
(Secured on Freehold property)	50,000		
Sundry Creditors	3,50,000		
	16,96,000		16,96,000

Problem No. 3 : A Co. Ltd. and B Co. Ltd agree to amalgamate and form a third company C Co. Ltd. which will take over all the assets and liabilities of the two existing companies.

In the case of A Co. Ltd. the assets and liabilities are to be taken over at book values for shares in C Co. Ltd. at the rate of 5 shares in C Co. Ltd. at a premium of 10% for every 4 shares in A Co. Ltd.

In the case of B co. Ltd.

i) The Debentures of B Co. Ltd. would be paid off by the issue of an equal number of debentures in C Co. Ltd. at a discount of 10%.

ii) The holders of 6% preference shares of B Co. Ltd. would be allotted 4 (four) 7% preference shares in C Co. Ltd. for every 5 (five) preference shares held in B Co. Ltd.

iii) The equity shareholders would be allotted sufficient shares to cover the balance on their accounts after adjusting assets values by reducing plant and machinery by 10% & Providing 5% on sundry debtors. Equity shares to B Co. Ltd. were also issued at 10% premium.

The summarised Balance sheet of A Co. Ltd. and B Co. Ltd. on the date of amalgamation were as follows :

Liabilities	'A' Co. Ltd. Rs.	'B' Co. Ltd. Rs.	Assets	'A' Co. Ltd. Rs.	'B' Co. Ltd. Rs.
Equity shares of			Plant and		
Rs. 10 each	4,00,000	5,00,000	Machinery	8,00,000	8,00,000
6% Preference	–	3,00,000	Stock	65,000	60,000
shares of Rs. 100 each			Sundry debtors	95,000	50,000
4% Debentures	–	2,00,000	Cash and bank		
profit & Loss A/c	5,00,000	–	Balances	65,000	40,000
Contingency Reserve	50,000	–	P & L A/c	–	1,40,000
Sundry Creditors	75,000	90,000		–	–
	10,25,000	10,90,000		10,25,000	10,90,000

Prepare necessary Ledger accounts in the books of A Co. Ltd. and B Co. Ltd. and opening balance sheet in C Co. Ltd. and also calculate the purchase consideration.

Solution :

Statement of Purchase Consideration

A Co. Ltd.

Whom payable	What and How payable	Rs.
1. Equity shareholders	i) Equity Shares (For every 4 shares 5 shares in C Ltd. Hence for 40,000 shares in A Ltd. 50,000 shares in C Ltd. Face value of 50,000 shares @ Rs. 10)	5,00,000
	ii) Premium @ 10%	50,000
	Purchase Price	5,50,000

B Co. Ltd.

Whom payable	What and How payable	Rs.
1. Equity Shareholder	i) Equity Shares (On the basis of final amount due on their account. The amount due is arrived at as under.) Share Capital	5,00,000
	ii) Discount from Debentures Repayment	20,000
	iii) Discount of 6% pref. shareholders Repayment	60,000
		5,80,000

	Less :		
	i) Depreciation of plant and machinery	80,000	
	ii) Provision for Doubtful Debts	2,500	
	iii) Profit & Loss A/c	1,40,000	
		2,22,500	
2. 6% Pref. Shareholders	i) 7% Preference shares For every 5 shares four 7% pref. shares. Hence for 3,000 pref. shares 2,400 7% pref. shares of Rs. 100 each.		2,40,000
3. 4% Debenture-holders	i) Debentures Equal number of debentures at 10% discount Hence for Rs. 2,00,000 Debentures		1,80,000
	Purchase price		7,77,500

In the Books of 'A' Co. Ltd.

Dr. **Realisation A/c** **Cr.**

	Rs.		Rs.
To Sundry Assets (Book value)		By Sundry Liab. A/c (Book value) (Sundry Creditors)	75,000
Plant & machinery	8,00,000	By 'C' Co. Ltd. A/c	5,50,000
Stock	65,000	By Equity shareholder A/c	4,00,000
Debtors	95,000	(Bal. Fig.)	
Cash	65,000		–
	10,25,000		10,25,000

Dr. **'C' Co. Ltd. A/c** **Cr.**

	Rs.		Rs.
To Realisation A/c	5,50,000	By Equity shares in 'C' Ltd.A/c	5,50,000
	–		–
	5,50,000		5,50,000

Dr. **Equity shares in 'C' Co. Ltd. A/c** **Cr.**

	Rs.		Rs.
To 'C' Co. Ltd. A/c	5,50,000	By Equity shareholders A/c	5,50,000
	–		–
	5,50,000		5,50,000

Dr. Equity shareholders A/c **Cr.**

	Rs.		Rs.
To Equity shares 'C' Co. Ltd.	5,50,000	By Equity shareholders A/c	4,00,000
To Realisation A/c	4,00,000	By Contingency Reserve A/c	50,000
	–	By Profit & Loss A/c	5,00,000
	9,50,000		9,50,000

In the Books of 'B' Co. Ltd.

Dr. Realisation A/c **Cr.**

	Rs.		Rs.
To Sundry Assets (Book value)		By Sundry Liab. A/c (Book value) (Sundry Creditors)	90,000
Plant & machinery	8,00,000	By Debentureholders A/c (Discount)	20,000
Stock	60,000		
Sundry Debtors	50,000	By Pref. Shareholders A/c (Discount)	60,000
Cash & Bank	40,000		
	–	By 'C' Company Ltd. A/c (P.C.)	7,77,500
		By Equity shareholders A/c(Loss)	2,500
	9,50,000		9,50,000

Dr. 'C' Co. Ltd. A/c **Cr.**

	Rs.		Rs.
To Realisation A/c	7,77,500	By Debentures in 'C' Co. Ltd. A/c	1,80,000
		By 7% preference shares in 'C' Co. Ltd. A/c	2,40,000
	–	By Equity shares in 'C' Co. Ltd. A/c	3,57,500
	7,77,500		7,77,500

Dr. 7% Pref. shares in 'C' Co. Ltd. A/c **Cr.**

	Rs.		Rs.
To 'C' Co. Ltd. A/c	2,40,000	By 6% pref. shareholders A/c	2,40,000
	–		–
	2,40,000		2,40,000

Dr. **Debentures in 'C' Co. Ltd. A/c** **Cr.**

	Rs.		Rs.
To 'C' Co. Ltd. A/c	1,80,000	By 4% Debentureholders A/c	1,80,000
	–		–
	1,80,000		1,80,000

Dr. **6% Pref. Shareholders A/c** **Cr.**

	Rs.		Rs.
To 7% Pref. shares in 'C' Co. Ltd. A/c	2,40,000	By 6% pref. share Capital A/c	3,00,000
To Realisation A/c	60,000		–
	3,00,000		3,00,000

Dr. **4% Debentures A/c** **Cr.**

	Rs.		Rs.
To Debentureholders A/c	2,00,000	By Balance b/d	2,00,000
	–		–
	2,00,000		2,00,000

Dr. **4% Debentureholders A/c** **Cr.**

	Rs.		Rs.
To Debentures in 'C' Co. Ltd.A/c	1,80,000	By 4% Debentures A/c	2,00,000
To Realisation A/c (Bal. fig.)	20,000		–
	2,00,000		2,00,000

Dr. **Equity shareholders A/c** **Cr.**

	Rs.		Rs.
To Realisation A/c	2,500	By Equity share capital A/c	5,00,000
To Profit & Loss A/c	1,40,000		
To Equity shares in 'C' Co. Ltd. A/c	3,57,500		
	5,00,000		5,00,000

In the Books of 'C' Co. Ltd.
Balance Sheet as on...

Liabilities	Rs.	Assets	Rs.
Share Capital		**Fixed Assets**	
Authorised,		Plant & Machinery	15,20,000
Issued, Subscribed and		**Current Assets**	
Paid-up Capital		Stock	1,25,000
82,500 Equity shares of		Sundry Debtors 1,45,000	
Rs. 10 each	8,25,000	Less R.D.D. 2,500	1,42,500
7% Pref. Shares of		Cash & Bank balance	1,05,000
Rs. 10 each	2,40,000	**Miscellaneous Expenditure**	
Reserve & Surplus :		Discount on issue of	20,000
Share premium	82,500	Debentures	
Capital reserve	4,00,000		
Secured Loans			
Debentures	2,00,000		
Current liabilities			
Sundry creditors	1,65,000		
	19,12,500		19,12,500

Working Notes :

1) Since the shares are issued at 10% premium, the number of shares issued.

is $\frac{3,57,500}{11}$ = 32,500 shares

Rs.

i.e. Share Capital	3,25,000
Premium	32,500
	3,57,500

2) **Capital Reserve**

Value of Net assets taken from A Ltd.

Rs.

Value of Assets	10,25,000
Less Sundry Creditors	75,000
Net assets	9,50,000
Purchase Price Paid	5,50,000
Capital Reserve	4,00,000

Problem No. 4 : Following are the balance sheets of X Ltd and Y Ltd. as on 31-12-2013

Balance Sheet of X Ltd.

Liabilities	Rs.	Assets	Rs.
6,000 Equity shares of		Land and buildings	2,00,000
Rs. 100 each	6,00,000	Plant & Machinery	3,00,000
1,000 6% Preference shares	1,00,000	Furniture	20,000
of Rs. 100 each		Stock	70,000
Contingency Reserve	20,000	Debtors	90,000
Creditors	70,000	Cash at Bank	15,000
Unclaimed Dividend	5,000	Preliminary Expenses	20,000
Contingent Liability for Bills		Discount on issue of shares	5,000
Discounted Rs. 4,000	–	Profit & Loss A/c	75,000
	7,95,000		7,95,000

Balance Sheet of Y Ltd.

Liabilities	Rs.	Assets	Rs.
7,000 Equity shares of		Freehold premises	4,00,000
Rs. 100 each	7,00,000	Plant & Machinery	2,10,000
General Reserve	18,000	Stock	29,000
Profit & Loss A/c	40,000	Debtors	1,90,000
Workmen's compensation		Cash at Bank	11,000
Fund	10,000		
Creditors	72,000		
	8,40,000		8,40,000

X Ltd. and Y Ltd. amalgamated as on 31-12-2013 and a new company Z Ltd. was formed with an authorised capital of 20,000 equity shares of Rs. 100 each. The amalgamation was agreed on the following conditions :

1) Z Ltd. took all assets of X Ltd at book values and creditors of X Ltd. The purchase consideration was discharged by issuing 3,000 equity shares of Rs. 100 each at Rs. 120 per share and the balance in cash.

2) Z Ltd., took all assets of Y Ltd. at book values except cash and also took the creditors. The purchase consideration was discharged by issuing 6,000 equity shares if Rs. 100 each at Rs. 120 per share and the balance in cash.

3) X Ltd. paid its preference capital back with arrears of preference dividend for the last two years.

4) Liability for bills discounted was settled at Rs. 2,500/-

5) Out of the unclaimed dividend Rs. 2,000 was paid to the rightful shareholders. The remaining unclaimed dividend was time barred and transferred to shareholders account.

6) Liability for workmen's compensation of Y Ltd. amounted to Rs. 7,500/-

7) The cost of liquidation of X Ltd was Rs. 5,000 and that of Y Ltd. was Rs. 6,000 which was paid by the respective companies.

You are required to prepare : a) Necessary accounts in the books of X Ltd.
b) Opening entries in the books of Z Ltd.
c) Balance Sheet of Z Ltd.

Solution :

Statement of Purchase Consideration

Particulars	X Ltd. Rs.	Y Ltd. Rs.
Sundry Assets (taken over)		
Land & Building	2,00,000	–
Plant & Machinery	3,00,000	2,10,000
Furniture	20,000	–
Stock	70,000	29,000
Debtors	90,000	1,90,000
Cash at Bank	15,000	–
Freehold Premises	–	4,00,000
	6,95,000	8,29,000
Less : Sundry Liabilities (taken over)		
Sundry Creditors	70,000	72,000
Purchase Price	6,25,000	7,57,000
Payment of Purchase Consideration		
i) 3,000 shares at Rs. 120 each - A Ltd.	3,60,000	–
ii) 6,000 shares at Rs. 120 each - B Ltd.	–	7,20,000
iii) Cash	2,65,000	37,000
	6,25,000	7,57,000

In the Books of X Ltd.

Dr.   **Realisation A/c**   **Cr.**

	Rs.		Rs.
To Sundry Assets (taken over)		By Creditors A/c	70,000
Land & Building	2,00,000	By Z Ltd. A/c	6,25,000
Plant & machinery	3,00,000	(Purchase consideration)	
Furniture	20,000	By Equity Shareholder's A/c	19,500
Stock	70,000	(Loss)	
Debtors	90,000		
Cash at Bank	15,000		
To Pref. Shareholders A/c	12,000		
(Dividend)			
To Cash A/c	2,500		
(Liability for bills discounted)			
To Cash A/c	5,000		
(Liquidation Expenses)	–		–
	7,14,500		7,14,500

Dr.   **Z Ltd. Account**   **Cr.**

	Rs.		Rs.
To Realisation A/c	6,25,000	By Shares in Z Ltd.	3,60,000
	–	By Cash	2,65,000
	6,25,000		6,25,000

Dr.   **Equity Shares in Z Ltd. A/c**   **Cr.**

	Rs.		Rs.
To Z Ltd. A/c	3,60,000	By Equity Shareholders A/c	3,60,000
	–		–
	3,60,000		3,60,000

Dr.   **Unclaimed Dividend A/c**   **Cr.**

	Rs.		Rs.
To Cash A/c	2,000	By Balance b/d	5,000
To Balance transferred to	3,000		
Equity shareholder's A/c	–		–
	5,000		5,000

Dr. **Cash Account** **Cr.**

	Rs.		Rs.
To Z Ltd. A/c	2,65,000	By Preference share capital A/c (Paid)	1,00,000
		By Preference dividend A/c (paid)	12,000
		By Realisation A/c (Bills discounted)	2,500
		By Unclaimed dividend A/c	2,000
		By Realisation A/c (Liquidation exp.)	5,000
		By Equity Shareholders A/c (Balancing figure)	1,43,500
	–		–
	2,65,000		2,65,000

Dr. **Preference Shareholders Account** **Cr.**

	Rs.		Rs.
To Cash A/c	1,00,000	By Preference share	
To Cash A/c (Dividend)	12,000	Capital A/c	1,00,000
	–	By Realisation A/c	12,000
	1,12,000		1,12,000

Dr. **Equity Shareholder's Account** **Cr.**

	Rs.		Rs.
To Profit & Loss A/c	75,000	By Equity Share Capital A/c	6,00,000
To Preliminary Expenses A/c	20,000	By Contingency Reserve A/c	20,000
To Discount on issue of shares A/c	5,000	By Unclaimed Dividend A/c	3,000
To Realisation A/c (Loss)	19,500		
To Shares in Z Ltd. A/c	3,60,000		
To Cash A/c	1,43,500		–
	6,23,000		6,23,000

In the Books of Y Ltd.

Dr. **Realisation Account** **Cr.**

	Rs.		Rs.
To Sundry Assets		By Creditors A/c	72,000
Freehold premises	4,00,000	By Z Ltd. A/c	7,57,000
Plant & machinery	2,10,000	(Purchase consideration)	
Stock	29,000	By Equity Shareholder's A/c	6,000
Debtors	1,90,000	(Loss)	
To Cash A/c	6,000		
(Liquidation Expenses)	–		–
	8,35,000		8,35,000

Dr.   **Z Ltd. Account**   **Cr.**

	Rs.		Rs.
To Realisation A/c	7,57,000	By Cash A/c	37,000
	–	By Shares in Z Ltd. A/c	7,20,000
	7,57,000		7,57,000

Dr.   **Cash Account**   **Cr.**

	Rs.		Rs.
To Balance b/d	11,000	By Workmen's	
To Z Ltd. A/c	37,000	compensation A/c	7,500
		By Realisation A/c	6,000
		(Liquidation Expenses)	
		By Equity shareholders A/c	34,500
	–	(Balancing figure)	
	48,000		48,000

Dr.   **Workmen's Compensation Fund Account**   **Cr.**

	Rs.		Rs.
To Cash A/c	7,500	By Balance b/d	10,000
To Equity shareholder's A/c	2,500		
(Balancing figure)	–		–
	10,000		10,000

Dr.   **Equity Shareholder's Account**   **Cr.**

	Rs.		Rs.
To Shares in Z Ltd. A/c	7,20,000	By Equity Share Capital A/c	7,00,000
To Realisation A/c (Loss)	6,000	By General Reserve A/c	18,000
To Cash A/c	34,500	By Profit & Loss A/c	40,000
		By Workmen's compensation	2,500
	–	Fund A/c	
	7,60,500		7,60,500

In the books of Z Ltd.
Journal Entries

Particulars		Dr. Rs.	Cr. Rs.
1. Business Purchase A/c	Dr.	13,82,000	
To Liquidator of X Ltd.			6,25,000
To Liquidator of Y Ltd.			7,57,000
(Being acquisition of the business of the two Companies as per the agreement)			
2. Land & Building A/c	Dr.	2,00,000	
Freehold premises A/c	Dr.	4,00,000	
Plant & Machinery A/c	Dr.	5,10,000	
Furniture A/c	Dr.	20,000	
Stock A/c	Dr.	99,000	
Debtors A/c	Dr.	2,80,000	
Cash at Bank	Dr.	15,000	
To Creditors A/c			1,42,000
To Business Purchase A/c			13,82,000
(Being various assets & liabilities of X Ltd. & Y Ltd. taken over)			
3. Liquidator of X Ltd. A/c	Dr.	6,25,000	
Liquidator of Y Ltd. A/c	Dr.	7,57,000	
To Equity share capital A/c			9,00,000
To share premium A/c			1,80,000
To Cash A/c			3,02,000
(Being Discharge of purchase consideration by issuing 9000 equity shares of Rs. 100 each of Rs. 120 each and balance in cash.)			

Balance Sheet of Z Ltd. as on 1-1-2014

Liabilities	Rs.	Assets	Rs.
Share Capital		Land & Building	2,00,000
9000 Equity share	9,00,000	Freehold premises	4,00,000
of Rs. 100 each.		Plant & Machinery	5,10,000
Share premium Account	1,80,000	Furniture	20,000
Creditors A/c	1,42,000	Stock	99,000
Bank Overdraft	2,87,000	Debtors	2,80,000
	15,09,000		15,09,000

Problem No. 5 : Ram Ltd. and Anand Ltd. agreed to transfer their business to a new company called Ramanand Ltd. which is, formed with an authorised capital of Rs. 15,00,000 divided into 10,000 equity shares of Rs. 100 each and 5000, 9% preference shares of Rs. 100 each. The Balance Sheets of the two companies as on 31st March 2014 were as follows :

Liabilities	Ram Ltd. Rs.	Anand Ltd. Rs.	Assets	Ram Ltd. Rs.	Anand Ltd. Rs.
8,000 Equity shares of Rs. 100 each, Rs. 75 Paid	6,00,000	–	Building	5,00,000	
			Premises	–	4,50,000
			Stock	–	2,00,000
			Debtors	32,000	70,000
6,000 Equity shares of Rs. 100 each fully paid	–	6,00,000	Cash	25,000	8,000
			Machinery	1,60,000	–
Share Premium	80,000	–	Preliminary Expenses	–	22,000
General Reserve	20,000	–	Profit & Loss A/c	25,000	
Profit & Loss A/c	–	20,000			
Dividend Equidisation Fund	–	30,000			
6% Debentures	–	50,000			
Sundry Creditors	40,000	35,000			
Provident Fund	–	15,000			
R.D.D.	2,000	–			
	7,42,000	7,50,000		7,42,000	7,50,000

The terms of amalgamation were as follows :

1) Buildings to be appreciated by Rs. 1,10,000
2) Premises to be reduced to Rs. 3,30,000
3) Other assets and liabilities to be taken up at book values.
4) Shareholders of Ram Ltd. are to receive one preference share at par and three equity shares (at a premium of 10%) fully paid for every four equity shares held in Ram Ltd.
5) Shareholders of Anand Ltd. to receive two preference shares at par and two equity shares (at a premium of 10%) fully paid for every five shares held in Anand Ltd.
6) Ramanand Ltd. (New company) to discharge the debentures by issue of 8% debentures at Rs. 100 each.
7) Liquidation expenses Rs. 1000 to be borne by Ramanand Ltd. and to be adjusted to goodwill account :

Prepare :

a) A statement showing purchase consideration of both the companies.

b) Realisation account, shareholders' account, Debentureholders' account and New company's account in the books of Anand Ltd.

c) Give opening journal entries of Ramanand Ltd. (New company)

Solution :

Note :

Purchase Consideration (Payment Method)

Whom Payable	What Payable	How Payable	Rs.
Ram Ltd.			
Equity shareholders	Preference Shares 9%	4 : 1 :: 8000 : 2000 (2000 × 100)	2,00,000
Equity shareholders	Equity shares	4 : 3 :: 8000 : 6000 (6000 × 100)	6,60,000
		Purchase consideration Rs.	8,60,000
Anand Ltd. :			
Equity shareholders	Preference shares 9%	5 : 2 :: 6000 : 2400 (2400 × 100)	2,40,000
Equity shareholders	Equity shares	5 : 2 :: 6000 : 2400 (2400 × 100)	2,64,000
Debentureholders	8% Debentures	–	50,000
		Purchase consideration Rs.	5,54,000

Accounts In the Books of Anand Ltd.

Dr. **Realisation Account** **Cr.**

	Rs.		Rs.
To Premises A/c	4,50,000	By Sundry creditors A/c	35,000
To Stock A/c	2,00,000	By Provident Fund A/c	15,000
To Debtors A/c	70,000	By Ramanand Ltd. A/c	
To Cash A/c	8,000	(P.C.)	5,54,000
	7,28,000		6,04,000
		By Equity shareholders A/c	1,24,000
	7,28,000		7,28,000

Dr. **Equity Shareholders' A/c** **Cr.**

	Rs.		Rs.
To Preliminary Exp. A/c	22,000	By Equity Share	
To Equity shares in		Capital A/c	6,00,000
Ramanand Ltd. A/c	2,64,000	By P & L A/c	20,000
To 9% pref. shares		By Dividend Equal	
in Ramanand Ltd. A/c	2,40,000	isation Fund A/c	30,000
To Realisation A/c	1,24,000		
	6,50,000		6,50,000

Dr. **Debentureholders' A/c** **Cr.**

	Rs.		Rs.
To 8% Debentures		By 6% Debentures A/c	50,000
in Ramanand Ltd. A/c	50,000		
	50,000		50,000

Dr. **Ramanand Ltd. A/c** **Cr.**

	Rs.		Rs.
To Realisation A/c	5,54,000	By Equity shares in	
		Ramanand Ltd. A/c	2,64,000
		By 9% Pref. shares	
		in Ramanand Ltd. A/c	2,40,000
		By 8% Debentures A/c	50,000
	5,54,000		5,54,000

Working Notes :

1) Provident Fund is an outside liability and transferred to the credit of Realisation A/c.
2) Preliminary expenses are losses which are transferred to Equity shareholders' A/c.
3) Liquidation expenses are paid by purchasing company. These are not recorded by vendor companies.
4) Students are advised to prepare the ledger accounts in the books of Ram Ltd.

Opening Journal Entries in the Books of Ramanand Ltd.

Particulars		L.F.	Dr. Rs.	Cr. Rs.
1) Business Purchase A/c	Dr.		8,60,000	
To liquidator of Ram Ltd.				8,60,000
(Being business of Ram Ltd. acquired)				

Particulars		L.F.	Dr. Rs.	Cr. Rs.
2) Building A/c	Dr.		6,10,000	
Debtors A/c	Dr.		32,000	
Cash A/c	Dr.		25,000	
Machinery A/c	Dr.		1,60,000	
Goodwill A/c	Dr.		75,000	
To S. Creditors A/c				40,000
To R.D.D. A/c				2,000
To Business purchase A/c				8,60,000
(Being assets & liabilities taken over)				
3) Liquidator of Ram Ltd. A/c	Dr.		8,60,000	
To Equity share capital A/c				6,00,000
To Share premium A/c				60,000
To 9% preference share capital A/c				2,00,000
(Being purchase consideration paid)				
For Purchase of Business of Anand Ltd.				
4) Business, Purchase A/c	Dr.		5,54,000	
To Liquidator of Anand Ltd. A/c				5,54,000
(Being business of Anand Ltd. acquired)				
5) Premises A/c	Dr.		3,30,000	
Stock A/c	Dr.		2,00,000	
Debtors A/c	Dr.		70,000	
Cash A/c	Dr.		8,000	
Goodwill A/c	Dr.		–	
To Sundry Creditors A/c				35,000
To Provident Fund A/c				15,000
To Business Purchase A/c				5,54,000
To Capital Reserve A/c				4,000
(Being assets and liabilities of Anand Ltd. taken over)				
6) Liquidator of Anand Ltd. A/c	Dr.		5,54,000	
To Equity share capital A/c				2,64,000
To Share premium A/c				24,000
To 9% preference share capital A/c				2,40,000
To 8% Debentures A/c				50,000
(Being purchase consideration of Anand Ltd. paid)				

7) Liquidation Expenses A/c	Dr.	1,000	
To Bank A/c			1,000
(Being Liquidation Expenses paid)			
8) Goodwill A/c	Dr.	1,000	
To Liquidation Expenses A/c			1,000
(Being Liquidation expenses transferred to goodwill A/c.)			

Note :   Rs.

Net Goodwill = Total Goodwill   = 76,000

           Less Capital Reserve   =   4,000

                                      72,000

Problem No. 6 : Following are the Balance Sheets of Anita Ltd. & Babita Ltd. as on 31st March, 2014.

Balance Sheet of Anita Ltd.

Liabilities	Rs.	Assets	Rs.
Share Capital :		Land & Building	1,00,000
3,000 Equity shares		Plant & Machinery	1,50,000
of Rs. 100 each	3,00,000	Furniture	10,000
500, 6% preference		Stock	35,000
shares of Rs. 100 each	50,000	Debtors	45,000
Contingency Reserve	10,000	Cash at Bank	7,500
Creditors	35,000	Preliminary Expenses	10,000
Unclaimed Dividend	2,500	Discount on issue of shares	2,500
Contingent Liability for		Profit & Loss A/c	37,500
Bill Discounted Rs. 2,000			
	3,97,500		3,97,500

Balance Sheet of Babita Ltd.

Liabilities	Rs.	Assets	Rs.
Share Capital :		Freehold Premises	2,00,000
3,500 Equity shares		Plant & Machinery	1,05,000
of Rs. 100 each	3,50,000	Stock	14,500
General Reserve	9,000	Debtors	95,000
Profit & Loss A/c	20,000	Cash at Bank	5,500
Workmen's Compensation Fund	5,000		
Creditors	36,000		
	4,20,000		4,20,000

Anita Ltd. & Babita Ltd. amalgamated as on 31st March, 2014 and a new company sunita Ltd. was formed with an authorised capital of 10,000 equity shares of Rs. 100 each. The amalgamation was agreed on the following conditions :

1. Sunita Ltd. took all assets of Anita Ltd. at book values and creditors of Anita Ltd. The purchase consideration was discharged by issuing 1,500 equity shares of Rs. 100 each Rs. 120 per share and the balance in cash.
2. Sunita Ltd. took all assets of Babita Ltd. at book values except cash and also took the creditors. The purchase consideration was discharged by issuing 3,000 Equity shares of Rs. 100 each at Rs. 120 per share and the balance in cash.
3. Anita Ltd. paid its preference capital back with arrears of preference dividend for the last two years.
4. Liability for bills discounted was settled Rs. 1,250.
5. Out of the unclaimed dividend, Rs. 1,000 was paid to the rightful shareholders. The remaining unclaimed dividend was time barred and thus transferred to shareholders account.
6. Liability for workmen's compensation of Babita Ltd. amounted to Rs. 3,750.
7. The cost of liquidation of Anita Ltd. was Rs. 2,500 and that of Babita Ltd. was Rs. 3,000, which was paid by the respective companies.

You are required to prepare :

a) Realisation Account, Sunita Ltd. A/c, Cash Account & Shareholders A/c in the books of Anita Ltd. and Babita Ltd.
b) Opening entries in the books of Sunita Ltd.

Solution :

Calculation of Purchase Consideration (Net Asset Method)

Particulars	Anita Ltd.	Babita Ltd.
Assets taken over at book values		
Land & Building	1,00,000	
Plant & Machinery	1,50,000	1,05,000
Furniture	10,000	–
Stock	35,000	14,500
Debtors	45,000	95,000
Cash at Bank	7,500	–
Freehold Premises	–	2,00,000
Total	3,47,500	4,14,500
Less Creditors	35,000	36,000
Purchase consideration	3,12,500	3,78,500
Payment of Purchase consideration		
1500 Equity shares at Rs. 100 each	1,50,000	–
3000 Equity shares at Rs. 100 each	–	3,00,000
Share premium at Rs. 20 per share	30,000	60,000
Cash	1,32,500	18,500
	3,12,500	3,78,500

In the Books of Anita Ltd.

Dr. **Realisation A/c** **Cr.**

Particulars		Rs.	Particulars	Rs.
To Land & Building A/c		1,00,000	By Creditors A/c	35,000
To Plant & Machinery A/c		1,50,000	By Sunita Ltd. A/c	3,12,500
To Furniture A/c		10,000	(Purchase price)	
To Stock A/c		35,000	By Equity shareholders A/c	9,750
To Debtors A/c		45,000	(Loss)	
To Bank A/c (transfer)		7,500		
To Bank A/c (Payments) :				
Pref. Dividend	6,000			
Liability for bills				
Discounted	1,250			
Cost of liquidation	2,500	9,750		
		3,57,250		3,57,250

Dr. **Sunita Ltd. A/c** **Cr.**

Particulars	Rs.	Particulars	Rs.
To Realisation A/c	3,12,500	By Equity shares A/c	1,80,000
		By Bank A/c	1,32,500
	3,12,500		3,12,500

Dr. **Bank A/c** **Cr.**

Particulars	Rs.	Particulars	Rs.
To Balance b/d	7,500	By Unclaimed Dividend A/c	1,000
To Sunita Ltd.'s A/c	1,32,500	By Realisation A/c (Transfer)	7,500
		By Realisation A/c (Payments)	9,750
		By Preference shareholders A/c	50,000
		By Equity shareholders A/c	71,750
	1,40,000		1,40,000

Dr. **Preference Shareholders A/c** **Cr.**

Particulars	Rs.	Particulars	Rs.
To Bank A/c	50,000	By pref. share capital A/c	50,000
	50,000		50,000

Dr. **Equity Shareholders A/c** **Cr.**

Particulars	Rs.	Particulars	Rs.
To Preliminary Expenses A/c	10,000	By Equity share capital A/c	3,00,000
To Discount on Issue of shares A/c	2,500	By Contingency Reserve A/c	10,000
To Profit & Loss A/c	37,500	By Unclaimed Dividend A/c	1,500
To Realisation A/c (Loss)	9,750		
To Equity Shares A/c	1,80,000		
To Bank A/c	71,750		
	3,11,500		3,11,500

In the Books of Babita Ltd.

Dr. **Realisation A/c** **Cr.**

Particulars	Rs.	Particulars	Rs.
To Freehold Premises A/c	2,00,000	By Creditors A/c	36,000
To Plant & Machinery A/c	1,05,000	By Sunita Ltd. A/c	3,78,500
To Stock A/c	14,500	(Purchase price)	
To Debtors A/c	95,000	By Equity shareholders A/c	3,000
To Bank A/c (Cost of Liquidation)	3,000		
	4,17,500		4,17,500

Dr. **Sunita Ltd. A/c** **Cr.**

Particulars	Rs.	Particulars	Rs.
To Realisation A/c	3,78,500	By Equity shares A/c	3,60,000
		By Bank A/c	18,500
	3,78,500		3,78,500

Dr. **Bank A/c** **Cr.**

Particulars	Rs.	Particulars	Rs.
To Balance A/c	5,500	By Realisation A/c	3,000
To Sunita Ltd. A/c	18,500	By Workmen's compensation A/c	3,750
		By Equity shareholders A/c	17,250
	24,000		24,000

Dr. **Equity Shareholders A/c** **Cr.**

Particulars	Rs.	Particulars	Rs.
To Realisation A/c	3,000	By Equity share capital A/c	3,50,000
To Equity shares A/c	3,60,000	By General Reserve A/c	9,000
To Bank A/c	17,250	By Workmen's Comp.Fund A/c	1,250
		By Profit & Loss A/c	20,000
	3,80,250		3,80,250

In the Books of Sunita Ltd.
Opening Entries

Particulars		Dr. Rs.	Cr. Rs.
Land & Building A/c	Dr.	1,00,000	
Plant & Machinery A/c	Dr.	1,50,000	
Furniture A/c	Dr.	10,000	
Debtors A/c	Dr.	45,000	
Bank A/c	Dr.	7,500	
Stock A/c	Dr.	35,000	
To Creditors A/c			35,000
To Liquidator of Anita Ltd. A/c			3,12,500
(Assets & liabilities taken over from Anita Ltd. at the values stated above.)			
Freehold Premises A/c	Dr.	2,00,000	
Plant & Machinery A/c	Dr.	1,05,000	
Stock A/c	Dr.	14,500	
Debtors A/c	Dr.	95,000	
To Creditors A/c			36,000
To Liquidator of Babita Ltd. A/c			3,78,500
(Assets & liabilities taken over from Babita Ltd. at the values of stated above.)			
Liquidator of Anita Ltd. A/c	Dr.	3,12,500	
Liquidator of Babita Ltd. A/c	Dr.	3,78,500	
To Equity share capital A/c			4,50,000
To Equity share premium A/c			90,000
To Bank A/c			1,51,000
(Issued 1,500 shares to Anita Ltd. and 3,000 shares to Babita Ltd. of Rs. 100 each at Rs. 120 per share & balance is paid in cash)			

Problem No. 7 : M Co. Ltd. and N. Co. Ltd. carry on similar business. They agreed to amalgamate. A new Co. L Ltd. is to be formed to which assets and liabilities of the existing companies with certain exceptions, are to be transferred on 31st December 2013. The balance sheets of the two companies were as follows :

Balance Sheet of M Co. Ltd.

Liabilities	Rs.	Assets	Rs.
Issued Capital		Freeholde property	1,05,000
15,000 shares of Rs. 10 each	1,50,000	Plant & Machinery	25,000
General Reserve	80,000	Motor Vehicles	10,000
Profit & Loss A/c	20,000	Stock	60,000
Sundry Creditors	75,000	Debtors	82,000
	–	Cash	43,000
	3,25,000		3,25,000

Balance Sheet of N Co. Ltd.

Liabilities	Rs.	Assets	Rs.
Issued Capital		Freeholde property	60,000
8,000 shares of Rs. 10 each	80,000	Plant & Machinery	15,000
Profit & Loss A/c	20,000	Stock	78,000
5% Debentures	60,000	Debtors	21,000
Sundry Creditors	32,000	Cash	18,000
	1,92,000		1,92,000

Assets and liabilities are to be taken over at book values with the following exceptions:

a) Goodwill of M Ltd. and N Ltd. is to be valued at Rs. 80,000 and Rs. 30,000 respectively.

b) Motor vehicles of M Ltd. are to be valued at Rs. 30,000.

c) Debentures of N Ltd. are to be discharged by the issue of 6% debentures of L Ltd. at a premium of 4%. The debtors and cash of N Ltd. are to be retained by the liquidators and the sundry creditors are to be paid out of the proceeds thereof.

Close the books of M Ltd. and N Ltd. and draw-up a Balance Sheet of L Ltd. as on 1-1-2014.

Solution :

Statement of Purchase Consideration

Particulars	M Ltd. Rs.	N Ltd. Rs.
Sundry Assets (taken over)		
Goodwill	80,000	30,000
Freehold property	1,05,000	60,000
Plant & Machinery	25,000	15,000
Motor Vehicles	30,000	–

Stock	60,000	78,000
Debtors	82,000	–
Cash	43,000	–
	4,25,000	1,83,000
Less : Sundry Liabilities (taken over) Creditors	75,000	–
Purchase Price	3,50,000	1,83,000

Payment of Purchase consideration	**M Ltd.**	**N Ltd.**
	Rs.	**Rs.**
i) 6% Debentures in L Ltd.	–	62,400
ii) Shares in L Ltd.	3,50,000	1,20,600

In the Books of M Ltd.

Dr.   **Realisation A/c**   **Cr.**

		Rs.		Rs.
To Sundry Assets A/c (taken over)			By Sundry Liab. A/c (taken over)	
Freehold property	1,05,000		(Sundry Creditors)	75,000
Plant & Machinery	25,000		By "L" Co. Ltd. A/c (P.C.)	3,50,000
Motor Vehicles	10,000			
Stock	60,000			
Debtors	82,000			
Cash	43,000	3,25,000		
To Equity shareholders A/c		1,00,000		
(Profit) (Bal. fig.)		–		–
		4,25,000		4,25,000

Dr.   **'L' Ltd. A/c**   **Cr.**

	Rs.		Rs.
To Realisation A/c	3,50,000	By Equity shares in L Ltd. A/c	3,50,000
	–		–
	350,000		3,50,000

Dr.   **Equity shares in L Ltd. A/c**   **Cr.**

	Rs.		Rs.
To L Ltd. A/c	3,50,000	By Equity shareholders A/c	3,50,000
	–		–
	3,50,000		3,50,000

Dr. Equity Shareholder's A/c **Cr.**

	Rs.		Rs.
To Equity shares in L Ltd. A/c	3,50,000	By Equity Share Capital A/c	1,50,000
		By General Reserve A/c	80,000
		By Profit & Loss A/c	20,000
		By Realisation A/c	1,00,000
	3,50,000		3,50,000

In the Books of N Ltd.

Dr. Realisation A/c **Cr.**

		Rs.		Rs.
To Sundry Assets A/c (Book value)			By Sundry Liab.A/c (Book value)	
Freehold property	60,000		(Sundry Creditors)	32,000
Plant & machinery	15,000		By 'L' Co. Ltd. A/c (P.C.)	1,83,000
Stock	78,000		By Cash A/c (Debtors realised)	21,000
Debtors	21,000	1,74,000		
To Cash A/c (creditors paid)		32,000		
To 5% Debentureholders A/c		2,400		
To Equity Shareholders A/c		27,600		
(Profit)				
(Bal. Fig.)		–		–
		2,36,000		2,36,000

Dr. 'L' Co. Ltd. A/c **Cr.**

	Rs.		Rs.
To Realisation A/c	1,83,000	By 6% Debentures in 'L' Ltd. A/c	62,400
		By Equity shares in 'L' Ltd. A/c	1,20,600
	1,83,000		1,83,000

Dr. 6% Debentures in 'L' Ltd. A/c **Cr.**

	Rs.		Rs.
To 'L' Co. Ltd. A/c	62,400	By 5% Debentureholders A/c	62,400
	–		–
	62,400		62,400

Dr.   **Equity shares in "L" Ltd. A/c**   **Cr.**

	Rs.		Rs.
To "L" Co. Ltd. A/c	1,20,600	By Equity shareholders A/c	1,20,600
	–		–
	1,20,600		1,20,600

Dr.   **Equity shareholders A/c**   **Cr.**

	Rs.		Rs.
To Equity shares in 'L' Ltd. A/c	1,20,600	By Equity share capital A/c	80,000
		By Profit & Loss A/c	20,000
To Cash A/c	7,000	By Realisation A/c	27,600
	1,27,600		1,27,600

Dr.   **5% Debentureholders A/c**   **Cr.**

	Rs.		Rs.
To 6% Debentures in 'L' Ltd. A/c	62,400	By 5% Debentures A/c	60,000
		By Realisation A/c (Bal. Fig.)	2,400
	62,400		62,400

Dr.   **Cash A/c**   **Cr.**

	Rs.		Rs.
To Balance b/d	18,000	By Realisation A/c	32,000
To Realisation A/c	21,000	By Equality shareholders A/c	7,000
	–	(Bal. Fig.)	–
	39,000		39,000

Balance Sheet of L Ltd. as on 1st Jan. 2014

Liabilities	Rs.	Assets	Rs.
Share Capital		**Fixed Assets**	
Shares	4,70,600	Goodwill	1,10,000
6% Debentures	62,400	Freehold property	1,65,000
Current Liability		Plant & Machinery	40,000
Creditors	75,000	Motor Vehicle	30,000
		Current Assets	
		Stock	1,38,000
		Debtors	82,000
		Cash	43,000
	6,08,000		6,08,000

Problem No. 8 : The following are the balance sheets of two companies Akash Ltd and Sagar Ltd. on 31 March 2014

Balance Sheet of Akash Ltd. (as on 31st March 2014)

Liabilities	Rs.	Assets	Rs.
Share Capital :		Good will	10,000
Equity shares of Rs. 1		Building	45,000
each fully paid	1,50,000	Machinery at cost 50,000	
Forfeited shares A/c	150	Less. Depreciation -15,000	35,000
4% Debentures	35,000	Sundry Debtors	25,850
Reserve Fund	10,000	Stock	68,276
Profit & Loss A/c	16,865	Cash at Bank	33,674
Sundry Creditors	5,785		
	2,17,800		2,17,800

Balance sheet of Sagar Ltd.
(as on 31st March 2014)

Liabilities	Rs.	Assets		Rs
Share Capital :		Good will		10,000
Equity Shares of Rs. 1		Building		13,000
each fully paid	39,000	Machinery at cost		11,000
5% Debentures	7,000	Sundry Debtors	10,000	
Sundry Creditors	25,700	Less : R.D.D. -	500	9,500
Bank Overdraft	600	Stock		15,200
		Profit & Loss A/c		13,600
	72,300			72,300

The two companies decided to amalgamate as on 31 st March, 2014 and a new company 'Sukhsagar Ltd' was formed with an authorised capital of Rs. 2,50,000 in shares of Rs. 1 each. The following terms were agreed.

1) The consideration was :

a) 6 Shares of Rs. 1 each at Rs. 1.10 fully paid in the New Company in exchange of every 5 shares in Akash Ltd. and Rs. 1,000 in cash.

On share of Rs. 1 each at Rs. 1.10 fully paid in the New Company in exchange for every 3 shares in Sagar Ltd. and Rs. 500 in cash.

b) The debentureholders were to be allotted such debentures in the new Company bearing interest at 3.5% as would bring them the same amount of interest.

2) Akash Ltd. to pay its own cost of winding up which amounted to Rs. 300 and the cost of winding up of Sagar Ltd. is to be paid by Sukhsagar Ltd. (not to include in purchase consideration) which amounted to Rs. 200.
3) Sukhsagar Limited to take over all assets and liabilities of both companies at book values.

Prepare :

i) Realisation A/c, Sukhsagar Ltd. A/c, Equity Shares in Sukhsagar Ltd A/c, 4% Debentureholders A/c, Cash A/c and Equity Shareholders A/c in the books of Akash Limited.
ii) Open Journal entries in the books of Sukhsagar Limited.   **(March 2010 PUP)**

Solution :

Calculation of purchase consideration

Akash Ltd.	Rs	Sagar Ltd.	Rs
1) Equity Shareholders (1,80,000 × 1.10)	1,98,000	1) Equity Shareholders (13,000 Share × Rs. 1.10)	14,300
2) Cash to Eq. Shareholders	1000	2) Cash to Eq. Share holder	500
3) 4% Debenture holders 35000 × 4% = 1400 Int. 3.5 - 100 1400 ? } 40,000	40,000	3) 4% Debentureholders 7000 × 5% = 350 Int. 3.5 - 100 1400 ? } 10,000	10,000
	2,39,000		24,800

In the books of Akash Ltd.
Realisation Account

Particulars	Rs	Particulars	Rs
To Good will	10,000	By Creditors	5,785
To Buidings	45,000	By Sukhsagar Ltd.	2,39,000
To Machinery	35,000		
To Sundry debtors	25,850		
To Stock	68,276		
To Cash at bank	33,674		
To Cash A/c (Exp)	300		
To 4% Debentureholders A/c	5,000		
To Equity Shareholder A/c (Profit)	21,685		
	2,44,785		2,44,785

Sukhsagar Limited A/c

Particulars	Rs	Particulars	Rs
To Realisation A/c (P.c)	2,39,000	By Equity Share in Sukhsagar (Ltd)	1,98,000
		By Cash A/c	1,000
		By 3.5% Debenture in Sukhsagar Ltd. A/c	40,000
	2,39,000		2,39,000

Equity Shares in Sukhsagar Ltd. A/C

Particulars	Rs	Particulars	Rs
To Sukhsagar Ltd A/c	1,98,000	By Equity Shareholder A/c	1,98,000
	1,98,000		1,98,000

4% Debentureholder A/c

Particulars	Rs	Particulars	Rs
To 3.5% Debentures in Sukhsagar Ltd A/c	40,000	By 4% Debentures A/c	35,000
		By Realisation A/c	5000
	40,000		40,000

Cash A/c

Particulars	Rs	Particulars	Rs
To Sukhsagar Ltd A/c	1000	By Realisation A/c (Exp)	300
		By Equity Shareholders A/c	700
	1000		1000

Equity Shareholders Account

Particulars	Rs	Particulars	Rs
To Equity Share in Sukhsagar Ltd A/c	1,98,000	By Equity Share capital A/c	1,50,000
To Cash A/c	700	By Forfeited share a/c	150
		By Reserve Funds	10,000
		By Profit & Loss A/c	16,865
		By Realisation A/c (Profit)	21,685
	1,98,700		1,98,700

Journal Entries in the books of Sukhsagar Ltd.

Particulars	L.F.	Dr. Rs.	Cr. Rs.
1) Business Purchase A/c		2,63,800	
To Liquidator a/c			
Akash Ltd			2,39,000
To Liquidator of sagar Ltd.			24,800
2) Good will A/c	Dr.	36,985	
Building A/c	Dr.	45,000	
Machinery A/c	Dr.	35,000	
Sundry Debtor A/c	Dr.	25,850	
Stock A/c	Dr.	68,276	
Cash at Bank A/c	Dr.	33,674	
To creditor A/c			5785
To Business Purchase A/c			2,39,000
(Asset & Liabilities of Akash Ltd)			
3) Good will A/c	Dr.	2,400	
Building A/c	Dr.	13,000	
Machinery A/c	Dr.	11,000	
Sundry debtor A/c	Dr.	10,000	
Stock A/c	Dr.	15,200	
To R.D.D. A/c			500
To Creditors A/c			25,700
To Bank Overdraft			600
To Business Purchase A/c			24,800
(Asset and Liabilities of Sagar Ltd)			
4) Liquidator of Akash Ltd A/c	Dr.	2,39,000	
To Eq. Share Capital A/c			1,80,000
To share premium			18,000
To cash A/c			1000
To 3.5 % Debenture A/c (P. C. Discharge)			40,000
5) Liquidator of Sagar Ltd A/c	Dr.	24,800	
To Eq. Share Capital			13,000
To share Premium			1,300
To cash A/c			500
To 3.5% Debentures			10,000
(Discharge of Pc sagar Ltd)			
6) Good will A/c	Dr.	200	
To cash A/c			200

Scheme of Marking :

1) Calculation of Pc each 2 Marks × 2   = 4 Mark

2) Realisation A/c & Equity Shareholders A/c

     2 Marks each × 2   = 4 Mark

3) Sukhsagar Ltd A/c

     Equity Shares A/c 4% Deb.

     Holder A/c, Cash A/c

     1 mark each × 4   = 4 Mark

4) Journal entries

     entry No. 1 & 6

     1 mark each   = 2 Mark

     entry No. 2, 3, 4 & 5   = 6 Mark

     $1\frac{1}{2}$ Mark each   = 6 Mark

                  20 Mark

Problem No. 9 : The Balance Sheet of Sagar Limited and Sarita Ltd. As on 31 st March 2014 was as follows.

Balance sheet as on 31 st March, 2014

Liabilities	Sagar Ltd (Rs)	Sarita Ltd (Rs)	Assets	Sagar Ltd (Rs)	Sarita Ltd (Rs)
Share Capital :			Good will	1,80,000	-
Equity Shares of					
Rs. 100 each	5,40,000	4,00,000	Plant & Machinery	1,00,000	1,60,000
			Land & Buildings	2,60,000	1,60,000
Dividend Equilisation			Furniture	-	30,000
Reserve	20,000	-	Vehicles	-	90,000
General Reserve	24,000	-	Stock	1,60,000	1,00,000
Profit & Loss A/c	36,000	-	Debtors	80,000	20,000
Creditors	1,60,000	1,40,000	Cash in hand	20,000	10,000
Bills Payables	10,000	40,000	Cash at Bank	80,000	-
Provision for Taxation	90,000	-	Profit & Loss A/c	-	10,000
	8,80,000	5,80,000		8,80,000	5,80,000

Sagar Ltd. And Sarita Ltd. Decided to amalgamate on that date and a New Company "Mahasagar Ltd' Was formed to carry on their business on the following terms.

1) Mahasagar Ltd took all assets of Sagar Ltd. Except Debtors Cash and Bank Balances, at 10% depreciation and agreed to pay Rs. 2,00,000 for Goodwill. It also took over creditors and Bills Payables.
2) Tax Liability for 2013-14 was paid at Rs. 76,000
3) Mahasagr Ltd. took all assets of Sarita Ltd. Except Debtors and Cash. Land & Buildings and Stock were taken at 20% appreciation and other assets were taken at book values. They also agreed to take over creditors of Sarita Ltd.
4) Sarita Ltd. Paid bills payables in full.
5) Purchase Consideration was satisfied as follows. Rs. 40,000 to Sagar Ltd. And Rs. 30,000 to Sarita Ltd. The balance of Purchase Consideration was paid in equity shares of Rs. 100 each.
6) Debtors of Sagar Ltd. Sarita Ltd. Realised Rs. 76,000 and Rs. 24,000 respectively

Prepare :

i) Realisation A/c, Mahasagar Ltd A/c, Equity Shares in Mahasagar Ltd A/c, Cash A/c, Equity Shareholders A/c & Provision for Taxation A/c in the books of Sagar Ltd.
ii) Acquisition entries of Mahasagar Ltd.   **(Oct 2011 - PUP)**

Solution :

Amalgamation
Calculation of Pc Sagar Ltd.

Net Assets taken over	Rs.	Less	Liab taken over	
Good will	2,00,000		Creditors	1,60,000
Land & Bld	2,34,000		Bills Payable	1,000
Plant & Machinery	90,000			1,70,000
Stock	1,44,000			
	6,68,000		P. C.	4,98,000

Calculation of Pc Sarita Ltd.

Assets taken over		Discharge of pc	
Plant & Machinery	1,60,000	in cash	30,000
Land & Building	1,92,000	in 4220 Shares of	4,22,000
Stock	1,20,000	Rs. 100 each	
Furniture	30,000		
Vehicles	90,000		
	5,92,000		
Less Liab taken over : Creditors	1,40,000		
Pc.	4,52,000		4,52,000

In the books of Sagar Ltd.
Realisation A/c

To Sundry Assets :		By Creditors	1,60,000
Good will	1,80,000	By Bills Payables	10,000
Land & Buildings	2,60,000	By Mahasagar Ltd. (Pc)	4,98,000
Plant & Machinery	1,00,000	By cash A/c (Debtors)	76,000
Stock	1,60,000	By Equity Shareholder A/c	36,000
Debtors	80,000	(Loss)	
	7,80,000		7,80,000

Mahasagar Ltd A/c

To Realisation A/c	4,98,000	By cash A/c	40,000
(Pc)		By Equity Shares in Mahasagar	4,58,000
	4,98,000		4,98,000

Equity Shares in Mahasagar Ltd. A/c

To Mahasagar Ltd. A/c	4,58,000	By Equity Shareholder A/c	4,58,000
	4,58,000		4,58,000

Cash A/c

To Bal. B/d	20,000	By Provision for Taxation	76,000
To cah at Bank	80,000	By Equity Shareholder A/c	1,40,000
To Mahasagar Ltd. A/c	40,000		
To Realisation A/c (Debtors)	76,000		
	2,16,000		2,16,000

Equity Shareholders A/c

To Realisation A/c (Loss)	36,000	By Equity Share Capital	5,40,000
To Equity Shares in Mahasagar Ltd. A/c	4,58,000	By Dividend Eq. Reserve	20,000
To Cash A/c	1,40,000	By General Reserve	24,000
		By Profit & Loss A/c	36,000
		By Provision for Taxation	14,000
	6,34,000		6,34,000

Provision of Taxation A/c

To Cash A/c	76,000	By Bal. B/d		90,000
To Equity Shareholder A/c	14,000			
	90,000			90,000

Jarnal Entries in the books of Mahasagar Ltd.

Date 31-3-2014	Particulars		L.F.	Dr. Rs.	Cr. Rs.
1.	Business Purchase A/c	Dr.		9,50,000	
	To Liquidator of Sagar Ltd.				4,98,000
	To Liquidator of Sarita Ltd.				4,52,000
2.	Good will A/c	Dr.		2,00,000	
	Land & Building A/c	Dr.		2,34,000	
	Plant & Machinery A/c	Dr.		90,000	
	Stock A/c			1,44,000	
	To Creditors A/c				1,60,000
	To Bills Payable A/c				10,000
	To Business Purchase A/c				4,98,000
3.	Plant & Machinery A/c	Dr.		1,60,000	
	Land & Building A/c	Dr.		1,92,000	
	Stock A/c	Dr.		1,20,000	
	Furniture A/c	Dr.		30,000	
	Vehicles A/c	Dr.		90,000	
	To Creditors A/c				1,40,000
	To Business Purchase A/c				4,52,000
4.	Liquidator of Sagar Ltd A/c	Dr.		4,98,000	
	To Cash A/c				40,000
	To Equity Share capital A/c				4,58,000
5.	Liquidator of Sarita Ltd. A/c	Dr.		4,52,000	
	To Cash A/c				30,000
	To Equity Share capital A/c				4,22,000

Problem No. 10 : The Balance Sheet of Kavita Ltd. and Savita Ltd. as on 31-3-2014 is as follows. A new Company was formed called Godawari Ltd. for Purchasing the business of the above two companies as on that date.

Balance Sheet
as on 31-3-2014

Liabilities	Kavita Ltd. Rs.	Savita Ltd. Rs.
Share Capital :		
1,500 Shares of Rs. 10 Each	15,000	-
800 Shares of Rs. 10 each	-	8,000
General Reserve	8,000	-
Profit and Loss	2,000	2,000
5% Debentures	-	6,000
Creditors	7,500	3,200
	32,500	19,200

Assets	Kavita Ltd. Rs.	Savita Ltd. Rs.
Building	10,500	6,000
Machinery	2,500	1,500
Motor Vehicles	1,000	-
Stock	6,000	7,800
Debtors	8,200	2,100
Cash	4,300	1,800
	32,500	19,200

The Following are the terms of Purchase of the business.

a) Good will of Kavita Ltd. and Savita Ltd. is to be valued at Rs. 8000 and Rs. 3000 Respectively.

b) All the assets and liabilities of Kavita Ltd. are to be taken over at their book values except motor vehicle which is valued at Rs. 3000

c) All the assets of Savita Ltd. are taken over at their book values except Debtors and cash but no the liabilities.

d) The Debentures of Savita Ltd. are to be discharged at a premium of 5% by issued them 9% Debentures of Godawari Ltd. as Part Payment of Purchase consideration.

e) The balance of Purchase Price to savita Ltd. and entire Purchase Price to Kavita Ltd is paid in Rs. 10 Fully paid Equity Shares of Godawari Ltd.

You are required to prepare.

i) Realisation Account, Shareholders Account and Godawari Ltd. Account in the books of Kavita Ltd.

ii) Opening Journal Entries and Balance Sheet of Godawari Ltd. as on 31-3-2014

(March 2013 - PUP)

Solution :

Statement of Purchase Consideration

Discharge of Purchase Consideration	Kavita (Rs.)	Savita (Rs.)	Particulars	Kavita (Rs.)	Savita (Rs.)
			Net Assets taken :		
3500 Eq. Shares of Rs. 10 each	35,000		Building	10,500	6,000
			Machinery	2,500	1,500
			Motar Vehicles	3,000	-
9% Debenture	-	6,300	Stock	6,000	7,800
To Debenture			Debtors	8,200	-
Holder			Cash	4,300	-
6000 + 300 Premium			Good will	8,000	3,000
100 Equity Shares of	-	12,000		42,500	18,300
Godawari Ltd at Fully paid			Less - Liabilities taken taken creditors Purchase Consideration	7,500	-
	35,000	18300		35,000	18300

Realisation A/c

Particulars	Rs	Particulars	Rs.
To Sundry Assets :			
Building	10,500	**By Sundry Liabilities :**	
Machinery	2,500	Creditors	7,500
Motar Vehicles	1,000	By Godawari Ltd	35,000
Stock	6,000	(P.C)	
Debtors	8,200		
Cash	4,300		
To Equity Shareholder (Profit)	10,000		
	42,500		42,500

Godawari Ltd. A/c

Particulars	Rs.	Particular	Rs.
To Realisation A/c	35,000	By Eq. Shares in Godawari Ltd. A/c	35,000
	35,000		35,000

Equity Shareholder A/c

Particulars	Rs.	Particulars	Rs.
To Eq. Shares in Godawari Ltd. A/c (3500 × 100)	35,000	By Eq. Share Capital A/c	15,000
		By General Reserve	8,000
		By P & L A/c	2,000
		By Realization A/c (Profit)	10,000
	35,000		35,000

Opening Entries in the Book of Godawari Ltd.

Date	Particulars		L.F.	Dr. Rs.	Cr. Rs.
1)	Business Purchase A/c	Dr.		53,300	
	To Liquidator of Kavita Ltd.				35,000
	To Liquidator of Savita Ltd.				18,300
2)	Building A/c	Dr.		16,5000	
	Machinery A/c	Dr.		4,000	
	Motar Vehicles A/c	Dr.		3,000	
	Stock A/c	Dr.		13,800	
	Sundry Debtors A/c	Dr.		8,200	
	Cash A/c	Dr.		4,300	
	Goodwill A/c	Dr.		11,000	
	To Creditors A/c				7,500
	To Business Purchase A/c				53,300
3)	Liquidator of Kavita Ltd A/c			35,000	
	Liquidator of Savita Ltd A/c			18,300	
	To Eq Share Capital A/c				47,000
	(4700 × 10)				
	To 9% Debenture A/c				6,300

In the Books of Godawari A/c
Balance sheet As on 31.3.2014

Liabilities	Rs.	Assets	Rs.
Share Capital : 4700 Fully Paid Eq. Shares of Rs. 10 each	47,000	**Fixed Assets :** Good will	11,000
		Building	16,500
Secured Loans :		Machinery	4,000
9% Debenture	6,300	Motor vehicles	3,000
Current Liabilities :		**Current Assets :**	
Creditors	7,500	Stock	13,800
		Sundry Debtors	8,200
		Cash	4,300
	60,800		60,800

5.6 EXERCISES

Objective Type Questions.

(a) Fill in the gaps.

1) Taking over the business of two or more companies is called...

2) Liabilities which are incurred on account of purchasing and selling are called as...

3) Assets less liabilities taken over by purchasing company is called...

Ans :- (1) Amalgamation, (2) Trade Liabilities, (3) Net assets.

(b) State Whether the following statement are true or false.

1) A new company need not to be formed in case of amalgamation.

2) Liabilities not taken over by the new company are not transferred to Realisation Account.

3) Accumulated losses and profits are transferred to realisation account in case of amalgamation of a company with another company.

Ans : (1) False, (2) True, (3) False

(c) Select the most appropriate answer.

1) The Share capital to the extent already held by purchasing company is closed by vendor company by crediting it to :

   (a) Investment account,

   (b) Purchasing Company's Account,

   (c) Share Capital Account.

2) Two Companies X Ltd. and Y Ltd. go into liquidation to form a new company, Z Ltd, it is a case of :

   (a) Absorption,

   (b) External Reconstruction,

   (c) Amalgamation.

Ans : (1) b, (4) c

A) Problems on Amalgamation

1) The Balance Sheets of Pune and Indapur Ltd. as on 31-3-2014 were as follows :

Balance Sheet of Pune Ltd. as on 31-3-2014

Liabilities	Rs.	Assets		Rs.
Share Capital :		Goodwill		22,500
675 Equity Shares		Land & Building		32,500
of Rs. 10 each	67,500	Plant & Machinery		12,500
General Reserve	3,000	Stock		20,000
Dividend Equalisation		Debtors	10,500	
Reserve	2,500	Less : R.D.D.	500	10,000
Profit and Loss A/c	4,500	Cash in hand		2,500
Creditors	20,000	Cash at Bank		10,000
Outstanding Exp.	1,250			
Provision for Taxation	11,250			
	1,10,000			1,10,000

Balance Sheet of Indapur Ltd. as on 31-3-2014

Liabilities	Rs.	Assets		Rs.
Share Capital :		Land & Building		20,000
500 Equity Shares of		Plant & machinery		20,000
Rs. 100 each	50,000	Furniture and Fittings		3,750
Bank Overdraft	5,000	Vehicles		11,250
Creditors	17,500	Stock		12,500
		Debtors	3,500	
		Less : R.D.D.	1,000	2,500
		Cash-in-Hand		1,250
		Profit and Loss A/c		1,250
	72,500			72,500

The companies amalgamated as on date of above Balance Sheet and new Company Satara Ltd. was formed to carry on the business of Pune Ltd. and Indapur Ltd. on the following terms :

1. Satara Ltd. took all Assets of Pune Ltd.except debtors, cash and bank balance at 10% Depreciation and agreed to pay Rs. 25,000 for goodwill. It also took over creditors and outstanding expenses.

2. Tax liability for 2014 was realised at Rs.9,500.

3. Satara Ltd. took all assets of Indapur Ltd. except Cash and Debtors. Land and Building and Stock were taken at 20% appreciation and other assets were taken at book value. Satara Ltd. also agreed to take over the creditors of Indapur Ltd.

4. Indapur Ltd. paid bank overdraft in full.

5. The purchase consideration was satisfied as follows :

   Cash of Rs. 5,000 to Pune Ltd. and Rs.3,750 to Indapur Ltd. The Balance of purchase consideration was paid in the Equity Shares of Satara Ltd. of Rs. 100 each.

6. Debtors of Pune Ltd. and Indapur Ltd. realised Rs. 9,500 and Rs. 3,000 respectively.

   You are Required to prepare :

   Realisation Account, Cash Accout, Satara Ltd. Account and Equity Shareholders Account in the books of Pune Ltd. and Indapur Ltd.

Ans :- Pune Ltd. - P. C. = Rs. 62,250

Realisation Loss Rs. 4,500

Indapur Ltd. P.C. = Rs. 56,500

Realisations Profit Rs. 7,000.

2) The following are the Balance Sheets of two companies, Sneha Ltd. and Prabha Ltd. as on 31st March 2014.

Liabilities	Sneha Ltd. Rs.	Prabha Ltd. Rs.	Assets	Sneha Ltd. Rs.	Prabha Ltd. Rs.
Share Capital	15,00,000	3,90,000	Goodwill	1,00,000	1,00,000
Share Premium A/c	1,500	-	Property	4,50,000	1,30,000
General Reserve	1,00,000	-	Machinery	3,50,000	1,10,000
P & L. A/c	1,68,650	-	Stock	6,82,760	1,52,000
10% Debentures	-	70,000	Sundry Debtors	2,58,500	95,000
8% Debentures	3,50,000	-	Bank Balance	3,36,740	-
Sundry Creditors	57,850	2,57,000	Profit & Loss A/c	-	1,36,000
Bank Overdraft	-	6,000			
	21,78,000	7,23,000		21,78,000	7,23,000

The two companies decided to amalgamate as on 31st March 2014 and a new company called "Sneha Prabha Ltd." was formed with an authorised capital of Rs. 25,00,000 in shares of Rs. 10 each.

The following terms were agreed upon :

Sneha Ltd.

1) The consideration was 6 shares of Rs. 10 each fully paid in the new company in exchange for every 5 shares in Sneha Ltd. and Rs. 10,000 in cash.

2) The debenture holders were to be alloted such debentures in the new company bearing interest at 7% as would bring them the same amount of interest.

3) The new company to take over all the assets and liabilities at their book values.

Prabha Ltd.

1) The consideration was one share of Rs. 10 each fully paid in the new company in exchange for every three shares in Prabha Ltd. and Rs. 5,000 in cash.

2) The debentureholders were to be allotted such debentures in the new company bearing interest at 7% as would bring them the same amount of interest.

3) The new company was to take over all the assets and liabilities at their book values. You are requested to calculate purchase consideration in case of each company and prepare the Balance Share of Sneha Prabha Ltd. after amalgamation.   (P.U.)

Ans : P.C. Sneha Ltd. Rs. 22,10,000

Prabha Ltd. Rs. 2,35,000

3) Fort Ltd. and Dadar Ltd. carry on business of a similar nature and it is agreed that they should amalgamate and form a new company Bombay Ltd. The position of the two companies was :

Fort Ltd.

Liabilities	Rs.	Assets	Rs.
Paid-up Capital :		Goodwill	14,000
600 Equity Shares of		Stock	40,000
Rs. 100 each	60,000	Debtors	36,000
Profit & Loss A/c	10,000		
Sundry Creditors	20,000		
	90,000		90,000

Dadar Ltd.

Liabilities	Rs.	Assets	Rs.
Paid-up Capital :		Stock	44,000
4,000 Equity Shares of		Debtors	16,000
Rs. 10 each	40,000		
Profit & Loss A/c	8,400		
Sundry Creditors	11,600		
	60,000		60,000

The average profits of the Fort Ltd. and the Dadar Ltd. have been Rs. 18,000 and Rs. 6,000 respectively. Mumbai Ltd. agrees with Fort Ltd. and Dadar Ltd. to take over both concerns for the sum of Rs. 1,20,000 and in addition to discharge all liabilities. Mumbai Ltd. agreed to issue shares at face value in discharge of purchase consideration.

It is agreed that the stock of Fort Ltd. and Dadar Ltd. before being taken over by Mumbai Ltd. will be written off to the extent of 10% of their respective book figures.

The profit on the conversion is to be divided between the shareholders of Fort Ltd. and Dadar Ltd. in the same proportion as the profit previously earned by them.

Show Realisation A/c and Shareholders A/c in the books of Fort Ltd. and Journal entries in the books of Mumbai Ltd.

Ans : Fort Ltd. - P. C. = Rs. 73,500

Realisation Profit Rs. 7,500

4) The following are the Balance Sheet of two companies A Ltd. and B Ltd. on 31st March, 2014.

A Ltd.

Liabilities	Rs.	Assets	Rs.
Equity Share of Rs. 1		Goodwill	10,000
each fully paid	1,50,000	Building	45,000
Forfeited shares A/c	150	Machinery at cost	
Reserve Fund	10,000	Less : Depreciation	35,000
4% Debentures	35,000	Sundry Debtors	25,850
Sundry Creditors	5,785	Stock	68,276
Profit & Loss A/c	16,865	Cash at Bank	33,674
	2,17,800		2,17,800

B Ltd.

Liabilities	Rs.	Assets		Rs.
Equity Shares of Rs. 1		Goodwill		10,000
each fully paid	39,000	Building		13,000
5% Debentures	7,000	Machinery		11,000
Sundry Creditors	25,700	Sundry Debtors	10,000	
Bank Overdraft	600	Less : R.D.D.	500	9,500
		Stock		15,200
		Profit & Loss A/c		13,600
	72,300			72,300

The two companies decided to amalgamate as on 31-3-2014 and a new company called XY Ltd. was formed with an authorised capital of Rs. 2,50,000 in shares of Re. 1 each. The following terms were agreed.

The Consideration was :

1. 6 shares of Re. 1 each at Rs. 1.10 fully paid in the new company in exchange for every five shares in A Ltd. and Rs. 1,000 in cash. One share of Re. 1 each at Rs. 1.10 fully paid in the new company in exchange for every 3 shares in B Ltd. and Rs. 500 in cash.

2. The debentureholders were to be allotted such debentures in the new company bearing interest at $3\frac{1}{2}$ % as would bring them the same amount of interest.

3. A Ltd. to pay its own cost of winding up which amounted to Rs. 300 and the cost of winding up of B Ltd. is to be paid by XY Ltd. (not included in purchase price) which amounted to Rs. 200.

4. The new company to take over all the assets and the liabilities at book values.

   You are requested to draw up necessary ledger accounts in the books of A Ltd. and B Ltd. and give journal entries and a Balance Sheet in the books of XY Ltd.

Ans : A Ltd. = P.C. Rs. 2,39,000

Realisation profit Rs. 21,685

B Ltd. = P.C. Rs. 24,800

Realisation Loss Rs. 10,600

5) Given below are the balance Sheets as on 31st March, 2014 of Alpha Ltd. and Beta Ltd. which are amalgamated to form a new company Gamma Ltd.

Liabilities	Alpha Rs.	Beta Rs.	Assets	Alpha Rs.	Beta Rs.
Share Capital in Shares of Rs.100 each fully paid	1,00,000	2,00,000	Fixed Assets Goodwill Building	- - 30,000	40,000 25,000
Reserves & Surplus			Plant	60,000	80,000
Capital Reserve	50,000	10,000	Furniture	5,000	10,000
Profit & Loss A/c	40,000	-	Current Assets		
General Reserve	10,000	-	Stock	1,14,000	1,50,000
Loans	80,000	60,000	Debtors	90,000	3,000
Other Liabilities	20,000	80,000	Cash at Bank	1,000	2,000
	-	-	Profit & Loss A/c	-	40,000
	3,00,000	3,50,000		3,00,000	3,50,000

The shareholders in the amalgamated companies are to be allotted fully paid equity shares in Gamma Ltd. for the amount of purchase consideration for which purpose all assets and liabilities are to be taken at book values except goodwill of Beta Ltd. which is considered worthless.

Give Journal Entries to close the books of Beta Ltd. and show the opening Balance Sheet of Gamma Ltd. (P.U.)

Ans : Purchase Consideration

Alpha Ltd.	Rs. 2,00,000
Beta Ltd.	Rs. 1,30,000
B/S Total	5,70,000

CHAPTER

6

Absorption of Joint Stock Company

6.1 Meaning
6.2 Problems on Absorption
6.3 Eercises

6.1 Meaning

Absorption :

The term absorption means taking over the business of one or more companies by a company already in existence.

In case of amalgamation a new company is formed to take over the business of one or more companies while in case of absorption, no new company is formed. According to companies Act 1956, the term amalgamation includes absorption. The same view has been taken by various courts in our country.

For example : A Ltd, an existing company, takes over the business of B Ltd.

This is the case of absorption. In this case, no new company is formed. A Ltd is already in existence and has taken over the business of B Ltd.

6.2 Problems on Absorption

Problem No. 1 : The following is the Balance Sheet of Black Ltd. as on 31st March, 2014.

Liabilities	Rs.	Assets	Rs.
Capital-		Goodwill	40,000
30,000 Equity shares		Plant & Machinery	3,00,000
of Rs. 10 each.	3,00,000	Stocks	1,60,000
20,000, 6% Cumulative		Sundry Debtors	2,40,000
Preference Shares		Cash at Bank	17,800
of Rs. 10 each	2,00,000	Profit & Loss A/c	80,200
1000, 5% Debentures		Preliminary Expenses	10,000
of Rs. 100 each	1,00,000	Commission and Brokerage	
Bank Overdraft	20,000	on shares	8,000
Employees' profit			
Sharing Account	28,000		

Liabilities	Rs.	Assets	Rs.
Sundry Creditors	1,83,000		
Interest Accrued on			
Debentures	5,000		
Depreciation Reserve	20,000		
Contingent liability			
Arrears of Cum. Pref.			
Dividend Rs. 24,000			
	8,56,000		8,56,000

With the view to avoid competition, Black Ltd. was taken over by White Ltd. as from 1st April 2014 on the following terms :

1) Take over all tangible assets with the exception of cash.
2) Pay the debentureholders at a premium of 10% by issue of its 6% cumulative preference shares of the face value of Rs. 10 each.
3) Issue one equity share of Rs. 10 each and make a payment of Rs. 4 in cash in exchange of every two equity shares in Black Ltd.
4) Sundry creditors to receive 90% of the sums due to then in fully paid equity shares of Rs. 10 each in White Ltd. in full settlement of all their claims.
5) Preference shareholders to be issued 5% Debentures in White Ltd. The preference shares of Black Ltd. are preferential as to capital and dividend in the event of winding up.
6) The Winding up expenses Rs. 2,000 are paid by White Ltd. separately.
7) The directors of white Ltd. subscribed 5,000 equity shares of Rs. 10 each and paid for the same in full.

Close the books of Black Ltd. by the way of passing journal entries and also the opening entries in the books of White Ltd. Prepare also purchase consideration statement in the books of White Ltd.

Solution : **Purchase Consideration (Payment Method)**

Whom Payable	What Payable	How Payable	Rs.
1) Debentureholders of Black Ltd.	6% Cum, Pref. shares in white Ltd.	1,00,000 + 10% + for Accrued Int.	1,10,000 + 5,000
			1,15,000
2) Equity Share holders of Black Ltd.	Equity shares in White Ltd. and Cash	2 : 1 :: 30,000 : 15000 (15,000 × 10) For 2 shares Rs. 4 (15,000 × 4)	1,50,000 60,000
3) Sundry Creditors of Black Ltd.	Equity Shares in White Ltd.	1,83,000 - 10%	1,64,700
4) Preference Share holders of Black Ltd.	5% Debentures in White Ltd.	2,00,000 + 24,000 (for dividend)	2,24,000
		Total Rs.	7,13,700

Journal Entries in the Books of Black Ltd. (Vendor Company)

Particulars		L.F.	Dr. Rs.	Cr. Rs.
1) Realisation A/c	Dr.		7,40,000	
To Goodwill A/c				40,000
To Plant & Machinery A/c				3,00,000
To Stock A/c				1,60,000
To Sundry Debtors A/c				2,40,000
(Being Assets taken over transferred.)				
2) Equity shareholders' A/c	Dr.		98,200	
To Profit & Loss A/c	Dr.			80,200
To Preliminary ExpensesA/c				10,000
To Commission & Brokerage				8,000
(Being Balance Sheet losses transferred)				
3) Equity Share Capital A/c	Dr.		3,00,000	
To Equity Shareholders' A/c				3,00,000
(Being Equity share capital transferred)				
4) 6% Cum. Pref. Share Capital A/c	Dr.		2,00,000	
To Preference Shareholders A/c				2,00,000
(Being preference share capital transferred)				
5) 5% Debentures A/c	Dr.		1,00,000	
Debenture Accrued Interest A/c	Dr.		5,000	
To Debentureholders' A/c				1,05,000
(Being Debentures and accrued interest transferred)				
6) Bank Overdraft A/c	Dr.		20,000	
Employees' profit Sharing A/c	Dr.		28,000	
To Realisation A/c				48,000
(Being remaining liabilities transferred to Realisation A/c)				
7) Depreciation Reserve A/c	Dr.		20,000	
To Realisation A/c				20,000
(Being Depreciation reserve on plant & Machinery transferred)				
8) White Ltd. A/c	Dr.		7,13,700	
To Realisation A/c				7,13,700
(Being purchase consideration due from white Ltd.)				
9) 6% Cum. pref. Shares in White Ltd. A/c	Dr.		1,15,000	
Equity Shares in White Ltd. A/c	Dr.		3,14,700	
5% Debenture in White Ltd. A/c	Dr.		2,24,000	
Bank A/c	Dr.		60,000	

	To White Ltd. A/c (Being purchase consideration received from White Ltd.)			7,13,700
10)	Debentureholders' A/c Dr. To 6% Cum. Pref. Shares in White Ltd. A/c (Being preference shares allotted to Debentureholders)	1,15,000		1,15,000
11)	Realisation A/c Dr. To Debentureholders A/c (Being loss on payment of debentures transferred)	10,000		10,000
12)	Equity shareholders' A/c Dr. To Equity shares in White Ltd. A/c (Being equity shares allotted to equity shareholders)	1,50,000		1,50,000

13)	Sundry creditors A/c Dr.
	     To Equity shares in White Ltd. A/c
	     To Realisation A/c
	(Being creditors allotted the equity shares and profit
	thereon transferred)
		1,83,000		1,64,700
				18,300

14)	Preference shareholders A/c Dr. To 5% Debentures in White Ltd. A/c (Being debentures allotted to preference shareholders)	2,24,000		2,24,000
15)	Realisation A/c Dr. To Preference shareholders A/c (Being loss on payment of preference shares transferred)	24,000		24,000
16)	Realisation A/c Dr. To Bank A/c (Being Bank overdraft and Employees' profit sharing A/c paid)	48,000		48,000
17)	Equity shareholders' A/c Dr. To Realisation A/c (Being realisation loss transferred)	22,000		22,000
18)	Equity shareholders' A/c Dr. To Bank A/c (Being final balance paid)	29,800		29,800

Working Notes :

1) Bank overdraft and employees' profit sharing account are the outside liabilities. These are not taken over by White Ltd. Hence, paid by Black Ltd.

2) Arrears of pref. dividends are payable on liquidation of Black Ltd. These are paid by White Ltd. in form of 5% Debentures.

3) Depreciation reserve is not a liability.

Journal Entries in the Books of White Ltd. (Purchasing Company)

Particulars	L.F.	Dr. Rs.	Cr. Rs.
1) Business Purchase A/c Dr.		7,13,000	
To Liquidator of Black Ltd. A/c			7,13,700
(Being business of Black Ltd. acquired)			
2) Goodwill A/c Dr.		13,700	
Plant & Machinery A/c Dr.		3,00,000	
Stocks A/c Dr.		1,60,000	
Sundry Debtors A/c Dr.		2,40,000	
To Business purchase A/c			7,13,700
(Being assets taken Over)			
3) Liquidator of Black Ltd. A/c Dr.		7,13,700	
To Bank A/c			60,000
To 6% cum. pref. share capital A/c			1,15,000
To Equity share capital A/c			3,14,700
To 5% Debentures A/c			2,24,000
(Being purchase consideration paid)			
4) a) Liquidation expenses A/c Dr.		2,000	
To Bank A/c			2,000
(Being liquidation expenses paid)			
b) Goodwill A/c Dr.		2,000	
To liquidation Expenses			2,000
(Being expenses transferred)			
5) Bank A/c Dr.		50,000	
To Equity share capital A/c			50,000
(Being 5,000 shares subscribed by directors)			

Problem No. 2 : The summarised Balance Sheets as on 31st March 2014 of Nitin Ltd. and Moti Ltd. were as under.

Nitin Ltd.

Liabilities	Rs.	Assets	Rs.
Share capital :		Buildings	6,00,000
15,000 Equity shares		Plant & Machinery	5,50,000
of Rs. 100 each.	15,00,000	Furniture	10,000
General Reserve	2,00,000	Stocks	3,80,000
Profit & Loss A/c	1,20,000	Sundry Debtors	2,30,000
Sundry Creditors	2,40,000	Cash & Bank balance	2,90,000
	20,60,000		20,60,000

Moti Ltd.

Liabilities	Rs.	Assets	Rs.
Share capital		Goodwill	1,00,000
5,000 Equity shares		Plant & Machinery	4,20,000
of Rs. 100 each.	5,00,000	Furniture	5,000
Capital Reserve	50,000	Stocks	1,80,000
Revenue Reserve	25,000	Sundry Debtors	1,80,000
Profit & Loss A/c	35,000	Expenses on new project	75,000
6% Debentures	3,00,000	Cash & Bank balances	45,000
Sundry Creditors	95,000		
	10,05,000		10,05,000

Moti Ltd. was absorbed by Nitin Ltd. on 1st April 2014 on the following terms :

a) Fixed assets other than goodwill to be valued at Rs. 5,00,000 including Rs. 6,000 for furniture.

b) Stock to be reduced by Rs. 20,000 in respect of obsolete items and sundry debtors by 5 per cent.

c) Nitin Ltd. to assume liabilities and pay cash to Moti Ltd. to enable it to discharge the debentures at 6% premium.

d) The new project was to be valued at Rs. 95,000.

e) The shareholders in Moti Ltd. to receive cash payment of Rs. 30 per share plus four equity shares in Nitin Ltd. for every five shares held.

f) Both the companies to declare and pay dividend of 6% prior to the merger.

g) Expenses of liquidation of Moti Ltd. were to be reimbursed by Nitin Ltd. to the extent of Rs. 5,000. The actual expenses amounted to Rs. 6,000.

Draft journal entries recording the scheme in the books of Moti Ltd. and prepare the Balance Sheet of Nitin Ltd. after absorption assuming that Nitin Ltd.'s authorised capital has been increased to Rs. 20,00,000.

Solution :

Calculation of Purchase consideration (Net Payment method)

For	Mode of Payment	Rs.
(i) Rs. 3,00,000 Debentures payment of cash at 6% premium	Cash	3,18,000
(ii) Liquidation Expenses	Cash	5,000
(iii) Shareholders, cash at Rs. 30 per share for 5,000 share	Cash	1,50,000
Total Cash		4,73,000
(iv) Shares in Nitin Ltd. @ four shares for every 5 shares in Moti Ltd. i.e. 4,000 shares @ Rs. 100 per share	Shares	4,00,000
Purchase Price Rs.		8,73,000

Journal Entries in the Books of Moti Ltd.

Date	Particulars	L.F.	Dr. Rs.	Cr. Rs.
	Realisation A/c Dr.		9,75,000	
	To Goodwill A/c			1,00,000
	To Plant & Machinery A/c			4,20,000
	To Furniture A/c			5,000
	To Stock A/c			1,80,000
	To Sundry Debtors A/c			1,80,000
	To New Project A/c			75,000
	To Cash & Bank A/c			15,000
	(Being transfer of assets to realisation)			
	Sundry Creditors A/c Dr.		95,000	
	To Realisation A/c			95,000
	(Being transfer of liabilities to Realisation)			
	Nitin Ltd. A/c Dr.		8,73,000	
	To Realisation A/c			8,73,000
	(Being Purchase price to be received from Nitin Ltd.)			
	Realisation A/c Dr.		6,000	
	To Bank A/c			6,000
	(Being Payment of Realisation Expenses.)			

Date	Particulars	L.F.	Dr. Rs.	Cr. Rs.
	Realisation A/c Dr.		18,000	
	To Debentureholders A/c			18,000
	(Being premium payable to debentureholders on Redemption of debentures.)			
	Equity Shareholders A/c Dr.		31,000	
	To Realisation A/c			31,000
	(Being loss on realisation is transferred to shareholders.)			
	Dividend A/c	Dr.	30,000	
	To Bank A/c			30,000
	(Being payment of Dividend @ 6% on Rs. 5,00,000.)			
	Bank A/c Dr.		4,73,000	
	Equity shares in Nitin Ltd. A/c Dr.		4,00,000	
	To Nitin Ltd.'s A/c			8,73,000
	(Being Receipt of 4,000 shares of Rs. 100 each as fully paid and cash Rs. 4,73,000 in settlement of purchase price from Nitin Ltd.)			
	6% Debenture A/c	Dr.	3,00,000	
	To Debentureholders A/c			3,00,000
	(Being transfer of balance on debentures to Debentureholders.)			
	Debentureholders A/c Dr.		3,18,000	
	To Bank A/c			3,18,000
	(Being Repayment of amount due to Debentureholders.)			
	Equity Share capital A/c Dr.		5,00,000	
	Capital Reserve A/c Dr.		50,000	
	Revenue Reserve A/c Dr.		25,000	
	Profit & Loss A/c Dr.		35,000	
	To Equity Shareholders A/c			6,10,000
	(Being balance on Share Capital, Reserves and Profit and Loss Account transferred to Equity Shareholders.)			

Date	Particulars	L.F.	Dr. Rs.	Cr. Rs.
	Equity Shareholders A/c Dr.		5,49,000	
	To Equity Shares in Nitin Ltd. A/c			4,00,000
	To Bank A/c			1,49,000
	(Being 4,000 shares issued of Rs. 100 each in Nitin Ltd. and paid cash to equity shareholders in satisfaction of their claim.)			

Working Notes :

1. After deduction of Realisation loss of Rs. 31,000 and Dividend A/c balance of Rs. 30,000, from Rs. 6,10,000. The final Net amount payable to shareholders is Rs. 5,49,000.

2. Out of original Bank balance of Rs. 45,000, Rs. 30,000 is paid as dividend and the balance of Rs. 15,000 is taken over by Nitin Ltd.

3. Out of Rs. 4,73,000 received from Nitin Ltd. Rs. 6,000 is paid towards expenses and Rs. 3,18,000 to debentureholders. Thus, the balance available to shareholders is Rs. 1,49,000 (i.e. 4,73,000 - 3,24,000)).

In the Books of Nitin Ltd.
Balance Sheet as on 1st April 2014

Liabilities	Rs.	Assets		Rs.
Share Capital :		Goodwill		27,000
Authorised :		Buildings		6,00,000
20,000 Equity shares of		Plant & Machinery		10,44,000
Rs. 100 each	20,00,000	Furniture		16,000
Issued & Paid-up :		New project		95,000
19,000 shares of Rs. 100 each		Stocks		5,40,000
of which 4,000 shares issued		Sundry Debtors	4,10,000	
to vendors as fully paid		Less : Provision	9,000	4,01,000
without receiving cash	19,00,000			
General Reserve	2,00,000			
Profit & Loss A/c	30,000			
Bank overdraft	2,58,000			
Sundry Creditors	3,35,000			
	27,23,000			27,23,000

Notes :

1. Goodwill

Agreed value of asset taken		9,41,000
Less : liabilities taken		95,000
Value of Net assets taken		8,46,000

Purchase price Rs. 8,73,000   Less : 8,46,000 = Rs. 27,000 Goodwill

2. Bank Overdraft -

Bank Balance taken over from Moti Ltd.		15,000
Original Bank Balance of Nitin Ltd.		2,90,000
Cash available		3,05,000
Cash paid to Moti Ltd.	4,73,000	
Dividend paid to shareholders of Nitin Ltd. @ 6%	90,000	5,63,000

As Rs. 5,63,000 cash required less Rs. 3,05,000 available = Overdraft Rs. 2,58,000

Problem No. 3 : Following is the Balance Sheet of Minal Ltd. as on 31st March 2014

Balance Sheet of Minal Ltd.
as on 31.3.2014

Liabilities	Rs.	Assets	Rs.
Share Capital		Land & Building	2,10,000
6,000 Share of		Plant & Machinery	1,60,000
Rs. 100 each	6,00,000	Vehicles	1,00,000
6% Debenture	20,000	Stock	80,000
Creditors	60,000	Debtors	60,000
Outstanding Expenses	4,000	Cash	64,000
		Underwriting Commission	10,000
	6,84,000		6,84,000

Nikita Ltd. absorbed Minal Ltd. on the following terms :

1. Nikita Ltd. acquired only the assets of Minal Ltd. except cash balance.

2. The purchase consideration was fixed as 5 equity shares of Rs. 100 each, at Rs. 140 per share for 7 equity shares of Minal Ltd. and 700, 6% preference shares of Rs. 100 each.

3. Realisation expenses amounted to Rs. 12,000 and were paid by Minal Ltd.

4. The Liquidator of Minal Ltd. transferred the preference shares, to creditors in full satisfaction of their claims.

5. Debentures were paid at a premium of 10%.

6. Outstanding expenses were paid in full and in addition Minal Ltd. had to pay Rs. 4,200 as compensation to the worker.

7. Nikita Ltd. valued Land & Building, Plant & Machinery at 10% appreciation, Vehicles at 10% depreciation, stock was reduced to its market value which was Rs. 64,000. Debtors were taken subject to 5% Reserve for Doubtful Debts.

    Prepare the necessary ledger accounts in the books of Minal Ltd. Pass the opening entries in the books of Nikita Ltd.

Solution :

Statement Showing Purchase Consideration (Net Payment method)

Discharge	Rs.	Net Assets taken over	Rs.
Equity Shares		Land & Building	2,31,000
Issued 5 Shares		Plant & Machinery	1,76,000
for every 7 shares, the number		Vehicles	90,000
of shares to be issued		Stock	64,000
for 6000 shares will be		Debtors 60,000	
$\dfrac{6,000 \times 5}{7} = 4285\dfrac{5}{7}$ shares		- R.D.D. 3000	57,000
So 4285 full shares		Net Worth	6,18,000
of Rs. 140 each	5,99,900	PC- Net Worth	
Fraction share paid in		= Goodwill	
cash at market price		hence balancing	
(Paid in cash)		figure is	
$\dfrac{5}{7} \times 140 =$	100	Goodwill	52,000
700 preference shares at Rs.			
100 each	70,000		
Purchase Consideration	6,70,000		6,70,000

In the Books of Minal Ltd.

Dr. **Realisation A/c** Cr.

Particulars	Rs.	Particulars	Rs.
To Land & Building A/c	2,10,000	By outstanding expenses A/c	4,000
To Plant & Machinery A/c	1,60,000	By Nikita Ltd. A/c	6,70,000
To Vehicle A/c	1,00,000		
To Stock A/c	80,000		
To Debtors A/c	60,000		
To Debentures (premium) A/c	2,000		
To Creditors (premium) A/c	10,000		
To Cash A/c :			
Outstanding Commission 4,000			
Realisation Expenses 12,000			
Compensation to Worker 4,200	20,200		
To Equity Shareholders (profit) A/c	31,800		
	6,74,000		6,74,000

Dr. **Nikita Ltd.'s A/c** Cr.

Particulars	Rs.	Particulars	Rs.
To Realisation A/c	6,70,000	By Equity shares A/c	5,99,900
		By Cash A/c	100
		By 6% preference shares A/c	70,000
	6,70,000		6,70,000

Dr. **Sundry Creditors A/c** Cr.

Particulars	Rs.	Particulars	Rs.
To 7% Pref. Shares in Nikita Ltd.' A/c	70,000	By Balance b/d	60,000
		By Realisation A/c	10,000
	70,000		70,000

Dr. **6% Debentures A/c** Cr.

Particulars	Rs.	Particulars	Rs.
To Cash A/c	22,000	By Balance c/d	20,000
		By Realisation A/c	2,000
	22,000		22,000

Dr. **7% Preference Shares in Nikita Ltd.'s A/c** Cr.

Particulars	Rs.	Particulars	Rs.
To Nikita Ltd.'s A/c	70,000	By Sundry Creditors A/c	70,000
	70,000		70,000

Dr. **Equity Shares in Nikita Ltd.' A/c** Cr.

Particulars	Rs.	Particulars	Rs.
To Nikita Ltd.'s A/c	5,99,900	By Equity Shareholders A/c	5,99,900
	5,99,900		5,99,900

Dr. **Cash A/c** Cr.

Particulars	Rs.	Particulars	Rs.
To Balance	64,000	By Realisation A/c	20,200
To Nikita Ltd.'s A/c	100	By Debentures A/c	22,000
		By Equity shareholders A/c	21,900
	64,100		64,100

Dr. **Equity Shareholders A/c** Cr.

Particulars	Rs.	Particulars	Rs.
To Underwriting commission A/c	10,000	By Equity Share Capital A/c	6,00,000
To Equity Shares		By Realisation A/c	31,800
in Nikita Ltd.'s A/c	5,99,900		
To Cash A/c	21,900		
	6,31,800		6,31,800

In the Books of Nikita Ltd.
Journal Entries

Date	Particulars	L.F.	Dr. Rs.	Cr. Rs.
	Business Purchase A/c Dr.		6,70,000	
	To Liquidators of Minal Ltd.'s A/c			6,70,000
	(Being purchase of business from Minal Ltd. &			
	price payable to the liquidator)			

Date	Particulars		L.F.	Dr. Rs.	Cr. Rs.
	Land & Buildings A/c	Dr.		2,31,000	
	Plant & Machinery A/c	Dr.		1,76.000	
	Vehicle A/c	Dr.		90,000	
	Stock A/c	Dr.		64,000	
	Debtors A/c	Dr.		60,000	
	Goodwill A/c	Dr.		52,000	
	To Reserve for Doubtful Debts. A/c				3,000
	To Business Purchase A/c				6,70,000
	(Being purchase of Assets from Minal Ltd. at the values stated above.)				
	Liquidator of Minal Ltd. A/c	Dr.		6,70,000	
	To Equity Share Capital A/c				4,28,500
	To 7% Preference Share Capital A/c				70,000
	To Equity Share Premium A/c				1,71.400
	To Cash A/c				100
	(Being issued 4,285 Equity share of Rs. 100 each at Rs. 140 per share, 700, 7% preference shares of Rs. 100 each and paid cash Rs. 100 in settlement of purchase consideration.)				

Problem No. 4 : Long Ltd. has agreed to acquire goodwill and assets (except investments) of Short Ltd. as at 31st March 2014. The Balance Sheet of Short Ltd. as on that date was as follows :

Liabilities	Rs.	Assets	Rs.
Share Capital (Rs. 10)	1,60,000	Goodwill	20,000
General Reserve	25,000	Land and Buildings	80,000
Profit & Loss A/c	18,000	Plant	80,000
8% Debentures	60,000	Investments	30,000
Creditors	37,000	Stock	40,000
Provision for Taxation	20,000	Debtors	50,000
		Bank	20,000
	3,20,000		3,20,000

Long Ltd. Will :

1. Discharge the Debentures @ 8% premium by issue of 7% Debentures in Long Ltd. at 10% Discount.
2. Issue 3 shares of Long Ltd. at market price of Rs. 11 for 2 shares of Short Ltd.;
3. Pay Rupees 2 in cash for each share of Short Ltd.; and
4. Pay absorption expenses Rs. 3,000.

Short Ltd. sells the investments for Rs. 32,000, one-third of the shares received from Long Ltd. are sold @ 10.50 each. Tax liability is determined at Rs. 24,000. Before transfer Short Ltd. declares and pays 10% provision.

Long Ltd. values Land and Buildings at Rs. 1,00,000. Plant at 10% below book value. Stock at Rs. 35,000 and Debtors subject to 5% provision.

Show : 1. Ledger Accounts in the books of Short Ltd.

2. Journal entries and Balance Sheet in the books of Long Ltd.

Solution :

Purchase Consideration
(Net Payment Method)

Whom Payable	What Payable	How Payable	Rs.
1) 8% Debentures in Long Ltd.	7% Debentures	60,000 + 8% premium i.e. 4,800	64,800
2) Equity shares Long Ltd.	Equity shares in Long Ltd.	2 : 3 i.e. 16,000 : 24,000 24,000 shares in long Ltd. at Rs. 11 per share	2,64,000
3) Equity Shares	Cash	Rs. 2 × 16,000	32,000
4) Short Ltd.	Cash (Absorption Expenses)	3,000	3,000
		Purchase Consideration	3,63,800

Calculation of Goodwill

Purchase consideration		3,63,800
Less Net Worth/Assets		
L & B	1,00,000	
Plant	72,000	
Debtors	47,500	
Stock	35,000	
Cash	4,000	2,58,500
Goodwill		1,05,300

In the Books of Short Ltd.

Dr.　　　　　　　　　　**Realisation A/c**　　　　　　　　　　Cr.

Particulars	Rs.	Particulars	Rs.
To Goodwill A/c	20,000	By Bank A/c (Sale of	
To Land & Buildings A/c	80,000	investments)	32,000
To Plant A/c	80,000	By Long Ltd.'s A/c (Purchase	
To Investments A/c	30,000	Price)	3,63,800
To Stock A/c	40,000		
To Debtors A/c	50,000		
To Bank A/c (Transfer)	4,000		
To Bank A/c (Expenses)	3,000		
To Income tax A/c	4,000		
To 8% Debentures A/c (premium)	4,800		
To Shares in Long Ltd.'s A/c (Loss on sale)	4,000		
To Shareholders A/c (profit)	76,000		
	3,95,800		3,95,800

Dr.　　　　　　　　　　**Long Ltd.'s A/c**　　　　　　　　　　Cr.

Particulars	Rs.	Particulars	Rs.
To Realisation A/c	3,63,800	By Shares A/c	2,64,000
		By 7% Debentures A/c	64,800
		By Bank A/c	35,000
	3,63,800		3,63,800

Dr.　　　　　　　　　　**8% Debentures A/c**　　　　　　　　　　Cr.

Particulars	Rs.	Particulars	Rs.
To 7% Debentures in Long Ltd.'s A/c	64,800	By Balance b/d	60,000
		By Realisation A/c	4,800
	64,800		64,800

Dr.   **Shares in Long Ltd. A/c**   Cr.

Particulars	Rs.	Particulars	Rs.
To Long Ltd.'s A/c	2,64,000	By Bank A/c (Sale of 8,000 Shares at Rs. 10.50)	84,000
		By Realisation A/c (Loss on sale)	4,000
		By Shareholders A/c	1,76,000
	2,64,000		2,64,000

Dr.   **Shareholders A/c**   Cr.

Particulars	Rs.	Particulars	Rs.
To Shares in Long Ltd.'s A/c	1,76,000	By Share Capital A/c	1,60,000
To Bank A/c	87,000	By General Reserve A/c	25,000
		By Profit & Loss A/c	2,000
		By Realisation A/c (Profit)	76,000
	2,63,000		2,63,000

Dr.   **Provision for Taxation A/c**   Cr.

Particulars	Rs.	Particulars	Rs.
To Income Tax A/c	24,000	By Balance	20,000
		By Realisation A/c (Excess over Provision)	4,000
	24,000		24,000

Dr.   **Bank A/c**   Cr.

Particulars	Rs.	Particulars	Rs.
To Balance	20,000	By Dividend (@ 10%) A/c	16,000
To Long Ltd.'s A/c	35,000	By Realisation A/c (Transfer)	4,000
To Realisation A/c (sale of Investments)	32,000	By Realisation A/c (Expenses)	3,000
		By Sundry Creditors A/c	37,000
To Shares in Long Ltd.'s A/c	84,000	By Provision for taxation A/c	24,000
		By Shareholders A/c	87,000
	1,71,000		1,71,000

Notes : 1. As 10% Dividend is paid before transfer to new company. Bank Balance and Profit & Loss A/c are reduced by the amount of Dividend i.e. Rs. 16,000.

In the Books of Long Ltd.
Journal Entries.

Date	Particulare		L.F.	Dr. Rs.	Cr. Rs.
	Business purchase A/c	Dr.		3,63,800	
	To Liquidator of Short Ltd. A/c				3,63,800
	(Being business Purchased)				
	Land & Buildings A/c	Dr.		100,000	
	Plant A/c	Dr.		72,000	
	Debtors A/c	Dr.		50,000	
	Stock A/c			35,000	
	Bank A/c	Dr.		4,000	
	Goodwill A/c	Dr.		1,05,300	
	(Balancing figure)				
	To Provision for				
	Bad debts A/c				2,500
	To Business Purchase A/c				3,63,800
	(Being Assets taken over)				
	Liquidator of short Ltd. A/c	Dr.		3,63,800	
	Dis. on issue of Debentures A/c	Dr.		7,200	
	To Share Capital A/c				2,40,000
	To Share Premium A/c				24,000
	To 7% Debentures A/c				72,000
	To Bank A/c				35,000
	(Being purchase consideration paid.)				

(**Note :** Debentures are issued at 10% discount. Therefore, to pay off Rs. 64,800 of the Debentureholders of Short Ltd. 7% Debentures of Rs. 72,000 must be issued i.e. face value of Rs. 72,000 less 10% discount Rs. 7,200 = 64,800.)

Balance Sheet of Long Ltd. (After Absorption) as on 1st April 2014

Liabilities	Rs.	Assets		Rs.
Share Capital :		Goodwill		1,05,300
24,000 shares of		Land & Building		1,00,000
Rs. 10 each	2,40,000	Plant		72,000
Share Premium	24,000	Stock		35,000
7% Debenture	72,000	Debtors	50,000	
Bank Overdraft	31,000	Provision for Bad Debts. 2500		47,500
		Discount on Issue of 7%		
		Debenture		7,200
	3,67,000			3,67,000

Problem No. 5 : Following is the Balance Sheet of Govind Ltd. as on 31st March, 2014.

Liabilities	Rs.	Assets	Rs.
Share Capital :		Goodwill	4,00,000
20,000 Equity Shares of		Land & Building	15,60,000
Rs. 100 each fully paid	20,00,000	Plant & Machinery	14,00,000
Reserve Fund	5,00,000	Patent Rights	3,50,000
Sinking Fund	1,00,000	Stocks	2,00,000
Workmen's accident Comp-		Sundry Debtors	4,00,000
ensation Fund (Estimated		Investment against	
Liabilities Rs. 9,000)	50,000	Sinking Fund	1,00,000
Employees Profit Sharing Fund	1,00,000	Cash at Bank	30,000
Staff provident Fund	1,50,000		
Sundry Creditors	1,40,000		
'A' Debentures	4,00,000		
'B' Debentures	10,00,000		
	44,40,000		44,40,000

Ramkrishna Ltd. absorbed Govind Ltd. on the date of its above Balance Sheet, the consideration being :

1. The Taking over of the liabilities.

2. The payment of cost of absorption (as part of purchase consideration) not exceeding Rs. 8,000.

3. The repayment of the 'B' Debentures at a premium 5% in cash.

4. The discharge of 'A' Debentures at a premium of 10% by the issue of 6% Debentures in Ramkrishna Ltd. at par.

5. A payment of Rs. 15 per share in cash.

6. Allotment of one 7% preference share of Rs. 100 each fully paid and five equity shares of Rs. 100 each fully paid for every four equity shares in Govind Ltd. The actual cost of absorption came to Rs. 10,000. Stock of Govind Ltd. includes goods valued at Rs. 56,000 purchased from Ramkrishna Ltd. which company invoices goods at cost plus $16\frac{2}{3}$ %. The creditors include Rs. 80,000 due by Govind Ltd. to Ramkrishna Ltd. The directors of Ramkrishna Ltd. decided to create a provision of 5% on sundry debtors against doubtful debts.

You are required to : (a) Prepare the following ledger accounts in the books of

Govind Ltd. (1) Realisation Account, (2) Ramkrishna Ltd. Account, (3) Sundry Shareholders Account.

(b) Pass Journal Entries in the books of Ramkrishna Ltd. and

(c) Show the working of purchase consideration.

Solution :

Calculation of Purchase Consideration

For whom	Mode of Payment	Rs.
1. Realisation Expenses	Cash	8,000
2. B Debentureholders @ 5% premium	Cash	10,50,000
3. A Debentureholders @ Rs. 10% premium	Debentures	4,40,000
4. Equity Shareholders @ Rs. 15 per share for 20,000 shares	Cash	3,00,000
7% Preference Shares @ 1 share for 4 shares i.e. 5,000 Pref. Shares of Rs. 100 each	Pref. shares	5,00,000
5. Eq. Shares for every 4 Shares i.e. 25,000 Shares of Rs. 100 each	Eq. shares	25,00,000
Total Purchase Price		47,98,000

Notes :

1. Since stock of Govind Ltd. includes Rs. 56,000 stock on which Ramkrishna Ltd. had made a profit $16\frac{2}{3}$ % on cost, the profit Rs. 8,000 included in this stock is cancelled while recording the stock in Ramkrishna Ltd.

2. Creditors of Govind Ltd. included Rs. 80,000 due to Ramkrishna Ltd. Hence, internal indebtedness is also cancelled.

In the Books of Govind Ltd.

Dr.   **Realisation A/c**   Cr.

Particulars	Rs.	Particulars	Rs.
To Sundry Assets A/c	44,40,000	By Creditors A/c	1,40,000
To Bank (Expenses) A/c	10,000	By Staff Provident Fund A/c	1,50,000
To A Debentureholders A/c	40,000	By Employees Profit	
To B Debentureholders A/c	50,000	Sharing Fund A/c	1,00,000
To Equity Shareholders A/c (Profit)	6,57,000	By Workmen's Accdt. Comp. Fund A/c	9,000
		By Ramkrishna Ltd.'s A/c	47,98,000
	51,97,000		51,97,000

Dr.   **Ramkrishna Ltd.'s A/c**   Cr.

Particulars	Rs.	Particulars	Rs.
To Realisation A/c	47,98,000	By Equity Shares A/c	25,00,000
		By 7% Pref. Shares A/c	5,00,000
		By 6% Debentures A/c	4,40,000
		By Bank A/c	13,58,000
	47,98,000		47,98,000

Dr.   **Shareholders A/c**   Cr.

Particulars	Rs.	Particulars	Rs.
To Equity shares in Ramkrishna Ltd.'s A/c	25,00,000	By Share Capital A/c	20,00,000
		By Res. Fund A/c	5,00,000
To 7% pref. Shares in Ramkrishna Ltd.'s A/c	5,00,000	By Sinking Fund A/c	1,00,000
		By Workmen's Comp. Fund A/c	41,000
To Bank A/c	2,98,000	By Realisation A/c	6,57,000
	32,98,000		32,98,000

Journal Entries in the books of Ramkrishna Ltd.

Date	Particulars	L.F.	Dr. Rs.	Cr. Rs.
1	Business Purchase A/c Dr.		47,98,000	
	To Liquidator of Govind Ltd. A/c			47,98,000
	(Being purchase of business of Govind Ltd.)			
2	Land & Buildings A/c Dr.		15,60,000	
	Plant & Machinery A/c Dr.		14,00,000	
	Patent Rights A/c Dr.		3,50,000	
	Stock A/c Dr.		1,92,000	
	Sundry Debtors A/c Dr.		4,00,000	
	Investments A/c Dr.		1,00,000	
	Bank A/c Dr.		30,000	
	Goodwill A/c Dr.		11,85,000	
	To Provision for D/Debts A/c			20,000
	To Sundry Creditors A/c			1,40,000
	To Staff Provident Fund A/c			1,50,000
	To Employees Profit Sharing Fund A/c			1,00,000

Date	Particulars	L.F.	Dr. Rs.	Cr. Rs.
	To Workmen's comp. Fund A/c			9,000
	To Business Purchase A/c			47,98,000
	(Being Assets & Liabilities taken over from Govind Ltd.)			
3	Sundry Creditors A/c Dr.		80,000	
	To Sundry Debtors A/c			80,000
	(Being cancellation of internal indebtedness)			
4	Liquidator of Govind A/c Dr.		47,98,000	
	To Equity Share Capital A/c			25,00,000
	To 7% pref. Share Capital A/c			5,00,000
	To 6% Debentures A/c			4,40,000
	To Bank A/c			13,58,000
	(Being settlement of purchase price.)			

Problem No. 6 : The Balance Sheet of Venus Co. Ltd. and Apollo Co. Ltd. as on 31st March, 2014.

Venus Ltd.

Liabilities	Rs.	Assets	Rs.
Share Capital :		Sundry Assets	3,37,000
900 shares of Rs. 270 each	2,43,000	Cash	700
General Reserve	80,700		
Profit & Loss A/c	3,000		
Sundry Creditors	11,000		
	3,37,700		3,37,700

Apollo Ltd.

Liabilities	Rs.	Assets	Rs.
Share Capital :		Sundry Assets	8,71,500
4,000 shares of Rs.150 each	6,00,000	Cash	5,500
General Reserve	2,57,000		
Profit & Loss A/c	7,000		
Sundry Creditors	13,000		
	8,77,000		8,77,000

It was proposed that Venus Ltd. be absorbed by Apollo Ltd. and the following arrangement was accepted by them.

The holder of every three shares in Venus Ltd. was to receive five shares in Apollo Ltd. plus as much cash as is necessary to adjust the right of shareholders of both the companies in accordance with the intrinsic value of the shares as per their Balance Sheets.

Show the working of purchase consideration and give journal entries and Balance Sheet of Apollo Ltd.

Solution :

$$\text{Intrinsic Value} = \frac{\text{Value of Net Assets}}{\text{No. of shares issued and subscribed}}$$

Accordingly, intrinsic value of each share of Venus Ltd. and Apollo Ltd. is arrived at as under :

	Venus Ltd.	Apollo Ltd.
Value of Assets	3,37,700	8,77,000
Less : Value of liabilities i.e. Creditors	11,000	13,000
Value of Net Assets	3,26,700	8,64,000
	3,26,700	8,64,000
Therefore, Intrinsic Value =	900	4,000
	Rs. 363	Rs. 216
	per share	per share

Purchase Consideration :

Venus Ltd. to receive five shares for its every three shares and balance in cash :

	Rs.
The Intrinsic value of 3 shares is =	1,089
(363 × 3)	
Less : Intrinsic Value of 5 shares =	1,080
(216 × 5)	
Difference to be received in cash =	9

This means Venus Ltd. is to receive cash at the rate of Rs. 9 per 3 shares. Hence, the total purchase price =

(i) For every 3 shares in Venus Ltd.
   5 Shares in Apollo Ltd.

   i.e. $\frac{900}{3} \times 5 = 1500$ Shares at Rs. 150 each =   2,25,000

(ii) Cash $= \dfrac{900 \times 9}{3}$ 2,700

   Purchase Consideration   2,27,700

Journal Entries in the books of Apollo Ltd.

Date	Particulars	L.F.	Dr. Rs.	Cr. Rs.
1	Business Purchases A/c Dr.		2,27,700	
	To Liquidator of Venus Ltd. A/c			2,27,700
	(Being Business of Venus Ltd. Acquired)			
2	Sundry Assets A/c Dr.		3,37,000	
	Cash A/c Dr.		700	
	To Sundry Creditors A/c			11,000
	To Capital Reserve A/c			99,000
	To Liquidator of Venus Ltd.'s A/c			2,27,700
	(Being Assets & Liabilities taken over form and purchase consideration payable to Venus Ltd.)			
3	Liquidator of Venus Ltd.'s A/c Dr.		2,27,700	
	To Share Capital A/c			2,25,000
	To Cash A/c			2700
	(Being payment of purchase Price in cash and by issue of 1500 shares of Rs. 150 each as fully paid)			

Note :

1) Calculation of Capital Reserve

	Rs.
Net Assets	
3,37,000 + 700 - 11000 =	3,26,700
Less Purchase consideration	2,27,700
Capital Reserve	99,000

In the Books of Apollo Ltd.
Balance Sheet as on 1-4-2014 (After Absorption)

Liabilities	Rs.	Assets	Rs.
Share Capital :		Sundry Assets	12,08,500
5,500 shares of Rs.150		Cash	3,500
each of which 1,500 issued to			
vendors without receiving cash	8,25,000		
Capital Reserve	99,000		
General Reserve	2,57,000		
Profit & Loss A/c	7,000		
Sundry Creditors	24,000		
	12,12,000		12,12,000

Problem No. 7 : Uptodate Ltd. has agreed to acquire the goodwill and assets (except stock) of Slowdown Ltd. as on 31st March, 2014 on which date the Balance Sheet of Slowdown Ltd. was as under :

Balance Sheet
as on 31-3-2014

Liabilities	Rs.	Assets	Rs.
Share Capital :		Fixed Assets	:
16,000 shares of Rs.100 each	1,60,000	Goodwill	20,000
Reserves	43,000	Freehold Property	80,000
9% Debentures	60,000	Machinery	80,000
Current liabilities & Provision	57,000	Current Assets :	
		Stocks	30,000
		Investments	40,000
		Sundry Debtors	50,000
		Bank Balance	20,000
	3,20,000		3,20,000

The consideration of acquisition agreed was as under :
  (a) Discharge of 9% debentures @ 10% premium by issue of 12% debentures in Uptodate Ltd.
  (b) Issue of 3 shares of Rs. 10 each in Uptodate Ltd. at market price of Rs. 12/- for every 2 shares of Slowdown Ltd.

(c) Payment of Rs. 2.50 in cash for each share in Slowdown Ltd.

(d) Acquisition expenses of Rs. 3,000/- to be met by Uptodate Ltd.

Slowdown Ltd. sold its stock (which was not taken over) at Rs. 32,000 and one third of the shares received from Uptodate Ltd; @ Rs. 12.50 each. Current Liabilities and Provisions (which were also not taken over) were settled at Rs. 55,000. Before the final liquidation it also declared a dividend of 12.50%.

Uptodate Ltd. valued freehold property at Rs. 1,20,000; machinery at Rs. 75,000; Investment at 10% increase and sundry debtors at 10% less. You are required to give -

(i) Ledger Accounts to close the books of Slowdown Ltd.

(ii) Opening Journal entries in the books of Uptodate Ltd.

Solution :

Calculation of Purchase Consideration

Purchase Consideration	Mode of Payment	Rs.
(i) Rs. 60,000 Debentures at 10% Premium	12% Debentures	66,000
(ii) For 16,000 shares, 24,000 shares at the rate of 3 shares for every 2 shares. Price of each share is Rs. 12 i.e. 24,000 × 12	Shares	2,88,000
(iii) Rs. 2.50 per share in cash i.e. 16,000 × 2.50	Cash	40,000
(iv) Acquisition Expenses	Cash	3,000
Purchase Consideration		3,97,000

Dr.   **Realisation A/c**   Cr.

Particulars	Rs.	Particulars	Rs.
To Goodwill A/c	20,000	By Uptodate Co. Ltd. A/c	3,97,000
To Freehold Property A/c	80,000	(Purchase Price)	
To Machinery A/c	80,000	By Cash A/c	32,000
To Investments A/c	40,000	(Sale of Stock)	
To Sundry Debtors A/c	50,000	By Current Liabilities A/c	2,000
To Bank A/c	20,000	(Discount)	
To Stock A/c	30,000		
To 9% Debentureholders A/c (Premium)	6,000		
To Cash (Expenses) A/c	3,000		
To Shareholders (Profit) A/c	1,02,000		
	4,31,000		4,31,000

Dr.   **Uptodate Ltd. A/c**   Cr.

Particulars	Rs.	Particulars	Rs.
To Realisation A/c (Purchase Price)	3,97,000	By Equity shares A/c By 12% Debentures A/c By Cash	2,88,000 66,000 43,000
	3,97,000		3,97,000

Dr.   **9% Debentureholders A/c**   Cr.

Particulars	Rs.	Particulars	Rs.
To 12% Debentures in Uptodate Ltd.'s A/c	66,000	By 9% Debentures A/c By Realisation (Premium) A/c	60,000 6,000
	66,000		66,000

Dr.   **Current Liabilities & Provisions**   Cr.

Particulars	Rs.	Particulars	Rs.
To Cash A/c To Realisation (Discount) A/c	55,000 2,000	By Balance b/d	57,000
	57,000		57,000

Dr.   **Equity Shares in Uptodate Ltd.**   Cr.

Particulars	Rs.	Particulars	Rs.
To Uptodate Co. Ltd.'s A/c To Equity shareholders A/c (Profit on sale of shares)	2,88,000 4,000	By Cash A/c (sale of 8,000 shares @ Rs. 12.50 each) By Equity Shareholders A/c	1,00,000 1,92,000
	2,92,000		2,92,000

Dr.   **Cash A/c**   Cr.

Particulars	Rs.	Particulars	Rs.
To Uptodate Co. Ltd.'s A/c To Shares in Uptodate Ltd.'s A/c (Sale) To Realisation A/c (Sale of Stock)	43,000 1,00,000 32,000	By Realisation A/c (Expenses) By Current Liabilities & Provisions A/c By Dividend A/c By Equity shareholders A/c	3,000 55,000 20,000 97,000
	1,75,000		1,75,000

Dr. **Equity shareholders A/c** Cr.

Particulars	Rs.	Particulars	Rs.
To Dividend A/c	20,000	By Equity share capital A/c	1,60,000
To Equity shares in		By Realisation (Profit) A/c	1,02,000
Uptodate Ltd. A/c	1,92,000	By Reserves A/c	43,000
To Cash A/c	97,000	By Profit on sale of shares	
		in Uptodate Ltd.'s A/c	4,000
	3,09,000		3,09,000

(**Note :** It is presumed that the dividend declared is paid out of cash subsequently received and the original Bank Balance is taken over by Uptodate Ltd. along with other assets)

Journal Entries in the books of Uptodate Ltd.

Date	Particulars		L.F.	Dr. Rs.	Cr. Rs.
1	Business Purchase A/c	Dr.		3,97,000	
	To liquidator of Slowdown Ltd.'s A/c				3,97,000
	(Being Business of Slowdown purchased)				
2	Freehold Property A/c	Dr.		1,20,000	
	Machinery A/c	Dr.		75,000	
	Investment A/c	Dr.		44,000	
	Sundry Debtors A/c	Dr.		50,000	
	Bank A/c	Dr.		20,000	
	Goodwill A/c	Dr.		93,000	
	To Provision for Doubtful Debt. A/c				5,000
	To Business Purchase A/c				3,97,000
	(Being Assets taken over)				
3	Liquidators of Slowdown Ltd. A/c	Dr.		3,97,000	
	To 12% Debentures A/c				66,000
	To Equity share capital A/c				2,40,000
	To Equity share premium A/c				48,000
	To Bank A/c				43,000
	(Being Purchase Consideration paid.)				

Balance Sheet of Uptodate Ltd.
as on 1-4-2014

Liabilities	Rs.	Assets	Rs.
Share Capital :		Freehold property	1,20,000
Equity Share Capital	2,40,000	Machinery	75,000
Share premium	48,000	Investment	44,000
12% Debenture	66,000	Sundry Debtors 50,000	
Bank Overdraft	23,000	- R.D.D. 5000	45,000
		Goodwill	93,000
	3,77,000		3,77,000

Problem No. 8 : The following is the Balance Sheet of Roopa Ltd. as on 31st March, 2014.

Balance Sheet

Liabilities	Rs.	Assets	Rs.
Share capital -		Land & Building	1,05,000
3,000 Shares of		Plant & Machinery	80,000
Rs. 100 each	3,00,000	Vehicles	50,000
6% Debentures	10,000	Stock	40,000
Creditors	30,000	Debtors	30,000
Outstanding Expenses	2,000	Cash	32,000
		Underwriting Commission	5,000
Total Rs.	3,42,000	Total Rs.	3,42,000

Sona Ltd. absorbed Roopa Ltd. on the following terms :

1) Sona Ltd. acquired only the assets of Roopa Ltd. except cash balance.
2) The purchase consideration was fixed as five equity shares of Rs. 100 each at Rs. 120 each for six equity shares of Roopa Ltd. and 350, 6% preference shares of Rs. 100 each.
3) Realisation expenses amounted to Rs. 6,000 and were paid by Roopa Ltd.
4) The liquidator of Roopa Ltd. transferred the preference shares to creditors in full satisfaction of their claims.
5) Debentures were paid at a premium of 10%.
6) Outstanding expenses were paid in full and in addition, Roopa Ltd. had to pay Rs. 2100 as compensation to the workers.
7) Sona Ltd. valued Land and Building and Plant and Machinery at 10% depreciation,

Stock was reduced to market value which was Rs. 32,000 and Debtors were taken subject to 5% Reserve for Doubtful Debts.

Prepare Realisation Account, Shareholders' Account and Cash Account in the books of Roopa Ltd. and Balance Sheet of Sona Ltd.

Solution :

Calculation of Purchase Consideration (Payment Method)

Particulars	Rs.
Equity share in Sona Ltd.	
$6 : 5 :: 3000 : 2500 \times 120 =$	3,00,000
6% preference Shares $= 350 \times 100 =$	35,000
Total Rs.	3,35,000

In the Books of Roopa Ltd.

Dr. **Realisation A/c** Cr.

Particulars	Rs.	Particulars	Rs.
To Land & Building A/c	1,05,000	By Sona Ltd.'s A/c	3,35,000
To Plant & Machinery A/c	80,000		
To Vehicles A/c	50,000		
To Stock A/c	40,000		
To Debtors A/c	30,000		
To Creditors A/c (Loss)	5,000		
To Bank A/c	6,000		
(Realisation Exp.)			
To Debentureholders A/c	1,000		
To Bank A/c	2,100		
(Compensation)			
To Equity Shareholders (Profit)	15,900		
	3,35,000		3,35,000

Dr. **Creditors' A/c** Cr.

Particulars	Rs.	Particulars	Rs.
To 6% Preference	35,000	By Balance b/d	30,000
Shares in Sona Ltd.'s A/c		By Realisation A/c	5,000
	35,000		35,000

Dr. **Outstanding Expenses A/c** Cr.

Particulars	Rs.	Particulars	Rs.
To Bank A/c	2,000	By Balance b/d	2,000
	2,000		2,000

Dr. **Debentureholders' A/c** Cr.

Particulars	Rs.	Particulars	Rs.
To Bank A/c	11,000	By Balance b/d	10,000
		By Realisation A/c	1,000
	11,000		11,000

Dr. **Equity Shareholders' A/c** Cr.

Particulars	Rs.	Particulars	Rs.
To Underwriting Com. A/c	5,000	By Equity Share Capital A/c	3,00,000
To Equity Shares in Sona Ltd.' A/c	3,00,000	By Realisation A/c	15,900
To Bank A/c	10,900		
	3,15,900		3,15,900

Dr. **Sona Ltd. A/c** Cr.

Particulars	Rs.	Particulars	Rs.
To Realisation A/c	3,35,000	By Equity shares in Sona Ltd.'s A/c	3,00,000
		By 6% Preference shares in Sona Ltd.'s A/c	35,000
	3,35,000		3,35,000

Dr. **Bank / Cash A/c** Cr.

Particulars	Rs.	Particulars	Rs.
To Balance b/d	32,000	By Realisation A/c	6,000
		By Debenture holders A/c	11,000
		By Realisation A/c	2,100
		By Outstanding Exp. A/c	2,000
		By Equity Shareholders A/c	10,900
	32,000		32,000

Note : Compensation paid Rs. 6,000 is shown on the debit side of Realisation A/c and credit side of cash A/c.

In the Books of Sona Ltd.
Balance Sheet (After Absorption) as on 1st April 2014

Liabilities	Rs.	Assets	Rs.
2500 Equity share		Goodwill	26,000
of Rs. 100 each	2,50,000	Land & Building	1,15,500
350, 6% preference		Plant & Machinery	88,000
Shares of Rs. 100 each	35,000	Vehicles	45,000
Share premium	50,000	Debtors 30000	
		- R.D.D. 1500	28,500
		Stock	32,000
	3,35,000		3,35,000

Note :-

Calculation of Goodwill		Rs.
Purchase consideration		3,35,000
Less Assets taken over		
Land & Building	1,15,500	
Plant & Machinery	88,000	
Vehicles	45,000	
Stock	32,000	
Debtors	28,500	3,09,000
Goodwill		26,000

Problem No. 9 : Following was the Balance Sheet of Apple Ltd. as on 31st March 2014

Balance Sheet as on 31-3-2014

Liabilities	Rs.	Assets	Rs.
Share Capital :		Land & Building	1,40,000
2,000 shares of Rs.100 each	2,00,000	Plant & Machinery	1,10,000
General Reserves	64,000	Stock	98,000
Profit & Loss A/c	60,000	Debtors	42,000
Bills Payable	42,000	Cash in Hand	14,000
Creditors	70,000	Advertising Suspenses A/c	32,000
	4,36,000		4,36,000

Apple Ltd. was absorbed by Banana Ltd. on the following terms :

1. Apple Ltd. agreed to write-off advertising suspense A/c against its own reserves.
2. Banana Ltd. revalued the assets of apple Ltd. as under :

   Land and Building Rs. 1,50,000, Plant & Machinery Rs. 1,04,000, Stock Rs. 1,20,000 and Debtors at Book value.
3. Banana Ltd. took over the assets and liabilities of Apple Ltd. and agreed to discharge the purchase consideration into 2,600 shares of Rs. 100 each at Rs. 110 per share and balance in cash.
4. Apple Ltd. paid its liquidation expenses of Rs. 4,000.

   Prepare Realisation A/c, Banana Ltd. A/c, Cash A/c and Shareholders A/c in the books of Apple Ltd. and opening Journal entries in the books of Banana Ltd.

Solution :

Calculation of Purchase Consideration

Particulars	Rs.	Rs.
Agreed Value of Assets taken		
Land & Building		1,50,000
Plant & Machinery		1,04,000
Stock		1,20,000
Debtors		42,000
Cash		14,400
Total		4,30,400
Less : Liabilities taken		
Creditors	70,000	
Bills Payable	42,000	1,12,400
Purchase Consideration		3,18,000

General Reserve Transferred to Shareholders' A/c as under

Particulars	Rs.
Balance as given	64,000
Less : Advertising Suspense A/c	32,000
Balance Transferred to Shareholders	32,000

In the Books of Apple Ltd.

Dr.   **Realisation A/c**   Cr.

Particulars	Rs.	Particulars	Rs.
To Land & Building A/c	1,40,000	By Creditors A/c	70,000
To Plant & Machinery A/c	1,10,000	By Bills Payable A/c	42,400
To Stock A/c	98,000	By Banana Ltd.'s A/c	3,18,000
To Debtors A/c	42,000	(Purchase Price)	
To Cash A/c	14,400		
To Cash A/c (Expenses)	4,000		
To Equity Shareholders A/c (profit)	22,000		
	4,30,400		4,30,400

Dr.   **Banana Ltd. A/c**   Cr.

Particulars	Rs.	Particulars	Rs.
To Realisation A/c	3,18,000	By Equity shares A/c	2,86,000
		By Cash A/c	32,000
	3,18,000		3,18,000

Dr.   **Cash A/c**   Cr.

Particulars	Rs.	Particulars	Rs.
To Balance b/d	14,400	By Realisation A/c (Transfer)	14,400
To Banana Ltd. A/c	32,000	By Realisation A/c (Expenses)	4,000
		By Equity Shareholders A/c	28,000
	46,400		46,400

Dr.   **Equity Shareholders A/c**   Cr.

Particulars	Rs.	Particulars	Rs.
To Equity Shares	2,86,000	By Share Capital A/c	2,00,000
To Cash	28,000	By General Reserve A/c	32,000
		By Profit & Loss A/c	60,000
		By Realisation A/c (Profit)	22,000
	3,14,000		3,14,000

In the Books of Banana Ltd. Journal Entries

Date	Particulars		L.F.	Dr. Rs.	Cr. Rs.
1	Business Purchase A/c	Dr,		3,18,000	
	To Apple Ltd. A/c				3,18,000
	(Purchase Price payable to Apple Ltd. for purchase of its business.)				
2	Land & Buildings A/c	Dr.		1,50,000	
	Plant & Machinery A/c	Dr.		1,04,000	
	Stock A/c	Dr.		1,20,000	
	Debtors A/c	Dr.		42,000	
	Cash A/c	Dr.		14,400	
	To Creditors A/c				70,000
	To Bills Payable A/c				42,400
	To Business Purchase A/c				3,18,000
	(Assets and Liabilities taken over from Apple Ltd. at the values stated above.)				
3	Apple Ltd.'s A/c	Dr.		3,18,000	
	To Equity Share capital A/c				2,60,000
	To Equity Share premium A/c				26,000
	To Cash A/c				32,000
	(Issued 2,600 Equity shares of Rs. 100 each at Rs. 110 per share as fully paid and paid cash in settlement of Purchase Price.)				

Problem No. 10 :

The following is the Balance sheet of Rupa Ltd. As on 31 st March, 2014

Liabilities	Rs.	Assets	Rs.
Share Capital :		Building	1,70,000
4000 Equity Shares of		Plant & Machinery	4,00,000
Rs. 100 each	4,00,000	Investment	50,600
General Reserve	50,000	Debtors	1,40,500
Profit & Loss A/c	5,600	Stock	80,700
5% Debentures	2,50,000	Cash at Bank	16,500
Creditors	1,28,700		
Dividend Equalisation Fund	24,000		
	8,58,300		8,58,300

Rupa Ltd. was absorbed by Dipa Ltd. on the above date, on the following terms and conditions, Dipa Ltd. to :

1) Assume all liabilities and to acquire all assets except investments which were sold by Rupa Ltd. For Rs. 45,500

2) Discharge the debentures at a discount of 5% by issue of 7% Debentures in Dipa Ltd.

3) Issue two shares of Rs. 60 each in Dipa Ltd. at Rs. 65 Per share and also pay Rs. 2 in cash to the shareholders of Rupa Ltd. in exchange for one share in Rupa Ltd.

4) Pay the cost of absorption for Rs. 1,500

With the consent of the shareholders, the Liquidator of Rupa Ltd. Sold off in open Market one fifth of the shares received from Dipa Ltd. at the average rate of Rs. 63 per share.

You are required to prepare.

i) Statement of Purchase Consideration

ii) Realisation A/c

iii) Shareholder A/c

iv) Bank A/c

v) 5% Debentureholder A/c

vi) Opening Journal Entries in the books of Dipa Ltd. **(March 2011 - PUP)**

Solution :

Statement of Purchase Consideration.

For	Amount (Rs.)	Form
5% Debentureholders (2,50,000-12,500)	2,37,500	7% Debentures
Shareholders		
i) (8000 × 65)	5,20,000	Equity Shares
ii) Cash (4000 × 2)	8000	Cash
Cost of Absorption	1500	Cash
Purchase Consideration	7,67,000	

In the book of Rupa Ltd.
Realisation A/c

Particular	Rs	Particular	Rs
To Sundry Asset	8,58,300	By S. Liabilities	1,28,700
To Cash	1500	By Cash sale of Investment	45,500
To Equity Shareholder	93,900	By Dipa Ltd.	7,67,000
		By Debentureholders	12,500
	9,53,700		9,53,700

Equity Shareholders A/c

Particular	Rs	Particular	Rs
To shares in Dipa Ltd	4000	By Share Capital	4,00,000
To shares in Dipa Ltd	3,90,000	By General Reserve	50,000
To Bank	1,79,500	By Profit & Loss A/c	5,600
		By Dividend Equalisation Fund	24,000
		By Realisation	93,900
	5,73,500		5,73,500

Cash Bank A/c

Particular	Rs	Particular	Rs
To Dipa Ltd.	9,500	By Realisation	1,500
To Shares in Dipa Ltd	1,26,000	By Equity Shareholders	1,79,500
To Realisation	45,500		
	1,81,000		1,81,000

5% Debenturesholder A/c

Particular	Rs	Particular	Rs
To 7% Debentures in Dipa Ltd.	2,37,500	By 5% Debentures	2,50,000
To Realisation A/c	12,500		
	2,50,000		2,50,000

Opening Journal Entries in the books of Dipa Ltd

Date	Particulars		L.F.	Dr. Rs.	Cr. Rs.
1)	Business Purchase A/c	Dr.		17,67,000	
	To Liquidator of Rupa Ltd				17,67,000
2)	Building A/c	Dr.		1,70,000	
	Plant & Machinery A/c	Dr.		4,00,000	
	Debtors A/c	Dr.		1,40,500	
	Stock A/c	Dr.		80,700	
	Bank A/c	Dr.		16,500	
	Good will A/c	Dr.		88,000	
	To Creditors A/c				1,28,700
	To Business Purchase A/c				7,67,000
3)	Liquidator of Rupa Ltd A/c	Dr		7,67,000	
	To Equity Share Capital A/c (8000 × 60)				4,80,000
	To Share Premium A/c (8000 × 5)				40,000
	To 7% Debentures A/c				2,37,500
	To Cash A/c				9,500

Problem No. 11 : The Following are the Balance sheets of Express Limited and Super Fast Limited as on 31st March 2014

Balance sheet of Express Limited as on 31.3.2014

Liabilities	Rs.	Assets	Rs
Share Capital		Good will	1,00,000
10,000 Equity Shares of		Fixed Assets	7,50,000
Rs. 100 each	10,00,000	Stock	2,60,000
5% Debentures (Rs. 100 each)	2,50,000	Debtors	2,00,000
Creditors	3,60,000	Profit & Loss A/c	3,00,000
	16,10,000		16,10,000

Balance Sheet of Super Fast Ltd. as on 31-3-2014

Liabilities	Rs.	Assets	Rs.
Authorised Capital		Good will	1,50,000
20,000 Equity Shares of		Fixed Assets	12,00,000
Rs. 100 each	20,00,000	Stock	2,50,000
Issued Capital		Debtors	2,00,000
15,000 Equity Shares of		Cash and Bank	2,00,000
Rs. 100 each	15,00,000		
Profit & Loss A/c	2,00,000		
Creditors	3,00,000		
	20,00,000		20,00,000

Super Fast Limited agreed to absorb Express Limited upon the following terms

1) Payment of cash of Rs. 15 for every share in Express Limited.
2) The shareholders of Express Limited to receive one share in Super Fast Limited for every two shares held by them.
3) Payment in cash at Rs. 110 for every debentureholder in full discharge of debentures.
4) Expenses of liquidation amounted to Rs. 10,000 Which were paid by Super fast Ltd. (not included in purchase consideration)

You are required to :

a) Prepare Realisation A/c, Super Fast Ltd A/c, Equity Shares in Super Fast Ltd A/c, Cash A/c, Equity Shareholders A/c, 5% Debentureholders A/c in the books of Express Limited.
b) Pass Opening entries in the books of Super Fast Limited and prepare Balance Sheet of Super Fast Limited after absorption. **(Oct. 2012 - PUP)**

Solution :

Statement of Purchase Consideration

Particulars	Rs.
1) Cash Payment to Shareholders (15 × 10,000)	1,50,000
2) Issue of Shares in Superfast Ltd. to Share holder. (5000 × 100)	5,00,000
3) Cash Payment to Debenture holders	2,75,000
Purchase Considration	9,25,000

In the Books of Express Ltd.
Realisation A/c

To Good will	1,00,000	By Creditors	3,60,000
To Fix Assets	7,50,000	By Super Fast Ltd	9,25,000
To stock	2,60,000		
To Debtors	2,00,000	By Eq. Shareholder A/c	50,000
To 5% Debentureholders A/c	25,000		
	13,35,000		13,35,000

Super Fast Ltd A/c

To Realisation A/c	9,25,000	By Share in Super Fast Ltd A/c	5,00,000
		By Cash A/c	4,25,000
	9,25,000		9,25,000

Equity Shares in Super Fast Ltd A/c

To Super Fast Ltd	5,00,000	By Equity Shareholder A/c	5,00,000
	5,00,000		5,00,000

Cash A/c

To Super Fast Ltd	4,25,000	By Eq. Shareholder A/c	1,50,000
		By Debentureholder	2,75,000
	4,25,000		4,25,000

5% Debenture A/c

To Cash A/c	2,75,000	By 5% Debenture A/c	2,50,000
		By Realisation A/c	25,000
	2,75,00		2,75,000

Eq. Share Holder A/c

To P & L A/c	3,00,000	By Eq. Share Capital A/c	10,00,000
To Share in Super fast Ltd A/c	5,00,000		
To Cash A/c	1,50,000		
To Realisation A/c	50,000		
	10,00,000		10,00,000

Opening Enteries in the Books of Superfast Ltd.

Date	Particulas	L.F.	Debit Rs.	Credit Rs.
1)	Business Purchase A/c		9,25,000	
	To Liquidator of Express Ltd A/c			9,25,000
2)	Fixed Assets A/c Dr.		7,50,000	
	Stock A/c Dr.		2,60,000	
	Debtors A/c Dr.		2,00,000	
	Good will A/c Dr.		75,000	
	To Business Purchase A/c			9,25,000
	To Creditors A/c			3,60,000
3)	Liquidator of Express Ltd A/c Dr.		9,25,000	
	To Share Capital A/c			5,00,000
	To Bank A/c			4,25,000
4)	Good will A/c Dr.		10,000	
	To Bank A/c			10,000

Balance Sheet of Super Fast Ltd A/c

Liabilities	Rs	Assets	Rs
Share Capital		Good will	2,35,000
Authorised Capital		Fixed Assets	19,50,000
20,000 Shares of	20,00,000	Debtors	4,00,000
Rs. 100 each		Stock	5,10,000
Issued and Subscribed			
20,000 Shares of Rs. 100 each	20,00,000		
Profit and loss A/c	2,00,000		
Bank Over draft	2,35,000		
(2,00,000 + 35,000)			
Crditors	6,60,000		
	30,95,000		30,95,000

6.3 EXERCISES

Objective Type Questions.

(a) Fill in the gaps.

1) Absorption means... Liquidation and one...
2) The amount payable by purchasing company to vendor company is called...

Ans : (1) One, formation, (2) Purchase consideration,

(b) State Whether the following statement are True or False.

1) Purchasing company is also knows as vendee company.
2) Outsiders liabilities are transferred to shareholders account.
3) The term trade liabilities includes debentures and outstanding salaries.
4) A new company is formed in case of absorption.

Ans : (1) True, (2) False, (3) False, (4) False.

(c) Select the most appropriate answer.

1) Accumulated profit includes :
   (a) Provision for doubtful debts.
   (b) Insurance Fund,
   (c) Employee's provident Fund.
2) Preliminary expenses are transferred by the vendor company at the time of absorption to :
   (a) Purchasing Company's account,
   (b) Realisation Account,
   (c) Equity Shareholders account.

Ans : (1) b, (2) c

Problems on Absorption

1) The Engineers Ltd. agreed to acquire the goodwill and assets, other than cash of Stainless Ltd. as on 31st March, 2014. A summary of the Balance Sheet of Stainless Ltd. as on 31st March, 2014 was as follows :

Liabilities	Rs.	Assets	Rs.
Share capital in Rs. 10/-		Goodwill	50,000
Equity share fully paid	5,00,000	Land, Building & Plant	6,70,000
General Reserve	1,80,000	Stock	1,04,000
Profit & Loss A/c	90,000	Debtors	38,000
8% Debentures	1,00,000	Cash	28,000
Creditors	20,000		
	8,90,000		8,90,000

The consideration payable by Engineers Ltd. was agreed as follows :

1. A cash payment equivalent to Rs. 5/- for every Rs. 10/- Equity Shares in Stainless Ltd.
2. The issue of 80,000 Rs. 10/- Equity Shares fully paid in Engineers Ltd. having an agreed value of Rs. 12.50 per share.
3. The issue of such an amount of fully paid 6% Debentures of Engineers Ltd. at Rs. 96/- as is sufficient to discharge the 8% Debentures of Stainless Ltd. at Rs. 120. The liabilities of Stainless Ltd. other than Debentures were discharged by that company.

When computing the agreed consideration, the directors of Engineers Ltd. valued the Land, Building and Plant at Rs. 11,50,000. The stock at Rs. 90,000 and the debtors at the amount stated on the Balance Sheet of Stainless Ltd. subject to allowance of 5% to cover doubtful debts. On the sales of its assets stainless Ltd. went into liquidation, the Equity Shareholders receiving cash and Equity Shares in Engineers Ltd. as repayments of their capital in Stainless Ltd.

You are required to draft the Journal entries, (a) To record the acquisition in the books of Engineers Ltd., (b) To close the books of Stainless Ltd.

Ans : - Purchase Consideration   Rs. 13,70,000

Realisations   Rs. 4,88,000

2) The summarised Balance Sheets of the Thick Ltd. and Thin Ltd. on 31st March, 2014 were as follows :

Liabilities	Thick Ltd. Rs.	Thin Ltd. Rs.	Assets	Thick Ltd. Rs.	Thin Ltd. Rs.
Shares of Rs. 10 each fully paid	2,00,000	1,50,000	Goodwill	-	30,000
			Fixed Assets	1,60,000	50,000
Trade Liabilities	25,000	60,000	Floating Assets	95,000	80,000
Profit & Loss A/c	30,000	-	Profit & Loss A/c	-	50,000
	2,55,000	2,10,000		2,55,000	2,10,000

The management of Thick Ltd. resolved to take over the business of Thin Ltd. with effects from April, 1st 2014. The shareholders of the company agreed to accept shares in the former company on the basis that the shares of Thick Ltd. were worth Rs. 12.50 each and that the shares of Thin Ltd. were worth Rs. 5 each. The purchasing company took over the fixed assets of Thin Ltd. together with the floating assets and the liabilities.

Assuming the necessary formalities were carried out, make journal entries necessary for these transactions in the books of Thick Ltd. and draw up its Balance Sheet immediately after the merger.

Ans : Purchase Consideration Rs. 75,000

B/S Total Rs. 3,85,000

3) Long Ltd. has agreed to acquire goodwill and assets (except investments) of Short Ltd. as at 31st March 2014. The Balance Sheet of Short Ltd. as on that date was as follows :

Liabilities	Rs.	Assets	Rs.
Share Capital	1,60,000	Goodwill	20,000
16,000 Equity shares of		Land and Buildings	80,000
Rs. 10 each		Plant	80,000
General Reserve	25,000	Investments	30,000
Profit & Loss A/c	18,000	Stock	40,000
8% Debentures	60,000	Debtors	50,000
Creditors	37,000	Bank	20,000
Provision for Taxation	20,000		
	3,20,000		3,20,000

Long Ltd. will :

1. Discharge the Debentures @ 8% premium by issue of 7% Debentures in Long Ltd. at 10% discount.

2. Issue 3 shares of Long Ltd. at market price of Rs. 11 for 2 shares of Short Ltd.

3. Pay Rupee 2 in cash for each share of Short Ltd.

4. Pay absorption expenses Rs. 3,000.

   Short Ltd. sells the investments for Rs. 32,000, one-third of the shares received from Long Ltd. are sold @ Rs. 10.50 each. Tax liability is determined at Rs.24,000. Before transfer Short Ltd., declares and pays 10% Dividend.

   Long Ltd. values Land & Buildings at Rs. 1,00,000. Plant at 10% below book value, stock at Rs. 35,000 and Debtors subject to 5% Provision.

   Show 1. Ledger Accounts in the books of Short Ltd.

   2. Journal Entries in the books of Long Ltd.

Ans : - 1) Purchase consideration Rs. 3,63,800

   Realisation profit Rs. 76,000.

4) The Assets of Rukmini Company Limited are purchased by the Shrikrishna Company Limited. The purchase consideration was agreed upon as under :

(a) A cash payment of Rs. 90/- per share for shares held by the members in the vendor company.

(b) Settlement of Debentures in the Rukmini Company Limited by repayments at Rs. 550/- per Debenture held.

(c) To exchange four shares of Shrikrishna Company Limited of Rs. 75/- each, quoted in the market at Rs. 140/- each for one share held by the members in the vendor company.

(d) Payments of Realisation expenses Rs. 12,000.

The Balance Sheet of Rukmini Company Limited as on 31st March, 2014 was as follows :

Capital & Liabilities	Rs.	Property & Assets		Rs.
Share Capital :		Land & Buildings		10,00,000
6,000 Equity Shares of		Plant & Machinery		16,00,000
Rs. 500 each fully paid	30,00,000	Furniture & Fixtures		3,10,000
Insurance Fund	65,000	Vehicles		2,40,000
General Reserve	2,75,000	Stock on Hand		8,10,000
Profit & Loss A/c	60,000	Bills Receivable		1,90,000
1,300 7%s Debenture of		Sundry Debtors	3,00,000	
Rs. 500 each	6,50,000	Less : Provision		
Sundry Creditors	1,10,000	For Doubtful Debts	35,000	2,65,000
Bills Payable	1,40,000	Cash in Hand		85,000
Bank Overdraft	2,00,000			
	45,00,000			45,00,000

You are required to prepare in the books of accounts of Rukmini Company Limited : (a) Realisation Account, (b) Equity Shareholders Account and (c) Cash Account and Journal Entries in the Books of the Purchasing Company including entries for cash.

Ans:- Purchase Consideration Rs.   30,67,000
Realisation Loss Rs.   15,10,000.

5) The following is the Balance Sheet of Pandurang Ltd. as on 31st March 2014.

Liabilities	Rs.	Assets	Rs.
Share Capital-		Goodwill	35,000
2,000 Shares of Rs. 100		Land & Building	85,000
each	2,00,000	Plant & ,Machinery	1,60,000
Reserve Fund	20,000	Stock	55,000
5% Debentures	1,00,000	Sundry Debtors	65,000
Loan from A (a director)	40,000	Cash & Bank	34,000
Sundry Creditors	80,000	Discount on Debentures	6,000
Total Rs.	4,40,000	Total Rs.	4,40,000

The business of the company is taken over by Eshwar company Ltd. as on that date on the following terms :

a) Eshwar Co. to take over all assets except cash, to value the assets at book values less 10% except Goodwill which is to be valued at 4 years' purchase of the excess of average (5 years) profits over 8% of the combined amount of share capital and reserves.

b) Eshwar Co. to take over trade liabilities which was subject to a discount of 5%.

c) The purchase consideration was to be discharged in cash to the extent of Rs. 1,50,000, and the balance in fully paid equity shares of Rs. 10 each valued at Rs. 12.50 per share. The average of the five years' profit was Rs. 30,100/-. The expenses of absorption Rs. 4,000 were paid by Pandurang Co. Ltd; but afterwards reimbursed by Eshwar Co. Ltd.

Show the necessary ledger accounts in the books of Pandurang Co. Ltd. and the working of Purchase consideration.

Ans :- Purchase Consideration   3,02,500
Realisation Loss A/c   17,500

6) The following is the Balance Sheet of Small Ltd. as on 31st March 2014.

Liabilities	Rs.	Assets	Rs.
4,000 Equity shares of	4,00,000	Buildings	1,70,000
Rs. 100 each		Plant & Machinery	4,00,000
General Reserve	50,000	Investments	50,600
Profit & Loss A/c	5,600	Debtors	1,40,500
5% Debentures	2,50,000	Stock	80,700
Creditors	1,28,700	Cash At Bank	16,500
Dividend Equilisation Ltd.	24,000		
	8,58,300		8,58,300

Small Ltd. was absorbed by Big Ltd. on the above on the following terms and conditions. Big Ltd. to

a) Assume all liabilities and to acquire all assets excepts investments which were sold by small Ltd. for Rs. 45,500/-

b) Discharge the debenture debt at a discount of 5% by issue of 7%s Debentures in Big Ltd.

c) Issue two shares of Rs. 60 each in Big Ltd. at Rs. 65 per share and also pay Rs. 2 in cash to the shareholders of Small Ltd. in exchange for one share in small Ltd.

d) Pay the cost of absorption Rs. 1,500.

With the consents of the shareholders, the liquidator of Small Ltd. sold off in open market, one-fourth of the shares received from Big Ltd. at the average rate of Rs. 63 per share.

Prepare :

i) Statement of purchase consideration.

ii) Realisation A/c.

iii) Shareholders' A/c.

iv) Bank A/c.

in the books of Small Ltd. (P.U.)

Ans : 1) Purchase consideration Rs. 7,67,000

2) Realisation Profit Rs. 93,900.

7) Abhay Ltd. is absorbed by Bharat Ltd. as 31st March 2014, when the Balance Sheet of Abhay Ltd. was as follows :

Liabilities	Rs.	Assets	Rs.
Share Capital -		Land & Building	17,50,000
20,000 Equity Shares		Plant & Machinery	18,00,000
of Rs. 100 each fully paid	20,00,000	Stock	2,00,000
Sinking Fund	3,00,000	Debtors	3,60,000
Share Premium	1,50,000	Sinking Fund investment	3,00,000
Provident Fund	1,50,000	Cash at Bank	30,000
Employees' Saving	3,00,000		
Sundry Creditors	1,40,000		
8% Debentures	4,00,000		
6% Debentures	10,00,000		
Total Rs.	44,40,000	Total Rs.	44,40,000

The purchase consideration for absorption was agreed as under :

a) Taking over of all liabilities.

b) Payment of cost of absorption not exceeding Rs. 8,000/-

c) Repayment of 6% Debentures at 5% premium.

d) Discharge of 8% Debentures at 10% premium by issue of 5% Debentures in Bharat Ltd.

e) A payment of Rs. 15 per share in cash and an allotment of one 7% preference share of Rs. 100 each and 5 equity shares of Rs. 100 each in Bharat Ltd. for every four shares in Abhay Ltd.

Actual cost of absorption was Rs. 10,000/- you are required to present necessary accounts in the books of Abhay Ltd. and opening entries in the books of Bharat Ltd.

(P.U.)

Ans : Purchase Consideration Rs. 47,98,000

Realisation profit Rs. 8,48,000.

CHAPTER 7

Reconstruction of Joint Stock Company

7.1 Meaning of Reconstruction

The term 'reconstruction' means reorganising the capital structure of a company including the reduction of the claims of both shareholders and creditors against the company. Such a reconstruction generally becomes necessary on account of bad financial position of a company. The reconstruction may be of following two types :-

i) External Reconstruction

ii) Internal Reconstruction

Internal Reconstruction :

In case of internal reconstruction, neither the old company is liquidated nor a new company is formed. To facilitate this process of internal reconstruction, the existing capital structure of the company is re-organised to infuse new life into it. The claims of various parties, viz. creditors, debentureholders, shareholders are suitably adjusted to write off accumulated losses, fictitious assets etc. In short, the existing company reconstitutes its capital structure and continues to carry on its business. The internal reconstruction is simpler than external reconstruction. The main objective of internal reconstruction is to write off miscellaneous expenses like preliminary expenses, Discount on issue of shares and debentures and underwriting commission etc. These assets are treated as 'lost capital' and hence capital reduction is required. Another objective of internal reconstruction is to write off fictitious assets like goodwill, patents etc. The reconstructed company may be in a position to carry forward its losses for income tax purposes against future profits. This will considerably reduce the income tax liability of the company in periods when good profits are made by it.

Internal reduction may require :
1) Alteration of Share Capital.
2) Reduction in Share Capital.

7.2 Alteration of Share Capital :

The Companies Act has used the word "Alteration Proper" for alteration of share capital. Alteration of share capital can be done under the provisions of Sections 94 to 97 of the Companies Act. The term alteration proper includes the following : –

1) Increase in share capital by issue of new shares.
2) Consolidation or sub-division of existing shares into shares of larger or smaller denomination.
3) Conversion of fully-paid shares into stocks and vice versa.
4) Cancellation of un-issued shares.

Alteration in share capital can be made by passing ordinary resolution, only if it is authorised by Articles of Association to do so. This change of alteration of capital must be communicated to the Registrar within 30 days of the date of passing the ordinary resolution.

Accounting Entries for Alteration of Share Capital :

1) Increase in share capital : This is similar to making a fresh issue of share capital and usual entries are to be passed for the increase in share capital.

2) Consolidation and conversion of shares into stock : In case of consolidation of shares, shares of smaller denominations are to be converted into shares of larger denomination. In such a case, the paid-up capital remains the same but the number of shares is reduced. For example : if the equity share capital Rs.1,00,000 of Rs.10 each, are to be consolidated into shares of Rs. 100 each, the entry will be as under :-

Equity share capital (Rs.10) Dr.   1,00,000
    To Equity share capital (Rs.100)   1,00,000
(Being conversion of 10,000 equity shares of
Rs.10 each into 1,000 shares of Rs.100 each)

3) Sub-division of shares : In case of sub-division of shares, larger denominations are converted into shares of smaller denominations. The journal entry in respect of such a conversion would be on the same pattern as explained in the case of consolidation of shares except that the number of shares would increase. For example : A company having equity share capital of Rs.1,00,000 divided into shares of Rs.100 each decides to convert it into shares of Rs.10 each, the journal entry will be as under :-

Equity Share Capital A/c (Rs. 100) ..... Dr.   1,00,000
   To Equity Share Capital A/c (Rs.10)   1,00,000
(Being conversion of 1,000 shares of Rs.100
each into 10,000 equity shares of Rs.10 each)

4) Conversion of shares into stock : A Company may convert its fully paid-up shares into stock or vice versa. In case, shares are converted into stock, the entry will be as under :-

Share Capital A/c .....Dr.
   To Capital Stock A/c
(Being conversion of shares into stock)

5) Cancellation of un-issued shares : As the un-issued shares are not recorded in the books of accounts, no entry is required to cancel them. Only the unauthorised capital is to be reduced to the extent of shares cancelled.

7.3 Reduction of Share Capital i.e. Internal Reconstruction

A Company can reduce its share capital as per provision of Sections 100 to 105 of the Companies Act. In order to effect share capital reduction, the following formalities must be completed :-

1) The Company must be authorised by its Articles of Association to reduce share capital. If there is no provision in the articles in this respect, it must pass a special resolution to alter its Articles of Association.

2) The Company must pass a special resolution to reduce share capital.

3) The Company must file a petition in the Court for seeking an order as regards confirming the reduction. If the Court is satisfied that the creditor's interest have been secured, it may confirm the reduction. However, it may impose the terms and conditions including a direction that the word "And Reduced" should be added after the name of the company for a certain period of time and that the company should publish the reasons for such reduction thereto. If the company fails to add the words **"And Reduced"**, a penalty of Rs.500 is payable.

4) The Company has to deliver to the Registrar, a certified copy of the Court's order and minutes approved by the Court showing the details of the shares for registration.

5) The Registrar will then register the order and the minutes.

6) After registration of these, the resolution to reduce capital shall take effect.

7) Notice of the registration shall be published in such a manner as the court may direct.

Causes for Internal Reconstruction

Following are the causes of capital reduction or internal reconstruction :-

1) Heavy accumulated losses
2) Over-valuation of assets
3) Declining turnover or profitability

4) Fall in the value of assets.

5) Increase in fictitious assets.

6) Future financial needs.

Forms of Capital Reduction

The reduction of share capital may take any of the following forms :-

a) Writing-off lost capital.

b) Refunding surplus of paid-up capital.

c) Reducing liability of members for uncalled capital.

7.4 Accounting Entries

a) Writing off lost capital

Internal reconstruction means the reduction of share capital to cancel any paid share capital which is lost i.e. not represented by the real value of assets. For example : The following is the balance sheet of a company.

Balance Sheet

Liabilities	Rs.	Assets	Rs.
7,000 shares of Rs.10 each	70,000	Fixed Assets	40,000
Creditors	30,000	Current Assets	30,000
		Profit & Loss A/c	10,000
		Goodwill	20,000
	1,00,000		1,00,000

The above balance sheet shows that the company has lost Rs. 30,000 (i.e. P & L A/C Rs. 10,000 + Goodwill Rs. 20,000) of its paid-up share capital. This will be written off by the help of following journal entry :-

Share Capital A/c .... Dr   30,000

   To Capital Reduction A/c   30,000

(Being loss of capital)

The share capital now stands reduced to Rs. 40,000. However, this reduction of share capital can be effected in two ways : One alternative could be only to reduce the paid-up value of the existing shares from Rs. 10 to Rs. 4 each without reducing the nominal value of the shares. This means the shareholders can be asked in future to pay Rs. 6 more, if the company requires additional capital. The journal entry in such a case will be the same as explained above.

Generally, the shareholders will be unwilling for the above alternative, since it puts an additional burden on them. Other alternative, can therefore be, to reduce both nominal as well as paid up value of shares to Rs. 4/- each. In such a case, the journal entry will be as under :

Share Capital A/c (Rs. 10)	...... Dr.	70,000	
To Share Capital A/c (Rs. 4)			40000
To Capital Reduction A/c			30,000
(Being value of share reduced to Rs. 4 each)			

b) Refunding Surplus paid-up capital

If a company has more funds than what it can profitably use, then it may decide to refund the surplus capital to shareholders. For example : A Company has a share capital of Rs. 1,00,000 divided into shares of Rs. 10 each and it decides to repay to its members Rs. 2 per share and make share as of Rs. 8 each fully paid. The journal entry will be as under :-

Share Capital A/c (Rs. 10)	... Dr	1,00,000	
To Share Capital A/c (Rs. 8)			80,000
To Bank A/c			20,000
(Being value of each share reduced to Rs. 8)			

c) Uncalled capital to be cancelled

In case the liability of members in respect of uncalled share capital is reduced, the paid-up value of the share capital will remain unchanged. However, the members will stand to gain since they will not have to pay money to the company to the extent of uncalled capital cancelled. For example : A company has a share capital of Rs. 1,00,000, divided into shares of Rs. 10 each called-up and paid-up Rs. 5 each. The company decides to cancel the liability of members to the extent of Rs. 5 per share thus making Rs. 5 paid-up. For this, following journal entry will be passed -

Share Capital A/c (Rs. 10)	Dr	50,000	
To Share Capital A/c (Rs. 5)			50,000
(Being uncalled capital cancelled)			

Note : In this case, no amount of capital is reduced and transferred to Capital Reduction Account

d) Surrender of Shares

In a reconstruction scheme, the shareholder may be required to surrender a part of their holding. Such a surrender can either be for immediate cancellation of the share capital or for issue of shares surrendered to some of the creditors of the company in satisfaction of their claims. The following accounting entries are to be passed in case of surrender of shares.

a) On Surrender of Shares
    Share Capital A/c   ..... Dr
       To Shares Surrendered A/c

b) On re-issue of Surrendered Shares
    Shares Surrendered A/c   ..... Dr
       To Share Capital A/c

c) On Cancellation of Surrendered Shares
    Shares Surrendered A/c   ..... Dr
       To Capital Reduction A/c

If a creditor or any other claimant reduces his claim, and in consideration, some of the shares surrendered are issued to him, the Capital Reduction Account is to be credited by the amount of claim waived by the creditor, irrespective of the consideration of shares surrendered issued to him. For e.g. If a creditor for Rs. 60,000 reduces his claim to Rs. 40,000 and in consideration, he is given shares surrendered amounting to Rs. 14,000, the Capital Reduction Account is to be credited with Rs. 20,000 (i.e. 60,000 less 40,000 reduction in his claim) and not by 6,000. It means the issue of shares surrendered Rs. 14,000 is not taken into account. Further, if a creditor agrees to accept additional shares surrendered of Rs. 10,000 in part payment of Rs. 40,000, this amount of Rs. 10,000 is also credited to Capital Reduction Account and the claim for creditors will be shown at Rs. 30,000 in the Balance Sheet. The entry for this will be as under :–

        Creditors A/c   .... Dr.   30,000
            To Capital Reduction A/c   30,000
        (Being reduction of the claims of creditors from Rs. 60,000 to Rs. 30,000)

Journal Entries

1) **On reduction of paid-up capital**
   Share Capital (old face value) A/c   ....Dr
       To Share Capital (new face value) A/c
       To Capital Reduction (with difference) A/c
   (Being face value changed and paid-up value of shares reduced)

2) **For reduction in shares without change in face value of shares.**
   Share Capital A/c   ....Dr
       To Capital Reduction A/c (with the amount of reduction)
   (Being capital reduced without change in the face value)

3) **If any sacrifice has been made by creditor i.e. reduction in the amount of credit.**
   Creditors A/c   ..... Dr
       To Capital Reduction A/c
   (Being liability on creditors reduced)

4) **For reduction in the amount of debentures or sacrifice made by debentureholders**
   Debentures A/c (with sacrifice)   .....Dr.
   Outstanding Interest on Debentures A/c (if any)   .....Dr
       To Capital Reduction A/c
   (Being liability of debentures reduced)

5) **For the appreciation in the value of Asset**
   Asset A/c (with appreciation)   .....Dr
       To Capital Reduction A/c
   (Being appreciation in the value of asset)

6) When the amount of capital reduction is utilised for writing off fictitious assets, past losses and excess value of other assets

Capital Reduction A/c	.....Dr

To Profit & Loss A/c
To Goodwill A/c
To Preliminary Expenses A/c
To Discount on issue of Shares or Debentures A/c
To Patents and Trademarks A/c
To Plant and Machinery A/c
To Land & Building A/c
To Stock A/c
To Debtors A/c
To Other Assets A/c
To Capital Reserve A/c (It any balance is left)
(Being the balance of capital reduced utilised for uniting off assets and losses)

7) For transfer of Reserves & Surplus, Share premium to Capital Reduction A/c

General Reserve or Reserve A/c	.... Dr
Profit & Loss A/c (credit balance) A/c	.... Dr
Share Premium A/c	.... Dr

To Capital Reserve A/c
(Being reserves and surplus and share premium account transferred)

8) For Sale of an asset

i) Sale of asset **at profit**

Bank A/c	.... Dr

To Asset A/c
To Capital Reduction A/c (Profit on Asset)
(Being asset sold on profit)

or

ii) Sale of an asset **at a loss**

Bank A/c	.... Dr
Capital Reduction A/c	.... Dr (with loss)

To Asset A/c
(Being asset sold at a loss)

9) Contingent liability paid

a)

Contingent Liability A/c	.... Dr

To Bank A/c
(Being contingent liability paid)

b)

Capital Reduction A/c	..... Dr

To Contingent Liability A/c
(Being loss on payment of contingent liability transferred.)

10) For payment of recorded liability
Liability A/c   ...... Dr
    To Bank A/c
(Being liability paid)

11) For payment of unrecorded liability
  i) Unrecorded liability A/c   ....Dr
      To Bank A/c
  (Being payment of unrecorded liability)
  ii) Capital Reduction A/c   ...... Dr.
      To Unrecorded Liability
  (Being balance of unrecorded liability transferred to capital reduction account)

12) For selling of unrecorded asset
  i) Bank A/c   .... Dr
      To Unrecorded Assets A/c
  ii) Unrecorded Asset A/c   ...... Dr
      To Capital Reduction A/c
  (Being balance of unrecorded asset transferred to capital reduction account)

13) For payment of Reconstruction Expenses
Capital Reduction A/c   ..... Dr
    To Bank A/c

14) For provision for taxation utilised for capital reduction
Provision for Taxation A/c   .... Dr
    To Capital A/c
(Being balances utilised for capital reduction)

15) For exchange of new debentures for old debentures
Debentures (old) A/c   .... Dr
    To Debenture (New) A/c
(Being debentures exchanged)

16) For Issue of new shares for cash
Bank A/c   .... Dr
    To Share Capital A/c
(Being fresh shares issued)

17) For assets given to loan creditors
Loan Creditors A/c   .... Dr
    To Asset A/c
(Being asset given to loan creditors.)

18) For changing the rate of dividend on preference shares
Preference Share Capital (old rate) A/c   ..... Dr
    To Preference Share Capital (New rate) A/c.
    (Being rate fo dividend on preference Share changed)

19) For arrears of preference share dividend cancelled -
* No Entry

20) For arrears of preference dividend are settled by issue of shares or cash -
Capital Reduction A/c   .... Dr
    To Cash A/c
    To Shares A/c
(Being arrears of dividend settled)

21) For penalty paid
Capital Reduction A/c   ..... Dr
    To Bank A/c
(Being penalty paid)

22) For fees refunded by directors
Bank A/c   ..... Dr
    To Capital Reduction A/c
(Being fees refunded by directors)

23) For taking over assets / shares by debentureholders
Debentureholders A/c   ... Dr
    To Asset A/c
    To Share Capital A/c
(Being assets / share taken by debentureholders)

24) For exchange of preference shares to equity share capital or debentures -
Preference Share Capital A/c   .... Dr
    To Equity Share Capital
    To Debentures A/c
(Being exchange of shares for debentures)

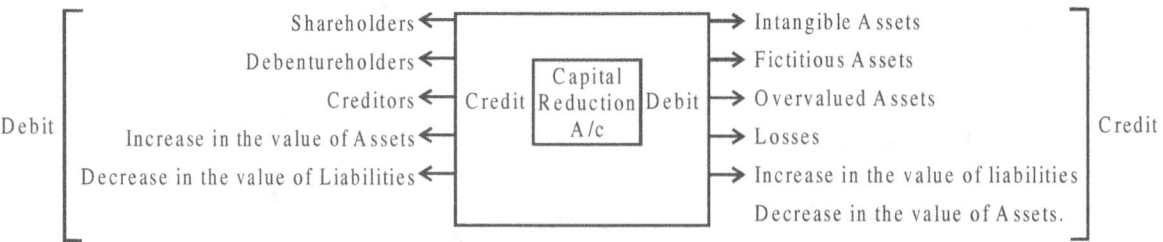

7.5 Capital Reduction Account

Capital reduction account is opened at the time of internal reconstruction of a company. The capital reduction account represents the sacrifice made by the different parties, i.e. shareholders, debentureholders and creditors. This sacrifice is used for writing off accumulated losses, intangible assets, over-valuation of assets etc. Similarly, any appreciation in the value of asset, capital profits etc are credited to this account. The balance of this account is transferred to capital reserve. If this account has no balance, it automatically tallies.

Proforma of Capital Reduction Account

Capital Reduction Account

Dr   Cr.

Particulars	Rs.	Particulars	Rs.

To P & L A/c
   (Loss written off)
To Goodwill A/c
   (Written off)
To Preliminary Expenses A/c
   (Written off)
To Discount on issue of
   Shares or Debentures
   (Written off)
To Asset A/c
   (Decrease in value)
To Bank A/c
   (Payment of unrecorded
   liability / reconstruction exp.)
To Bank A/c
   (Refund of Directors' fees)
To Capital Reserves A/c
   (Balancing figure)
		By Share Capital A/c
		   (Reduction in capital)
		By Debentures A/c
		   (Reduction in debentures)
		By Creditors
		   (Sacrifice of creditors)
		By Asset A/c
		   (Increase in the value)
		By Bank A/c
		   (Sale of unrecorded asset)	

7.6 Preparation of Balance Sheet after Internal Reconstruction

After implementation of Capital Reduction Scheme, the balance sheet is prepared by considering the changes in the assets and liabilities. There must be the word **"And Reduced"** after the name of the balance sheet of ..... Co Ltd. as on .....

For example : Balance Sheet (and Reduced) as on.....

Generally, the following points should be taken into consideration while preparing the balance sheet :-

1) The capital reduced is shown at reduced paid-up value.
2) The liabilities reduced are shown at reduced value. If some liabilities are paid, they will not be shown in the Balance Sheet.
3) All fictitious assets are not shown.
4) Intangible assets written off are not shown.
5) Past losses / accumulated losses are not shown.
6) Tangible assets are shown at reduced figures.
7) The assets and liabilities which are not affected by capital reduction scheme are intact

and they are shown by their original values.
8) Change in authorised capital is shown in the Balance Sheet. Of course, no entry is passed for change in the authorised capital.
9) The balance of Capital Reserve is shown on the liability side of Balance Sheet.
10) If any call made, it increases the cash at bank as well as paid value of capital.

Important Note :

Under the capital reduction scheme, the words "To" and "By" play a very important role. They should not be misinterpreted. The word "To" implies the reduction as required to that amount. For example : If a share of Rs. 10 is reduced to Rs. 3, it means there is a reduction (10-3) of Rs. 7 per share and the paid-up capital will be Rs. 3 per share. The word "By" implies that there is a reduction by the amount given. For example : If a share of Rs. 10 is reduced by Rs. 7 per share, it means there is a reduction of Rs. 7 per share and the paid-up value will be Rs. 3 per share.

7.7 Problems on Internal Reconstruction

Problem No. 1 : The Balance Sheet of "S". Co. Ltd. as on 31st March 2014 was as follows :

Liabilities	Rs.	Assets	Rs.
Share Capital		Goodwill	15,000
2,000 Preference Shares of		Freehold Properties	2,00,000
Rs. 100 each	2,00,000	Plant and Machinery	3,00,000
4,000 Equity Shares of		Stock-in-trade	50,000
Rs. 100 each	4,00,000	Debtors	40,000
5% Mortgage Debentures	1,00,000	Profit and Loss A/c	2,45,000
Bank Overdraft	50,000		
Creditors	1,00,000		
	8,50,000		8,50,000

The company got the following scheme of capital reduction approved by the Court :
1. The Preference Shares to be reduced to Rs. 75 per share; fully paid-up and the Equity Shares to Rs. 37.50.
2. The debentureholders took over the stock-in-trade and the book debts in full satisfaction of the amount due to them.
3. The Goodwill Account to be eliminated.
4. The freehold properties to be depreciated by 50%
5. The value of the Plant and Machinery to be increased by Rs. 50,000

Pass the journal entries required to record the effect of the order of the Court and to draw up an amended Balance Sheet and Capital Reduction Account. **(P.U.)**

Solution

In the Books of "S" Co. Ltd.
Journal Entries

Date	Particulars	L.F.	Dr. Rs.	Cr. Rs.
2014 Mar.31	Preference Share Capital A/c Dr. To capital Reduction A/c (Being the reduction of 2,000 preference shares of Rs. 100 to an equal number of shares of Rs. 75 each)		50,000	50,000
Mar. 31	Equity Share Capital A/c Dr. To Capital Reduction A/c (Being the reduction of 4,000 equity shares of Rs. 100 each to an equal number of shares of Rs. 37.50 each)		2,50,000	2,50,000
Mar. 31	Debenture A/c Dr. To Stock-in-trade A/c To Debtors A/c To Capital Reduction A/c (Being stock and debtor taken over by debentureholders in full satisfaction of their claims)		1,00,000	50,000 40,000 10,000
Mar. 31	Plant and Machinery A/c Dr. To Capital Reduction A/c (Being the appreciation in the value of plant and machinery)		50,000	50,000
Mar. 31	Capital Reduction A/c Dr. To Goodwill A/c To Freehold Properties A/c To Profit and Loss A/c (Being the assets and losses written off out of capital reduction account)		3,60,000	15,000 1,00,000 2,45,000

In the books of "S" Ltd.

Dr.   **Capital Reduction A/c**   Cr.

Particulars	Rs.	Particulars	Rs.
To Goodwill A/c	15,000	By Preference Share Capital A/c	50,000
To Freehold Properties A/c	1,00,000	By Equity Share Capital A/c	2,50,000
To Profit & Loss A/c	2,45,000	By Debentures A/c	10,000
		By Plant & Machinery A/c	50,000
	3,60,000		3,60,000

In the books of "S" Co. Ltd.
Balance Sheet (And Reduced) As at 31st March 2014

Liabilities	Rs.	Assets	Rs.
		Fixed Assets	
Share Capital		Freehold Properties	1,00,000
2,000 Preference		Plant and Machinery	3,50,000
Shares of Rs. 75 each	1,50,000		
4,000 Equity Shares of			
Rs. 37.50 each	1,50,000		
Current Liabilities :			
Bank Overdraft	50,000		
Creditors	1,00,000		
	4,50,000		4,50,000

Problem No. 2 : Uptodate Company Ltd. presents you with the following Balance Sheet as on 31st March 2014.

Liabilities	Rs.	Assets	Rs.
Share Capital :		Goodwill	30,000
Equity Share of Rs. 100		Land & Building	75,000
each, fully paid	2,00,000	Plant & Machinery	1,50,000
7% Preferences Shares		Patents	15,000
of Rs. 100 each	1,50,000	Stock	1,10,000
Profit prior to Incorporation	5,000	Sundry Debtors	75,000
6% Debentures	1,50,000	Cash	2,500
Sundry Creditors	1,00,000	Preliminary Expenses	12,500
		Profit & Loss A/c	1,35,000
	6,05,000		6,05,000

The following scheme of reconstruction was duly approved :
1. 7% Preference Shares be converted into 9% Preference Shares, the amount being reduced by 30%
2. Equity shares be reduced to fully paid shares of Rs. 50 each.
3. Land and Building be appreciated by 20%
4. Debentures be reduced by 20%
5. All intangible assets and fictitious amounts including Patents be written off. Utilise profit prior to incorporation, if necessary.
6. Equity Shareholders to subscribe equity shares of Rs. 50,000. The amount to be utilised for acquiring new Plant and Machinery.

Assuming the whole scheme to have been put through, give journal entries resulting from it and prepare the resultant Balance Sheet.   **(P.U)**

Solution   **Inter Book of Uptodate Co. Ltd.**

Journal Entries

Date	Particulars	L.F.	Dr. Rs.	Cr. Rs.

31.3.2014	7% Preference Share Capital A/c Dr.
	  To 9% Preference Share Capital
	  To Capital Reduction A/c
	(Being 7% preference shares of Rs. 100 each converted into 9% preference shares and reduced to Rs. 70 each.)
			1,50,000	1,05,000
				45,000

31.3.2014	Equity Share Capital A/c Dr. To Capital Reduction A/c (Being equity shares of Rs. 100 each fully paid reduced to Rs. 50 each fully paid)		1,00,000	1,00,000
31.3.2014	Land & Buildings A/c Dr. Debentures A/c Dr. To Capital Reduction A/c (Being land and building appreciated by 20% and debentures reduced to Rs. 1,20,000)		15,000 30,000	45,000

31.3.2014	Capital Reduction A/c Dr.
	Profit prior to Incorporation A/c Dr.
	  To Goodwill A/c
	  To Patents A/c
	  To Preliminary Expenses A/c
	  To Profit & Loss A/c
	(Being intangible and fictitious assets written off)
			1,90,000
			2,500
				30,000
				15,000
				12,500
				1,35,000

Date	Particulars	L.F.	Dr. Rs.	Cr. Rs.
31.3.2014	Bank A/c Dr. To Equity Shares Application & Allotment money A/c (Being application and allotment money received)		50,000	50,000
31.3.2014	Equity Share Application and Allotment A/c Dr. To Equity Shares Capital A/c (Being application and allotment money transferred to share capital account)		50,000	50,000

Balance Sheet of Uptodate Ltd.
as on 1st April 2014 (And Reduced)

Liabilities	Rs.	Assets	Rs.
		Fixed Assets :	
Share Capital :		Land & Building	90,000
Equity Shares of Rs. 50 each	1,50,000	Plant & Machinery	1,50,000
9% Preference Shares		Stock	1,10,000
of Rs. 70 each	1,05,000	Sundry Debtors	75,000
Profit prior to Incorporation	2,500	Cash at Bank	52,500
6% Debentures	1,20,000		
Sundry Creditors	1,00,000		
	4,77,500		4,77,500

Problem No. 3 : Following is the Balance Sheet of Krinti Ltd.

Balance Sheet as at 31.3.2014

Liabilities	Rs.	Assets	Rs.
Share Capital :		Goodwill	50,000
1,500 6% Preference Shares		Debtors	30,200
of Rs. 100 each	1,50,000	Leasehold Property (at cost)	80,000
2,000 Equity Shares of		Plant and Machinery (at cost)	2,10,000
Rs. 100 each	2,00,000	Stock-in-trade	79,175
Capital Reserve	36,000	Profit and Loss A/c	1,10,375
Creditors	42,500	Preliminary Expenses	7,250
Bank Overdraft	51,000		

Liabilities	Rs.	Assets	Rs.
Depreciation Provision :			
Leasehold Property	30,000		
Plant and Machinery	57,500		
	5,67,000		5,67,000

The approval of the Court was obtained for the following scheme for reduction of capital -

i) The Preference Shares to be reduced to Rs. 50 per share.

ii) The Equity shares to be reduced to Rs. 12.50 per share.

iii) The balance in Capital Reserve Account should not be utilised.

iv) Plant and Machinery to be written down to Rs. 75,000.

v) The Profit and Loss Account balance and all intangible assets including preliminary expenses to be written off.

Pass the necessary journal entries in the books of Krinti Ltd. Also prepare Capital Reduction A/c and Balance Sheet.   **(P.U.)**

Solution

Journal Entries in the books of Krinti Ltd.

Date	Particulars	L.F.	Dr. Rs.	Cr. Rs.
2014 Mar. 31	6% Preference Share Capital A/c Dr.		75,000	
	To Capital Reduction A/c			75,000
	(Being reduction of 1,500 preference shares of Rs. 100 each to Rs. 50 each.)			
Mar.31	Equity Share Capital A/c Dr.		1,75,000	
	To Capital Reduction A/c			1,75,000
	(Being reduction of 2,000 equity shares of Rs. 100 each to Rs. 12.50 each)			
Mar. 31	Capital Reduction A/c Dr.		2,50,000	
	To Goodwill A/c			50,000
	To Profit and Loss A/c			1,10,375
	To Preliminary Expenses A/c			7,250
	To Plant and Machinery A/c			77,500
	To Capital Reserve A/c			4,875
	(Being utllisation of capital reduction account to write off the fictitious and intangible assets)			

Working Note :

1) Valuation of Plant and Machinery	Rs.
Cost price of Plant and Machinery	2,10,000
- Depreciation	57,500
	1,52,500
- Written down	75,000
Plant and Machinery written off	77,500

In the books of Krinti Ltd.

Dr. **Capital Reduction A/c** Cr.

Particulars	Rs.	Particulars	Rs.
To Goodwill A/c	50,000	By 6% Pref. Share Capital A/c	75,000
To Profit & Loss A/c	1,10,375	By Equity Share Capital A/c	1,75,000
To Preliminary Expenses A/c	7,250		
To Plant & Machinery A/c	77,500		
To Capital Reserve A/c	4,875		
(Balancing Figure)			
	2,50,000		2,50,000

Balance Sheet (And Reduced)
as on 1-4-2014

Liabilities	Rs.	Assets	Rs.
1,500, 6% Preference		Leasehold Property (at cost)	80,000
Shares at Rs. 50 each	75,000	Debtor	30,200
2,000 Equity Shares	25,000	Stock-in-trade	79,175
at Rs. 12.50 each		Plant & Machinery	75,000
Creditors	42,500		
Bank Overdraft	51,000		
Depreciation provision on			
Leasehold Property	30,000		
Capital Reserve	40,875		
	2,64,375		2,64,375

Problem No. 4 : The following is the summarised Balance Sheet of RMS Ltd. as on 31st March, 2014

Liabilities	Rs.	Assets	Rs.
Authorised & Issued Capital :		Goodwill	1,20,000
30,000 6% Preference Shares		Land & Building	2,67,000
of Rs. 10 each	3,00,000	Plant	2,55,000
6,00,000 Equity Shares		Shares in Subsidiary Ltd. (at Cost)	75,000
of Re. 1 each	6,00,000	Stock	2,25,000
8% Debentures (Secured		Debtors	2,70,000
on Land & Building) 1,20,000		Profit & Loss A/c	2,64,000
Accrued Interest 6,000	1,26,000		
Bank Overdraft		**Deferred Expenditure :**	
(Secured on Stock)	1,65,000	Advertisement	60,000
Directors' Loans	75,000		
Creditors	2,70,000		
	15,36,000		15,36,000

(**Note :** There is a contingent liability for damages of Rs. 30,000)

Preference Shares are cumulative and dividends are in arrears for three years.

A Capital Reduction Scheme setting the following terms was duly approved –

i) The preference shares to be reduced to Rs. 8 per share and the equity shares to 25 paise each and to be consolidated as shares of Rs. 10 each and Re. 1 each fully paid, respectively. The preference shareholders waive two-thirds of the dividend arrears and receive equity shares for the balance. The authorised capital to be restored to : 30,000 preference shares of Rs. 10 each and 6,00,000 equity shares of Re. 1 each.

ii) The shares in Subsidiary Ltd. are sold to an outside interest for Rs. 1,50,000

iii) All intangible assets are to be eliminated and bad debts of Rs. 21,000 and obsolete stock of Rs. 30,000 to be written off.

iv) The debentureholders to take over one of the company's properties (book value Rs. 54,000) at a price Rs. 60,000 in part satisfaction of the debentures and to provide further cash Rs. 45,000 on a floating charge. The arrears of interest are paid.

v) Directors refund Rs. 10,000 of the fees previously received by them.

vi) The contingent liability materialised in the sum stated but the company recovered Rs. 15,000 of these damages in action against one of its directors. This was debited to his Loan A/c of Rs. 24,000, the balance of which was paid in cash on his resignation.

vii) The remaining Directors agreed to take equity shares in satisfaction of their loans.

You are required to : (i) give the necessary journal entries, including cash transactions, and (ii) set out the revised Balance Sheet.

Solution

Journal Entries in the books of RMS Ltd.

Date	Particulars	L.F.	Dr. Rs.	Cr. Rs.
2014 Mar. 31	6% Preference Share Capital A/c Dr.		60,000	
	Equity Share Capital A/c Dr.		4,50,000	
	To Capital Reduction A/c			5,10,000
	(Being share capital reduced)			
Mar. 31	Capital Reduction A/c Dr.		18,000	
	To Equity Share Capital A/c			18,000
	(Being equity shares issued against 1/3rd arrears of preference share dividends.)			
Mar. 31	Bank A/c Dr.		1,50,000	
	To Shares in Subsidiary Co. A/c			75,000
	To Capital Reduction A/c			75,000
	(Being investment sold and profits credited to capital reduction account)			
Mar. 31	8% Debentures A/c Dr.		60,000	
	To Land & Building A/c			54,000
	To Capital Reduction A/c			6,000
	(Being cancellation of debentures by transfer of land building at profit)			
Mar. 31	Bank A/c Dr.		10,000	
	To Capital Reduction A/c			10,000
	(Being refund of fees by Directors)			
Mar. 31	Accrued Interest A/c Dr.		6,000	
	Outstanding Claim A/c Dr.		30,000	
	To Bank A/c			36,000
	(Being interest paid accrued on debentures and contingent liability materialised)			
Mar. 31	Bank A/c Dr.		45,000	
	To 6% Debentures A/c			45,000
	(Being debentures issued against loan from Debentureholders)			

Date	Particulars	L.F.	Dr. Rs.	Cr. Rs.
Mar. 31	Director's Loan A/c Dr.		24,000	
	To Outstanding Claim A/c			15,000
	To Bank A/c			9,000
	(Being contingent liability charged to director and balance of his loan paid in cash.)			
Mar. 31	Director's Loan A/c Dr.		51,000	
	To Equity Share Capital A/c			51,000
	(Being issued shares to directors in payment of their loan.)			
Mar. 31	Capital Reduction A/c Dr.		5,83,000	
	To Goodwill A/c			1,20,000
	To Stock A/c			30,000
	To Bad Debts A/c			21,000
	To Advertisement A/c			60,000
	To Outstanding Claim A/c			15,000
	To Profit & Loss A/c			2,64,000
	To Capital Reserve A/c			73,000
	(Being utilisation of capital reduction account to write off the various accounts as stated above and transfer of excess to capital reserve)			

Balance Sheet of RMS Ltd. (And Reduced)
as on 1st April, 2014

Liabilities	Rs.	Assets	Rs.
Authorised Capital :		**Fixed Assets :**	
30,000, 6% Preference Shares		Land & Building	2,13,000
of Rs. 10 each	3,00,000	Plant	2,55,000
6,00,000 Equity Shares		**Current Assets :**	
of Re. 1 each	6,00,000	Stock	1,95,000
Issued & Paid-up :		Debtors	2,49,000
24,000, 6% Preference Shares		Bank	1,60,000
of Rs. 10 each	2,40,000		
2,19,000 Equity Shares of			
Re. 1 each	2,19,000		
Reserves and Surplus :			
Capital Reserve	73,000		

Liabilities		Rs.	Assets	Rs.
Secured Loans :				
6% Debentures				
(Old)	60,000			
(New)	45,000	1,05,000		
Bank Overdraft		1,65,000		
Current Liabilities :				
Creditors		2,70,000		
		10,72,000		10,72,000

(Note : (1) Bank Overdraft is presumed to have been paid off)

Problem No. 5 : The following was the Balance Sheet of Hopeful Ltd. as on 31-3-2014

Liabilities	Rs.	Assets	Rs.
Share Capital :		Freehold	23,75,000
15,000 7% Cumulative		Plant and Machinery	8,00,000
Preference Shares of		Goodwill	3,00,000
Rs. 100 each	15,00,000	Stock	3,50,000
2,75,000 Equity Shares		Debtors	2,25,000
of Rs. 10 each	27,50,000	Preliminary	2,50,000
Share Premium A/c	4,00,000	Profit and Loss A/c	7,50,000
Sundry Creditors	4,00,000		
	50,50,000		50,50,000

Dividend on preference shares was in arrears as from 1st January, 2012. The following scheme of reconstruction was approved and duly sanctioned.

a) Preference shares to be reduced to Rs. 80 per share.

b) Equity Shares to be reduced to Rs. 5 per share.

c) Write off all intangible assets and premium account.

d) One equity share of Rs. 5 each to be issued for Rs. 10 of gross preference dividend in arrears.

e) Freehold to be written down to Rs. 18,50,000.

Give necessary journal entries and prepare a revised balance sheet. **(P.U.)**

Solution :   **Journal Entries in the books of Hopeful Ltd**

Date	Particulars		L.F.	Dr. Rs.	Cr. Rs.
2014 Mar. 31	7% Preference Share Capital A/c	Dr.		3,00,000	
	Equity Share Capital A/c	Dr.		13,75,000	
	To Capital Reduction A/c				16,75,000
	(Being 15,000, 7% preference shares of Rs. 100 each reduced to Rs. 80 each and 2,75,000 equity shares of Rs. 10 each reduced to Rs. 5 each)				
Mar. 31	Preference Shares Dividend A/c	Dr.		1,57,500	
	To Equity Share Capital A/c				1,57,500
	(Being issued 31,500 equity shares of Rs. 5 each in full payment of arrears of dividend for last 3 years)				
Mar. 31	Capital Reduction A/c	Dr.		16,75,000	
	Share Premium A/c	Dr.		4,00,000	
	To Goodwill A/c				3,00,000
	To Preliminary Expenses A/c				2,50,000
	To Preference Share Dividend A/c				1,57,500
	To Profit and Loss A/c				7,50,000
	To Freehold A/c				5,25,000
	To Capital Reserve A/c				92,500
	(Being intangible assets written off and value of freehold reduced)				

Balance Sheet of Hopeful Ltd., (And Reduced) as on 1st April, 2014

Liabilities	Rs.	Assets	Rs.
Share Capital :		**Fixed Assets :**	
15,000 7% Preference		Freehold	18,50,000
Shares of Rs. 80 each	12,00,000	Plant and Machinery	8,00,000
3,06,500 Equity Shares		**Current Assets :**	
of Rs. 5 each	15,32,500	Debtors	2,25,000
Reserves and Surplus :		Stock	3,50,000
Capital Reserve	92,500		
Current Liabilities :			
Sundry Creditors	4,00,000		
	32,25,000		32,25,000

Problem No. 6 : The following is the Balance Sheet of Uma Ltd., as on 31st March 2014

Liabilities	Rs.	Assets	Rs.
Share Capital :		Goodwill	70,000
4,000 Equity Shares		Land and Building	1,50,000
of Rs. 100 each	4,00,000	Plant and Machinery	3,50,000
3000 - 8% Preference		Patents	20,000
Shares of Rs. 100 each	3,00,000	Stock	2,20,000
Profit prior to Incorporation	10,000	Sundry Debtors	1,00,000
4% Debentures	3,00,000	Cash at Bank	5,000
Sundry Creditors	2,00,000	Preliminary Expenses	21,000
		Profit and Loss A/c	2,74,000
	12,10,000		12,10,000

The following scheme of reconstruction was approved :

1. 8% preference shares be converted into 9% preference shares, the amount being reduced by 30%.
2. Equity share be reduced to fully-paid shares of Rs. 50 each.
3. Land and Buildings be appreciated by 20%.
4. The debentureholders are agreeable to have their claims reduced by 20%.
5. All intangible assets and fictitious amounts including patents written off. Utilise profit prior to incorporation, if necessary.
6. The Company issued 2,000 equity shares of Rs. 50 each to the public and all were subscribed, the amount to be utilised for acquiring new plant and machinery.

Pass the journal entries in the books of the Company and draw a balance sheet. (P.U.)

Solution :

Journal Entries in the books of Uma Ltd.

Date	Particulars	L.F.	Dr. Rs.	Cr. Rs.
31.3.2014	8% Preference Share Capital A/c Dr.		3,00,000	
	To 9% Preference Share Capital A/c			3,00,000
	(Being the convertion of 8% preference shares into 9% preference shares)			

Date	Particulars		L.F.	Dr. Rs.	Cr. Rs.
31.3.2014	9% Preference Share Capital A/c	Dr.		90,000	
	To Share Capital Reduction A/c				90,000
	(Being the reduction of 3,000 9% preference shares of Rs. 100 each to equal number of shares of Rs. 70 each)				
31.3.2014	Equity Share Capital A/c	Dr.		2,00,000	
	To Share Capital Reduction A/c				2,00,000
	(Being the reduction of 4,000 equity shares of Rs. 100 each to an equal number of shares of Rs. 50 each)				
31.3.2014	Land and Building A/c	Dr.		30,000	
	To Share Capital Reduction A/c				30,000
	(Being the appreciation in the value of land and building)				
31.3.2014	4% Debentures A/c	Dr.		60,000	
	To Share Capital Reduction A/c				60,000
	(Being the sacrifice by debentureholders)				
31.3.2014	Bank A/c	Dr.		1,00,000	
	To Equity Share Capital A/c				1,00,000
	(Being the issue of 2,000 equity shares of Rs. 50 each to the public)				
31.3.2014	Share Capital Reduction A/c	Dr.		3,80,000	
	Profit prior to Incorporation A/c	Dr.		10,000	
	To Goodwill A/c				70,000
	To Patents A/c				20,000
	To Preliminary Expenses A/c				21,000
	To Capital Reserve A/c				5,000
	To Profit & Loss A/c				2,74,000
	(Being the assets and losses written off out of capital reduction account)				

In the books of Uma Ltd.,
Balance Sheet (And Reduced)
As on 1st April 2014

Liabilities	Rs.	Assets	Rs.
Share Capital :		**Fixed Assets :**	
6,000 Equity Shares of		Land and Buildings	1,80,000
Rs.50 each	3,00,000	Plant and Machinery	3,50,000
3000 - 9% Preference Shares		**Current Assets :**	
of Rs.70 each	2,10,000	Stock	2,20,000
Reserves and Surplus :		Sundry Debtors	1,00,000
Capital Reserve	5,000	Cash at Bank	1,05,000
Secured Loans :			
4% Debentures	2,40,000		
Current Liabilities :			
Creditors	2,00,000		
	9,55,000		9,55,000

Problem No. 7 : Given below is the Balance Sheet of Amrut Ltd. as on 31st March 2014.

Liabilities	Rs.	Assets	Rs.
2,000 Preference Shares of		Land and Building	80,000
Rs.100 each	2,00,000	Fixtures	70,000
3,000 Equity Shares		Machinery	1,20,000
of Rs.100 each	3,00,000	Investments	90,000
Workmen Compensation		(Market Value Rs.65,000)	
Fund	10,000	Stock	78,000
Loans	75,000	Sundry Debtors	58,000
Secured Creditors		Cash	1,000
against Machinery	12,000	Profit and Loss A/c	1,88,000
Sundry Creditors	88,000		
	6,85,000		6,85,000

The scheme of reconstruction is prepared and approved as under :

1) Land and Building should be brought upto the present market value of Rs.1,50,000.
2) Equity shares to be reduced to Rs.20 per share paid-up cancelling Rs.80 per share and preference shares to be reduced to Rs.60 each cancelling Rs. 40 per share. The face value of these shares remain the same.

3) The equity shareholders to pay the call money of Rs. 40 per share and preference shareholders to pay the call money of Rs. 20 per share immediately.

4) Unsecured creditors are paid 10% of their dues and they accept a reduction of 30% of their claims.

5) Loans are paid off completely.

6) Liabilities to the workmen's compensation materialised to Rs.15,000.

7) Out of the funds available, the assets are to be written off as under :

    a) Profit and Loss A/c and fixtures totally.

    b) Machinery to the extent of Rs.80,000.

    c) Investments to its market value.

    d) Stock to its cost price of Rs.50,000.

    e) Creating a reserve for doubtful debts at 10% of the sundry debtors.

Pass the necessary journal entries in the books of Amrut Ltd., and give its balance sheet after reconstruction. **(P.U.)**

Solution :

Journal Entries
In the books of Amrut Ltd.

Date	Particulars		L.F.	Dr. Rs.	Cr. Rs.
31.3.2014	Land and Building A/c	Dr.		70,000	
	To Capital Reduction A/c				70,000
	(Being the appreciation in the value of land and building)				
31.3.2014	Equity Share Capital A/c	Dr.		2,40,000	
	Preference Share Capital A/c	Dr.		80,000	
	To Capital Reduction A/c				3,20,000
	(Being Rs. 80 per share on 3,000 equity shares at Rs.40 per share and on 200 preference shares at Rs.20 per share)				
31.3.2014	Bank A/c	Dr.		1,60,000	
	To Equity Share Capital A/c				1,20,000
	To Preference Share Capital A/c				40,000
	(Being call money received on 3,000 equity shares at Rs.40 per share and on 2,000 preference shares at Rs.20 per share)				

Date	Particulars	L.F.	Dr. Rs.	Cr. Rs.
31.3.2014	Loan A/c Dr.		75,000	
	To Bank A/c			75,000
	(Being loans paid off)			
31.3.2014	Creditors A/c Dr.		35,200	
	To Bank A/c			8,800
	To Capital Reduction A/c			26,400
	(Being 10% unsecured creditors are paid and 30% unsecured creditors are reduced)			
31.3.2014	Workmen's Compensation Fund A/c Dr.		10,000	
	Capital Reduction A/c Dr.		5,000	
	To Bank A/c			15,000
	(Being workmen's compensation paid)			
31.3.2014	Capital Reduction A/c Dr.		4,11,400	
	To Profit and Loss A/c			1,88,000
	To Fixtures A/c			70,000
	To Machinery A/c			80,000
	To Investment A/c			25,000
	To Stock A/c			28,000
	To R.D.D A/c			5,800
	To Capital Reserve A/c			14,600
	(Being various assets and losses written off)			

Balance Sheet of Amrut Ltd. (And Reduced)
as on 1st April 2014

Liabilities	Rs.	Assets		Rs.
Share Capital :		**Fixed Assets :**		
2,000 Preference Shares of		Land and Building		1,50,000
Rs.100 each,	1,60,000	Machinery		40,000
Rs.80 paid up		Investment (Market Price)		65,000
3,000 Equity Shares of Rs.100		**Current Assets :**		
each, Rs.60 paid up	1,80,000	Stock (Cost Price)		50,000
Reserves and Surplus :		Debtors	58,000	
Capital Reserve	14,600	**Less : R.D.D.**	5,800	52,200
Current Liabilities :		Cash		62,200
Creditors (including Rs.12,000 fully secured against machinery)	64,800			
	4,19,400			4,19,400

Problem No. 8 : A special resolution was passed by Sneha Ltd. and was sanctioned by the Court to the following effects :

1) 10,000, 6% preference shares of Rs.10 each, Rs.8/- paid-up to be reduced to 10,000, 6% preference shares of Rs.10 each, Rs.6/- paid up.
2) 30,000 equity shares of Rs.10 each fully paid to be reduced to Rs.2 each, fully paid.
3) 600, 7% debentures of Rs.100 each fully paid to be reduced to 600, 6% debentures of Rs. 80/- each, fully paid.
4) The debentureholders agreed to forgo the outstanding interest due to them.
5) Sundry creditors agreed to forgo 20% of their claims in exchange for fully paid equity shares for the balance.
6) The sum available will be applied :
   a) To write off preliminary expenses and profit and loss account balance.
   b) To reduce the value of plant by 25% and buildings by 40%.

The Balance Sheet of Sneha Ltd., as on 31st March 2014, was as follows :

Balance Sheet

Liabilities	Rs.	Assets	Rs.
Authorised Capital		Plant	2,00,000
50,000 Equity Shares	5,00,000	Buildings	1,00,000
30,000 Preference Shares	3,00,000	Stock	45,000
Issued Capital			
30,000 Equity Shares of		Debtors	35,000
Rs.10 each	3,00,000	Bills Receivable	12,000
10,000 6% Preference Shares		Cash at Bank	7,000
of Rs,10 each, Rs.8/-		Profit and Loss A/c	99,000
paid-up	80,000	Preliminary Expenses	1,200
600, 7% Debentures			
of Rs.100 each	60,000		
Interest outstanding on			
Debentures	4,200		
Creditors	50,000		
Bills Payable	5,000		
	4,99,200		4,99,200

You are required to prepare Capital Reduction Account in the books of the Company and its balance sheet immediately after the implementation of the scheme and also pass the Journal Entries. **(P.U.)**

Solution :

Journal Entries
In the books of Sneha Ltd.

Date	Particulars	L.F.	Dr. Rs.	Cr. Rs.

31.3.2014	6% Preference Share Capital A/c Dr.
	  To Share Capital Reduction A/c
	  (Being the reduction of 10,000 6% preference shares of Rs. 10 each, Rs. 8 paid up to an equal number of shares of Rs. 10 each, Rs. 6 paid-up)
			20,000	20,000

31.3.2014	Equity Share Capital A/c Dr.
	  To Share Capital Reduction A/c
	  (Being the reduction of 30,000 equity shares of Rs.10 each to an equal number of shares of Rs.2 each fully paid)
			2,40,000	2,40,000

31.3.2014	7% Debentures A/c (Rs.100) Dr.
	  To 6% Debentures A/c (Rs.80)
	  To Share Capital Reduction A/c
	  (Being the reduction of debentures)
			60,000	48,000
				12,000

31.3.2014	Interest Outstanding on Debentures A/c Dr.
	  To Share Capital Reduction A/c
	  (Being interest outstanding on debentures has been sacrificed by debentureholders)
			4,200	4,200

31.3.2014	Sundry Creditors A/c Dr.
	  To Equity Share Capital A/c
	  To Share Capital Reduction A/c
	  (Being the equity shares accepted by sundry creditors)
			50,000	40,000
				10,000

31.3.2014	Share Capital Reduction A/c Dr.
	  To Preliminary Expenses
	  To Profit and Loss A/c
	  To Plant A/c
	  To Building A/c
	  To Capital Reserve A/c
	  (Being the assets and losses written off out of capital reduction account)
			2,86,200	1,200
				99,000
				50,000
				40,000
				96,000

Capital Reduction A/c

Dr.   Cr.

	Rs.		Rs.
To Preliminary Expenses	1,200	By Preference Share	
To Profit and Loss A/c	99,000	Capital A/c	20,000
To Plant A/c	50,000	By Equity Share	
To Building A/c	40,000	Capital A/c	2,40,000
To Capital Reserve A/c		By Debentures A/c	12,000
(Transfer)	96,000	By Interest Outstanding	
		on Debentures A/c	4,200
		By Creditors A/c	10,000
	2,86,200		2,86,200

Inter Books of M/s. Sneha Ltd.,
Balance Sheet (And Reduced)
as at 1st April 2014

Liabilities	Rs.	Assets	Rs.
Share Capital :		**Fixed Assets :**	
10,000, 6% Preference Shares		Plant	1,50,000
of Rs. 10 each, Rs. 6 paid-up	60,000	Building	60,000
50,000 Equity Shares of		**Current Assets :**	
Rs. 2 each	1,00,000	Stock	45,000
Reserves and Surplus :		Debtors	35,000
Capital Reserve	96,000	Bills Receivable	12,000
Secured Loans :		Cash at Bank	7,000
6% Debentures	48,000		
Current Liabilities :			
Bills Payable	5,000		
	3,09,000		3,09,000

Problem No. 9 : Swati Ltd., has been suffering heavy losses in the past. It is now considered that the worst is over and a sound re-organisation will enable its business to run successfully in the future. The Balance Sheet of the company immediately before the reconstruction is as follows :

Balance Sheet as on 31st March 2014

Liabilities	Rs.	Assets	Rs.
Share Capital :		Goodwill	3,00,000
Authorised Capital :		Fixed Assets	15,85,000
20,000 Equity Shares		Stock-in-trade	95,000
of Rs. 100 each	20,00,000	Sundry Debtors	50,000
5,000, 6% Preference Shares of		Investment	20,000
Rs. 100 each.	5,00,000	Cash at Bank	12,000
Issued Capital :		Preliminary Expenses	
10,000 Equity Shares of		(not written off)	5,000
Rs. 100 each	10,00,000	Discount on issue of Shares	3,000
2,000, 6% Preference Shares		Profit & Loss A/c	12,90,000
of Rs. 100 each	2,00,000		
(dividend in arrears for 5 years)			
5% Debentures of Rs. 100 each	16,60,000		
Sundry Creditors	4,80,000		
Liabilities for			
Income Tax	20,000		
	33,60,000		33,60,000

The following scheme of reconstruction was agreed upon and duly confirmed by the Court :

i) The equity shares shall be reduced to the shares of Rs. 10 each, Rs. 5 per share being paid-up.

ii) The preference shareholders shall forgo 90% of their claims in shares and the remaining shares shall be converted to 7% preference shares of Rs. 10 each, while their claim for arrears of dividend shall be reduced to one year's dividend and the same shall be discharged by the issue of fully paid equity shares.

iii) The debentureholders agreed to have 60% of their claims, which shall be discharged by the issue of 7½% debentures of Rs. 100 each.

iv) The sundry creditors are required to forgo 60% of their claims.

v) The assets to be revalued as follows : Fixed Assets Rs. 12,00,000, Stock-in-trade Rs. 70,000, Sundry Debtors Rs. 40,000, Investment Rs. 10,000.

vi) In order to provide sufficient working capital, the equity shareholders are to pay the balance amount due against each share.

Show the journal entries in the books of the company and also the balance sheet after implementation of the scheme.

Solution :   **Journal Entries**

Date	Particulars		L.F.	Dr. Rs.	Cr. Rs.
31.3.2014	Equity Shares Capital A/c	Dr.		9,50,000	
	To Capital Reduction A/c				9,50,000
	(Being 10,000 equity shares of Rs. 100 each fully paid are reduced to Rs. 10 each, Rs. 5 paid-up as per special resolution and court sanction.)				
31.3.2014	6% Preference Share Capital A/c	Dr.		2,00,000	
	To 7% Preference Share Capital A/c				20,000
	To Capital Reduction A/c				1,80,000
	(Being 6% preference shares of Rs. 100 each are reduced to 7% preference shares of Rs. 10 each, cancelling 90% of the original capital as per special resolution and court sanction.)				
31.3.2014	Preference Share Dividend A/c	Dr.		12,000	
	To Equity Share Capital A/c				12,000
	(Being issued 1,200 equity shares of Rs. 10 each fully paid in satisfaction of preference dividend in arrears.)				
31.3.2014	5% Debentures A/c	Dr.		16,60,000	
	To 7½% Debentures A/c				9,96,000
	To Capital Reduction A/c				6,64,000
	(Being issued 7½% debentures of 9,96,000 in full satisfaction of Rs. 16,60,000 due to 5% debentureholders.)				
31.3.2014	Sundry Creditors A/c	Dr.		2,88,000	
	To Capital Reduction A/c				2,88,000
	(Being sundry creditors forgo 60% of their claim.)				
31.3.2014	Capital Reduction A/c	Dr.		20,82,000	
	To Profit & Loss A/c				12,90,000
	To Discount on Issue of Shares A/c				3,000
	To Preliminary Expenses A/c				5,000
	To Goodwill A/c				3,00,000
	To Fixed Assets A/c				3,85,000
	To Stock-in-trade A/c				25,000
	To Sundry Debtors A/c				10,000

Date	Particulars	L.F.	Dr. Rs.	Cr. Rs.
	To Investments A/c			12,000
	To Dividend on Preference Share A/c			42,000
	To Capital Reserve A/c			10,000
	(Being use of capital reduction account to write off losses and to reduce values of assets as stated above, balance being transferred to capital.)			
31.3.2014	Equity Share Final Call A/c Dr.		50,000	
	To Equity Share Capital A/c			50,000
	(Being final call made of Rs. 5 per share on 10,000 equity shares.)			
31.3.2014	Bank A/c Dr.		50,000	
	To Equity Share Final Call A/c			50,000
	(Being received on account of final call.)			

Balance Sheet of Swati Ltd., as on 1st April 2014 (And Reduced)

Liabilities	Rs.	Assets	Rs.
Share Capital :		**Fixed Assets :**	12,00,000
Authorised :		Investments	10,000
20,000 Equity Shares of		Stock-in-trade	70,000
Rs 10 each	2,00,000	Sundry Debtors	40,000
5,000, 7% Preference Shares of		Cash at Bank	62,000
Rs. 10 each	50,000		
Issued, Subscribed & Paid-up :			
11,200 Equity Shares of Rs. 10 each fully paid, of which 1,200 issued in satisfaction of Dividend-in-Arrears	1,12,000		
2,000, 7% Preference Shares of Rs. 10 each	20,000		
Reserves and Surplus :			
Capital Reserve	42,000		
Secured Loan :			
7½% Debentures	9,96,000		
Current Liabilities :			
Sundry Creditors	1,92,000		
Income Tax Liability	20,000		
	13,82,000		13,82,000

(**Note** - It is presumed creditors and income tax are not yet paid.)

Problem No. 10 : The following is the Balance Sheet of Kamini Ltd. as on 31 March 2014

Liabilities	Rs.	Assets	Rs.
Share Capital :		Goodwill	15,000
5%, 2,000 Cumulative Preference		Freehold Property	2,00,000
Shares of Rs. 100 each	2,00,000	Plant and Machinery	3,00,000
4,000 Equity Shares of		Stock-in-trade	50,000
Rs. 100 each	4,00,000	Debtors	40,000
6% Mortgage Debenture	1,00,000	Profit and Loss A/c	2,40,000
Bank Overdraft	50,000	Cash	5,000
Creditors	1,00,000		
	8,50,000		8,50,000

The Company got the following scheme of capital reduction approved by the court.

1) The Preference Shares to be reduced to Rs. 75 per share fully paid up and Equity Shares to Rs. 40 fully paid-up.
2) The Debentureholders took over the stock-in-trade and the book debts in full satisfaction of the amount due to them.
3) The Goodwill Account is to eliminated.
4) The Freehold Properties to be increased by 30%.
5) The value of Plant and Machinery to be depreciated by $33\frac{1}{3}$%.
6) The expenses of reconstruction amounted to Rs. 3,000.

Give the journal entries for the above and prepare the revised Balance Sheet and also prepare Capital Reduction Account.   (**P.U.**)

Journal Entries in the books of Kamini Ltd.

Date	Particulars	L.F.	Dr. Rs.	Cr. Rs.
2014				
Mar. 31	Cumulative Preference Share Capital A/c Dr.		50,000	
	To Capital Reduction A/c			50,000
	(Being the reduction of 2,000 preference shares at Rs. 75 each)			
Mar. 31	Equity Share Capital A/c Dr.		2,40,000	
	To Capital Reduction A/c			2,40,000
	(Being the reduction of 4,000 equity shares at Rs. 40 each)			

Date	Particulars	L.F.	Dr. Rs.	Cr. Rs.
Mar. 31	6% Mortgage Debenture A/c Dr. To Stock in trade A/c To Debtors A/c To Capital Reduction A/c (Being stock and debtors taken over by debentureholders in full satisfaction of their claim)		1,00,000	50,000 40,000 10,000
Mar. 31	Freehold property A/c Dr. To Capital Reduction A/c (Being the appreciation in the value of property)		60,000	60,000
Mar. 31	Re-construction Expenses A/c Dr. To Cash A/c (Being reconstruction expenses paid)		3,000	3,000
Mar. 31	Capital Reduction A/c Dr. To Goodwill A/c To Plant and Machinery A/c To Profit and Loss A/c To Reconstruction Expenses A/c To Capital Reserve A/c (Being assets and losses written off out of capital reduction account)		3,60,000	15,000 1,00,000 2,40,000 3,000 2,000

Capital Reduction Account

Dr.   Cr.

Particulars	Rs.	Particulars	Rs.
To Goodwill A/c	15,000	By Cumulative Preference shares A/c	50,000
To Plant & Machinery A/c	1,00,000	By Equity Share Capital A/c	2,40,000
To Profit & Loss A/c	2,40,000	By Freehold Property A/c	60,000
To Reconstruction Expenses A/c	3,000	By 6% Mortgage Debentures A/c	10,000
To Capital Reserve A/c	2,000		
	3,60,000		3,60,000

In the books of Kamini Ltd.
Balance Sheet As on 1st April, 2014 (And Reduced)

Liabilities	Rs.	Assets	Rs.
Share Capital :		**Fixed Assets :**	
5%, 2,000 Cumulative Preference		Freehold Property	2,60,000
Shares of Rs. 75 each	1,50,000	Plant and Machinery	2,00,000
4,000 Equity Shares of		**Current Assets :**	
Rs. 40 each	1,60,000	Cash	2,000
Reserves and Surplus :			
Capital Reserve	2,000		
Current Liabilities :			
Bank Overdraft	50,000		
Creditors	1,00,000		
	4,62,000		4,62,000

7.8 EXERCISES :

Objective type questions :

a) State whether each of the following statements is True or False

1) Permission of the Court is not required for the increase of share capital.
2) The term "Alteration Proper" and reduction of capital are synonymous.
3) Refunding surplus capital do not amount to reduction of share capital.
4) Reconstruction necessarily involves liquidation of the Company concerned.
5) The balance in the share premium account can be transfered to capital reduction account.
6) The Company can carry forward accumulated losses for taxation purposes in case of internal reconstruction.

Ans. 1) True   2) False   3) False   4) False   5) True   6) True

b) Fill in the gaps

1) The main purpose of internal reconstruction is to ..... capital of a Company.
2) The sacrifice made by different parties are shown in ..... account.
3) The balance of capital reduction account is transferred to .... account.
4) Expenses on reconstruction account are transferred to ..... account.
5) A share of Rs. 10 is reduced to Rs. 2, it means there is a reduction of ..... in the value of share.

Ans : 1) reduce   2) Capital Reduction Account   3) Capital Reserve Account   4) Capital Reduction Account   5) Rs. 8

c) **Select the most appropriate answer :**

i) The accumulated losses under the scheme of internal reconstruction are written off against :

   (a)   Share Capital Account

   (b)   Capital Reduction Account

   (c)   None of the above.

ii) A Contingent Liability not provided for, if not materialised is credited to :

   (a)   Capital Reduction Account

   (b)   Profit and Loss Account

   (c)   None of the two.

iii) The balance of Capital Reduction Account after writing off accumulated losses is transferred to :

   (a) General Reserve   (b) Share Capital   (c) Capital

iv) Reduction in Share Capital requires the permission of :

   (a) The Central Government   (b) Court

   (c) Controller of Capital Issues.

Ans : i) (b)   ii) (c)   iii) (c) iv) (b)

Practical Problems

1) The Unsuccessful Company Ltd., prepared a scheme for reconstruction, which was duly approved by the Court. The terms of reconstruction were as under :

1. The shareholders to receive in lieu of their present holding (viz. 50,000 shares of Rs. 10 each) the following :

   a)   Fully-paid Equity Share equal to 2/5th of their holding.

   b)   5% Preference Shares, fully paid, to the extent of 1/5th of the above new Equity.

   c)   Rs. 60,000 in 6% second Debentures.

2. An issue of Rs. 5,00,000 5% Debentures was made and allotted, payment for the same have been received in cash.

3. The Goodwill which stood at Rs. 3,00,000 was written down to Rs. 1,50,000; the Plant and Machinery standing at Rs. 1,00,000 was written down to Rs. 75,000; Freehold and Leasehold Premises standing at Rs. 1,50,000 were written down to Rs. 1,25,000

   Pass journal entries to give effect to the above scheme.

Ans : Capital Reduction Account total Rs. 2,00,000

2) Following is the Balance Sheet of Kiran Ltd.

Balance Sheet as on 31-3-2014

Liabilities	Rs.	Assets	Rs.
Share Capital :		Goodwill	50,000
1,500, 6% Preference Shares		Debtors	30,200
of Rs. 100 each	1,50,000	Leasehold Property	
2,000 Equity Shares of		(at cost)	80,000
Rs. 100 each	2,00,000	Plant & Machinery	
Capital Reserve	36,000	(at cost)	2,10,000
Creditors	42,500	Stock-in-trade	79,175
Bank Overdraft	51,000	Profit & Loss A/c	1,10,375
Depreciation Provision :		Preliminary Exp.	7,250
Leasehold Property	30,000		
Plant & Machinery	57,500		
	5,67,000		5,67,000

The approval of the Court was obtained for the following scheme for reduction of capital –

i) The Preference Shares to be reduced to Rs. 50 per share.

ii) The Equity Shares to be reduced to Rs. 12.50 per share.

iii) The balance on Capital Reserve Account should not be utilised.

iv) Plant and Machinery to be written down to Rs. 75,000.

v) The Profit and Loss Account balance and all Intangible Assets including preliminary expenses to be written off.

Pass the journal entries in the books of Kiran Ltd.

Ans. : Capital Reserve Rs. 4,875

3) The Following was the Balance Sheet of "AB" Ltd. as on 31-3-2014

Liabilities	Rs.	Assets	Rs.
Share Capital :		Freehold	23,75,000
15,000, 7% Cumulative		Plant & Machinery	8,00,000
Preference Shares of		Goodwill	3,00,000
Rs. 100 each	15,00,000	Stock	3,50,000
2,75,000 Equity Shares of		Debtors	2,25,000
Rs. 10 each	27,50,000	Preliminary Expenses	2,50,000
Share Premium A/c	4,00,000	Profit & Loss A/c	7,50,000
Sundry Creditors	4,00,000		
	50,50,000		50,50,000

Dividend on Preference Shares was in arrears as from 1st April, 2008. The following scheme of reconstruction was approved and duly sanctioned.

a) Preference Shares to be reduced to Rs. 80 per share.
b) Equity Shares to be reduced to Rs. 5 per share.
c) Write off all intangible assets and premium account.
d) One Equity Share of Rs. 5 each to be issued for Rs. 10 of gross Preference Dividend in arrears.
e) Freehold to be written down to Rs. 18,50,000.

Give necessary journal entries and prepare revised Balance Sheet. **(P.U.)**

Ans : Capital Reserve Rs. 92,500

4) On 31st March 2014, the following balances appeared in the books of Kartiki Co. Ltd.

Particulars	Debit (Rs.)	Credit (Rs.)
Share Capital - Authorised and Issued		
6000 - 7% Cumulative Preference Shares of		
Rs. 100 each		6,00,000
1,10,000 Ordinary Shares of Rs. 10 each		11,00,000
Share Premium A/c		1,60,000
Freehold Premises at cost	12,00,000	
Plant and Machinery at cost	4,00,000	
Depreciation Account		
Freehold Premises		2,50,000
Plant and Machinery		80,000
Goodwill	1,20,000	
Stock on Hand as on 31.3.2014	1,40,000	
Sundry Debtors	90,000	
Preliminary Expenses	1,00,000	
Profit and Loss A/c	3,00,000	
Creditors		1,60,000
	23,50,000	23,50,000

Dividends on Preference Shares are in arrears as from 1st April 2012

The following terms were settled under a duly approved scheme –

a) Preference Shares to be reduced to Rs.80 each and the Ordinary Shares to Rs. 5 each.
b) One Rs. 5 Ordinary Share to be issued for each Rs. 10 of gross Preference Share Dividend arrears.
c) All intangible assets and the Share Premium Account to be written off.

d) Freehold premises to be written down upto Rs. 7,40,000.

You are required to give : a) necessary journal entries; and b) Balance Sheet after reconstruction. **(P.U.)**

Ans. Capital Reserve Rs. 37,000

5) Abhishek Company Ltd., has been suffering heavy losses in the past. It is now considered that the worst is over and a sound re-organisation will enable its business successfully in the future. The Balance Sheet of the company immediately before the reconstruction is as folllows :-

Balance Sheet as on 31st March 2014

Liabilities	Rs.	Assets	Rs.
Share Capital		Goodwill	3,00,000
Authorised Capital		Fixed Assets	15,85,000
20,000 Equity Shares of		Stock-in-trade	95,000
Rs. 100 each	20,00,000	Sundry Debtors	50,000
5,000, 6% Preference Shares		Investment	20,000
of Rs. 100 each	5,00,000	Cash at Bank	12,000
Issued Capital		Preliminary Expenses	
10,000 Equity Shares of		(not written off)	5,000
Rs. 100 each	10,00,000	Discount on issue of Shares	3,000
2,000, 6% Preference Shares		Profit and Loss A/c	12,90,000
of Rs. 100 each	2,00,000		
(dividend in arrears for			
5 years)			
5% Debentures of Rs. 100 each	16,60,000		
Sundry Creditors	4,80,000		
Liabilities for Income Tax	20,000		
	33,60,000		33,60,000

The following scheme of reconstruction was agreed upon and duly confirmed by the Court –

i) The Equity Shares shall be reduced to the shares of Rs. 10 each, Rs. 5 per share being paid-up.

ii) The Preference shareholders shall forgo 90% of their claims in shares and the remaining shares shall be converted to 7% Preference Shares of Rs. 10 each, while their claim for arrears of dividend shall be reduced to one year's dividend and the same shall be discharged by the issue of fully paid Equity Shares.

iii) The debentureholders agreed to have 60% of their claims which shall be discharged by the issue of 7½% debentures of Rs. 100 each.

iv) The sundry creditors are required to forgo 60% of their claims.

v) The assets to be revalued as follows.

Fixed Assets Rs. 12,00,000, Stock-in-trade Rs. 70,000, Sundry Debtors Rs. 40,000, Investment Rs. 10,000.

vi) In order to provide sufficient working capital, the equity shareholders are to pay the balance amount due against each share.

Show the journal entries in the books of the company and also the Balance sheet after implementation of the scheme. **(P.U.)**

Ans. : Capital Reserve Rs. 42,000

CHAPTER

8

Holding Company's Balance Sheet

Introduction :

A holding company is the one that holds either the whole of the share capital or a majority of the shares in one or more companies. A holding company acquires majority of the shares of another company or having direct or indirect power to appoint majority of the directors of another company. Thus, a company acquires majority shares or acquires a power to appoint a majority of directors, is called a Holding Company. The other company which is controlled by a holding company is called a subsidiary a company. The object of holding company is to promote combination movement so that competition may be eliminated, advantages of monopoly or near monopoly may be enjoyed and economies in production and management may be secured. Such advantages can be enjoyed by amalgamation or absorbing two or more companies into one, but in such a case, the companies which are being amalgamated or absorbed have to liquidate themselves and lose their identity. But a holding company is one of the pattern of combination, so under this pattern a Holding Company and its subsidiaries continue to have their independent existence and thereby their trade names, reputation, goodwill etc. are retained with them. The holding may be wholly-owned subsidiary or partly-owned subsidiary company.

a) Wholly-owned Subsidiary :

When a holding company acquires all the shares of the subsidiary, such a subsidiary is called as wholly-owned subsidiary.

b) Partly-owned Subsidiary :

When a holding company acquires not all but major portion (generally more than 51%) of the shares of a subsidiary, such-subsidiary is known as "partly-owned subsidiary."

The remaining shares of such company are held by outsiders, who are known as minority shareholders and their interest is called minority interest.

8.1 Definition of Holding Company :

A holding company is better defined in the context of the definitions of a subsidiary company. Section 4 of the Companies Act, 1956, defines a subsidiary company. According to this Section (1), a company shall be deemed to be a subsidiary company of another if, and only, if :–

a) that other company controls the composition of its board of directors; or b) that other -

i) When the first mentioned company is an existing company in respect of which the holders of preference shares issued before the commencement of this Act have the same voting rights in all respects as the shareholders of equity shares, exercises or controls more than half of the total voting power of such a company;

ii) when the first mentioned company is another comapny, holds more than half in nominal value of its equity share capital : or

c) the company is the subsidiary of any company which is that other company's subsidiary."

For example :

a) "S" Ltd., is having a share capital of Rs. 1,00,000 divided into shares of Rs. 100 each. So the number of shares come to 1,000. If H Ltd. acquires 700 shares in "S" Ltd., then "H" Ltd. will be called as a holding company and "S" Ltd., will be the subsidiary of "H" Ltd.

b) If "H" Ltd., purchases only 400 shares or less than 50% of the shares, then "H" Ltd., will not be treated as a Holding Company.

8.2 Final Accounts

Financial year of holding and subsidiary companies :

It seems to be the intention of the Companies Act that the financial year of a holding company and subsidiary company should end on the same date. Section 213(1) of the Companies Act, therefore, provides that the Central Government, may, if considered desirable, issue the necessary direction to the holding or subsidiary company to extend its financial year, if necessary.

According to Section 219(2) (c), the time gap between the close of the financial year of the holding company and that of its subsidiary company should not be more than 6 months. If it is more than 6 months, the Central Government is bound to give the necessary directions to reduce the time gap to not more than 6 months on the application of the directors of the Holding Company or its subsidiary.

Consolidated Final Accounts

In India, it is not compulsory for the holding company to make consolidated balance sheet and consolidated profit and loss account incorporating its own operations as well as operations of the subsidiary companies. However, according to Section 212 of the Companies

Act, the holding company has to attach the following documents with its Balance Sheet in respect of each of its subsidiaries –
  i) a copy of the balance sheet of the subsidiary,
  ii) a copy of its profit and loss account,
  iii) a copy of the report of its board of directors,
  iv) a copy of the report of its auditor and
  v) a statement showing : (i) The extent of holding companies interest in the subsidiary at the end of financial year (ii) The profits (after deduction of losses of the subsidiary) separately for the current financial year and for the previous financial year and separately so far as they concern the holding company for profits already dealt with i.e. profit earned by the subsidiary after the date of acquisition of shares by a holding company.

However, it is preferred to prepare a consolidated balance sheet and a consolidated profit and loss account in order to make it necessary to understand by the members of the holding company, in addition to holding company's separate final accounts.

8.3 Preparation of Consolidated Balance Sheet

In India, although a Holding Company is not required by law to prepare a consolidated Balance Sheet and consolidated Profit and Loss Account, preparation of consolidated Balance Sheet and consolidated Profit and Loss Account is of much help to the holding company to show the clear picture, so in addition to the "legal" Balance Sheet as prescribed in Schedule VI, the holding company may also publish the Balance Sheet in which the assets and liabilities of all subsidiaries are given alongwith its own assets and liabilities as the Balance Sheet of head office incorporates the assets and liabilites of its branches.

Shareholders of the holding company are interested in knowing the affairs of the subsidiary company as part of their money given to the holding company is invested in the subsidiary company. So, it becomes safe for the directors of the holding company to disclose to the shareholders of the holding company, the extent to which they are entitled to the net assets of the subsidiary company.

In the preparation of Consolidated Balance Sheet, many important problems are involved. They are as follows :–
  1) Elimination of investment in shares of subsidiaries account.
  2) Minority Interest
  3) Cost of control
  4) Capital Profits and Revenue profits
  5) Inter-Company transactions.
  6) Contingent Liabilities.
  7) Unrealised Profits.
  8) Revaluation of Assets and Liabilities
  9) Preference Shares in Subsidiaries.
  10) Bonus shares
  11) Dividends

12) Share Premium, Capital Reserve etc.
13) Preliminary Expenses.

8.4 Treatement to important items in Consolidated Balance Sheet

1) Elimination of Investment in shares of subsidiaries Account or Cancellation of Investment and Share Capital –

Consolidated Balance Sheet can be prepared by combining all the assets and liabilities of the holding company and its subsidiaries. It will certainly balance, but it is not the consolidated Balance Sheet. This is because the inter-company balances have first to be eliminated. The "Investment in Subsidiary company" by holding company should cancel out the share capital of the subsidiary company. It will be clear from the following example:-

Balance Sheets

Liabilities	Holding Co.	Subsidiary Co.	Assets	Holding Co.	Subsidiary Co.
Equity Shares of Rs. 10 each	2,00,000	1,00,000	Fixed Assets Investment	2,50,000	1,20,000
Liabilities	1,50,000	20,000	in subsidiary company – 10,000 shares	1,00,000	-
	3,50,000	1,20,000		3,50,000	1,20,000

All the shares of subsidiary company have been purchased by the holding company. So, all the assets and liabilities of subsidiary company belong to the holding company.

In this case, the subsidiary company is wholly-owned subsidiary company of the holding company. The consolidated Balance Sheet will be prepared as follows :

Consolidated Balance Sheet

Liabilities	Rs.	Assets	Rs.
20,000 Equity Shares of Rs. 10 each Liabilities (1,50,000 + 20,000)	2,00,000 1,70,000	Fixed Assets 2,50,000 + 1,20,000 Investment in 10,000 shares of Rs 10 each of the subsidiary company (All the shares held)	3,70,000 –
	3,70,000		3,70,000

From the above example, it follows that while preparing the consolidated balance sheet, investment of the holding company in the subsidiary company should be replaced by the assets and liabilities of the subsidiary company if all the shares of the subsidiary company have been purchased by the holding company.

2) Minority Interest :

A holding company may not hold the entire share capital of the subsidiary company : Generally, a majority portion of Share Capital is purchased by the holding company and remaining shares are purchased by outsiders. These outsiders have less than 50% of the shares of the subsidiary company and hence they are called minority shareholders. The interest of minority shareholders is known as Minority Interest and it must be shown on the liability side of the consolidated balance sheet. For example : If a holding company holds only 3/4ᵗʰ of the equity share capital of the subsidiary company, it will be entitled to only 3/4ᵗʰ of the net assets of the subsidiary company, while other 1/4ᵗʰ of net assets belong to outsiders or minority shareholders. It is a usual practice to incorporate all assets and liabilities of the subsidiary company in the consolidated balance sheet and show the interest of minority in the subsidiary company as a separate liability under the heading "Minority Interest."

The minority interest is calculated as follows :

Particulars	Rs.
Paid-up value of Equity and Preference Shares held by outsiders.	× × ×
Add : 1) Proportionate share in all undistributed profit or General Reserve / Capital Profit of subsidiary comapny	× × ×
2) Proportionate share in Revenue Profit of subsidiary company.	× × ×
3) Proportionate increase in the value of assets of subsidiary company.	× × ×
Total	× × ×
Less : 1) Proportionate share of losses of the subsidiary company.	× × ×
2) Proportionate decrease in the value of assets of the subsidiary company	× × ×
Minority Interest	× × ×

If the preference shares are held by outsiders, the paid-up value of such shares together with dividend thereon (if there are profits) is also added to the value of minority interest or shown separately. Proportionate share of the subsidiary company's profits and reserves belonging to the outsiders is calculated, keeping in view the value of equity shares held by them and the value of preference shares held is not considered because profits and reserves belong to equity shareholders and not to preference shareholders.

3) Cost of Control (Goodwill or Capital Reserve)

In case the subsidiary company has accumulated profits or accumulated losses, the holding company may acquire the shares of subsidiary company at a premium or at a discount, as the case may be. In other words, the price paid by the holding company for the shares of the subsidiary company is also affected by the accumulated profits or accumulated losses in the subsidiary company's balance sheet on the date such of acquisition. Such excess or less payment of net worth of assets represent cost of control. So such losses or profits should be taken into consideration while preparing the consolidated balance sheet.

If a holding company pays higher price then the net worth of assets of the subsidiary company, then is called **Goodwill**. If the price paid is less than its net worth of the assets, it is a profit which is earned prior to acquisition of shares and hence treated as **Capital Reserve.**

Calculation of Goodwill

Particulars	Rs.
Market price of shares acquired in subsidiary company (Investment in subsidiary company)	×××
Add : Holding company's share in capital losses	×××
Total	×××
Less : 1) Face value of shares acquired by holding company	×××
2) Holding company's share in capital profit	×××
3) Dividend received by holding company from the capital profit of subsidiary company	×××
Goodwill / Cost of Capital	×××

If there is a goodwill, in the balance sheets of both companies, it will be added to this Goodwill.

Note : If the balance is negative, it will be considered as Capital Reserve.

4) Capital Profits and Revenue Profits :

The holding company may acquire the shares in the subsidiary company either on the balance sheet date or any date earlier than the balance sheet date. If the holding company acquires shares in the subsidiary company on the balance sheet date, all profits earned by the subsidiary company have been taken as capital profits for the holding company. In case the holding company acquires the shares on the date other than balance sheet date of the subsidiary company, the profits of the subsidiary company will have to be apportioned between capital profits and revenue profits from the point of view of the holding company. The profit earned by the subsidiary company before holding company acquires its shares or control is known as capital profit or pre-acquisition profit. Undrawn pre-acquisition profit is taken into consideration for the calculation of goodwill or capital reserve.

The profit earned by the subsidiary company after the holding company acquires the shares or its control is known as Revenue Profits or Post-acquisition Profits of the subsidiary company and do not form part of goodwill or Capital Reserve calculation. In other words, while preparing the consolidated balance sheet, capital profits or losses should be adjusted with the cost of control and revenue profits should be merged with the balance in profit and loss account of the holding company.

Minority shareholders are not concerned whether the profits are pre-acquisition or post-acquisition. Post-acquisition profit is apportioned between the holding company and minority shareholders. The share of the holding company is added with its profit, while the share of minority shareholders form a part of the calculation of minority interest.

5) Inter-company Transactions :

While preparing a consolidated Balance Sheet, common transactions appearing in both the balance sheets of holding company and the subsidiary company should be eliminated. Such transactions may be –

1) **Goods sold on credit** by the holding company to subsidiary company or vice-versa will appear as debtors in the balance sheet of the company selling goods and as creditors in the balance sheet of the company purchasing goods.

2) **Bills drawn** by one company and accepted by the other company are eliminated while preparing consolidated balance sheet but bill discounted will continue to appear as liability, because the company which has accepted bills, will have to make the payment to an outsider i.e. bank on the due date.

3) **Loans advanced** by the holding company to the subsidiary company or vice versa appears as an asset in the balance sheet of the Company which gives such loans and as a liability in the balance sheet of the Company that takes these loans.

4) **Debentures issued** by one Company and held by the other Company.

6) Contingent Liability :

Contingent liability is a liability which may or may not arise or happen. It is customary to show contingent liabilities as a footnote to the balance sheet. Contingent Liability may be of two types :

a) External Contingent Liability

b) Internal Contingent Liability

External contingent liability is on account of a transaction between the Company and the third party while internal contingent liability is on account of a transaction between the companies of the same group. While preparing a consolidated balance sheet, the external contingent liabilities are shown as a footnote to the balance sheet, while internal contingent liabilities are eliminated from the footnote, since they appear as actual liabilities in the consolidated balance sheet.

7) Unrealised profit

When the goods are sold by the holding company to subsidiary company or vice-versa and if the goods remain unsold at the end of financial year, such goods are included in stock and appear as an asset in the balance sheet of the purchasing company. The profits earned by the selling company cannot be considered as a real profit. So, while preparing the consolidated balance sheet such unrealised profits on inter-company sales should be deducted from the profit of the selling company and also by deducting it from stock of the buying company. It is recorded as under :–

i) Ascertain the total amount of unrealised profit included in the stock lying with purchasing company. For example, if the goods costing Rs.10,000 were sold by "H" Ltd., to "S" Ltd., for the sum of Rs.12,000 and 40% of the goods are still in stock with "S" Ltd., the amount of unrealised profit will be as follows :–

Selling price - cost price = profit.

Rs.12,000 - Rs.10,000 = Rs.2,000

40% goods are still in stock, so, $\dfrac{2,000 \times 40}{100}$ = Rs.800

Unrealised profit is Rs. 800

ii) Reduce the amount of unrealised profit to the extent of the interest of the holding, company. For example, if in the above case, "H" Ltd., holds $\frac{3}{4}^{th}$ of the share capital of "S" Ltd., it will be advisable to reduce the unrealised profit to $\frac{3}{4}^{th}$ of Rs.800 i.e. Rs.600

It has become a common practice these days to consider the total profit on stock as unrealised without taking note of minority interest. For example, in the above case, the unrealised profit can also be taken as Rs.800. However, the former course is preferable.

iii) Finally deduct the unrealised profit from the profit of the company selling the goods and from the stock of the company purchasing the goods.

8) Revaluation of Assets and Liabilities :

If the assets and liabilities of the subsidiary company are revalued at the time of acquisition of shares in the subsidiary company, profit or loss on account of such revaluation is treated as capital profit or capital loss and is divided among minority shareholders and the holding company, according to the proportion of equity shares held by them. The holding company's share of such capital profit is transferred to capital reserve or deducted from cost of control or Goodwill and vice-versa, if there is a loss on revaluation. Share of profit of minority shareholders is added to the minority interest and a deduction is made from the minority interest, if there is a loss on revaluation.

9) Preference Shares in Subsidiaries :

(i) When preferenee shares are held by the holding company : If the holding company holds preference share in the subsidiary company, the difference between the price paid for these shares and their paid-up value is adjusted against Goodwill or Capital Reserve as the case may be, as is done in case of equity shares.

For example : If the holding company purchases 100 preference shares of Rs.100 each fully paid for a sum of Rs. 13,000 the excess of Rs. 3,000 of the cost of shares over paid-up value will be charged to Goodwill. However, if the cost of acquiring preference shares in the above case is only Rs. 8,000, the sum of Rs. 2,000, excess paid-up value over the cost of shares will be shown as Capital Reserve in the consolidated Balance Sheet.

ii) When shares are held by outsiders : In case the preference shares are held by outsiders, the paid-up value of such shares will be included in minority interest.

iii) Arrears of preference Dividend : In case the preference dividend are in arrears and the profits of the subsidiary company are adequate for making provision for such dividend, the amount of arrears should be provided out of the profits. The share of holding company in such arrears should be taken to its profit and loss account, if they have been provided out of post-acquisition profits. However, if such arrears or dividend have been provided out of pre-acquisition profits, they should be taken to cost of control. The shares of minority should be added to minority interest. In case the profits are not adequate to provide for all the arrears of dividend, there is no necessity of providing for the arrears of preference dividend.

10) Bonus Shares :

If the subsidiary company issues bonus shares to the existing shareholders, the holding company as well as minority shareholders will be receiving additional shares without making any Payment. The bonus shares may be issued out of pre-acquisition profits and reserves or post-acquisition profits and reserves.

Treatment to Bonus Shares :

a) Issue of Bonus Shares out of pre-acquisition profit - If the subsidiary company has issued bonus shares out of pre-acquisition profit or reserve, it will have no effect on the consolidated balance sheet. It is so because the holding company's share in pre-acquisition profits is reduced as bonus shares are issued out of it. But on the other hand, the paid-up value and number of shares held by the holding company will increase. The cost of control i.e. Goodwill or Capital Reserve will ultimately remain the same as it was before the issue of bonus shares.

b) Issue of Bonus Shares out of post-acquisition profits : If the bonus shares are issued by the subsidiary company out of post-acquisition profits, the balance of post-acquisition profits will be reduced to the extent of bonus shares issued. The remaining balance of post-acquisition profits will be divided between the holding company and minority shareholders.

11) Dividends :

The holding company owns majority of the shares of its subsidiary. When a dividend is paid out of profits of the subsidiary company, the holding company is likely to receive majority portion of it as a shareholder. It should be noted that, such a dividend may be paid out of the pre-acquisition profits or post-acquisition profits. The accounting treatment in the books of the holding company may vary accordingly.

a) Dividend paid out of pre-acquisition profits of a subsidiary company : If the subsidiary company has paid the dividend out of pre-acquisition profits, the holding company's share therein is required to be credited to Investment Account (shares in subsidiary company) reducing the cost of shares of subsidiary company in the holding company. Thus, dividend received by the holding company from subsidiary company out of pre-acquisition profits is added to Capital Reserve, which in turn, reduces the value of Goodwill. Since such a dividend is not available for distribution to the shareholders of the holding company, it is not credited to its profit and loss account.

b) Dividend paid out of post-acquisition profits by subsidiary company : Dividend received by the holding company from a subsidiary out of post-acquisition profits is treated as investment income and credited to profit and losss account of the holding company.

It should be noted that any Interim Dividend paid by subsidiary company is also treated in the books of holding company in the same manner as discussed above.

c) Unclaimed Dividend : Out of the total amount, the proportion belonging to the inter-company is cancelled in the consolidated Balance Sheet, being the mutual indebtedness and the amount payable to outsiders only is shown as a liability.

d) Proposed Dividend : When the dividend is proposed by the holding company, it will be deducted from the post-acquisition profits of the holding company (if it is not appearing in B/S of holding company) and will be shown in the consolidated Balance Sheet as a current liability.

The holding company's share of such proposed dividend is added with the profit and loss account of the holding company. Minority's share of proposed dividend can be added with the minority interest or it can be shown as a current liability in the consolidated balance sheet alongwith the proposed dividend of holding company, if any.

12) Share Premium, Capital Reserve etc.

In consolidated Balance Sheet, generally only the Share Premium Account of the holding company appears. However, it will be appropriate to adjust any share premium charged by the holding company, in respect of issue of its own shares in exchange for the shares of subsidiary company, against cost of control in the consolidated balance sheet.

The share premiun or any capital reserve appearing in the books of the subsidiary company on the date of acquisition of shares should be taken as a pre-acquisition profit and may be adjusted against cost of control. However, any share premium or capital reserve arising in the books of subsidiary company after acquisition, should not be taken as pre-acquisition profit. The holding company's share in such profits should be merged with the share premium or capital reserve. The proportionate share of minority should be included in the minority interest.

13) Provision for Taxation :

Any provision for taxation in the books of the subsidiary company should be taken to the consolidated balance sheet and be shown on the liability side.

14) Preliminary Expenses :

The preliminary expenses of the subsidiary company may be taken as an item of capital loss and treated accordingly. Alternatively, the amount may be added with the amount of preliminary expenses of the holding company.

8.5 Problems on Consolidated Balance Sheet

Problem No. 1 : Following are the balance sheets of 'H' Ltd., and 'S' Ltd., as on 31st, March, 2009

Balance Sheets

Liabilities	'H' Ltd. Rs.	'S' Ltd. Rs.	Assets	'H' Ltd. Rs.	'S' Ltd. Rs.
Share Capital			**Fixed Assets**	3,00,000	1,00,000
Share of Rs. 10 each	5,00,000	2,00,000	Plant & Machinery	1,00,000	1,00,000
General Reserve	1,00,000	50,000	60% Shares in 'S' Ltd.	1,62,400	—
P. & L. A/c	60,000	35,000	Debtors	52,600	39,000
Creditors	80,000	80,000	Bills Receivables	—	20,000
Bills payable	40,000	-	Current Assets	1,65,000	1,00, 000
			Preliminary Expenses	-	6,000
	7,80,000	3,65,000		7,80,000	3,65,000

'H' Ltd., acquires shares on 1st April, 2008 on which date the General Reserve and profit and loss Account showed balances of Rs. 40,000 and Rs. 8,000 respectirely. No part of the preliminary expenses was written off during the year ending 31st March, 2009. The fixed assets are undervalued by Rs. 20,000 The Plant and Machinery was overvalued by Rs. 10,000. Debtors of 'S' Ltd. include Rs. 9,000 due from 'H' Ltd., in respect of goods supplied. Bills Receivable held by 'S' Ltd., accepted by 'H' Ltd.

Prepare a consolidated Balance sheet.   **(P.U.)**

Solution :

Working Notes

1) Calculation of Shareholding Ratio

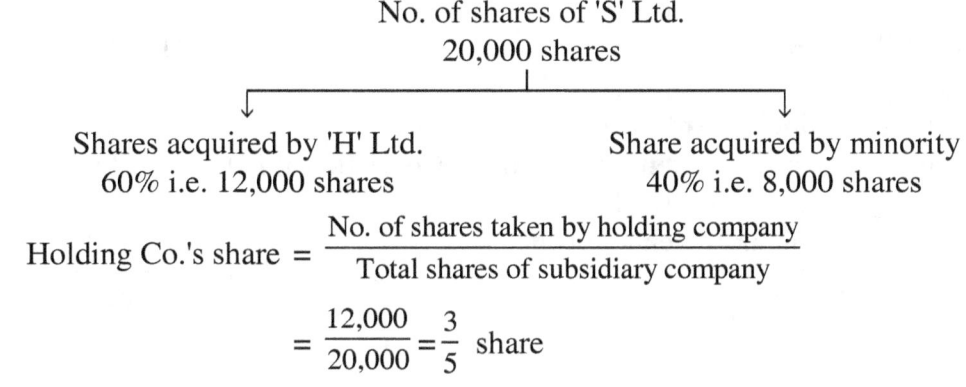

$$\text{Holding Co.'s share} = \frac{\text{No. of shares taken by holding company}}{\text{Total shares of subsidiary company}}$$

$$= \frac{12,000}{20,000} = \frac{3}{5} \text{ share}$$

Subsidiary Company's share (i.e. minority) : $1 - \frac{3}{5} = \frac{2}{5}$ share

2) Calculation of Capital Profit

i)	General Reserve (1-4-2008)	40,000
ii)	Profit & Loss A/c (cr. bal) 1-4-2008)	8,000
iii)	Increase in fixed Assets	20,000
	(i.e. under-valuation)	68,000

Less

i)	Decrease in Plant & Machinery (i.e. over-valuation)	10,000	
ii)	Preliminary Expenses (written off)	6,000	16,000
	Capital Profit		52,200

Holding co's share in capital profit

$52,000 \times \frac{3}{5} =$ 31,200

Minority's share in capital profit

$52,000 \times \frac{2}{5} =$ 20,800

3) Calculation of Revenue Profit

		Rs.
1)	General Reserve (50,000 - 40,000) =	10,000
2)	Profit & Loss A/c (35,000 - 8,000) =	27,000
	Revenue Profit	37,000

Holding Company's share in Revenue Profit

$\left(37,000 \times \frac{3}{5} \right) =$ 22,200

Minority's Shares in Revenue Profit

$\left(37,000 \times \frac{2}{5} \right) =$ 14,800

4) Calculation of Minority Interest

		Rs.
1)	Face value of shares taken by Subsidiary Co. (8,000 × 10)	80,000
2)	Minority's Share in Capital Profit	20,800
3)	Minority's Share in Revenue Profit	14,800
	Minority Interest	1,15,600

5) Calculation of cost of control i.e. Goodwill

i) Market value of shares taken by
holding Company i.e. Investments   1,62,400

Less :

i) Face value shares taken by holding company 1,20,000

ii) Holding Co's share in Capital Profit   31,200   1,51,200

Goodwill   11,200

Consalidated Balance Sheet as on 31-3-2009

Liabilities		Rs.	Assets		Rs.
Share capital			**Fixed Assets.**		
Shares of Rs. 10 each.		5,00,000	'H' Ltd.	3,00,000	
General Reserve		1,00,000	'S' Ltd.	1,00,000	
Profit & Loss A/C	60,000			4,00,000	
+ Holding Co's share	22,200		+ Interest	20,000	4,20,000
in Revenue Profit		82,200	Plant & Machinery		
Minority Interest		1,15,600	'H' Ltd.	1,00,000	
Creditors 'H' Ltd.	80,000		'S' Ltd.	1,00,000	
'S' Ltd	80,000		Less	2,00,000	
	1,60,000		Decrease	10,000	1,90,000
Less Mutual owing	9,000	1,51,000	**Debtors**		
			'H' Ltd.	52,600	
Bills Payable	40,000	20,000	'S' Ltd.	39,000	
– B. R.	20,000		Less	91,600	
			Mutual owing	9,000	82,600
			Current Asset.		
			'H' Ltd.	1,65,000	
			'S' Ltd.	1,00,000	2,65,000
			Goodwill		11,200
		9,68,800			9,68,800

Problem No. 2 : From the following balance sheets of 'H' Ltd. and 'S' Ltd. as on 31st March, 2009 and the additional information thereon, prepare a consolidated Balance Sheet.

Liabilities	'H' Ltd. Rs.	'S' Ltd. Rs.	Assets	'H' Ltd. Rs.	'S' Ltd. Rs.
Share Capital					
Shares of Rs. 10 each			Fixed Assets	11,62,000	1,80,000
Fully paid	10,00,000	2,00,000	70% Shares of S Ltd.		
General Reserve	3,10,000	-	at cost	1,42,000	-
Prolit & Loss Account	1,50,000	40,000	Current Assets	3,86,000	1,24,000
Creditors	2,30,000	69,000	Preliminary Expenses	-	5,000
	16,90,000	3,09,000		16,90,000	3,09,000

'H' Ltd., acquired the shares on 31st Dec., 2008. On 1st April, 2008, profit and loss account showed a debit balance of Rs. 8,000. On 31st March, 2009, 'S' Ltd., decided to revalue its fixed assets at Rs. 2,00,000. **(P.U.)**

Solution :

Working Notes :

1) Calculation of Shareholdings

i) Holding Co's Share $= \dfrac{\text{Shares held by Holding Company}}{\text{Total shares of Sub. Company}}$

$= \dfrac{14,000\,\text{shares}}{20,000\,\text{shares}}$

ii) Minority's Share $= 1 - \dfrac{7}{10} = \dfrac{3}{10}$

2) Calculation of profit earned during the year.

Profit & Loss Appro. A/c

Particulars	Rs.	Particulars	Rs.
To Opening balance (Loss)	8,000	By Profit earned during the year	48,000
To Closing balance of profit	40,000		
	48,000		48,000

Alternalively : Profit on 31 st March, 2009 is Rs. 40,000. It is calculated after adjusting the loss. Hence, total profit may be Rs. 48,000. After deduction of loss, the profit is i.e. 48,000 - 8,000 = Rs. 40,000

Thus, total profit earned during the year is Rs. 48,000.

Date of acquisition of business is 31st Dec., 2008

Pre-acquisition period	Post-acquisition period
31st March, 2008 to 31st Dec., 2008 i.e. 9 months	31st Dec., 2008 to 31st March, 2009 i.e. 3 months

The profit earned during the pre-acquisition period is Capital Profit and profit earned during post-acquisition period is Revenue Profit. Such profits are calculated as under :–

$$48,000 \times \frac{9}{12} = \text{Rs. } 36,000 \text{ Capital Profit}$$

$$48,000 \times \frac{3}{12} = \text{Rs. } 12,000 \text{ Revenue Profit}$$

i) Calculation of total Capital Profit

	Rs.
Capital profit before acquisition	36,000
+ Appreciation in the value of fixed assets	
(Rs. 2,00,000 - Rs. 11,80,000)	20,000
	56,000
Less	
i) Loss on 1st April, 2008 Rs.8,000	
ii) Preliminary Expenses 5,000	13,000
Total Capital Profit	43,000

a) Holding Co's share in capital profit

$$\text{Rs. } 43,000 \times \frac{7}{10} = \text{Rs. } 30,100$$

b) Minority's share in capital profit

$$\text{Rs. } 43,000 \times \frac{3}{10} = \text{Rs. } 12,900$$

ii) Distribution of Revenue Profit

a) Holding Co's share = $\text{Rs. } 12,000 \times \frac{7}{10} = \text{Rs. } 8,400$

b) Minority share = $\text{Rs. } 12,000 \times \frac{3}{10} = \text{Rs. } 3,600$

3) Calculation of Minority Interest

	Rs.
1) Face value of shares taken by subsidiary company (6,000 × 10)	60,000
2) Minority'share in capital profit	12,900
3) Minority's share in Revenue profit	3,600
Minority Interest	76,500

4) Calculation of Capital Reserve

	Rs.
Face value of shares taken by holding company 14,000 shares × 10	1,40,000
+ Holding Co's share in capital profit	30,100
	1,70,100
Less	
Cost value of shares taken by holding company	
i.e. investments	1,42,000
Capital Reserve	28,100

Consolidated Balance Sheet
as on 31-3-2009

Liabilities	Rs.	Assets		Rs.
Share Capital		**Fixed Assets**		
Shares of Rs. 10 each	10,00,000	'H' Ltd.	11,62,000	
		'S' Ltd.	+ 1,80,000	
General Reserve	3,10,000		13,42,000	
P & L. A/c 1,50,000		Add. Income	20,000	13,62,000
+ Holding Co's Share in		Current Assets		
Revenue Profits 8,400	1,58,400	'H' Ltd.	3,86,000	
Creditors		'S' Ltd.	+ 1,24,000	5,10,000
'H' Ltd. 2,30,000				
'S' Ltd. + 69,000	2,99,000			
Capital Reserve	28,100			
Minority Interest	76,500			
	18,72,000			18,72,000

Problem No. 3 : The following are the summarised Balance Sheets of 'H' Ltd., and 'S' Ltd., on 31-3-2009

Liabilities	'H' Ltd. Rs.	'S' Ltd. Rs.	Assets	'H' Ltd. Rs.	'S' Ltd. Rs.
Share Capital :			Sundry Assets	1,90,000	80,000
Shares of Rs. 10 each	1,80,000	1,00,000	Debtors	50,000	25,000
Profit & Loss A/c	35,000	–	Investments, Shares in		
Creditors	80,000	30,000	'S' Ltd. (8,000 shares)	55,000	–
			Profit & Loss A/c	–	25,000
	2,95,000	1,30,000		2,95,000	1,30,000

'H' Ltd., acquired the shares in 'S' Ltd., on 1st August, 2008. The Balance Sheet of 'S' Ltd., as on 31st March, 2008, showed a Debit Balance on Profits & Loss A/c Rs. 40,000.

The debtors of 'H' Ltd., include Rs. 10,000 due from S Ltd, whereas the creditors of 'S' Ltd., include Rs. 5,000 due to 'H' Ltd. As a cheque of Rs. 5,000 remitted by 'S' Ltd., to 'H' Ltd., being in transit.

Prepare a consolidated Balance Sheet. **(P.U.)**

Solution :

Working Notes

1) Pre and Post Acquisition period

Holding company acquires shares on 1st Aug., 2008 of 'S' Ltd.

i) Pre-acquisition period – 1-4-2008 to 31-7-2008 = 4 months.

ii) Post acquisition period – 1-8-2008 to 31-3-2009 = 8 months.

2) Shareholding Ratio

No. of shares of 'S' Ltd.
10,000 Shares
↓

Shares acquired by 'H' Ltd.	Shares acquired by minority
8,000 shares	2,000 Shares

'H' Ltd.'s share = $\dfrac{8,000}{10,000} = \dfrac{4}{5}$

'S' Ltd.'s share = $1 - \dfrac{4}{5} = \dfrac{1}{5}$

3) Calculation of Capital Loss

	'H' Ltd.	'S' Ltd.	
	4	1	
Loss on 1-4-2008			40,000
Loss profit upto 1-8-2008 $\dfrac{1}{3}$ of 15,000			5,000
			35,000

(Loss of Rs. 40,000 is reduced to Rs. 25,000 at the end of the year. It means during the year, Company earned profit of Rs. 15,000)

Division of capital loss between 35,000 28,000 7,000
'H' Ltd., and 'S' Ltd., in the ratio of 4:1

4) Revenue Profit

Profit from 1-8-2008 to 31-3-2009

$15,000 \times \dfrac{2}{3}$ 10,000

Division of Revenue profit between 'H' Ltd., & 'S' Ltd., in the ratio of 4 : 1   10,000   8,000   2,000

5) Goodwill

Market price of shares held by 'H' Ltd. (Investment)	55,000
Add : 'H' Co's share in capital loss	28,000
	83,000
Less : Face value of shares held by holding company (8,000 × 10)	80,000
Goodwill	3,000

6) Minority Interest

Face value of shares taken by minority (2,000 × 10)	20,000
Subsidiary's (minority) Share Revenue	2,000
Profit	22,000
Less : Subsidiary Co's (minority) shares in capital loss	7,000
Minority Interest	15,000

Consolidated Balance Sheet
of 'H' Ltd., and its subsidiary 'S' Ltd., as on 31st March, 2009

Liabilities		Rs.	Assets		Rs.
Share Capital :			Goodwill		3,000
18,000 Shares of Rs. 10 each		1,80,000	Sundry Assets		
Profit & Loss A/c			'H' Ltd.	1,90,000	
'H' Ltd.	35,000		'S' Ltd.	80,000	2,70,000
Add : 'H' Ltd's Share in			Debtors		
Revenue Profits of Ltd. Co.	8,000	43,000	'H' Ltd.	50,000	
Creditors			Less : Due from		
'H' Ltd.		80,000	'S' Ltd.	10,000	
'S' Ltd.	30,000			40,000	
Less : Due to			'S' Ltd.	25,000	65,000
'H' Ltd.	5,000	25,000	25,000	Cash in Transit		5,000
Minority Interest		15,000			
		3,43,000			3,43,000

Problem No. 4 : 'H' Ltd., acquired shares in 'S' Ltd., on 1-4-2008. Their Balance Sheet as on 31-3-2009 were :

Balance Sheets as on 31-3-2009

Liabilities	'H' Ltd. Rs.	'S' Ltd. Rs.	Assets	'H' Ltd. Rs.	'S' Ltd. Rs.
Share Capital :			Land & Building	1,00,000	20,000
Shares of Rs. 100			Plant & Machinery	1,50,000	30,000
each, fully paid	2,50,000	50,000	Investment :		
General Reserve	50,000	20,000	400 shares in		
(as on 1-4-2008)			'S' Ltd. (at cost)	50,000	–
Profit & Loss A/c	70,000	25,000	Stock	40,000	25,000
Creditors	30,000	5,000	Debtors	30,000	15,000
			Cash	30,000	10,000
	4,00,000	1,00,000		4,00,000	1,00,000

Additional Information :

1. Sundry Debtors of 'H' Ltd. include Rs. 5,000 due from 'S' Ltd.
2. Stock of 'S' Ltd., includes goods purchased from 'H' Ltd., for Rs. 20,000 on which 'H' Ltd., made a profit of 25% on sale
3. On 1-4-2008, Profit & Loss A/c of 'S' Ltd., showed a credit balance of Rs. 5,000
   Prepare a consolidated Balance Sheet of 'H' Ltd., and it's subsidiary 'S' Ltd. **(P.U.)**

Solution :

Working Notes

1) Shareholding Ratio :

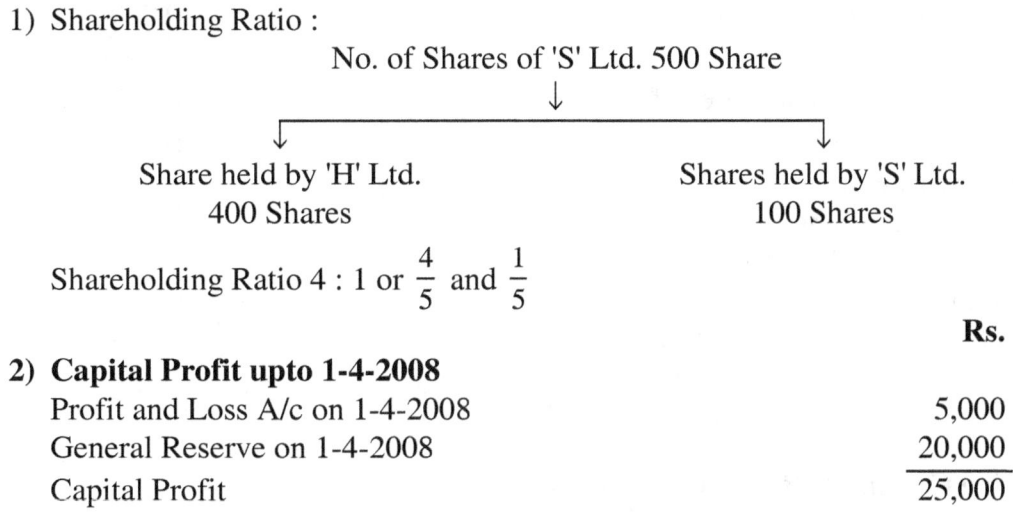

No. of Shares of 'S' Ltd. 500 Share

Share held by 'H' Ltd.   Shares held by 'S' Ltd.
400 Shares   100 Shares

Shareholding Ratio 4 : 1 or $\frac{4}{5}$ and $\frac{1}{5}$

	Rs.
2) Capital Profit upto 1-4-2008	
Profit and Loss A/c on 1-4-2008	5,000
General Reserve on 1-4-2008	20,000
Capital Profit	25,000

i) Holding Co's share in Capital Profit

$$25,000 \times \frac{4}{5} = \text{Rs. } 20,000$$

ii) Minority's share in Capital Profit

$$25,000 \times \frac{1}{5} = \text{Rs. } 5,000$$

3) Revenue Profit

	Rs.
Profit & Loss A/c on 31-3-2009	25,000
Less : Profit & Loss on 1-4-2008	5,000
Revenue profit	20,000

i) Holding Co's share in Revenue Profit

$$20,000 \times \frac{4}{5} = \text{Rs. } 16,000$$

ii) Minority's share in Revenue Profit

$$20,000 \times \frac{1}{5} = \text{Rs. } 4,000$$

4) Minority Interest

	Rs.
Face value of shareholding by Minority (100×100)	10,000
Add : Capital Profit of Minority	5,000
Revenue Profit of Minority	4,000
Minority Interest	19,000

5) Capital Reserve

	Rs.
Face value of shares held by minority ('S' Ltd.)	40,000
Add : Capital Profit of 'H' Ltd.	20,000
	60,000
Less : Market value of shares of 'S' Ltd.	50,000
Capital Reserve	10,000

6) Unrealised Profit

25% Profit on selling price

cost + profit = selling price

100 + 25 = 125

Selling Price = Rs. 125 and Profit = Rs. 25

$$20,000 \text{ selling price } \frac{20,000 \times 25}{125} = \text{Rs. } 5,000$$

Holding Co's share Rs. $5,000 \times \frac{4}{5} = \text{Rs. } 4,000$

Consolidated Balance sheet
as on 31-3-2009

Liabilities	Rs.	Assets		Rs.
Share Capital		**Fixed Assets**		
2500 Equity Shares		Land & Building		
of Rs. 100 each	2,50,000	'H' Ltd.	1,00,000	
		'S' Ltd.	20,000	1,20,000
Reserve & Surplus				
General Reserve	50,000	Plant & Machinery		
Capital Reserve	10,000	'H' Ltd.	1,50,000	
Profit & Loss A/c 70,000		'S' Ltd.	30,000	1,80,000
Add : Revenue				
Profit of 'H' Ltd. 16,000		**Current Assets**		
86,000		Stock		
Less : unrealised profit 4,000	82,000	'H' Ltd.	40,000	
		'S' Ltd.	25,000	
Current Liabilities			65,000	
Sundry Creditors		Less : Unrealised profit 4,000		61,000
'H' Ltd. 30,000		Sundry Debtors		
'S' Ltd. 5,000		'H' Ltd.	30,000	
35,000		'S' Ltd.	15,000	
Less Internal owing 5,000	30,000		45,000	
Minority Interest	19,000	Less : Internal owing	5,000	40,000
		Cash		
		'H' Ltd.	30,000	
		'S' Ltd.	10,000	40,000
	4,41,000			4,41,000

Problem No. 5 : The following are the Balance Sheets of two companies as at 31st December, 2008

Liabilities	'AB' Ltd. Rs.	'CD' Ltd. Rs.	Assets	'AB' Ltd. Rs.	'CD' Ltd. Rs.
Equity Share Capital			Land and Building	2,00,000	1,50,000
Shares of Rs. 10 each	10,00,000	5,00,000	Machinery	3,00,000	3,00,000
General Reserve			Stock	75,000	50,000
on 1.1.2008	1,00,000	1,00,000	Sundry Debtors	50,000	60,000

Liabilities	'AB' Ltd. Rs.	'CD' Ltd. Rs.	Assets	'AB' Ltd. Rs.	'CD' Ltd. Rs.
Profit & Loss A/c on 1.1.2008	50,000	30,000	Investment at cost Shares in 'CD' Ltd.	5,00,000	
Profit for the year 2008	60,000	40,000	Bills Receivable	10,000	5,000
Sundry Creditors	70,000	50,000	Cash at Bank	1,55,000	1,60,000
Bills Payable	10,000	5,000			
	12,90,000	7,25,000		12,90,000	7,25,000

1) 'AB' Ltd., acquired 40,000 equity shares of 'CD' Ltd., on 1.1.2008
2) Bills Receivable of 'AB' Ltd., includes Rs. 3,000 accepted by 'CD' Ltd.
3) Sundry Debtors of 'AB' Ltd., includes Rs. 10,000 due from 'CD' Ltd.
4) Stock of 'CD' Ltd., includes goods purchased from 'AB' Ltd., for Rs. 30,000 which were invoiced by 'AB' Ltd., at a profit of 25% on invoice price.
   Prepare a consolidated Balance Sheet of 'AB' Ltd., and its subsidiary 'CD' Ltd., as at 31.12.2008, giving the necessary workings. **(P.U.)**

Solution :
Working Notes :

1) Shares Acquisition Ratio : 4 : 1

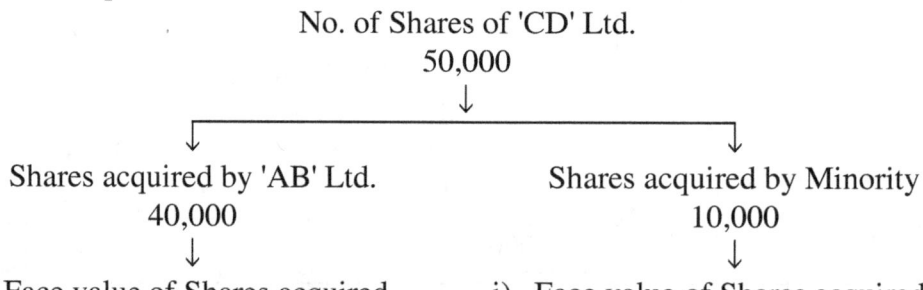

No. of Shares of 'CD' Ltd.
50,000

Shares acquired by 'AB' Ltd.
40,000

i) Face value of Shares acquired by 'AB' Ltd. = Rs. 4,00,000
ii) Market price of shares acquired by 'AB' Ltd. = Rs. 5,00,000

Shares acquired by Minority
10,000

i) Face value of Shares acquired by Minority = Rs. 1,00,000

Shareholding Ratio = 'AB' Ltd. $\frac{4}{5}$ and 'CD' Ltd. $\frac{1}{5}$

2) Capital Profit (upto 1.1.2008)

	Rs.
Profit and Loss A/c on 1.1.2008	30,000
General Reserve on 1.1.2008	1,00,000
Capital Profit	1,30,000

i)   Holding Co's share in Capital Profit = $1,30,000 \times \dfrac{4}{5}$ = Rs. 1,04,000

ii) Subsidiary Co's share in Capital Profit = $1,30,000 \times \dfrac{1}{5}$ = Rs. 26,000

3) Revenue Profit (1.1.2008 to 31.12.2008)

	Rs.
Profit & Loss Account	40,000
Revenue Profit	40,000

i)   Holding Co's share in Revenue Profit

$4,00,000 \times \dfrac{4}{5}$ = Rs. 32,000

ii) Subsidiary Co's (minority) share in Revenue Profit

$40,000 \times \dfrac{1}{5}$ = Rs. 8,000

4) Minority Interest :

	Rs.
Face value of shares acquired by Minority	1,00,000
Add : i) Capital Profit of Minority	26,000
ii) Revenue Profit of Minority	8,000
Minority Interest	1,34,000

5) Goodwill Capital Reserve :

	Rs.
Market Price of shares acquired by 'AB' Ltd.	5,00,000
Less : Face value of shares acquired by 'AB' Ltd.	4,00,000
	1,00,000
Less : Capital Profit of 'AB' Ltd.	1,04,000
Capital Reserve	4,000

6) Unrealised Profit

Stock of 'CD' Ltd., includes Rs. 30,000 worth goods purchased from 'AB' Ltd., on which 'AB' Ltd., charged profit @ 25% on invoice price.

Hence, Profit on invoice price = $30,000 \times \dfrac{25}{100}$

$= 7,500$

Holding Co's Shares 4/5th of 7,500; i.e. Rs. 6,000.

Consolidated Balance Sheet of 'AB' Ltd., together with its Subsidiary 'CD' Ltd., as on 31-12-2008

Liabilities		Rs.	Assets		Rs.
Share Capital			**Fixed Assets**		
1,00,000 equity shares of			Land and Building		
Rs. 10 each		10,00,000	'AB' Ltd.	2,00,000	
Reserves and Surplus :			'CD' Ltd.	1,50,000	3,50,000
General Reserve		1,00,000	Machinery		
Profit and Loss A/c			'AB' Ltd.	3,00,000	
(1.1.2008)	50,000		'CD' Ltd.	3,00,000	6,00,000
Add : i) Profit during			**Current Assets**		
2008	60,000		**Loans and Advances :**		
ii) Revenue Profit			Stock		
('AB' Ltd.)	32,000		'AB' Ltd.	75,000	
	1,42,000		'CD' Ltd.	50,000	
Less : Unrealised Profit	6,000	1,36,000		1,25,000	
Capital Reserve		4,000	Less : Unrealised Profit	6,000	1,19,000
Current Liabilities & Provisions :			Debtors		
Sundry Creditors			'AB' Ltd.	50,000	
'AB' Ltd.	70,000		'CD' Ltd.	60,000	
'CD' Ltd.	50,000			1,10,000	
	1,20,000		Less : Inter co. owing	10,000	1,00,000
Less : Inter-Co. owing	10,000	1,10,000	Bills Receivable		
Bills payable			'AB' Ltd.	10,000	
'AB' Ltd.	10,000		'CD' Ltd.	5,000	
'CD' Ltd.	5,000			15,000	
	15,000		Less : Inter-Co. owing	3,000	12,000
Less : Inter-Co. owing	3,000	12,000	Cash at Bank		
Minority Interest		1,34,000	'AB' Ltd.	1,55,000	
			'CD' Ltd.	1,60,000	3,15,000
		14,96,000			14,96,000

Problem No. 6 : From the following Balance Sheet of 'H' Ltd., and its subsidiary 'S' Ltd., drawn on 31st December 2008, prepare a consolidated Balance Sheet as on that date.

Liabilities	'H' Ltd. Rs.	'S' Ltd. Rs.	Assets	'H' Ltd. Rs.	'S' Ltd. Rs.
Share Capital :			**Fixed Assets :**	3,50,000	1,50,000
in Shares of			Stock	90,000	40,000
Rs. 100 each	5,00,000	2,00,000	Debtors	60,000	30,000
General Reserve	1,00,000	–	9% Debentures		
Profit & Loss A/c	80,000	–	in 'S' Ltd. at par	60,000	–
9% Debentures	–	1,00,000	1,500 shares of 'S' Ltd		
Trade Creditors	75,000	45,000	@ Rs. 80 each	1,20,000	–
			Bank	75,000	25,000
			Profit and Loss A/c	–	1,00,000
	7,55,000	3,45,000		7,55,000	3,45,000

'H' Ltd., acquired the shares on 1st May, 2008. The Profit and Loss Account of 'S' Ltd., showed a debit balance of Rs. 1,50,000 on 1st January, 2008. During March, 2008, goods costing Rs. 6,000 were destroyed against which the insurers paid Rs. 2,000. Trade Creditors of 'S' Ltd., include Rs. 20,000 for goods supplied by 'H' Ltd., on which H. Ltd. made a profit Rs. 2,000. Half of the goods were still in stock on 31st December, 2008.

(CS Inter, and P.U)

Solution :

Working Notes :
1) Pre and Post Acquisition Period Ratio : 1 : 2
   Holding Co. 'H' Ltd. acquired shares of 'S' Ltd. on 1.5.2008
   i)   Pre acquisition period is 1.1.2008 to 1.5.2008 i.e. 4 months
   ii) Post acquisition is 1.5.2008 to 31.12.2008 i.e. 8 months
2) Share Acquisition Ratio : 3 :1 (1500 : 500)

No. of Shares of 'S' Ltd.

2,000

↓

Shares acquired by 'H' Ltd. 1,500	Shares acquired by Minority 500
i) Face value of shares acquired by H Ltd. = Rs. 1,50,000	i) Face value of shares acquired by Minority = Rs. 50,000
ii) Market price of shares acquired by H Ltd. = Rs. 1,20,000	

Note :

	Rs.
Profit Prior and after purchase of shares	
Profit and Loss A/c on 1.1.2008 (Loss)	1,50,000
Less : Profit and Loss A/c on 31.12.2008 (Loss)	1,00,000
Profit during the year	50,000

But, it is after deducting loss of goods Rs. 4,000. It means the profit before loss was Rs. 54,000. The period ratio is 1 : 2. Hence, division of profit is Rs. 18,000 and Rs. 36,000. The Loss of Rs. 4,000 is before the purchase of shares. Hence, Profit from 1.1.2008 to 1.5. 2008 = 18,000 - 4,000 = Rs. 14,000

3) Capital Loss upto 1-5-2008

	Rs.
Profit & Loss A/c (Loss on 1-1-2008)	1,50,000
Less - P and L A/c (Profit) 1-1-08 to 1-5-08	14,000
Capital Loss	1,36,000

Division of Capital Loss between 'H' Ltd. & 'S' Ltd.

i)	Holding Co's shares in capital loss $(1,36,000 \times \frac{3}{4})$	1,02,000
ii)	Minority's share in capital loss $(1,36,000 \times \frac{1}{4})$	34,000

4) Revenue Profit (1-5-2008 t0 31-12-2008)

Profit & Loss A/c (see note)		36,000

Division of Revenue Profit between 'H' Ltd. & 'S' Ltd.

i)	Holding Co's share in Revenue Profit $(36,000 \times \frac{3}{4})$	27,000
ii)	Minority share in Revenue Profit $(36000 \times \frac{1}{4})$	9,000

5) Minority Interest

	Rs.
Face value of shares held by Minority	50,000
Add - Revenue Profit of Minority	9,000
	59,000
Less - Capital Loss of Minority	34,000
Minority Interest	25,000

6) Goodwill

	Rs.
Cost price of shares held by 'H' Ltd.	1,20,000
Add - Capital Loss of 'H' Ltd.	1,02,000
	2,22,000
Less - Face value of shares held by 'H' Ltd.	1,50,000
Goodwill	72,000

7) Unrealised Profit

Stock of 'S' Ltd., includes Rs. 10,000, goods purchased from 'H' Ltd., on which 'H' Ltd., charged profit is Rs. 1,000.

Hence, Holding Companies shares $3/4^{th}$ of 1,000 i.e. Rs. 750.

Consolidated Balance Sheet of 'H' Ltd., with its subsidiary 'S' Ltd. as on 31-12-2008

Liabilities		Rs.	Assets		Rs.
Share Capital			Good will		72,000
5,000 equity shares of			Fixed Assets		
Rs. 100 each		5,00,000	'H' Ltd.	3,50,000	
Reserves and Surplus			'S' Ltd.	1,50,000	5,00,000
General Reserve		1,00,000			
Profit and Loss A/c	80,000		**Current Assets and**		
Add - Revenue Profit	27,000		**Loans and Advances**		
	1,07,000		Stock		
Less - Unrealised			'H' Ltd.	90,000	
Profit	750	1,06,250	'S' Ltd.	40,000	
Creditors				1,30,000	
'H' Ltd.	75,000		Less - Unrealised		
'S' Ltd.	45,000		Profit	750	1,29,250
	1,20,000		Debtors		
Less - Inter-Co. owing	20,000	1,00,000	'H' Ltd.	60,000	
Secured Loans :			'S' Ltd.	30,000	
6% Debenture	1,00,000			90,000	
Less - held by 'H' Ltd.	60,000	40,000	Less Inter-Co. owing	20,000	70,000
Minority Interest		25,000	Cash at Bank		1,00,000
		8,71,250			8,71,250

Problem No. 7 : Prepare a Consolidated Balance Sheet with necessary workings from the Balance Sheet of 'H' Ltd. and 'S' Ltd. and additional information given below :–

Balance Sheet as on 31-12-2008

Liabilities	'H' Ltd. Rs.	'S' Ltd. Rs.	Assets	'H' Ltd. Rs.	'S' Ltd. Rs.
Share Capital :			Land & Buildings	2,00,000	1,00,000
Share of Rs. 100			Plant & Machinery	1,50,000	2,00,000
each	5,00,000	3,00,000	Investment in		
General Reserve	40,000	10,000	2,700 shares of		
Profit & Loss A/c	70,000	5,000	'S' Ltd.	2,97,000	
Bills Payable	50,000	25,000	Stock	40,000	30,000
Creditors	1,40,000	60,000	Debtors	50,000	60,000
			Bills Receivable	63,000	10,000
	8,00,000	4,00,000		8,00,000	4,00,000

Additional Information :

1) On the date of purchase of shares there was no balance in General Reserve and Profit and Loss A/c showed a debit balance of Rs. 10,000 in the books of 'S' Ltd.
2) Sundry Debtors of 'S' Ltd., include Rs. 40,000 due from 'H' Ltd.
3) Bills Payable of 'S' Ltd., include Rs. 18,000/- in favour of 'H' Ltd., which has discount of Rs. 3,000/- of them.
4) Stock of 'S' Ltd., includes Rs. 4,000 being purchased from 'H' Ltd., on which the later company made a profit of $33\frac{1}{3}$ on Cost.   **(P.U.)**

Solution :

Working Notes : -

1) Shares Acquisition Ratio - 9 : 1

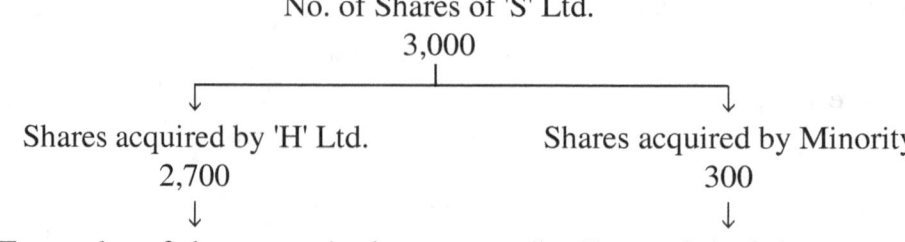

No. of Shares of 'S' Ltd.

3,000

Shares acquired by 'H' Ltd.   Shares acquired by Minority

2,700   300

i)   Face value of shares acquired by 'H' Ltd. = Rs. 2,70,000

           i)   Face value of shares acquired by Minority = Rs. 30,000

ii)   Market price of shares acquired by 'H' Ltd. = Rs. 2,97,000

2) Capital Loss -

	Rs.
Profit and Loss A/c (loss)	10,000
Capital Loss =	10,000

i) Holding Co's shares in Capital Loss

$$10,000 \times \frac{9}{10} = \text{Rs. } 9,000$$

ii) Minority's shares in Revenue Profit

$$10,000 \times \frac{1}{10} = \text{Rs. } 1,000$$

3) Revenue Profit

Profit and loss A/c (loss)	10,000
Add : Profit and Loss A/c (Profit) 31-12-2008	5,000
	15,000
Add : General Reserve on 31-12-2008	10,000
Revenue Profit	25,000

i) Holding Co's shares in Revenue Profit.

$$25,000 \times \frac{9}{10} = \text{Rs. } 22,500$$

ii) Minority's shares in Revenue Profit

$$25,000 \times \frac{1}{10} = \text{Rs. } 2,500$$

4) Minority Interest

Face value of shares acquired by Minority	30,000
Add : Revenue Profit of Minority	2,500
	32,500
Less : Capital Loss of Minority	1,000
Minority Interest	31,500

5) Goodwill

	Rs.
Market price of shares acquired by 'H' Ltd.	2,97,000
Add : Capital Loss of 'H' Ltd.	9,000
	3,06,000
Less : Face value of shares acquired by 'H' Ltd.	2,70,000
Goodwill	36,000

6) Unrealised Profit

Stock of 'S' Ltd., includes Rs. 4,000 worth goods purchased from 'H' Ltd., on which

'H' Ltd., charged profit @ $33\frac{1}{3}\%$ on cost.

Hence, Cost price + Profit = Selling price

$$100 \quad + \quad 33\frac{1}{3} \quad = 133\frac{1}{3}$$

$\therefore$ Profit on selling price $= \dfrac{33\frac{1}{3}}{133\frac{1}{3}} = \dfrac{1}{4}$

$\therefore$ Profit in Rs. 4,000 is $\dfrac{1}{4}$th of 4,000; i.e. Rs. 1,000.

Holding Co's Shares $\dfrac{9}{10}$th of 1,000; i.e. Rs. 900.

Consolidated Balance Sheet
of 'H' Ltd., together with its Subsidiary 'S' Ltd.
as on 31-12-2008

Liabilities		Rs.	Assets		Rs.
Share Capital			**Fixed Assets**		
5,000 Equity Shares of			Goodwill		36,000
Rs. 100 each		5,00,000	Land and Building		
Reserves and Surplus			'H' Ltd.	2,00,000	
General Reserve		40,000	'S' Ltd.	1,00,000	3,00,000
Profit and Loss A/c	70,000		Plant and Machinery		
Add - Revenue profit	22,500		'H' Ltd	1,50,000	
	92,500		'S' Ltd	2,00,000	3,50,000
Less - Unrealised			**Current Assets Loans**		
Profit	900	91,600	**and Advances**		
Current Liabilities			Stock		
and Provisions			'H' Ltd.	40,000	
Bills Payable			'S' Ltd.	30,000	
'H' Ltd.	50,000			70,000	
'S' Ltd.	25,000		Less - Unrealised		
	75,000		Profit	900	69,100

Liabilities		Rs.	Assets		Rs.
Less - Inter-Co.			Debtors		
Owing	15,000	60,000	'H' Ltd.	50,000	
Sundry Creditors			'S' Ltd.	60,000	
'H' Ltd.	1,40,000			1,10,000	
'S' Ltd.	60,000		Less - Inter-Co.		
	2,00,000		Owing	40,000	70,000
Less - Inter-Co.			Bills Receivable		
Owing	40,000	1,60,000	'H' Ltd.	63,000	
Minority Interest		31,500	'S' Ltd.	10,000	
				73,000	
			Less - Inter-Co.		
			Owing	15,000	58,000
		8,83,100			8,83,100

Problem No. 8 : From the following information, prepare the consolidated Balance Sheet of 'H' Ltd., and its subsidiary 'S' Ltd., as at 31st December, 2008, giving detailed workings.

Balance Sheet as at 31st December, 2008

Liabilities	'H' Ltd. Rs.	'S' Ltd. Rs.	Assets	'H' Ltd. Rs.	'S' Ltd. Rs.
Share Capital			Goodwill	1,00,000	—
Equity Shares of			Fixed Assets	2,00,000	2,50,000
Rs. 10 each	4,00,000	2,00,000	Investments		
General Reserve	2,00,000	60,000	16,000 Shares of		
Profit and Loss A/c	1,00,000	40,000	Rs. 10 each in 'S'		
6% Debentures	—	1,00,000	Ltd. (at Cost)	2,00,000	
Loan from 'H' Ltd.	—	10,000	6% Debentures of		
Sundry Creditors	1,00,000	40,000	'S' Ltd. (Face Value		
Bills Payable	50,000	30,000	Rs. 60,000)	60,000	—
			Govt. Securities		50,000
			Stock	1,00,000	40,000
			Sundry Debtors	80,000	40,000
			Bills Receivable	40,000	—
			Bank Balance	60,000	1,00,000
			Loan to 'S' Ltd.	10,000	—
	8,50,000	4,80,000		8,50,000	4,80,000

1) Sundry Creditors of 'H' Ltd., include Rs. 20,000 due to 'S' Ltd.

2) The Closing Stock of 'H' Ltd., includes stock worth Rs. 30,000 supplied by 'S' Ltd., which was invoiced at cost plus 20% profit on cost.

3) Bills payable of 'S' Ltd., include Rs. 24,000 issued in favour of 'H' Ltd., which was discounted but not yet matured Rs. 4,000 of them.

4) 'H' Ltd., acquired 16,000 equity shares in 'S' Ltd., on 1st January, 2008 on which date the Balance Sheet of 'S' Ltd., showed General Reserve at Rs. 20,000 and Profit and Loss A/c Credit balance of Rs. 10,000.

5) 'H' Ltd., revalued Fixed Assets of 'S' Ltd., as on 1st January, 2008, at Rs. 2,60,000.

(P.U.)

Solution :

Working Notes

1) Shares Acquisition Ratio = 4 : 1

No. of shares of 'S' Ltd.

20,000

Shares acquired by 'H' Ltd. 16,000	Shares acquired by Minority 4,000
i) Face value of shares held by 'H' Ltd. = Rs. 1,60,000	i) Face value of shares held by Minority = Rs. 40,000
ii) Market price of shares held by 'H' Ltd. = Rs. 2,00,000	

2) Capital Profit (upto 1-1-2008)

General Reserve on 1-1-2008	20,000
Profit and Loss A/c on 1-1-2008	10,000
Appreciation of Fixed Assets	10,000
Capital Profit	**40,000**

i) Holding Co's Share in Capital Profit

$$40,000 \times \frac{4}{5} = Rs. 32,000$$

ii) Minority's share in Capital Profit'

$$40,000 \times \frac{1}{5} = Rs. 8,000$$

3) Revenue Profit (1-1-2008 to 31-12-2008)

i) General Reserve on 31-12-2008	60,000	
Less - General Reserve on 1-1-2008	20,000	40,000
ii) Profit and Loss A/c on 31-12-2008	40,000	
Less = Profit and Loss A/c 1-1-2008	10,000	30,000
Revenue Profit		70,000

i) Holding Co's share in Revenue Profit

$$70,000 \times \frac{4}{5} = 56,000$$

ii) Minority share in Revenue Profit

$$70,000 \times \frac{1}{5} = \text{Rs. } 14,000$$

4) Minority Interest

Face value of shares held by Minority	40,000
Add - i) Capital Profit of Minority	8,000
ii) Revenue Profit of Minority	14,000
Minority Interest	62,000

5) Goodwill   Rs.

Market price of Shares held by 'H' Ltd.	
Face value of Shares held by 'H' Ltd.	2,00,000
Less - Face value of Bonus Shares held by 'H' Ltd.	1,60,000
	40,000
Less - Capital Profit of 'H' Ltd.	32,000
Goodwill	8,000

6) Unrealised Profit

Unsold stock with 'H' Ltd.	
(of goods purchased from 'S' Ltd.)	30,000
Unrealised Profit included in this stock cost plus 20%	
i.e. 1/6 on Sale	5,000

'H' Ltd's share in Unrealised Profit $\frac{4}{5}$ th of 5,000 = 4,000

Consolidated Balance sheet of 'H' Ltd., with its Subsidiary 'S' Ltd., as on 31-12-2008

Liabilities		Rs.	Assets		Rs.
Share Capital			**Fixed Assets**		
40,000 equity shares of			Goodwill		1,08,000
Rs. 10 each		4,00,000	Fixed Assets		
Reserves and Surplus			'H' Ltd.	2,00,000	
General Reserve		2,00,000	'S' Ltd.	2,50,000	
Profit and Loss A/c	1,00,000		**Add :** Appreciation	10,000	4,60,000
Add - Revenue profit	56,000		**Investments**		
	1,56,000		Govt. Securities		50,000
Less - Unrealised Profit	4,000	1,52,000	**Currents Assets**		
Secured Loans			**Loans and Advances**		
6% Debentures	1,00,000		'H' Ltd.	1,00,000	
Less - internal	60,000	40,000	'S' Ltd.	40,000	
Current Liabilities and				1,40,000	
Provisions			**Less -** Unrealised		
Sundry Creditors			Profit	4,000	1,36,000
'H' Ltd.	1,00,000		Sundry Debtors		
'S' Ltd.	40,000		'H' Ltd.	80,000	
	1,40,000		'S' Ltd.	40,000	
Less - Inter-Co.				1,20,000	
Owing	20,000	1,20,000	Less - Inter-Co.		
Bills Payable			Owing	20,000	1,00,000
'H' Ltd.	50,000		Bills Receivable	40,000	
'S' Ltd.	30,000		Less - Inter-Co.		
	80,000		Owing	20,000	20,000
Less - Inter-Co.					
Owing	20,000	60,000	Bank Balance		
Minority Interest		62,000	'H' Ltd.	60,000	
			'S' Ltd.	1,00,000	1,60,000
		10,34,000			10,34,000

Problem No. 9 : The following are the Balance Sheets of Satara Ltd., and Pune Ltd., as on 31st March, 2009.

Balance Sheets

Liabilities	Satara Ltd. Rs.	Pune Ltd. Rs.	Assets	Satara Ltd. Rs.	Pune Ltd. Rs.
Share Capital			Goodwill	60,000	20,000
Shares of Rs.10 each	10,00,000	4,00,000	Machinery	7,32,000	2,72,000
General Reserve	1,50,000	—	Stock	1,80,000	90,000
Profit & Loss A/c	1,42,000	60,000	Debtors	2,95,000	1,23,000
Creditors	1,82,000	87,000	Cash	35,000	27,000
Bills Payable	20,000	—	Investment (24,000 shares of Pune Ltd. at Cost)	1,92,000	—
			Bills Receivable	—	15,000
	14,94,000	5,47,000		14,94,000	5,47,000

Other Information -

a) Satara Ltd., acquired the shares in Pune Ltd., on 1st Oct., 2008

b) The Profit & Loss Account of Pune Ltd., showed a debit balance of Rs. 20,000 on 1st April, 2008

c) Included in the Stock of Pune Ltd., are goods of Rs. 20,000 which were supplied by Satara Ltd., as cost plus 25%.

d) The Bills payable in Satara Ltd., represented Rs. 15,000 issued in favour of Pune Ltd. Prepare a consolidated Balance Sheet with full working. **(P.U.)**

Solution

Working Notes :

1) Calculation of Shareholding Ratio.

i) Holding Co's share $= \dfrac{\text{Shares held by Holding Company}}{\text{Total shares of Subsidiary Company}}$

$= \dfrac{24,000 \text{ Shares}}{40,000 \text{ Shares}} = \dfrac{3}{5}$ Share

ii) Minority's share $= 1 - \dfrac{3}{5} = \dfrac{2}{5}$ Share.

Shareholding Ratio $= 3 : 2$

2) Pre and post acquisition period

i) Pre-acquisition period - 1st April, 2008 to 1st Oct., 2008 = 6 months.

ii) Post-acquisition period - 1st Oct., 2008 to 31-3-2009 = 6 months.

3) Capital Profit

Profit & Loss Account 1-4-2008 to 1-10-2008	Rs.
(Rs. 60,000 + 20,000 ÷ 2)	40,000
Less Profit and Loss A/c (Loss on 1-4-2008)	20,000
Capital Profit	20,000

i) Holding Co's share in Capital Profit

$$20,000 \times \frac{3}{5} = \text{Rs. } 12,000$$

ii) Minority's share in Capital Profit

$$20.000 \times \frac{2}{5} = \text{Rs. } 8,000$$

4) Revenue Profit

Profit & Loss Account	
(1-10-2008 to 31-3-2009)	40,000

i) Holding Co's share in Revenue Profit.

$$40,000 \times \frac{3}{5} = \text{Rs. } 24,000$$

ii) Minority's share in Revenue Profit

$$40,000 \times \frac{2}{5} = \text{Rs. } 16,000$$

5) Minority Interest

Face value of shares held by Minority	1,60,000
Add - i) Capital Profit of Minority	8,000
ii) Revenue Profit of Minority	16,000
Minority Interest	1,84,000

6) Goodwill

Balance of Goodwill		
Satara Ltd., 60,000 + Poona Ltd., 20,000		80,000
Add : Market price of shares held.		
(Investment) by Satara Ltd.		1,92,000
		2,72,000
Less : i) Face value of shares held by Satara Ltd.	2,40,000	
ii) Capital Profit of Satara Ltd.	12,000	
		2,52,000
Goodwill		20,000

7) Unrealised Profit

Stock of Poona Ltd., includes Rs. 20,000 worth goods purchased from Satara Ltd., on which Satara Ltd., charged profit at cost plus 25%.

Hence, cost + profit = selling price

Rs. 100 + Rs. 25 = Rs.125

∴ Selling price is Rs.125 and profit Rs. 25

$$20,000 \text{ selling price } = \frac{20,000 \times 25}{125} = \text{Rs. } 4,000$$

$$\text{Holding Co's share } = 4,000 \times \frac{3}{5} = \text{Rs. } 2,400$$

Consolidated Balance Sheet
as on 31-3-2009

Liabilities		Rs.	Assets		Rs.
Share Capital			**Fixed Assets**		
1,00,000 Equity shares		10,00,000	Goodwill		20,000
of Rs. 10 each			Machinery		
Reserves & Surplus		1,50,000	'S' Ltd.	7,32,000	
General Reserve			'P' Ltd.	2,72,000	10,04,000
P & L A/c	1,42,000		**Current Assets**		
Add. Revenue profit	24,000		Stock		
	1,66,000		'S' Ltd.	1,80,000	
Less			'P' Ltd.	90,000	
Unrealised profit	2,400	1,63,600	Less	2,70,000	
Current Liabilities			Unrealised Profit	2,400	2,67,600
Creditors			Cash – 'S' Ltd.	35,000	
'S' Ltd.	1,82,000		'P' Ltd.	27,000	62,000
'P' Ltd.	87,000	2,69,000	Debtors		
Bills payable			'S' Ltd.	2,95,000	
'S' Ltd	20,000		'P' Ltd.	1,23,000	4,18,000
Less Internal owing	15,000	5,000	Bills Receivable		
Minority Interest		1,84,000	Poona Ltd.	15,000	
			Less Internal owing	15,000	
		17,71,600			17,71,600

Problem No. 10 : 'A' Ltd., acquired 2,000 Equity Shares of Rs. 100 each in 'B' Ltd., on 1st January, 2008.

The summarised Balance Sheets of the two companies as on 31st December, 2008 were as follows :

Liabilities	'A' Ltd. Rs.	'B' Ltd. Rs.	Assets	'A' Ltd. Rs.	'B' Ltd. Rs.
Share Capital			Fixed Assets	7,00,000	2,50,000
Equity Shares of			Current Assets	4,00,000	2,00,000
Rs. 100 each	8,00,000	2,50,000	2,000 Shares		
Reserves	3,00,000	50,000	in 'B' Ltd., at cost	3,00,000	
Profit & Loss A/c	1,00,000	1,00,000			
Creditors	2,00,000	50,000			
	14,00,000	4,50,000		14,00,000	4,50,000

'B' Ltd., had a credit balance of Rs. 50,000 in the Reserves and Rs. 20,000 in the Profit and Loss Account when 'A' Ltd., acquired shares in 'B' Ltd.

'B' Ltd., issued bonus shares in the ratio of one for every five shares held out of the profit earned during 2008. This is not shown in the above Balance Sheet of 'B' Ltd.

Prepare a consolidated Balance Sheet of 'A' Ltd., and its subsidiary, as on 31st December, 2008, giving all necessary workings. **(P.U.)**

Solution :

Working Notes :

1. Shares Acquisition Ratio : 4:1

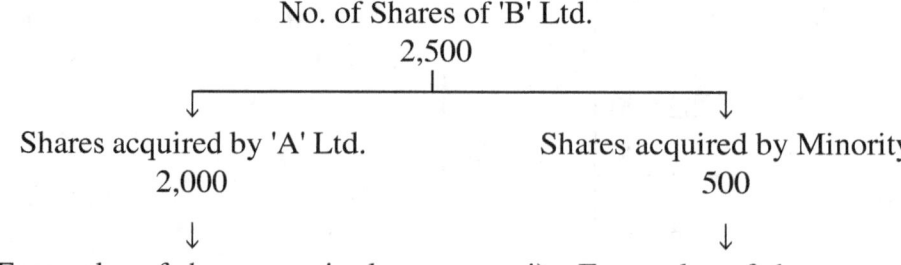

No. of Shares of 'B' Ltd.

2,500

Shares acquired by 'A' Ltd. 2,000	Shares acquired by Minority 500
i) Face value of shares acquired by 'A' Ltd. = Rs. 2,00,000	i) Face value of shares acquired by Minority = Rs. 50,000
ii) Market price of shares acquired by 'A' Ltd. = Rs. 3,00,000	

2. Capital Profit (upto 1-1-2008)   Rs.

Reserve on 1-1-2008	50,000
Profit and Loss A/c on 1-1-2008	20,000
Capital Profit	70,000

i) Holding Co's share in Capital Profit

$$20,000 \times \frac{4}{5} = 56,000$$

ii) Minority Share in Capital Profit

$$70,000 \times \frac{1}{5} = 14,000$$

3. Revenue Profit (1-1-2008 to 31-12-2008)   Rs.

Profit & Loss A/c on 31-12-2008	1,00,000
Less : Profit and Loss A/c on. 1-1-2008	20,000
	80,000
Less : Issue of Bonus Shares	50,000
Revenue Profit	30,000

Division of Revenue Profit   Division of Bonus Shares.

i) Holding Co's share in Revenue

$$30,000 \times \frac{4}{5} = Rs.\ 24,000$$

i) Holding Co's share in Bonus shares

$$50,000 \times \frac{4}{5} = Rs.\ 40,000$$

ii) Minority's share in Revenue Profit

$$30,000 \times \frac{1}{5} = Rs.\ 6,000$$

ii) Minority's Bonus Shares

$$50,000 \times \frac{1}{5} = Rs.\ 10,000$$

4. Minority Interest :   Rs.

Face value of shares acquired by Minority	50,000
Add : i) Bonus Shares	10,000
ii) Capital Profit of Minority	14,000
iii) Revenue Profit of Minority	6,000
Minority Interest	80,000

Goodwill

Market price of shares held by 'A' Ltd.		3,00,000
Less : i) Face Value of Shares held by 'A' Ltd.	2,00,000	
ii) Face value of Bonus shares held by 'A' Ltd.	40,000	2,40,000
		60,000
Less : Capital Profit of 'A' Ltd.		56,000
Goodwill		4,000

Consolidated Balance Sheet of 'A' Ltd., with its Subsidiary 'B' Ltd., as on 31-12-2008

Liabilities		Rs.	Assets		Rs.
Share Capital :			**Fixed Assets :**		
8,000 equity Shares of			Goodwill		4,000
Rs. 100 each		8,00,000	Fixed Assets		
Reserves and Surplus :			'A' Ltd.	7,00,000	
Reserve		3,00,000	'B' Ltd.	2,50,000	9,50,000
Profit and Loss A/c	1,00,000		**Current Assets**		
Add : Revenue Profit	24,000	1,24,000	'A' Ltd.	4,00,000	
Current Liabilities			'B' Ltd.	2,00,000	6,00,000
and Provisions :					
Creditors					
'A' Ltd.	2,00,000				
'B' Ltd.	50,000	2,50,000			
Minority Interest		80,000			
		15,54,000			15,54,000

8.6 EXCERCISES

1) From the following Balance Sheets and particulars given below prepare a consolidated Balance Sheet of 'S' Ltd., and 'T' Ltd., as on 31-3-2009

Balance Sheets as on 31-3-2009

Liabilities	'S' Ltd. Rs.	'T' Ltd. Rs.	Assets	'S' Ltd. Rs.	'T' Ltd. Rs.
Share Capital			Goodwill	12,000	9,000
Equity Shares of			Land & Building	37,500	30,000
Rs.100 each, fully paid	1,50,000	60,000	Plant & Machinery	60,000	33,000
General Reserve	30,000	18,000	Furniture	10,500	3,000
Profit & Loss A/c	42,000	27,000	Investment :		
Bills Payable	–	12,000	450 Equity Shares		
Creditors	27,000	21,000	in 'T' Ltd.	72,000	–
			Stock	30,000	27,000
			Debtors	9,000	28,500
			Cash at Bank	18,000	7,500
	2,49,000	1,38,000		2,49,000	1,38,000

Additional Information :

a) 'S' Ltd., acquired the shares in 'T' Ltd., on 1st July, 2008

b) The balance on Profit & Loss A/c of 'T' Ltd., as on 1st April, 2008, was Rs. 6,000 (credit) and on General Reserve Rs. 15,000

c) The Bills Payable of 'T' Ltd., were all issued in favour of 'S' Ltd., of which company got bills discounted.

d) The Stock of 'T' Ltd., included goods worth Rs. 2,400 which were supplied by 'S' Ltd., at a profit of 25% on cost. **(P.U.)**

Ans. : B/S Total Rs. 3,21,290

2) 'H' Ltd., acquired 4,000 shares of 'S' Ltd., on 1st July, 2008. Their Balance Sheets as on 31st December, 2008, stood as follows :

Balance Sheet as on 31-12-2008

Liabilities	'H' Ltd. Rs.	'S' Ltd. Rs.	Assets	'H' Ltd. Rs.	'S' Ltd. Rs.
Share Capital :			**Assets :**		
Equity shares of			Fixed Assets	6,00,000	5,00,000
Rs. 100 each	10,00,000	5,00,000	Investments		
General Reserve	2,50,000	1,50,000	4,000 Equity Shares		
Profit & Loss A/c	1,00,000	50,000	(at Rs. 120 each)	4,80,000	—
Creditors	1,50,000	50,000	**Current Assets :**		
			Sundry Debtors	2,50,000	1,50,000
			Stock	1,50,000	50,000
			Cash at Bank	20,000	50,000
	15,00,000	7,50,000		15,00,000	7,50,000

On 1-1-2008, the Profit and Loss A/c and the General Reserve of 'S' Ltd., showed the Credit Balance of Rs. 30,000 and Rs. 1,00,000 respectively. Debtors of 'H' Ltd., include Rs. 15,000 due from 'S' Ltd.

Stock of 'H' Ltd., includes Rs. 20,000 purchased from 'S' Ltd., which made 20% profit on selling price.

Prepare a consolidated Balance Sheet of 'H' Ltd., and it's Subsidiary 'S' Ltd., as on that date. **(P.U.)**

Ans. B/S Total 17,51,800

3) From the following Balance Sheets and particulars given below, prepare a consolidated Balance Sheet of 'H' Ltd., and 'S' Ltd., as on 31-3-2009

Balance Sheets as on 31-3-2009

Liabilities	'H' Ltd. Rs.	'S' Ltd. Rs.	Assets	'H' Ltd. Rs.	'S' Ltd. Rs.
Share Capital :			Goodwill	8,000	6,000
Equity Shares of			Land & Building	25,000	20,000
Rs. 100 each,			Plant & Machinery	40,000	22,000
fully paid	1,00,000	40,000	Furniture	7,000	2,000
General Reserve	20,000	12,000	300 Equity		
Profit & Loss A/c	28,000	18,000	Shares in 'S'		
Bills Payable		8,000	Ltd., at cost	48,000	—
Creditors	18,000	14,000	Stock	20,000	18,000
			Debtors	6,000	19,000
			Cash at Bank	12,000	5,000
	1,66,000	92,000		1,66,000	92,000

a) 'H' Ltd., acquired the shares in 'S' Ltd., on 1-10-2008
b) The balance on Profit and Loss Account of 'S' Ltd., as on 1-4-2008 was Rs. 4,000 (credit) and on General Reserve Rs. 10,000
c) The Bills Payable of 'S' Ltd., were all issued in favour of 'H' Ltd., of which company got bills discounted.
d) The stock of 'S' Ltd., included goods worth Rs. 1,600 which were supplied by 'H' Ltd., as a profit of 25% on cost. **(P.U.)**

Ans. B/S Total 2,11,260

4) Following are the Balance Sheets of 'P' Ltd., and 'R' Ltd., as at December, 2008 :

Liabilities	'P' Ltd. Rs.	'R' Ltd. Rs.	Assets	'P' Ltd. Rs.	'R' Ltd. Rs.
Share Capital :			Goodwill	20,000	10,000
(Rs. 10 each)	2,50,000	1,00,000	Fixed Assets	2,00,000	1,20,000
General Reserve	75,000	30,000	Stock	80,000	30,000
P & L A/c	70,000	60,000	Debtors	60,000	50,000
Creditors	50,000	20,000	Investments 6,000		
Bills Payable	5,000	2,000	Shares of 'R' Ltd.	85,000	—
			Cash	5,000	2,000
	4,50,000	2,12,000		4,50,000	2,12,000

Additional Information :

1) Shares in 'R' Ltd., were acquired by 'P' Ltd., on 1st July 2008.

2) 'R' Ltd., had on 1-1-2008 Rs. 18,000 in General Reserve and Rs. 14,000 in Profit and Loss Account.

3) Included in the Creditors of 'R' Ltd., is Rs. 12,000 for goods supplied by 'P' Ltd.

4) Included in stock of 'R' Ltd., are the goods to the value of Rs. 6,000, Which were supplied by 'P' Ltd., at the profit of 25% on cost.

Prepare consolidated Balance Sheet as at 31-12-2008 Showing necessary working.

(P.U.)

Ans. B/S Total Rs. 5,64,280.

5) The following are the Balance Sheets of 'H' Ltd., and 'S' Ltd., as at 31st March, 2009

Liabilities	'H' Ltd. Rs.	'S' Ltd. Rs.	Assets	'H' Ltd. Rs.	'S' Ltd. Rs.
Equity Shares			Machinery	3,90,000	1,35,000
of Rs. 10 each	6,00,000	2,00,000	Furniture	80,000	40,000
General Reserve	3,40,000	80,000	80% shares		
P & L A/c	1,00,000	60,000	in 'S' Ltd., at cost	3,40,000	—
Creditors	70,000	35,000	Stock	1,80,000	1,20,000
			Debtors	50,000	30,000
			Cash at Balance	70,000	50,000
	11,10,000	3,75,000		11,10,000	3,75,000

The following additional information is provided to you.

1) Profit and Loss Account of 'S' Ltd., stood at Rs. 30,000 on 1-4-2008, whereas General Reserve has remained unchanged since that date.

2) 'H' Ltd., acquired 80% shares in 'S' Ltd., on 1-10-2008 for Rs. 3,40,000 as mentioned above.

3) Included in debtors of 'S' Ltd., is a sum of Rs. 10,000 due from 'H' Ltd., for goods sold at a profit of 25% on cost price. Till 31-3-2009, only one-half of the goods had been sold while the remaining goods were lying in the godown of 'H' Ltd., as on that date.

You are required to prepare a consolidated Balance sheet as at 31st March, 2009. Show all calculations.

(P.U.)

Ans. B/S Total Rs. 12,14,200.

6) The following are the Balance Sheets of 'X' Ltd., its subsidiary 'Y' Ltd., as at 31st Dec., 2008.

Liabilities	'X' Ltd. Rs.	'Y' Ltd. Rs.	Assets	'X' Ltd. Rs.	'Y' Ltd. Rs.
Share Capital			Land & Building	50,000	30,000
Equity shares of Rs. 10			Plant & Machinery	40,000	—
each, fully paid	1,00,000	50,000	Furniture & Fixtures	20,000	15,000
General Reserve	50,000	25,000	Stock-in-trade	20,000	30,000
P & L. A/c	–	25,000	Sundry Debtors	5,000	10,000
6% Debentures			Cash in Hand	5,000	5,000
of Rs. 100 each	20,000	–	Cash at Bank	40,000	20,000
Sundry Creditors	60,000	10,000	Investment		
			4,000 Equity Shares		
			in 'P' Ltd.	50,000	—
	2,30,000	1,10,000		2,30,000	1,10,000

The following information is supplied :–
1) 'X' Ltd., acquire is shares in 'Y' Ltd., on 1st Jan., 2008, when 'Y' Ltd., had Rs. 25,000 in General Reserve and Rs. 20,000 in Profit & Loss A/c (credit balance)
2) Stock-in-trade of 'Y' Ltd., include the goods of the value of Rs 20,000 purchased from 'X' Ltd., on which 'X' Ltd., charged cost plus 25%.
3) Debtors of 'Y' Ltd., includes Rs. 2,000 due from 'X' Ltd.
4) The proper value of Land & Building which stood at Rs. 30,000 in the books of 'Y' Ltd., as at the date of acquisition was Rs.50,000. **(P.U.)**

Ans : B/S Total 3,04,800

7) Following are the Balance Sheets of Poona Ltd., and Mumbai Ltd., as on 31st Dec., 2008.

Liabilities	Pune Ltd. Rs.	Mumbai Ltd Rs.	Assets	Pune Ltd. Rs.	Mumbai Ltd Rs.
Share Capital			Land & building	3,00,000	1,06,000
Equity Shares			Plant & Machinery	1,50,000	1,80,000
of Rs.100 each	6,00,000	3,00,000			
General Reserve	40,000	10,000	Investments		
P & L A/c	70,000	5,000	(2,700 shares in		
Bills Payable	25,000	31,000	Mumbai Ltd., at cost)	2,97,000	—
Sundry Creditors	1,42,000	60,000	Stock	40,000	50,000
Bank Overdraft	25,000	—	Sundry Debtors	52,000	60,000
			Bills Receivables	63,000	10,000
	9,02,000	4,06,000		9,02,000	4,06,000

Additional Information :

1) Poona Ltd., acquires shares in Mumbai Ltd., on 1st January, 2008, on which date the Profit and Loss A/c showed a debit balance Rs.10,000 in the books of Mumbai Ltd., and there was no balance in General Reserve.

2) Sundry debtors of Mumbai Ltd., included Rs.40,000 due from Poona Ltd.

3) Bills Payable of Mumbai Ltd., include Rs.18,000 issued in favour of Poona Ltd., which was discounted at Rs. 3,000 by them.

   Prepare a consolidated Balance Sheet. **(P.U.)**

Ans : B/S Total Rs.10,28,000

8) Hard Ltd., acquired 80% shares of Soft Ltd., on 1st January, 2008, at the total cost of Rs.3,25,000. The Balance Sheets of the two Companies on 31st Dec. 2008 were as follows :

Liabilities	'H' Ltd. Rs.	'S' Ltd. Rs.	Assets	'H' Ltd. Rs.	'S' Ltd. Rs.
Equity shares			Land and Building	4,50,000	1,50,000
of Rs.10 each	6,00,000	2,00,000	Plant and Machinery	3,50,000	1,00,000
Preference Shares			Stock	1,50,000	70,000
of Rs.100 each	2,00,000	—	Investment	3,25,000	
General Reserve	2,50,000	30,000	Debtors	1,20,000	60,000
P & L A/c	3,00,000	1,50,000	Bank Balance	5,000	20,000
Creditors	50,000	20,000			
	14,00,000	4,00,000		14,00,000	4,00,000

The following further information is relevant –

1) Creditors of Hard Ltd., include Rs.20,000 for goods purchased from Soft Ltd., on which Soft Ltd., made a profit of Rs.5,000.

2) Half of the goods sold as above were still included in the stock of Hard Ltd.

3) The General Reserve of Soft Ltd., represents balance as on 1st Jan., 2008.

4) Profit and Loss A/c balance as on 1st Jan., 2008 was Rs.60,000, out of which dividend at 15% was paid for the year 2007.

   Prepare a consolidated Balance Sheet.

Ans : B/S Total 15,46,000

CHAPTER 9

Liquidation of Joint Stock Company

Preparation of Liquidators Final Statement of Account

PREPARATION OF LIQUIDATORS FINAL STATEMENT OF ACCOUNT

A limited company is an artificial person created by law. Its existence is not perpetual. As the company is formed by law, it is dissolved through the process laid down by the law. The company cannot have a natural death. A solvent or insolvent company can be liquidated or dissolved. It can be brought to an end, if the directors of the company desire to dissolve the company. On dissolution, the company's name shall be struck off by the Registrar from the Register of the Company and he shall also get the fact published in the Official Gazette.

9.1 Meaning of Liquidation:

Liquidation or winding up of a company is a process by which the dissolution of a company is brought about and its property is administered for the benefits of its creditors and members. An administrator called liquidator is appointed to carry out the work related to liquidation and he is vested with the control of the company. Assets are realised, calls-in-arrears are collected, besides uncalled capital, if any, is called up, if necessary. Debts are paid off and finally the surplus, if any, is distributed among the members of the company in accordance with their rights. Thus, liquidation or winding up ultimately leads to dissolution of a company.

9.2 Modes of Winding Up

A Company can be liquidated in any of the following three ways :

1) Compulsory winding up.
2) Voluntary winding up.
3) Winding up under the supervision of Court.

1) Compulsory Winding Up :

The winding up of a Company by an order of the Court is known as compulsory winding up. According to Section 433 of the Company's Act, the Court may order for the compulsory winding up of a company in the following circumstances –

1) If the company passes a special resolution for winding up.
2) If the company is insolvent.
3) If the company commits a default in holding a statutory meeting.
4) If the company does not commence its business within a year of its incorporation or suspends business for a year.
5) If the company is unable to pay its debts.
6) If the number of the members of a company falls below 7 in case of a public company and 2 in case of a private company.
7) If the court is of the opinion that it is just and equitable that the company should be wound up.

The petition for winding up to the Court can be made by the company itself, any of its creditors, a contributory, the Registrar or any person authorised by the Central Government to make such a petition.

2) Voluntary Winding Up

A liquidation without intervention of the Court is known as "voluntary liquidation". A company may be wound up voluntarily –

i) by passing an ordinary resolution in the general meeting; or –
   a) when the period for the duration for which the company was constituted has expired or over; or –
   b) when the event or happening on which depended the termination of the existence of the company has happened.
ii) by passing a special resolution to wind up voluntarily for any reason whatsoever.

Types of Voluntary Liquidation

There are two types of voluntary liquidation. These are as follows :

1)   Voluntary liquidation by members.
2)   Voluntary liquidation by creditors.

   1)   Voluntary liquidation by members : In this type, the member of the Company voluntarily decides to wind up the company. The company may be solvent and able to pay all its debts from realisation of its assets to all claimants, but members may yet want to dissolve the company.

Legal provisions regarding voluntary winding up –

1) At least two or more directors must file a statutory declaration for the winding up of a company to the Registrar.

2) The statutory declaration must be made within 5 weeks immediately preceding the date of the passing of the resolution for winding up of a company.

3) Special resolution must be passed in the general meeting of members.

4) The special resolution is to be advertised in the Official Gazette within 14 days of the passing of such resolution.

5) The company must give a notice to the liquidator within 10 days from the passing of such resolution, regarding the appointment of liquidator.

6) If the process of winding up takes more than a year, the liquidator is expected to call a meeting of the company at the end of each year and give the information in respect of its act and dealing regarding the realisation of assets.

After completing all the formalities, the decision of liquidation of the company is taken and the business of the company comes to an end.

2) Voluntary liquidation by creditors : In this case, the creditors them selves convene the meeting of voluntarily to initiate the process of winding up of the company. This meeting is convened only after the meeting of the members of the company takes place. At the meeting, the resolution of wind up the company is passed and the same is sent it to the Registrar within 10 days from the date on which such a resolution is passed. A voluntary liquidation by creditor's may be initiated only if the company is not in a position to pay off its liabilities.

3) Winding up under the supervision of the Court : According to Section 522 of the companies Act, at any time, after a company has passed a resolution for voluntary winding up, the court may make an order that the voluntary winding up shall continue subject to the supervision of the Court. Such an order is passed by the Court on the application of any creditor or contributory or liquidator or the company itself under the following circumstances –

i) The liquidator under voluntary winding up is prejudiced or is negligent in collecting the assets of a company.

ii) The resolution for winding up was obtained by fraud.

9.3 Consequences of Liquidation (Effects of Liquidation)

The following are the consequences which generally follow a company's winding up decision :-

1) An official designated as a liquidator will take over the administration of the Company. In case of compulsory winding up, the official liquidator attached to High Court

functions as a liquidator of the company. In case of voluntary winding up, such an official is appointed by the members or the creditors depending upon members or creditor's voluntary winding up.

2) The powers of the Board of Directors will terminate and will not vest in the liquidator.

3) The winding up order or resolutions of voluntary winding up shall operate as a notice of discharge to all members of the company. The members of the company will be termed as contributories on the commencement of company's winding up. The liquidator will prepare a list of all such contributories who may be made liable to contribute towards the company on account of deficiency in the assets of the company. In case there is a surplus in the asset, the liquidator shall prepare a list of those members, who are entitled to share this surplus. The term contributory include members of both the above categories.

4) The liquidator will realise the assets of the company and distribute the proceeds among various claimants.

9.4 Preparation of Liquidator's Final Statement of Account

After the winding up of the company, the main duty of the liquidator is to collect the assets of the company and realise them and distribute the money so realised among right claimants. For this purpose, he maintains a cash book for recording the receipts and payments and is required to submit an abstract of the cash book to the Court in case of compulsory winding up, and to the Company in case of voluntary winding up. The liquidator is also required to prepare an account of winding up known as "Liquidator's Final Statement of Account" after the affairs of the Company are fully wound up. This account takes the form of Cash Account and the following receipts and payments are shown in this account –

Receipts:

During the process of winding up, the liquidator receives the amount from :

1) Realisation of assets of the Company.
2) Realisation from debtors of the Company.
3) Surplus from fully secured creditors.
4) Contribution received from directors and officers of the Company.
5) Calls made and received from contributers.

Payment:

On the credit side of this account, he records the payments made in the following priority order :

1) Payment to fully secured creditors.
2) Payment of legal expenses.
3) Liquidator's remuneration.
4) Liquidation expenses or cost of winding up.

5) Payment to preferential creditors.
6) Payment to debentureholders including outstanding interest and other creditors having a floating charge on the assets of the Company.
7) Payment to unsecured creditors.
8) Payment to shareholders.
   a) Preference shareholders.
   b) Equity shareholders

Proforma of Liquidator's Final Statement of Account is as follows :-

Form No. 156
(See Rule 329)
Companies Act, 1956

* Strike out what does not apply

* Here state whether the winding up is a members' or creditors' voluntary winding up or a winding up under the supervision of the Court. If under the supervision of the Court, mention the number of the petition in which the order was made and the date of the order.

Liquidator's Statement of Account of the Winding up
(Members' / Creditors' Voluntary Winding up)
(Pursuant to Section 318 / 497)

1. Name of the Company ...... Ltd.
2. Nature of proceeding :
3. Date of commencement of the winding up :
4. Name and address of the Liquidator :

Statement showing how the winding up has been conducted and the property of the Company has been disposed off from .... 20.... (commencement of winding-up) to ...... 20.... (Close of winding up.)

Receipts	Estimated Value Rs. P.	Value realised Rs. P.	Payments	Rs. P.	Payments Rs. P.
Assets :			Legal charges		
Cash at Bank			Liquidator's remuneration :		
Cash in Hand			When applicable -		
Marketable Securities			% on Rs. ...... realised		
Bills Receivable			% on Rs. ...... distributed		
Trade Debtors			Total	.....	
Loans and Advances					
Stock-in-trade					
Work-in-progress					

Receipts	Estimated Value Rs. P.	Value realised Rs. P.	Payments	Rs. P.	Payments Rs. P.

Freehold property
Leasehold property
Plant and Machinery
Furniture, Fittings,
    Utensils, etc.
Patents, Trade Marks etc.
Investments other than
    Marketable Securities
Surplus from Securities
Unpaid Calls at commen-
    cement of winding up
Amounts receivable from
    calls on contributories
    made in the winding up
Receipts as per Trading
    Account
Other property, viz...
 	
        Total
 	
Less
    Payments to redeem
      securities
    Costs of execution
    Payments as per
      Trading Accounts
			(By whom fixed ......)
			Auctioneers' and Valuers'
			    charges
			Liquidation expenses
			Costs of possession and
			    maintenance of estate
			Costs of notices in Gazette
			    and newspapers
			    Incidental outlay
			    (establishment charges
			    and other expenses of
			    liquidation)
			Total costs and charges
			i) Debentureholders :
			    Payment of Rs. .... per
			    Rs. ..... debenture
			    Payment of Rs. .... per
			    Rs. ..... debenture
			    Payment of Rs. .... per
			    Rs. ..... debenture
			ii) Creditors :
			    ...... * Preferential
			    ...... * Unsecured :
			    Dividend(s) .... P. in the
			      rupee on Rs.
			    (The estimate of the
			    amount expected to rank
			    for dividend was Rs. ......)
			iii)Returns to contributories :
			    (Equity and preferential
			    shareholders)
			    .... P. per rupee ....*share ....
			    .... P. per rupee ....*share ....
			    .... P. per rupee ....*share ....
			    Add balance		

Explanations of some important item and order of payment

1) Legal Expenses:

The expenses which are incurred by the Company during the period of its winding up on meeting the legal requirements are known as legal expenses.

2) Liquidator's Remuneration:

A liquidator gets his remuneration in the form of commission based on assets realised and payment made to creditors or contributories. This remuneration is fixed in the general meeting of members. The liquidator gets the following type of remuneration –

a) Fixed remuneration.

b) Commission on realisation of assets.

c) Commission on payment to –

i) Unsecured creditors.

ii) Equity shareholders.

a)   Fixed remuneration : A fixed amount may be given as a commission or remuneration to the liquidator.

b) Commission on realisation of assets : Realisation of assets means the amount receivable from sale of assets of the Company. While calculating the commission on realisation of asset, the following points must be taken into consideration :

i) The amount of cash in hand and cash at bank are not included in the realisation proceeds. If it is specially mentioned that these should be included, only then, they are to be included in the realisation proceeds.

ii) The liquidator gets commission on the surplus from the asset given to creditors after making payment to secured creditors. The liquidator makes an effort for realising the surplus from such asset from secured creditors. However, if he sells the asset himself, he gets commission on the total proceeds of such assets.

iii) Commission on Unsecured Creditors.

The creditors who have not been given any asset of the company as a security are called unsecured creditors. As the preferential creditors are unsecured, the amount of preferential creditor is also included in the unsecured creditors. But, if it is specially mentioned that, the commission is payable excluding preferential creditors, then the commission of liquidator is to be charged only on the amount paid to unsecured creditor.

If the amount is sufficient to make payment of unsecured creditors, the commission is charged after making the payment of unsecured creditors.

For example : Suppose the amount available is Rs. 40,000 and unsecured creditors are Rs. 30,000, and the rate of commission is 2%, the commission will be charged on Rs. 30,000 i.e. $\dfrac{30,000 \times 2}{100}$ = Rs. 600. Thus, the unsecured creditors will be paid Rs. 30,000 and the liquidator will be paid a commission of Rs. 600.

If cash is insufficient

If cash is not sufficient to pay secured creditors / contributories and the remuneration to liquidator, the remuneration is calculated as under :-

Suppose liquidator's remuneration is fixed at 2% on the amount paid to unsecured creditors, unsecured creditors are Rs. 30,000 and the cash available is Rs. 30,294. If Rs. 30,000 are to be paid to unsecured creditors, the liquidator must get Rs. 600 at 2% on the payment of Rs. 30,000 to unsecured creditors. But after the payment of Rs. 30,000, cash available is only Rs. 294 and as such Rs. 600 cannot be paid to liquidator. Hence, in such a case, the remuneration is calculated by using the following formula :

$$\text{Liquidator's Remuneration} : \frac{\text{Cash available for unsecured Creditors} \times \% \text{ of commission}}{100 + \% \text{ of commission}}$$

Cash		Cash	Remuneration
102	:	30,294	2% i.e. Rs. 2

$$= \frac{30,294 \times 2}{102} = \text{Rs. } 594$$

Rs. 30,294 less Rs. 594 = Rs. 29,700 cash available for payment to unsecured creditors and 2% of 29,700 is Rs. 594.

Thus, in such a case, the rate of remuneration is to be added to 100 and then remuneration is calculated on cash available as shown above.

iv) Commission on payment to equity shareholder

Sometimes, instead of giving a commission on amount paid to unsecured creditors, the liquidator is paid a commission on the amount paid to equity shareholders. If the amount available is sufficient to make the payment of Equity shareholder's capital, commission is charged on the principle of 'Berere charging' but if the amount is net sufficient to make capital payment of equity shareholder's capital the commission is charged on the principle of 'After charging' and the balance will be paid to equity shareholders.

3) Liquidation expenses :

After the payment of liquidator's remuneration, liquidation expenses or cost of winding up is paid. Liquidation expenses include cost of possession and maintenance of estate and cost of notices in Gazette and newspapers.

4) Fully secured creditors :

Fully secured creditors are those creditors, whose amount of loan is fully secured. They are given asset as a security and generally the realisable value of this asset is more than the amount of loan.

For example : If the amount of loan is Rs. 30,000 and the value of asset is Rs. 50,000, the creditors are termed as fully secured creditors.

Generally, the payment made to the fully secured creditor and the amount realised from the sale of security are not shown in the liquidator's final statement of account. The fully secured creditors recover the amount of asset and hand over the surplus to the liquidator. This surplus is shown in the liquidator's final statement of account.

Partly secured creditors : If the amount realised from the security is less than the claim of the creditor, his unsatisfied balance is added to the unsecured creditor.

For example : If the claim of a creditor is for Rs. 15,000 and the amount realised from the security is Rs. 10,000, the unsatisfied balance of claim Rs. 5,000 is added to unsecured creditors. Such creditors are treated as partly secured creditors.

5) Preferential Creditors :

The following are the preferential creditors who are paid after meeting the cost of winding up including the liquidator's remuneration but in priority to all other debts :

i) All revenue taxes, ceases and rates due and payable by the Company to the Government or local authority within 12 months before the date of commencement of winding up.

ii) All wages or salaries of any employee due for the period not exceeding 4 months, within 12 months before the commencement of winding up and any compensation payable to any workmen under any of the provisions of Chapter V(A) of the Industrial Disputes Act, 1947, provided the amount payable to any one claimant will not exceed Rs. 1,000.

iii) All accrued holiday remuneration becoming payable to an employee on account of the termination of his employment before or on account of winding up.

(Note : Persons who advance money for the purpose of preferential payment under (ii) and (iii) above will be treated as preferential creditors)

iv) Unless the company is being wound up voluntarily for the purpose of reconstructions or amalgamation, all contributions payable during the 12 months previous to winding up, by the company as the employer of any person, under Employee's State Insurance Act, 1948, or any other law for the time being in force.

v) All sums due as compensation under Workmen's Compensation Act, 1923.

vi) All sums due to any employee from a provident fund, a pension fund, a gratuity fund or any other fund for the welfare of the employees maintained by the Company.

vii) The expenses of any investigation held under Sections 235 or 237, insofar as they are payable by the Company.

If the cash is insufficient to pay in full all the preferential creditors, then the cash available is paid proportionately to all of them.

6) Debentureholders and creditors having floating charge :

When no specific asset of the Company is given as security to debentureholders or creditors but all assets of the Company are given as a security to them, they are called as debentureholders and creditors having a floating charge. They have no right to sell any specific asset and get the amount realised for their loans. They will rank as unsecured and will be paid after the payment of preferential creditors.

7) Interest on Debentures :

If the company is solvent, interest is paid upto the date of actual payment of principal, and if the company is insolvent, the interest is payable only upto the date of the commencement of winding up.

8) Payment to unsecured creditors :

After the payment to debentureholders, unsecured creditors rank for payment. Unsecured creditors may get full amount of their claim, if the surplus is available. On the other hand, if sufficient cash is not available, they may get part payment for the settlement of their dues.

9) Payment to Contributories :

The contributories in the event of winding up of a company may be :
i) Preferential shareholders.
ii) Equity shareholders.

Payment to preferential shareholders with arrears of dividend :

Preference shareholders have a preference to receive their capital and dividend over equity shareholders. While paying the dividend on preference shares, the following points should be taken into account –

i) No dividend is payable for the period falling after commencement of winding up. It means arrears of dividend upto the date of commencement of winding up are only considered.

ii) If dividend was declared but not paid, it is to be paid as debt of the Company and not as arrears and it is paid in priority of returns of even preference share capital.

iii) If dividend is in arrears and has not been declared, it is paid only if there remains any surplus after repayment of equity share capital in full.

However, if the Articles state that arrears of dividend on preference shares are to be paid before anything is paid to equity shareholders, the payment of dividend is to be made accordingly. In this case, if it is felt necessary, the required amount is collected by making a call on partly-paid equity shares.

10) Payment to Equity Shareholders

After having paid all the claims of preference shareholders, all the cash available is paid to equity shareholders. If there are various types of equity shares i.e. fully paid and partly paid equity shares, but no provision is made for giving priority to any class of them, the excess amount paid on any share then is returned first and the balance is distributed proportionately among all classes of shares.

Calls on partly paid shares :

If the amount available by realisation of assets is not sufficient to pay the claims of all claimants, the liquidator can make a call on these shares which are partly paid up.

Calls-in-Advance :

Sometimes, some equity shareholders pay the amount without the call being made by the Company, Such an amount is called as "Calls-in-advance". In case of winding up of the Company, the amount of calls-in-advance will be paid before making the payment to equity shareholders.

9.5 PROBLEMS

Problem No. 1 : Poona Ltd. passed a resolution to wind up voluntarily on 30th June, 2014, when its Balance Sheet stood as under :-

Balance Sheet as on 30-6-2014

Liabilities	Rs.	Assets	Rs.
Share Capital :		Land	50,000
Authorised and Subscribed		Plant & Machinery	1,15,000
1,000, 6% Preference Shares		Patents	30,000
of Rs. 100 each	1,00,000	Stock at Cost	27,500
500 Equity Shares of Rs. 100	-	Sundry Debtors	55,000
each, Rs. 75 paid-up	37,500	Cash at Bank	15,000
1,500 Equity Shares of Rs. 100	-	Profit & Loss A/c	60,000
each, Rs. 60 paid-up	90,000		
5% Debentures (Floating			
charge on all assets)	50,000		
Interest on Debentures	2,500		
Creditors	65,000		
Income Tax	7,500		
	3,52,500		3,52,500

a) The preference dividends were in arrears for two years. The arrears are payable on liquidation as per the Articles of Company. Creditors include a loan of Rs. 25,000 on the mortgage of land.

b) The Assets realised is as follows :
   Land Rs. 60,000; Plant and Machinery Rs. 87,500; Patents 27,500; Stock Rs. 30,000 and Sundry Debtors Rs. 40,000.

c) The Expenses of Liquidation amounted to Rs. 5,450.

d) The liquidator is entitled to a commission of 3% on all assets realised and 2% on amounts distributed among unsecured creditors except preferential creditors.

e) All payments were made on 31st December, 2014.

You are required to prepare Liquidator's Statement of Account.

Solution

Liquidator's Final Statement of Account

Receipts		Rs.	Payments		Rs.
To Cash at Bank		15,000	By Liquidator's Remuneration		
To Assets Realised			3% × 2,45,000 =	7,350	
Land	60,000		2% × 40,000 =	800	8,150
Plant and Machinery	87,500		By Liquidation Expenses		5,450
Patents	27,500		By Preferential Creditors (Income tax)		7,500
Stock	30,000		By Debentureholders together		
Debtors	40,000	2,45,000	with interest upto 31-12-08		53,750
			(50,000 + 2,500 + 1,250)		
			By Unsecured Creditors		40,000
			By 6% Preference Shareholders		
			Dividend	12,000	
			Capital	1,00,000	1,12,000
			By Equity Shareholders holding		
			500 shares of Rs. 100 each		
			Rs. 75 paid up		
			(Rs. 15 per share refunded)		
			(500 × 15)		7,500
			By Equity Shareholders holding		
			2,000 shares of Rs. 100 each		
			Rs. 60 paid up		25,650
			(Paid Rs. 12.825 per share)		
			(2000 × 12.825)		
		2,60,000			**2,60,000**

Notes :

1) Income tax is treated as preferential creditors.

2) Payment to equity shareholders.

	Rs.
Total amount Realised	2,60,000
Less : Paid to claimant except equity shareholders	2,26,850
Amount payable to equity shareholders	33,150
Less : Amount paid to 500 equity shareholders of Rs. 75 each Rs. 15 per share refunded	7,500
Balance paid to all	25,650
Equity shareholders at Rs. 12.825 per share (12.825 × 2,000)	25,650

Problem No. 2 : The Breakfast Food Ltd. went into voluntary liquidation on 31st December, 2013. Its Balance Sheet as on that date was as under :

	Rs.		Rs.
5,000 Preference Shares of Rs. 100 each	5,00,000	Land & Building	2,50,000
		Machinery and Plant	6,25,000
2,500 Equity Shares of		Patents	1,00,000
Rs. 100 each, Rs. 75 paid-up	1,87,500	Stock	1,37,500
7,500 Equity shares of		Debtors	2,75,000
Rs. 100 each, Rs. 60 paid-up	4,50,000	Cash	75,000
5% Mortgage Debentures	2,50,000	Profit & Loss A/c	2,80,000
Interest Outstanding on above	12,500	Discount on Debentures	20,000
Creditors	3,62,500		
	17,62,500		17,62,500

The Liquidator is entitled to a commission of 3% on all assets realised and surplus from security except cash and 2% on the amount distributed among the unsecured creditors other than preferential creditors. Creditors include preferential creditors Rs. 37,500 and loans for Rs. 1,25,000/- secured by mortgage on Land and Building.

Assets realised as under :

Land and Building Rs. 3,00,000/-, Machinery and Plant Rs. 5,00,000/-, Patents Rs. 75,000/- Stock Rs. 1,50,000, Debtors Rs. 2,00,000/- Expenses of liquidation amounted to Rs. 17,250 and legal expenses Rs. 10,000/-

Prepare liquidator's final statement of Account. (P.U.)

Solution :

Liquidator's Final Statement of Account

Receipts	Rs.	Payments	Rs.
To Cash at Bank	75,000	By Legal Expenses	10,000
To Sundry Debtors	2,00,000	By Liquidator's Remuneration	
To Stock	1,50,000	3% on Rs. 11,00,000 = 33,000	
To Patents	75,000	2% on Rs. 2,00,000 = 4,000	37,000
To Machinery and Plant	5,00,000	By Cost of liquidation	17,250
To Surplus from Land and Building	-	By Preferential Creditors	37,500
(3,00,000 - 1,25,000)	1,75,000	By Debentureholders having	
		floating charge - principal 2,50,000	
		Interest Outstanding 12,500	2,62,500
		Unsecured Creditors (3,62,500	
		- 37,500 - 1,25,000)	2,00,000
		By Preference shareholders	
		capital 5,00,000	5,00,000
		By Equity Shareholders Rs. 15	
		per share on 2,500 shares 37,500	
		All shareholders 73,250	1,10,750
		(on 10,000 shares)	
	11,75,000		**11,75,000**

Note :

1) Liquidator's Remuneration on assets realised

Land and Building (3,00,000 - 1,25,000)	1,75,000
Plant and Machinery	5,00,000
Patents	75,000
Stock	1,50,000
Debtors	2,00,000
Total assets realised	11,00,000

Problem No. 3 : Following is the Balance Sheet of Reena Ltd., as on 30th June, 2013

Balance Sheet

Liabilities	Rs.	Assets	Rs.
Share Capital :	-	Land and Building	75,000
1,500, 8% Preference Shares	-	Plant and Machinery	1,80,000
of Rs. 100 each	1,50,000	Furniture	30,000
4,500 Equity Shares of Rs. 100	-	Fitting	15,000
each Rs. 50 paid-up	2,25,000	Moulds	1,50,000
6% Debentures (having a	-	Stock	75,000
floating charge on all assets)	1,20,000	Debtors	37,500
Outstanding Debenture Interest	7,200	Cash in Hand	1,500
Sundry Creditors :	-	Profit and Loss A/c	1,12,500
On Mortgage of Plant			
and Machinery	90,000		
Preferential	9,300		
Unsecured	75,000		
	6,76,500		**6,76,500**

The company went into voluntary liquidation as on the above Balance Sheet date. Preference dividend was in arrears for one year and as per the Articles of the company, it was to be paid.

The Liquidator realised the assets as under :-

Land and Building	-	1,50,000
Plant and Machinery	-	1,65,000
Moulds	-	1,27,500
Furniture	-	18,000
Stock	-	63,000
Debtors	-	31,500

Fittings were worthless.

The Liquidation Expenses amounted to Rs. 8,190.

The liquidator is entitled to a remuneration at 2% on the assets realised, 2% on the amount distributed to unsecured creditors and 10% on the amount returned to equity shareholders. In addition to the above liabilities, the liquidtor had to pay Rs. 2,700 as repairs bill of Plant and Machinery.

The Liquidator made payments on 31st December, 2013. Prepare, Liquidator's Final Statement of Accounts. (P.U.)

Solution

Liquidator's Final Statement of Account

Receipts	Rs.		Payments		Rs.
To Cash Balance		1,500	By Liquidator's Remuneration		
			on Assets Realised		
To Assets Realised 5,55,000			2% × 5,50,000 =	11,100	
Less : Secured Creditors 90,000	4,65,000		on Unsecured Creditors		
			2% × 87,000 =	1,740	
			on Equity Shareholders		
			10% × 59,700 =	5,970	18,810
			By Liquidation Expenses		8,190
			By Preferential Creditors		9,300
			By Debentures together		
			with interest upto		
			31st Dec., 2008		1,30,800
			By Unsecured Creditors		77,700
			By Preference Shareholders		
			Dividend	12,000	
			Capital	1,50,000	1,62,000
			By Equity Shareholders		59,700
	4,66,500				4,66,500

Notes : Remuneration to Liquidator :

i) Preferential creditors, being unsecured are taken into consideration. Amount due for repairs is also included in unsecured creditors.

ii) Cash in hand is not considered while taking the assets realised. As Plant and Machinery is realised by the liquidator himself, it is considered for calculation and remuneration.

Problem No. 4 : Swati Co. Ltd. passed a resolution to wind up voluntarily on 31st March, 2014, when its Balance Sheet stood as follows :

Liabilities	Rs.	Assets	Rs.
Share Capital :		**Fixed Assets :**	
8,000 Preference Shares of			
Rs.10 each	80,000	Freehold Property	80,000
12,000 Equity Shares		Plant and Machinery	70,000
of Rs. 10 each fully paid	1,20,000	**Current Assets :**	
Secured Loan :		Stock	80,000
5% Debentures secured		Cash	250
on Freehold Property	60,000	Debtors	59,750
Current Liabilities :		Profit and Loss A/c	73,000
Bank Overdraft	30,000		
Trade Creditors	68,500		
Preferential Creditors	4,500		
(Dividend on Preference Shares was			
in arrears for 3 years at 6%p.a.)			
	3,63,000		3,63,000

Freehold property was sold for Rs. 1,00,000, Plant and Machinery realised Rs. 60,000. Stock realised Rs. 75,000 and Debtors realised Rs. 50,000. Debentures were paid off out of the sale proceeds of freehold property. Cost of liquidation was Rs. 5,000 and liquidator's remuneration was fixed at Rs. 2,531 plus 2% on all assets realised except cash and 10% on the amount returned to equity shareholders.

Prepare the liquidator's final statement of the account. (P. U.)

Solution : **Liquidator's Final Statement of Account**

Receipts	Rs.	Payments		Rs.
To Cash	250	By Legal Expenses		
To Debtors	50,000	By Liquidator's Remuneration		
To Stock	75,000	Fixed =	2,531	
To Plant and Machinery	60,000	2% on Rs. 2,85,000 =	5,700	
To Surplus from Freehold		10% on Rs. 13,290 =	1,329	9,560
Property (1,00,000-60,000)	40,000	By Liquidation Expenses		5,000
		By Preferential Creditors		4,500
		By Unsecured Creditors		
		Bank Overdraft	30,000	
		Trade Creditors	68,500	98,500
		By Preference		
		Shareholders capital	80,000	
		Dividend Arrears	14,400	94,400
		By Equity Shareholders		13,290
Tatal Rs.	2,25,250			2,25,250

Notes :

1) **Liquidator's remuneration on payment to equity shareholders :**
   Balance available after payment of preference shareholders :
   2,25,250 - 2,10,631 = Rs. 14,619/-
   Commission = 14,619 × 10/110 = Rs. 1,329.
   Net Balance to be paid to equity shareholders = 14,619 - 1,329 = Rs. 13,290/-
   Thus 10% of Rs. 13,290 = Rs. 1,329/-

2) Debentureholders are secured. Their payment is not shown in the Liquidator's Final Statement of Account.

Problem No. 5 : Following was the Balance Sheet of Star Ltd., as on 31st March, 2014.

Balance Sheet

Liabilities	Rs.	Assets	Rs.
Share Capital :		Land and Building	2,00,000
2,000, 10% Preferences Shares		Plant and Machinery	1,50,000
of Rs. 100 each, fully paid	2,00,000	Furniture	20,000
3,000 Equity Shares of Rs. 100		Stock	1,00,000
each, Rs. 90 paid-up	2,70,000	Debtors	1,20,000
1,000 Equity Shares of Rs. 100		Bills Receivable	20,000
each, Rs. 85 paid-up	85,000	Cash in Hand	5,000
7% Debentures (floating charge		Profit and Loss A/c	2,40,000
on all assets)	1,00,000		
Creditors	2,00,000		
	8,55,000		8,55,000

The Company went into voluntary liquidation as on above date.

The preference share dividend was in arrears for two years and as per the Articles, it was to be paid before returning the equity share capital.

The debenture interest was paid upto 31st March, 2014. However, the debentureholders were repaid on 30th Sept., 2014

Included in the sundry creditors, a loan of Rs. 20,000 secured on the hypothecation of Plant and Machinery and preferential creditors of Rs. 10,000.

The liquidator realised the assets as follows : Land and Building Rs. 1,90,000; Plant and Machinery Rs. 1,30,000; Furniture Rs. 10,000, Stock Rs. 90,000; Debtors Rs. 1,15,000; Bills Receivable Rs. 14,000.

Legal charges on liquidation Rs. 2,000 and liquidation expenses Rs. 1,300. The liquidator's remuneration was fixed at Rs. 500 plus 2.5% on the amount realised by him, plus 2% on the amount distributed to unsecured creditors, including preferential creditors. The liquidator made all payments on 30th Sept., 2014.

Prepare Liquidator's Final Statement of Account. (P.U.)

Solution

Liquidator's Final Statement of Account

Receipts		Rs.	Payments		Rs.
To Cash		5,000	By Legal Expenses		2,000
To Assets realised	5,49,000		By Liquidator's Remuneration		
Less : Paid to	20,000	5,29,000	Fixed	500	
Secured Creditors			On Assets Realised		
			2.5% × 5,49,000	13,725	
			On Unsecured Creditors		
			2% × 1,80,000	3,600	17,825
To Calls received on			By Liquidation Expenses		1,300
Equity Shares			By Preferential Creditors		10,000
on 3,000 × 1.406		4,218	By Debentures	1,00,000	
on 1,000 × 6.407		6,407	Interest	3,500	1,03,500
			By Unsecured Creditors		1,70,000
			By Preference Shareholders		
			Dividend	40,000	
			Capital	2,00,000	240,000
		5,44,625			5,44,625

Note : Call to be made on Equity Shares.

Face value of equity shares Rs. 4,00,000; paid-up value Rs. 3,55,000 + Rs. 10,625, falling short to pay preference shareholders. Hence, the total deficiency is Rs. 3,65,625. Hence, each shareholder is required to lose Rs. 91.406 as under :

$$\frac{3,65,625}{4,00,000} \times 100 = 91.40625$$

Thus, shareholder who has paid Rs. 85 has to pay Rs. 6.407 and shareholder who has paid Rs. 90 has to pay 1.406 (.001 is adjusted instead of taking exact figure ·40625)

Problem No. 6 : The Oversmart Co. Ltd. went into liquidation on 31st December, 2013, when the following Balance Sheet was prepared:

Balance Sheet as on 31ˢᵗ December, 2013

Liabilities		Rs.	Assets	Rs.
Share Capital :			**Fixed Assets :**	
Authorised :			Goodwill	50,000
30,000 shares of			Leasehold Property	48,000
Rs. 10 each		3,00,000	Plant and Machinery	65,500
Issued and Paid up :			**Current Assets :**	
19,500 shares of			Stock on Hand	56,800
Rs. 10 each		1,95,000	Sundry Debtors	64,820
Unsecured loans :			Cash in Hand	2,500
Bank Overdraft		12,000	Profit and Loss A/c	98,680
Current Liabilities :				
Sundry Creditors				
Preferential	24,200			
Partly Secured	55,310			
Unsecured	99,790	1,79,300		
		3,86,300		3,86,300

The liquidator realised the assets as follows :

Leasehold property which was used in the first instance to pay partly secured creditors pro-rata Rs. 35,000.

Plant and Machinery Rs. 51,000

Stock in Hand Rs. 39,000

Sundry Debtors Rs. 58,500

The expenses of liquidation amounted to Rs. 1,000 and the remuneration of the liquidator was agreed at 2.5% on the amount realised including cash and 2% on the amount paid to the unsecured creditors, including preferential creditors.

Prepare the liquidator's Final Statement of Accounts showing distribution.   (P.U.)

Solution : **Liquidator's Final Statement of Accounts.**

Receipts	Rs.	Payments		Rs.
To Cash in Hand	2,500	By. Legal Expenses		
To Sundry Debtors	58,500	By Liquidator's Remuneration		
		on Assets Realised		
To Stock in Hand	39,000	2.5% on creditor 1,86,000 =	4,650	
To Plant and Machinery	51,000	2% on 24,200 =	484	
		2% on 1,18,300 =	2,366	7,500

Receipts	Rs.	Payments		Rs.
		By Liquidation Expenses		1,000
		By Debenture holders having floating charge		–
		By Preferential Creditors		24,200
		By Unsecured Creditors		
		Creditors	99,790	
		Unsatisfied Claim	20,310	
		Bank Overdraft	12,000	
		(See Note 2)		
			1,32,100	1,18,300
	1,51,000			1,51,000

Note :

1) Liquidator's Remuneration

2.5% on Assets Realised

Assets Realised	Rs.
Leasehold Property	35,000
Plant and Machinery	51,000
Stock	39,000
Debtors	58,500
Cash	2,500
	1,86,000

2.5% on 1,86,000 = Rs. 4,650

2) Commission on Payment to unsecured creditors.

	Rs.
Total amount Realised	1,51,000
Less : (Preferential Crs. + commission + liquidation exps)	
= 24,200 + 4,650 + 484 + 1,000 =	30,334
Balance available for unsecured creditors.	1,20,666
But actual unsecured creditors are	
Rs. 99,790 + 20,310 + 12,000 =	1,32,100

As the available cash is insufficient for payment to unsecured creditors, the commission to be paid on unsecured creditors will be calculated as under :

$$= \frac{\text{Balance available} \times \% \text{ of commission}}{100 + 2}$$

$$= \frac{1,20,666 \times 2}{102} = \text{Rs. } 2,366$$

	Rs.
Balance of Cash available	1,20,666
Less : Commission to be paid	2,366
Unsecured Creditors	1,18,300

Problem No. 7 : On 1st April, 2014 'P' Ltd., went into voluntary liquidation. The position at the commencement of winding up was as follows :

Balance Sheet as on 1-4-2014

Liabilities	Rs.		Assets	Rs.
Paid-up Capital :			Building	2,10,000
1,000, 8% Preference Shares			Debtors	65,000
of Rs. 100 each		1,00,000	Stock	35,000
1,500 Equity Shares of			Cash	8,775
Rs. 100 each		1,50,000	Machinery	50,000
5% Debentures (having a			Furniture	40,000
floating charge)	1,00,000		Profit and Loss A/c	46,225
Interest Accrued	2,500	1,02,500		
Sundry Creditors	63,500			
Bank Overdraft	30,000			
Trade Debts				
Income Tax for				
Assessment Year				
2013-14	5,000			
Rates	3,500			
Electricity	500	1,02,500		
		4,55,000		4,55,000

The liquidator realised the following amounts :

Buildings Rs. 4,00,000; Debtors Rs. 57,000; Stock Rs. 25,000; Machinery Rs. 36,000; Furniture Rs. 32,000.

The liquidator's remuneration was 5% on the amount realised by him and 1% on the amounts paid to unsecured creditors. His expenses amounted to Rs. 2,000, 5% debentures were paid on 1st July, 2014. In the event of liquidation, the preference shareholders were entitled to 10% of any surplus, left after discharging all liabilities and costs, the balance belonging to the equity shareholders.

Prepare the Liquidator's Final Statement of Account.

Solution :

Liquidator's Final Statement of Account.

Receipts	Rs.	Payments	Rs.
To Cash	8,775	By Liquidator's remuneration	
To Assets realised	5,50,000	5% × 5,50,000 = 27,500	
		1% × 1,02,500 = 1,025	28,525
		By Liquidation Expenses	2,000
		By Debentureholders	
		(together with interest)	1,03,750
		By Unsecured Creditors	1,02,500
		By Preference Shareholders	1,07,200
		(See Note)	
		By Equity Shareholders	2,14,800
		(See Note)	
	5,58,775		5,58,775

Note : Payment to Preference Shareholders and equity Shareholders

	Rs.
Total Cash Received	5,58,775
Less : Total Cost and liabilities	
(28,525 + 2,000 + 1,03,750 + 1,02,500)	2,36,775
Surplus	3,22,000
Paid Preference shareholders and equity shareholders	
(1,00,000 + 1,50,000)	2,50,000
	72,000

Preference Shareholders get Rs.	1,00,000	- 7,200
+ 10% of 72,000	7,200	64,800
	1,07,200	

Balance Rs. 64,800 will be paid to equity shareholders. They get
Rs. 1,50,000 + 64,800 = 2,14,800.

Problem No. 8 : The following is the position of "X" Ltd. as on 30th June, 2014 on which date the company is taken into voluntary liquidation.

Particulars	Rs.	Rs.
Share Capital - Issued and Subscribed		
2,500 Preference shares of Rs. 100 each fully paid		2,50,000
20,000 Equity shares of Rs. 10 each fully paid		2,00,000
Land and building	75,000	
Machinery	1,00,000	
Furniture	5,000	
Vehicles	15,000	
Secured Loans -		
From Bank against mortgage of Land and Buildings		50,000
Others against a floating charge on the		
Company's undertaking		25,000
Cash	5,000	
Other current assets	2,50,000	
Sundry Liabilities		25,000
Profit and Loss A/c	1,00,000	
	5,50,000	5,50,000

The realisation were :

1) Land and Buildings (realised by Bank) for Rs. 60,000.

2) Machinery Rs. 90,000

3) Furniture Rs. 5,000

4) Vehicles Rs. 20,000

5) Other current assets Rs. 2,25,000.

Sundry liabilities included preferential claims of Rs. 2,500. The liquidator is entitled to a fixed remuneration of Rs. 125 increased by 1% of the amounts disbursed to unsecured creditors (excluding preferential claims) and ¼% of the amounts realised by him in respect of company's assets.

You are required to show the liquidator's final statement of account to record his dealings.

Liquidator's Final Statement of Account

Receipts	Rs.	Payments		Rs.
To Cash in Hand	5,000	By Legal Expenses		–
To Assets Realised :		By Liquidator's remuneration :		
Current Assets	2,25,000	Fixed	125	
Machinery	90,000	On Assets realised		
Furniture	5,000	¼% on 3,40,000	850	
		On Unsecured Creditors		
Vehicles	20,000	1% on 22,500	225	1,200
Surplus Received from		By Liquidation Expenses		–
Land and Buildings (60,000-50,000)	10,000	By Preferential Creditors		2,500
		By Secured Creditors		
		having floating charge		25,000
		By Unsecured Creditors		22,500
		By Preference Shareholders		2,50,000
		By Equity Shareholders		53,800
	3,55,000			3,55,000

Notes :

1) Liquidator's remuneration on realisation of assets is calculated on those assets only which are realised by liquidator except cash in hand. As land and buildings are realised by Bank, it is not considered. (i.e. Rs. 90,000 + 5,000 + 20,000 + 2,25,000 = Rs. 3,40,000)

2) Liquidator's commission (remuneration) on payment to unsecured creditors is calculated on the amount excluding preferential creditors.
(unsecured Creditors 2,500 = Rs. 25000 - Preferential Creditors 2500 = 22,500)

3) Payment to secured creditors is not shown in the liquidator's statement.

Problem No. 9 : Following was the Balance Sheet of Alpha Ltd., as on 31st December, 2013

Liabilities	Rs.	Assets	Rs.
Share Capital :		Goodwill	2,24,000
2,000, 8% Preference Shares		Land and Building	4,36,000
of Rs. 100 each fully paid	2,00,000	Plant and Machinery	1,80,000
4,000 Equity Shares of Rs. 100		Furniture	20,000
each, Rs. 80 paid-up	3,20,000	Office Equipments	40,000
6,000 Equity Shares of Rs. 100		Stock	1,98,000
each, Rs. 70 paid-up	4,20,000	Debtors	1,70,000

Liabilities	Rs.	Assets	Rs.
8% Debentures (having a Floating charge on all assets)	2,00,000	Bills Receivable	44,000
Debentures Interest	8,000	Cash in Hand	16,000
Creditors	3,20,000	Profit and Loss A/c	1,40,000
	14,68,000		14,68,000

The company went into voluntary liquidation as on that date :

a) The preference dividend was in arrears for 3 years and as per the articles it was to be returned before returning equity capital.

b) Sundry creditors include a loan of Rs. 80,000 secured on the hypothecation of plant and Machinery and preferential creditors of Rs. 20,000.

c) The liquidator realised the assets as follows :
Land and Building Rs. 4,30,000; Plant and Machinery Rs. 1,00,000; Office Equipments Rs. 25,000; Furniture Rs. 16,000; Stock Rs. 1,40,000; Debtors Rs. 1,20,000 and Bills Receivable Rs. 28,000

d) Legal Charges on Liquidation amounted to Rs. 2,000. The liquidation expenses were Rs. 5,200. The Liquidator's remuneration was fixed at Rs. 2,000 plus 2% on sale of assets, plus 4% on the amount distributed to unsecured creditors.

e) There was a typewriter which was completely written off from the books of accounts but liquidator sold it for Rs. 1,000, which was not included in the amount of office equipments above.

Prepare Liquidator's statement of account if the amounts were paid on 31st March, 2014 (P.U.)

Liquidator's Final Statement of Account

Receipts	Rs.		Payments		Rs.
To Cash in hand		16,000	By Legal Expenses		2,000
To Assets realised :			By Liquidator's		
Land and Building	4,30,000		Remuneration :		
Office Equipments			Fixed	2,000	
including Typewriter	26,000		On Sales of Asset		
Furniture	16,000		8,60,000 × 2%	17,200	
Stock	1,40,000		On Unsecured Creditors		
Debtors	1,20,000		2,40,000 × 4%	9,600	28,800
Bills Receivable	28,000		By Liquidation Expenses		5,200
Plant and Machinery			By Preferential Creditors		20,000

Receipts		Rs.	Payments		Rs.
Balance after payment			By Debentureholders 2,00,000		
to Secured Creditors	20,000	7,80,000	Interest upto 31-8-2014 12,000		2,12,000
			By Unsecured Creditors		2,20,000
			By Preference Shareholders		
			Capital	2,00,000	
			Dividend Arrears	48,000	2,48,000
			By Equity Shareholders holding		
			4,000 shares on which Rs. 80		
			per share are paid are refunded		
			@ Rs. 10 per share to make		
			them Rs. 70 per share paid.		40,000
			By Equity Shareholders		
			holding 10,000 shares, Rs. 2		
			per share are refunded		20,000
		7,96,000			7,96,000

Notes :

1) Liquidator realised following assets.

	Rs.
Land and Building	4,30,000
Plant and Machinery	1,00,000
Office Equipment including Typewriter	26,000
Furniture	16,000
Stock	1,40,000
Debtor	1,20,000
Bills Receivable	28,000
Total	8,60,000

2) Liquidator's remuneration on unsecured creditors is calculated on the amount including preferential creditor and excluding secured creditors.

Problem No. 10 : Mr. Raj was appointed as the liquidator of Badluck Ltd., on 1st January, 2014, on which date Balance Sheet of the Company stood as under :

Balance Sheet
as at 1ˢᵗ January, 2014

Liabilities	Rs.	Assets	Rs.
Share Capital :		**Fixed Assets :**	90,000
10,000 Equity Shares		**Current Assets :**	
of Rs. 10 each, Rs. 8 per		Loans and Advances	20,000
share called-up 80,000		**Miscellaneous Expenditure :**	
Less : Calls-in-arrears 5,000	75,000	Profit & Loss A/c	37,000
5,000, 6% Cumulative			
Preference Shares of			
Rs. 10 each	50,000		
Secured Loan	10,000		
Current Liabilities :			
(including unpaid Income Tax			
Rs. 2,000)	12,000		
Contingent Liability			
Arrears of Cumulative			
Preference Dividend			
Rs. 9,000			
	1,47,000		1,47,000

The calls-in-arrears were duly collected. The assets realised Rs. 82,000. The liquidation expenses amounted Rs. 2,980. The remuneration of the liquidator was fixed at Rs. 2,000 plus 2% of the amount distributed among the equity shareholders.

You are required to prepare the liquidator's final statement of Account.

Solution

Liquidator's Final Statement of Account

Receipts	Rs.	Payments	Rs.
To Assets Realised	82,000	By Secured Loan	10,000
To Loans and Advances	20,000	By Liquidator's Remuneration	
To Calls in Arrears	5,000	Fixed 2,000	
		2% on 20,068 412	2,412
		By Liquidation Expenses	2,980
		By Preferential Creditors	2,000
		(Income Tax)	
		By Unsecured Creditors	10,000

Receipts	Rs.	Payments	Rs.
		By Preference Shareholders	
		Dividend Arrears 9,000	
		Capital 50,000	59,000
		By Equity Shareholders	20,608
	1,07,000		1,07,000

Note :

(i) It is presumed that Loans and Advances are recovered in full; (ii) the preference share dividend was declared and as such ranks for payment before paying anything to equity shareholder :

Problem No. 11 : The Breakfast Food Ltd., went into voluntary liquidation on 31st March, 2014.

Balance Sheet as on 31-3-2014

Liabilities	Rs.	Assets	Rs.
Share Capital :		Land and Building	2,50,000
5000, 6% Cumulative Preference		Plant and Machinery	6,25,000
Shares of Rs. 100 each	5,00,000	Patents	1,00,000
2,500 Equity Shares of		Stock	1,37,500
Rs. 100 each, Rs. 75 paid	1,87,500	Sundry Debtors	2,75,000
7,500 Equity Shares of 100 each		Cash at Bank	75,000
Rs. 60 paid	4,50,000	Profit and Loss A/c	2,80,000
5% Mortgage Debentures	2,50,000	Discount on Issue of Debentures	20,000
Interest Outstanding	12,500		
Creditors	3,62,500		
	17,62,500		17,62,500

The liquidator is entitled to a commission of 3% on all assets realised except cash and 2% on amounts distributed among unsecured creditors other than preferential creditors. Creditors include preferential creditors Rs. 37,500 and a Loan for Rs. 1,25,000 secured by a mortgage on land and buildings. The preference dividends were in arrears for two years. The assets realised, as follows:

Land and Building Rs. 3,00,000; Machinery and Plant Rs. 5,00,000; Patents Rs. 75,000; Stock Rs. 1,50,000; Sundry Debtors Rs. 2,00,000. The expenses of liquidation amounted to Rs. 17,250 and legal expenses Rs. 10,000.

Prepare the Liquidator's Final Statement of Account.

Solution   Liquidator's Final Statement of Account

Receipts		Rs.	Payments	Rs.
To Bank Balance		75,000	By Legal Expenses	10,000
To Assets realised			By Liquidator's Remuneration	
Machinery and Plant	5,00,000		12,25,000 × 3% = 36,750	
Patents	75,000		2,00,000 × 2% = 4,000	40,750
Stock	1,50,000		By Liquidation Expenses	17,250
Debtors	2,00,000	9,25,000	By Preferential Creditors	37,500
To Surplus from			By Debentureholders	2,62,500
secured Creditor		1,75,000	By Unsecured Creditors	2,00,000
			By Preference Shareholders	5,00,000
			By Equity Shareholders	
			holding 2,500 shares on which	
			Rs. 75 per share were paid,	
			Rs. 15 per share refunded	37,500
			By Equity Shareholders	
			holding 10,000 shares refunded	
			Rs. 6.95 per share	69,500
		11,75,000		11,75,000

Problem No. 12 : Following balances appeared in the book of Goodluck Ltd., as on 1st April, 2014.

Land and Building		2,00,000
Plant and Machinery		5,80,000
Stock		1,10,000
Debtors		2,20,000
Cash at Bank		60,000
Profit and Loss A/c		30,000
		12,00,000
Less Liabilities -		
9% Debentures (having floating charge on all assets)	2,00,000	
Creditors	2,90,000	4,90,000
		7,10,000
Share Capital (paid-up)		
a) 2,000, 6% Preference Shares of Rs. 100 each		2,00,000
b) 2,000, Equity Shares of Rs. 100 each, Rs. 75 per share paid-up		1,50,000
c) 6,000 Equity Shares of Rs. 100 each, Rs. 60 per share paid-up		3,60,000
		7,10,000

The Company went into voluntary liquidation on 1-4-2014.

The assets were realised as under :

Land and Building Rs. 2,40,000, Plant and Machinery Rs. 4,60,000, Stock Rs. 1,20,000 and Debtors Rs. 1,60,000

The preference dividends were in arrears for two years. Creditors include :

a) Rs. 30,000 preferential

b) Rs. 1,00,000 loan on the mortgage of land and buildings.

Cost of liquidation Rs. 13,800

Liquidator's Remuneration -

a) 3% on all assets realised except Cash at Bank, and

b) 2% on distribution to unsecured creditors.

Prepare the liquidator's statement of account assuming that the payment was made on 30th September, 2014.

Solution :   **Liquidator's Final Statement of Account**

Receipts	Rs.	Payments		Rs.
To Cash at Bank	60,000	By Legal Expenses		
To Debtors	1,60,000	By Liquidator's Remuneration		
To Stock	1,20,000	3% on Rs. 9,80,000 =	29,400	
To Plant	4,60,000	2% on Rs. 1,90,000 =	3,800	33,200
To Surplus from Land and		By Liquidation Expenses		13,800
Buildings (2,40,000 - 1,00,000)	1,40,000	By Debenture having		
		a floating		
		charge on assets	2,00,000	
		Interest Accrued for		
		6 months	9,000	2,09,000
		By Preferential Creditors		30,000
		By Unsecured Creditors		1,60,000
		By Preference		
		Shareholders	2,00,000	
		Arrears of Dividend	24,000	2,24,000
		By Equity Shareholders		
		Rs. 15 per share on		
		2,000 shares =	30,000	
		Rs. 30 on all shares	2,40,000	2,70,000
	9,40,000			9,40,000

Note :

1) Liquidator's remuneration on payment to unsecured creditors is calculated on the amount including preferential creditors.

2) Payment to preferential creditors is shown after the payment to debenture holders having floating charge.

Problem No. 13 :

Balance Sheet of Brightless Ltd.
as on 31-3-2014

Liabilities	Rs.	Assets	Rs.
20,000, 6% Non-cumulative		Land and Building	1,90,000
Preference Shares of Rs. 10	2,00,000	Plant and Machinery	1,20,000
10,000 Equity Shares of		Patents	10,000
Rs. 10 each, Rs. 9 paid	90,000	Stock	45,000
10,000 Equity Shares of		Debtors	90,000
Rs. 10 each, Rs. 5 paid	50,000	Bank	29,950
6% Mortgage Debentures		Investment	40,000
Secured by Land and Building	1,00,000	Profit and Loss A/c	70,550
Outstanding Interest			
on Debentures	6,000		
Loan secured by Hypothecation			
of Stock	40,000		
Trade Creditors	80,000		
Creditors for Salaries	15,000		
Liability for Workmen's			
Compensation	2,000		
Owing to Government for			
Telephone and Taxes	12,500		
	5,95,500		5,95,500

The company went into voluntary liquidation on 1-4-2014 and a liquidator was appointed with a remuneration of 2% of assets realised with the exception of cash and 2% of the amount distributed amongst unsecured creditors (excluding preferential creditors). Stock realised Rs. 30,000, Land and Building Rs. 1,60,000 and other assets Rs. 2,40,000. All assets were realised and payments made on 30-9-2014.

Prepare liquidator's final statement of account assuming the expenses were Rs. 4,450.

Solution

Liquidator's Statement of Account

Receipts		Rs.	Payments		Rs.
To Bank Balance		29,950	**By Secured Creditors:**		
To Assets realised			Debentures with Interest		
Land and Building	1,60,000		upto 30-9-2008	1,09,000	
Stock	30,000		Loan	30,000	1,39,000
Others	2,40,000	4,30,000	**By Liquidator's Remuneration**		
To Call proceeds on			2% on Rs. 4,30,000	8,600	
10,000 shares on which			2% on Rs. 90,000	1,800	10,400
Rs. 5 paid (@ Rs. 2.67 per		26,700	By Liquidation Expenses		4,450
share)			By Preferential Creditors		29,500
			By Unsecured Creditors		90,000
			By Preference Shareholders		2,00,000
			By Ordinary Shareholders		13,300
			holding 10,000 shares		
			on which Rs. 9 were paid		
			(@ Rs. 1.33 per share)		
		4,86,650			4,86,650

Notes :

1. Loan creditor for Rs. 40,000 was given security of stock, which realised Rs. 30,000. Therefore, uncovered balance of debt Rs. 10,000 is added to unsecured creditors.
2. After payment of unsecured creditors, cash available is Rs. 1,86,600. As the pref. shares have priority for repayment of capital, necessary calls must be made on equity shares and the preference shareholders must be paid. On 10,000 equity shares of Rs. 10 each Rs. 9 are paid, whereas on other 10,000 Equity Shares Rs. 5 paid. Therefore, to pay Preference shareholders in full and to bring the paid-up capital on equity shares to equal, a call of Rs. 2.67 is required to be made on 10,000 equity shares on which Rs. 5 were paid. The amount of call is arrived at as under :

Paid amount on equity shares (90,000 plus 50,000)	1,40,000
Amount falling short to pay preference shareholders	13,400
Total amount required	1,53,400

Hence, the total deficiency Rs. 1,53,400 is to be divided between 20,000 equity shares. The deficiency per share comes to Rs. 7.67 which means Rs. 2.67 to be called on 10,000 equity shares on which Rs. 5 were paid and the other 10,000 equity shares on which Rs. 9 were paid are to get Rs. 1.33 so that the loss suffered by them per share will also be 7.67.

9.6 EXERCISES

A) Objective type questions

Fill in the gaps :

1) Liquidation means ...... of a company
2) Liquidation without intervention of the Court is known as ......
3) For passing a special resolution, a notice of ...... days must be given.
4) The creditors who receive full amount of loan are called as ......
5) The creditors who are paid prior to any payment to unsecured creditors are known as ......

Ans. : 1) dissolution 2) voluntary liquidation 3) 14 4) fully secured creditors 5) Preferential creditors.

B) State whether the following statements are True or False

1) Voluntary liquidation is done with the help of Court.
2) Liquidator gets commission on assets realised by him.
3) Compulsory liquidation is done with the help of Court.
4) Equity shareholders receive their dues before preference shareholders.
5) A Liquidator is appointed for liquidation of a company.

Ans. : 1) False 2) True 3) True 4) False 5) True

PROBLEMS :

1) Ahmednagar Ltd. passed a resolution to wind up voluntarily on 30th June, 2014, when its Balance Sheet stood as under :-

Balance Sheet

Liabilities	Rs.	Assets	Rs.
Share capital		Land	1,00,000
Authorised and		Plant and Machinery	2,30,000
Subscribed 2000, 6% Preference		Patents	60,000
shares of Rs. 100 each	2,00,000	Stock at Cost	55,000
1,000 Equity Shares of Rs. 100		Sundry Debtors	1,10,000
each, Rs. 75 paid	75,000	Cash at Bank	30,000
3,000 Equity Shares of Rs.100		P and L A/c	1,20,000
each, Rs. 60 paid	1,80,000		
5% Debentures (Floating			
charge on all assets)	1,00,000		
Interest on Debenture	5,000		
Creditors	1,30,000		
Income Tax	15,000		
	7,05,000		7,05,000

a) The preference dividends were in arrears for two years. The arrears are payable on liquidation as per the Articles of Company. Creditors include a loan for Rs. 50,000 on the mortgage of land.

b) The assets realised is as follows :
Land Rs. 1,20,000, Plant and Machinery Rs. 1,75,000, Patents Rs. 55,000, Stock Rs. 60,000 and Sundry Debtors Rs. 80,000

c) The expenses of liquidation amounted to Rs. 10,900.

d) The liquidator is entitled to a commission of 3% on all assets realised and 2% on amounts distributed among unsecured creditors.

e) All payments were made on 31st December, 2014. You are required to prepare Liquidator's Statement of Account. (P.U.)

Answer : Total of Liquidator's Account Rs. 4,70,000

2) Altra-optimist Ltd., went into voluntary liquidation on 31st March, 2014. The following Balance Sheet was prepared.

Liabilities	Rs.	Assets	Rs.
Subscribed Capital :		Goodwill	40,000
19,500 Equity Shares of		Patents	10,000
Rs. 10 each fully paid	1,95,000	Freehold Building	48,000
Sundry Creditors :		Plant	65,500
Preferential	24,200	Stock-in-trade	56,800
Partly Secured		Sundry Debtors	64,820
(Against Freehold Property)	55,310	Bills Receivable	2,500
Unsecured	99,790	Profit and Loss A/c	98,680
Bank Overdraft (Unsecured)	12,000		
	3,86,300		3,86,300

The Liquidator realised the assets as follows :

a) Freehold Property (used to pay partly secured creditors)   Rs. 35,000
b) Plant   Rs. 51,000
c) Stock in Trade   Rs. 39,000
d) Bills Receivable   Rs. 2,500
e) Debtors   Rs. 58,500

The expenses of liquidation amounted to Rs. 1,000 and the Liquidator's remuneration was agreed at 2½% on the amount realised and 2% on the amount paid to unsecured creditors.

You are required to prepare :

1. Liquidator's Final Statement of Account.

2. The Working of Liquidator's remuneration.

Ans : Total of Liquidator's A/c Rs. 1,51,000

3) From the following information relating to Star Company Ltd., prepare Liquidator's Final Statement of Account.

1.   Share Capital :

(a) 1,000, 6% Preference Shares of Rs. 100 each fully paid.

(b) 40,000 'A' Equity Shares of Rs. 10 each fully paid

(c) 30,000 'B' Equity Shares of Rs. 10 each, Rs 8 paid.

(d) 20,000 'C' Equity Shares of Rs. 5 each, Rs. 3 paid up

2.   Debentures of Rs. 50,000

3.   Creditors –

Preferential Creditors Rs. 20,000

Unsecured Creditors Rs. 70,000

The preference dividends were in arrears for two years.

The Assets realised Rs. 3,20,000

Cost of liquidation amounted to Rs. 4,000 and the liquidator's remuneration is fixed at 5% on assets realised. (P.U.)

Ans. : Total of Liquidator's Final Statement of Account Rs. 3,40,000

4) The Mumbai Co. Ltd. went into voluntary liquidation on 31st March, 2014 with the following assets and liabilities :-

	Rs.
Cash in Hand	750
Stock which realised	29,600
Book Debts which realised	49,200
Furniture which realised	1,050
Investments lodged with the Bank against	
Overdraft which were sold by the Bank for -	4,900
Unsecured Creditors	53,775
Preferential Creditors	5,295
Bank Overdraft	4,000
6% Debentures secured by a floating charge on the	
undertaking interest paid on 30th September, 2013	44,000

The excess amount realised by the Bank was remitted to the Liquidator. Debentures were paid off on 20th Sept., 2014 together with interest to the date of winding up and a first and final dividend distributed to the creditors.

The Liquidator's remuneration is to be calculated at 3% on the net amount realised (including cash in hand but excluding the amount paid to the secured creditors out of the proceeds of the security) and 2% on the amount distributed to the Unsecured creditors excluding preferential creditors. The expenses of winding up amounted to Rs. 1,014.75.

Prepare the Liquidator's Final Statement of Account showing the rate and the amount of the final dividend payable to the unsecured Creditors.

Ans : Liquidator's Statement : Rs. 81,500

5) A Limited Company passed a resolution to wind up voluntarily on 31st March, 2014, when its Balance Sheet stood as follows :

Liabilities	Rs.	Assets	Rs.
Share Capital :		**Fixed Assets :**	
Issued and Subscribed :		Freehold Property	80,000
8,000 Preference Shares	80,000	Plant and Machinery	70,000
12,000 Equity Shares	1,20,000	**Current Assets :**	
Secured Loans :		Stock	80,000
5% Debenture secured		Cash	250
on Freehold Property	60,000	Debtors	59,750
Current Liabilities :		Profit and Loss A/c	70,000
Bank Overdraft	30,000		
Trade Creditors	65,500		
Income Tax	4,500		
	3,60,000		3,60,000

The interest on debentures is paid upto 31-3-2013 but dividend on preference shares @ 6% is in arrears for three years.

The Freehold Property was sold for Rs. 1,00,000, Plant and Machinery realised Rs. 60,000, Stock Rs. 75,000 and Debtors realised Rs. 50,000, The debentures were paid off out of sale proceeds of assets. Cost of liquidation was Rs. 5,000 and the Liquidator's remuneration was fixed at Rs. 2,530 plus 2% on the amount realised and 10% on the amount returned to equity shareholders.

The Company's Articles give the Preference Shares priority over Equity Shares both for dividend and capital. Draft the Liquidator's Final Statement of Account to show the distribution.

Ans. : Total of Liquidator's A/c Rs. 2,85,250

6) The position of Goodluck Ltd. in liquidation is as follows :

Balance Sheet

Liabilities	Rs.	Assets	Rs.
Share Capital :		Cash	1,16,000
1,000, 6% Preference Shares of		(Left after paying all other	
Rs. 100 each fully paid	1,00,000	Liabilities and Liquidation Expenses)	
1,000 Equity Shares of		Deficiency	66,000
Rs. 50 each fully paid	50,000	(Excluding Arrears of one year's	
1,000 Equity Shares of Rs. 40 each,		dividend on Preference Shares)	
Rs. 30 per Share called 30,000			
Less : Calls in Arrears 4,000	26,000		
Calls in Advance	6,000		
	1,82,000		1,82,000

Prepare Liquidator's Final Statement of Account presuming that the Articles of Association provide for payment of preference dividend in arrears before payment to Equity Shareholders.

Ans. : Total of Liquidator's Final Statement of Account - Rs. 1,22,000.

7) A Company passed a Special Resolution for voluntary winding on 31st March, 2014, when its Balance Sheet stood as under :-

Balance Sheet

Liabilities	Rs.	Assets	Rs.
Share Capital :		Plant and Machinery	4,00,000
5,000 Equity Shares of Rs. 100		Fittings and Furniture	1,000
each fully paid	5,00,000	Stock in trade	50,000
1,000 Equity Shares of		Debtors	1,50,000
Rs.100 each,		Cash in Hand	5,000
Rs.75 called up and paid-up	75,000	Profit and Loss A/c	4,21,000
1,000, 6% Cumulative Preference			
Shares of Rs. 100 each			
fully paid-up	1,00,000		
7% Debentures (secured on			
Plant and Machinery)	1,00,000		
Unsecured Creditors	2,52,000		
	10,27,000		10,27,000

Dividend on preference shares remained unpaid for full one year. Interest (payable annually on December 31) on debentures was paid upto December 31, 2013. Unsecured creditors included Rs. 2,000 of preferential Creditors.

Plant and Machinery realised Rs.3,60,000, Stock Rs.1,00,000 and Debtors Rs.1,40,000. Furniture and Fitting realised nothing. The expenses of winding up amounted to Rs.19,500.

The Liquidator's remuneration is to be @ 4% on realisation of assets and @2% on distribution among unsecured creditors excluding preferential Creditors. The winding up was completed on 30th June, when the Debentures were repaid. The necessary call was made and received in full from all shareholders.

Please draw up the Liquidator's Statement of Account.

Answer :- Total – Liquidator's Final statement of Account Rs. 5,06,500

8) The following is the position as on 31-12-2013 of Overwise Ltd., which goes into voluntary liquidation as on that date:

Liabilities	Rs.	Assets	Rs.
Share Capital :		Fixed Assets	90,000
3,000 Equity Shares		Stock	2,40,000
of Rs.50 each	1,50,000	Debtors	1,80,000
100 Preference Shares		Cash at Bank	10,000
of Rs.100 each	10,000	Loans and Advances	40,000
General Reserve	10,000		
Loan from Strong Bank			
Ltd. (Secured)	20,000		
5% Debentures (Secured)	2,80,000		
Creditors	90,000		
	5,60,000		5,60,000

The following information is given:

a) The loan from Strong Bank Ltd., is secured by first charge on fixed assets.

b) 5% debentures are secured by pledge of goods, hypothecation of all current assets and a second charge on fixed assets.

c) Creditors include preferential creditors of Rs. 20,000. On 15-1-2014, stocks are sold. Stocks in the pledge/godown realised Rs. 1,40,000 and other stocks were sold for Rs. 40,000. On 31-1-2014, expenses of liquidation amounting to Rs.300 are met and fixed assets are sold for Rs.1,30,000 on 15-2-2014, all other current assets realised for Rs.1,91,000 and liquidator's remuneration amounting to Rs.700 are paid.

There was a moped which was completely written off from the books of accounts but Liquidator sold it for Rs.1,000 which was not included in the amount of fixed assets above.

In addition to the above liabilities, the Liquidator had to pay Rs. 1,500 as repair bill of Plant and Machinery.

Prepare Liquidator's Cash Account and Liquidator's Final Statement of Account presuming that all payments are made in order of preference on earliest availability of cash.

Ans :- Total of Liquidator's Final statement of Account Rs. 2,12,000

9) A Company passed a special Resolution for winding up on 31st March, 2014, when its Balance Sheet stood as under:

Liabilities	Rs.	Assets	Rs.
Share Capital -		Plant and Machinery	2,00,000
2,500 Equity Shares of		Furniture and Fittings	500
Rs.100 each fully paid	2,50,000	Stock-in-trade	25,000
500 Equity Shares of		Debtors	75,000
Rs.100 each, Rs. 75		Cash in Hand	2,500
per share called and paid-up	37,500	Profit and Loss A/c	2,10,500
500, 6% Cumulative			
Preference Shares of Rs.100			
each fully paid	50,000		
7% Debentures (Secured on			
Plant and Machinery)	50,000		
Unsecured Creditors	1,26,000		
	5,13,500		5,13,500

Dividend on preference shares remained unpaid for full year. Interest (payable annually on December 31) on debentures was paid upto December 31, 2013. Unsecured creditors include Rs. 1,000 of preferential creditors.

Plant and Machinery realised Rs.1,80,000/-, Stock Rs.50,000/- and Debtors Rs. 70,000/- Furniture and fittings realised nothing.

The expenses of winding up amounted to Rs. 9,750/-

The Liquidator's remuneration is to be @ 4% on realisation of assets and at 2% on distribution among unsecured creditors excluding preferential creditors. The winding up was completed on 30th June 2014, when the debentures were repaid. The necessary call was made and received in full from all shareholders.

Please draw up the Liquidator's Account.

Ans : Total of Liquidator's Final Statement of Account – Rs. 2,63,250

10) You are asked by a Liquidator of a Company to prepare a Statement of Account to be laid before a meeting of the shareholders from the following :-

Balance Sheet of the Company as on the date of liquidation i.e. 1-1-2014

Liabilities	Rs.	Assets	Rs.
Share Capital :		Fixed Assets	4,00,000
4,000 Equity Shares of Rs.100		Book Debts	3,00,000
each, called Rs. 80	3,20,000	Loss todate	1,00,000
1,000 Pref. Shares of Rs.100			
each, called up Rs. 70	70,000		
Secured Loans from Banks			
on Building and Machinery	1,50,000		
Trade Creditors	2,60,000		
	8,00,000		8,00,000

The assets realised as follows on 1-4-2014 : fixed assets Rs.1,00,000 book debts Rs.1,00,000, expenses paid Rs. 4,000 on 1-6-2014. Fixed Assets (final) Rs.2,00,000, Book Debts Rs.1,00,000 on 1-8-2014, book debts (final payment) Rs.50,000. The liquidator is entitled to a commission at 5% on collection and 2% on the amount paid to equity shareholders. Prepare a statement on the assumption that disbursements are made in accordance with law, as and when cash is available.

Ans :- Total of Liquidator's Statement of Account Rs. 4,00,000

Objective Type

Theory Questions

1) Write Short Notes on :
   a)   Issue of debentures at discount

KEY TERMS

Isuue, Forfeiture and Their Re - Issue :

1) **Company :** A Company is a particular kind of association. It is a voluntary and autonomous association formed to carry out a particular purpose in comnon. A company is an artificial person created by law having a common seal and perpetual succession.

2) **Share Capital :** The Capital collected by the Company through the issue of shares is called as "Share Capital".

3) **Share :** The Capital of a Company is divided into small parts called as "Shares".

4) **Authorised Capital :** It is the maximum amount of share capital which the Company is authorised to raise by way of public subscription.

5) **Issued Capital :** It is represented by the number of shares that have been issued to the public for Cash and to the vendors as fully or partly paid against purchase consideration.

6) **Subscribed Capital :** It is that part of issued capital for which applications are received from the public.

7) **Called-up Capital :** The amount on the shares which is actually demanded by the Company to be paid is called "Called-up Capital".

8) **Paid-up Capital :** It is that part of called-up capital which is actually paid by the shareholders.

9) **Equity Shares :** It is those shares, the holders of which are entitled to profits after all prior charges have been paid.

10) **Preference Shares :** It is those shares, the holders of which enjoy the preferential rights as to dividend and repayment of capital in the event of winding up of the company.

11) **Calls-in-arrears :** It is that part of called-up capital which has not been paid by the shareholders fully or partially.

12) **Calls-in-advance :** The amount received before making the calls is called as "calls-in-advance"

13) **Cumulative Preference Shares :** It is those shares on which the arrears of dividend are carried forward and accumulated and are payable in future when the company earns the profit.

14) **Non - Cumulative Preference Shares :** It is those shares on which arrears of dividend cannot be accumulated.

15) **Redeemable Preference Shares :** It is thore shares, which are to be redeemed after expiry of certain term as per agreement.

16) **Irredeemable Preference Shares :** It is those shares the amount of which are not to be redeemed during the lifetime of the company.

17) **Participative Preference Shares :** It is those shares which carry the right of sharing profits left after paying preference and equity dividends at a fixed rate.

18) **Non-Participating Preference Shares :** It is those shares which do not carry the right of sharing in the surplus left after paying equity dividend.

19) **Convertible Preference Shares :** It is those shares which can be converted into equity shares.

20) **Non-convertible Preference Shares :** It is those shares which cannot be converted into equity shares.

21) **Issue of Shares at Par :** When a shareholder is required to pay the face value of the shares of the company, it is called "issue of shares at par".

22) **Issue of Shares at Premium :** When a shareholder is required to pay more than the face value of the shares of the company, it is called "issue of shares at premium".

23) **Issue of Shares at a Discount :** When a shareholder is required to pay less amount than the face value of shares, it is called "issue of shares at discount."

24) **Right Issue :** When in further issue, the shares are given only to the existing shareholders in proportion of their holdings is called as "right issue".

25) **Prospectus :** It is a document in which the Company invites the public for subscription of shares or debentures of the Company.

26) **Share Allotment :** It is an act of distributing shares to the applicants.

27) **Pro-rata Allotment :** In case of over-subscription, when the Company reduces the, demand of each

applicant proportionately on the basis of their total demand and number of shares issued it is called as "pro-rata allotment".

28) **Forfeiture of Shares :** When a shareholder fails to pay the calls made on him, his shares may be taken away as cancelled as a penalty. It is called "forfeiture of shares".

29) **Re-issue of Forfeited Shares :** When forfeited shares are issued to others by a Company it is called as "re-issue of forfeited shares'.

30) **Debentures :** It is a document issued by a Company acknowledging the debt under its common seal.

31) **Secured Debentures :** Those debentures which are secured by a charge on the assets of the Company.

32) **Unsecured Debentures :** Those debentures which are not secured by charge or pledge on the assets of the Company.

33) **Redeemable Debentures :** The debentures which are to be redeemed after the expiry of certain term as per agreement.

34) **Registed Debentures :** Those debentures which are registered in the Register of Company.

35) **Bearer Debentures :** Those debentures which are not registered with the Company, and hence Rare payable to the bearer of debentures.

36) **Sinking Fund :** It is a specific fund created by a Company against the profits

37) **Profit prior to Incorporation :** Profits earned from the date of purchase of running business till the date of incorporation is called as Capital Profit.

38) **Post-incorporation Profit :** Profits earned from the date of incorporation to the date of closing the accounts is known as revenue profit.

39) **Loss prior to Incorporation :** The loss incurred from the date of purchase of running business till the date of incorporation is treated as capital loss.

40) **Post-incorporation loss :** The loss incurred from the date of incorporation to the date of closing the Accounts is treated as capital loss.

41) **Profit and Loss Account :** The account which shows a true and fair view of the profit or loss of the company at the end of accounting year.

42) **Profit and loss Appropriation Account :** The account which shows the disposal of profits.

43) **Divisible Profit :** Profits available for dividend to shareholders is known as "Divisible Profit".

44) **Balance Sheet :** A Balance Sheet is a statement of Assets & Liabilities on a particular date.

45) **Dividend :** The share in the profits payable to sharehoders is known as Dividend.

46) **Interim Dividend :** An interim Dividend is a dividend paid by the directors at any time between two Annual General Meetings.

47) **Proposed Dividend :** A dividend recommended or proposed by Board of Directors at certain rate on paid-up capital is known an "proposed dividend".

48) **Unclaimed Dividend :** Dividend declared but not claimed is known as "unclaimed dividend".

49) **Contingent Liabilities :** Contingent liabilities are those liabilities which are not the actual liabilities on the date of balance sheet. They may or may not turn into liabilities depending upon the happening of the certain events in the future.

50) **Current Liabilities :** Current liabilities are those which are to be paid out within a span of short period.

51) **Provisions :** Provision means any amount written off or retained by way of providing for depreciation renewal etc., or for any known liability.

52) **Fixed Assets :** Fixed assets are those which are of the permanent nature and which are acquired by the business for its own use and which are not for resale.

53) **Redemption :** Redemption means repayment.

54) **Preliminary Expenses :** Those expenses which are incurred on the formation of the company.

55) **Accounting Standards :** Accounting Standards are the authoritative bases for preparation and presentation of financial statements of the enterprises.

56) **Liquidation :** Liquidation is one of the processes by which, dissolution of Company is brought about.

57) **Compulsory winding up :** Winding up of a Company by Court is called compulsory winding up.

58) **Voluntary winding up :** Winding up of a Company by the members or creditors without any intervention

of the Court is called voluntary winding up.

59) **Liquidator :** The commencement of winding up of a Company does not put an end to the existence of the Company. Its assets are to be realised and distributed among the creditors, debentureholders and shareholders. For this purpose, somebody has to act as an agent of the company. Such an agent is called liquidator.

60) **Liquidator's Final Statement of Account :** The liquidator is required to prepare an account of winding up of a Company and such account is called Liquidator's Final Statement of Account.

61) **Liquidator's Remuneration :** The Liquidator normally gets the commission for winding up of a company. Such commission is called liquidator's remuneration.

62) **Fully Secured Creditors :** The creditors who are given security for the full payment of their loan, are called fully secured creditors.

63) **Unsecured Creditors :** The creditors who are not given any security for the payment of loan, are called unsecured creditors.

64) **Preferential Creditors :** The creditors who get preference or priority in respect of returning the amount, over other creditors are called preferential creditors.

65) **Amalgamation :** Amalgamation refers to the merger of two or more existing companies into a single new Company.

66) **Absorption :** The term absorption means taking over of the business of one or more companies by the Company already in existence.

67) **Reconstruction :** When a Company has accumulated huge losses or in financial difficulties or is over-capitalised, then it is reconstructed. This is called reconstruction of a company.

68) **Internal Reconstruction :** Internal reconstruction means reduction of capital of a Company which is to be reconstructed.

69) **External Reconstruction :** External reconstruction takes place when a new Company of similar name is formed to take over the business of the existing Company.

70) **Purchase Consideration :** Purchase consideration is the amount which is paid by the purchasing Company for the purchase of the business of the vendor Company.

71) **Net worth of business :** Assets taken over - Liabilities taken over.

72) **Holding Company :** A Company which holds more than 51% of shares of another Company is called a holding company.

73) **Subsidiary Company :** A Company whose shares have been acquired by a holding company is called Subsidiary Company.

74) **Minority Interest :** The interest of minority shareholders are called as minority interest.

75) **Goodwill on consolidation :** When the value of "investment in Subsidiary" in the holding Company's Balance Sheet is more than the book value of the net assets acquired, the difference represents Goodwill on consolidation.

76) **Capital Reserve on Consolidation :** If the value of investment in Subsidiary is less than book value of net assets acquired, the difference represents capital reserve on consolidation.

77) **Capital Profit :** The profit earned by a subsidiary company before the holding company acquires its control is known as capital profit or pre-acquisition profit.

78) **Revenue Profit :** The profit earned by a subsidiary company after the holding company acquires its control is known as revenue or post-acquisition profit.

79) **Unrealised Profit :** If the goods are sold by the subsidiary company to the holding company or vice-versa, remain unsold at the close of financial year, the profit charged by the Company on unsold goods remains unrealised. This is called unrealised profit.

80) **Inter - company Debts and Acceptance :** It is very common that member companies have business dealing not only with outsiders but also with each other. Inter-company transactions may lead to inter-company debts and acceptances. These transactions are to be the cancelled in consolidated balance sheet.